D1480180

ALLEN DRURY

PUBLIC MEN

A NOVEL

A LISA DREW BOOK

SCRIBNER

A Lisa Drew Book/Scribner
1230 Avenue of the Americas
New York, NY 10020

This book is a work of fiction. Names, characters, places, and incidents
either are products of the author's imagination or are used fictitiously. Any resemblance
to actual events or locales or persons, living or dead, is entirely coincidental.

SCRIBNER and design are registered trademarks of Simon & Schuster Inc.
A LISA DREW BOOK is a trademark of Simon & Schuster Inc.

DESIGNED BY ERICH HOBBING

Text set in Fairfield

Manufactured in the United States of America

1   3   5   7   9   10   8   6   4   2

Library of Congress Cataloging-in-Publication Data
Drury, Allen.
Public Men: a novel/Allen Drury.
p.   cm.
"A Lisa Drew Book."
I. Title.
PS3554.R8P83   1998
813'54—dc21   98–6729
CIP

ISBN 0-684-80703-3

Dedicated to
LISA DREW,
fine editor, loyal friend,
staunch supporter for thirty-nine contentious years

MEMBERS OF THE HOUSE
Final Roster, Year 2000

Class of 1939: TIMOTHY MERRILL BATES, the *Washington Inquirer*. TIM
EDWARD PAUL HAGGERTY, Rome, Italy. HACK
DR. NORTH McALLISTER, Salt Lake City. NORTH
THEODORE KRASNIK MUSAVICH, the University. MOOSE
DR. CLYDE GAIUS UNRUH, Honolulu. GUY
HON. RICHARD EMMETT WILSON, U.S. Senate. WILLIE

Class of 1940: ANTONIO ANDRADE, Collina Bella Winery, Rutherford,
California. TONY
DR. GALEN BRYCE, "Shady Oaks," Hollywood. GALE
LOREN DAVIS, Davis Oil Company, Long Beach, California. LOR
DR. ALAN FREDERICK OFFENBERG, the University. DUKE
DR. RENÉ SURATT, the University. RENNY

Class of 1941: JEFFERSON DAVIS BARNETT, Barnett Plantations,
Charleston, South Carolina. JEFF
RANDOLPH CARDINAL CARRERO, the Vatican. RANDY
DR. ROGER LEIGHTON, International Atomic Energy
Agency, Vienna. RODGE
MARCUS ANDREW TAYLOR, Taylorite Corporation,
Pittsburgh, Pennsylvania. MARC

The college days and midlife battles of the members of the House will be found in the novels *Toward What Bright Glory?* and *Into What Far Harbor?*

9

1

**"We live in the Republic of Feel-Good,
in a time when all the scum of America
is rising to the top."**

15

2

The Very Occasional Newsletter, **Vol. 2**

129

3

"Always the judges, never the judged."

143

4

**"An awesomely broad-gauged intellect,
truly one of the masterminds of the twentieth century . . .
a glowing flame in the great eternal struggle between good
and evil in our land. With such a one to give us counsel,
good's triumph may sometimes be delayed.
It can never be denied."**

167

5

**"A futile gesture, as befits a futile politician,
foredoomed to failure, as he has always been foredoomed
to failure, by his faulty perception of events."**
217

6

The Very Occasional Newsletter, **Vol. 3**
307

7

**The last reunion:
home, in a different season**
319

PUBLIC MEN

1

"We Live in the Republic of Feel-Good, in a Time When All the Scum of America Is Rising to the Top."

1

"We live in the Republic of Feel-Good, in a time when all the scum of America is rising to the top.

"The worried voices of the honest, the decent, the good-hearted and the levelheaded express their concerned dismay. Ever louder rises the chorus of the scum to drown them out. Down, and further down, sinks America as the scum steadily gain ground."

So asserted Timothy Bates, that famous and famously controversial columnist for Anna Hastings's *Washington Inquirer,* in one of his many blasts at those who, in his judgment, were sapping (often deliberately) the strength of his beleaguered and beloved country in the closing decades of the twentieth century.

Before faxing it to Anna he read it over the phone to his fraternity brother, lifelong friend, loyal supporter and sometimes necessary critic, Senator Richard Emmett Wilson of California.

Willie Wilson's reaction was appropriately wry.

"My *goodness!*" he exclaimed. "You're outdoing yourself, Timmy. You sound even more doomsday than usual."

Tim was only moderately amused. Willie, he remarked with some asperity, sounded like all Tim's other critics "on the left side of nonsense."

"That's me," Willie agreed with mock solemnity born of half a century of familiarity with Tim's frequently expressed indignations.

"Wait until I read you the rest of it," Tim said from his comfortable bachelor's apartment in the Watergate. In his charming Federal-era town house on Capitol Hill, Willie prepared to listen. Tim proceeded with relish:

"The influence of the perpetrators of scum, who by any standards of decency and common sense are scum themselves, is becoming ever more pervasive in politics, academe, Hollywood, Broadway, publishing, advertising, the legal profession, talk-radio, pop music, the media—all the areas that affect the good taste, common decency and mutual tolerance of the nation. The scum-merchants are reducing America rapidly to the lowest common denominator. They are encouraging, inspiring and creating an ugly decay of morals and manners, an uncaring and irresponsible flaunting of standards and steadiness, a wanton destruction of the fabric that holds an enduring—and endurable—society together. Language and conduct are increasingly vulgar and crude in major areas of public communication. Good taste and kindly behavior are increasingly nonexistent. The necessary goodwill, tolerance and respect that people must have for one another—and for themselves—if they are to live together peaceably and constructively, are being deliberately and ruthlessly destroyed.

"In politics, an increasing incivility, a harsh and inexcusable unfairness, degrade debate and destroy that elemental courtesy that is necessary for the successful conduct of democratic government. All rocks are turned over, all foibles ruthlessly dug up, all weaknesses mercilessly exploited. Fairness, decency and tolerance are destroyed in the pursuit of voters who are ever more disgusted and turned off as they are more and more hysterically wooed. The process is aided, abetted, encouraged and exploited by the media.

"In the highest places of government, scum betray the public trust they say they serve by proclaiming the noblest of intentions while performing the shabbiest and most immoral of deeds. Character has become a mockery, integrity a joke.

"In academia, principles are mocked, standards denigrated and destroyed, independent minds forced into conformity or crushed.

"In newspaper columns and editorials, in magazine articles, in television and radio programs and commentaries, the independent mind, the independent analysis, the independent challenge to the accepted wisdom, are ruthlessly censored, suppressed and, if possible, destroyed.

"In the worlds of literature and the arts, the ugly, the repellent, the deliberately unstructured and self-indulgent, are hailed and worshiped as the epitome of artistic expression, the ultimate achievement of American genius. The scum prevail and what is fashionable with the scum prevails over all.

"In the legal profession, high-priced scum run amuck in their fevered pursuit of ever bigger headlines, ever greater profits.

"In commerce, famous names flaunt their sexual obsessions with steadily diminishing taste and restraint as they present their products and use their latest girl- or boyfriends to advertise them.

"In Hollywood, capital of four-letter words and similar sophomoric substitutes for intelligence and charm, juvenile minds in control of a worldwide medium strive to outdo each other in the presentation of unnecessary and uncalled-for filth, with devastating effects upon other juvenile minds as they replace wit with vulgarity and offer as evidence of maturity violence piled upon violence to an extreme that would be laughable were it not so pathetic and so destructive of society.

"On talk-radio the lowest common denominators of American vulgarity trumpet their scum, smut and political and personal crudities with childish relish and a smugly self-gratulatory air.

"In general-circulation magazines, the scum present the various forms of sexual expression in graphic language that provokes from the decent a bewildered 'Who needs it?' but presumably evokes gratified response from the erotically bereft.

"And in general conversation, the foulest of fishwives' language slips easily from the lips of lovely ladies, thereby raising the level of social intercourse to heights untouched, one suspects, since the days of Elizabeth I.

"Nor is it enough to destroy current stabilities. History and past stabilities must be destroyed too.

"Hollywood, Broadway, academia, publishing, critics, commentators, the media in general, deliberately reconstruct history, join forces to twist, subvert and pervert facts to conform to 'politically correct,' monstrously mangled misinterpretations of past events to suit present prejudices.

"The perpetrators of scum are riding high these days. The cancer they create has already eaten deep into the fabric of American life. It is eating up America itself—the decent, stable, worthwhile America that the earnest and good-hearted still want to see achieved for themselves and their children. The influence of the scum seeps through the nation like runaway sewage."

Tim paused. Using the irony with which he sometimes greeted Tim's more extreme effusions, Willie murmured, "Wow! You tell 'em, boy!"

"And that isn't all," Tim assured him cheerfully. "There's more. The scum hate my guts anyway. I might as well let them know I'm as dreadful as always."

And he concluded his reading with a certain grim satisfaction, knowing that he would once more, as so often, drive his critics into near incoherent rage:

"A great interlocking directorate of clever minds, facile pens, movies, plays, TV programs, articles, recklessly unprincipled and irresponsible books, editorials, columns, headlines, sound bites, enhance and increase the scum's power. With incessant mutual praise and nonstop mutual promotion they support one another and their shabby purposes. Scum calls to scum. They cling together like amoebas, secure in their smug agglutination.

"No group is more successful at profiting from America; no group despises her more; no group is less worthy of her tolerance and her bounty. Yet somehow she manages—just—to survive them.

"So far.

"To applaud this ultimate triumph of the American spirit is to infuriate them. To note that the great republic still stands and somehow continues to stagger forward in spite of their attacks is to inflame them to the point of gibberish.

"They cannot abide an America successful on America's own terms. So they toil away, never stopping in their busy task of destroying their own country. Increasingly their blighting hands and warped perspectives derange America's past and present.

"It is no wonder the past is increasingly besmirched, the present increasingly unstable. It is no wonder the future becomes increasingly uncertain."

Tim stopped, with a wicked little chuckle that indicated he was enjoying this.

"You *really* don't like them, do you?" Willie inquired in mock awe. Tim's chuckle dissolved into genuine laughter.

"I despise them," he said. "And they despise me." His tone became thoughtful.

"I'm always blowing their cover. I'm always saying their emperors have no clothes. I don't waste time on the tabloid sensations of sex and money which they overemphasize to divert attention from their own devious games. I don't deal in those journalistic clichés. I go deeper than that.

"I've always been after bigger game.

"All my professional life I've written about the genuine corruptions and conspiracies that truly threaten America. The attempts to control minds. The attempts to impose attitudes. The agreed-upon campaigns to dominate the national agenda and twist it into whatever skewed direction the scum decide it should go. The smooth hypocrisies that condemn one side of the ideological argument and suavely forgive all the vicious trespasses of the other. Subversion—not cliché subversion but *real* subversion, late twentieth century style, of the American mind and the American hope.

"And it isn't really organized conspiracy, either. Peer pressure alone is quite enough to dragoon the faithful into line and produce a single massive yawp on any agreed-upon, fashionable subject."

He stopped and laughed again.

"And *that,* damned scum," he said, "is what I think of *you!*"

"You always amaze me," Willie remarked. "You get these fits of enormous indignation and you always sound terribly fierce, but then you come out of them with a laugh and what appears to be quite rational stability. How do you do it?"

"That's my Mr. Hyde side," Tim said cheerfully. "Now that he's had his say, Dr. Jekyll will resume control."

"I hope so," Willie said with a fervor exaggerated but not entirely humorous. "I've known you for half a century and you haven't died of spontaneous combustion yet. But someday, Timothy—"

"Never," Tim said.

Willie's tone became quizzical.

"Are they really all that bad? Aren't there any good people in the enemy camp, as you'd probably call it, who are trying to do good? Are they *all* confirmed subverters of our not-always-so-perfect society? I find that hard to believe."

Tim conceded with an impatient sound.

"Oh, no, of course not. One has to exaggerate some when making a case, just as they exaggerate about me and about all who refuse to follow their automatic mind-set. I hit hard because they hit hard. But don't worry about their tender little souls, Willie. Others, like me, keep trying. But the scum prevail more and more these days."

And as the millennium hurried toward its close and the world sank ever further into chaos foreign, domestic, national, international, large, small, whatever, wherever—from the smallest crime in the smallest street in the smallest village to the massive genocide of tribe against tribe and nation against nation—Timmy's World War II generation had all too many opportunities to test his thesis and find it valid.

He and others struggled to maintain some level of social decency, moral stability and responsible individual conduct.

But more often than not, the scum prevailed.

2

And now the century has ended—the millennium has ended—the lives of the members of the house, whose disparate journeys began together so many years ago at the beautiful University in the foothills of the San Francisco Peninsula, are, one by one, ending too.

As the call goes out for a last reunion, eleven of the original twenty-six members of the World War II Alpha Zeta house of 1939 are gone. An average of sixty years has passed since most of them left the lovely campus to enter a world rushing headlong into the abyss of global war. Some of the survivors, not all of whom have stayed in touch in recent years, are surprised that so many are left.

The call for reunion goes out, on a sudden sentimental impulse, from the Capitol Hill office of the Honorable Richard Emmett Wilson, senior Senator from the state of California (which he will be until he leaves office, voluntarily retiring at age eighty-two, when the 107th Congress convenes at noon on the upcoming January 5 of the year 2001).

His suggestion ("full of the old Willie hype," as that distinguished oncologist, Dr. Clyde Gaius Unruh, remarks to his ever-faithful, ever-plump Maggie in their spectacular home overlooking Honolulu) reaches all of his remaining fourteen fraternity brothers. Of these, only twelve are still capable of understanding and acknowledging it. The other three, while still physically present, have vanished into the living twilight of the dead-in-life that claims so many who once strode, vigorous, laughing, confident and secure in the possession of all their faculties, across the happy fields of memory in the golden haze of youth.

Willie is still the most famous member of the house, although Guy Unruh, his closest college friend and more recently co-winner of the Nobel Prize in medicine for his contributions to cancer research, is not so far behind. But it is Willie who, in the public eye and in the eyes of his fraternity brethren and classmates still living, is, as always, the most dominant, the most famous, the best known, the graduate who has brought most credit to his own name and most reflected honor on the University.

This does not surprise those who have traversed contemporaneously with him the savage chaos of the twentieth century.

"There goes Willie again," Duke Offenberg has often remarked to gentle Shahna when some new report of Willie's doings has reached them in their beautiful retirement home on "President's Knoll" overlooking the campus.

"He never stops," Shahna agrees in the affectionate tone in which they always mention Willie. His staunch defense of Duke through Duke's difficult years as president of the University has made them his for life.

The same cannot be said for another fraternity brother, that perennial, and perennially hostile, gadfly, Dr. René Suratt, self-appointed scourge of all those who are skeptical of that self-sanctifying "establishment" which Renny has always supported and which, in turn, has always supported him.

Renny is not one of those whose brain and personality have been dimmed by time. Far from it. Approaching eighty-one, he is as waspish, savage and unfair (as many see it) as he has always been. "Such a pity nothing has damaged his brain," Guy Unruh observed once when back on campus for a year's stint as visiting lecturer in the school of medicine. "What a shame he can still think."

Renny still thinks; and being, now as always, as sensitive to slights as he is adept at giving them, he knows perfectly well what his remaining fraternity brothers think of him. He despises them; and sensing with complete accuracy the depth of their dislike for him, he never fails to raise whatever hell he can for them. At almost eighty-one this is still quite substantial enough to make them pause before crossing him.

"Just be sure that if you have to pick up a skunk, you pick him up by the tip of his tail and hold him at arm's length," Willie once ironically advised Duke when Renny had launched one of his many savage attacks on Duke from his tenured sanctuary in the political science department. "Otherwise his hind legs will get purchase and then you're dead, man. You'll smell as bad as he does."

"I know," Duke agreed ruefully. "I try to ignore him. But," he sighed, "that's easier said than done."

For that reason—and just because of Renny's generally unlovely characteristics—his lifelong reputation as a campus seducer of young minds and young bodies, his harshly intolerant, ruthless, unforgiving personality—Willie has thought for quite a while before directing his secretary to send an invitation to the reunion to Dr. Suratt. But then, as he remarks to Tim, Renny is, after all, a brother. And old fraternity loyalties, even though faded by time and other difficult aspects of advancing age, still carry some sentimental weight.

"Oh, hell," Timmy says. "Put him on the list. You can't very well snub him altogether, that would be a little too much. And he can't do any more harm there than he's done to you and Duke and me and Rodge and who knows how many thousands of others over the years."

"I'm not so sure," Willie says, drawing another analogy from the family ranch in the San Joaquin Valley, where he and his younger brother, Billy, grew up. "Even an old rattler still has his venom."

"Renny has venom, all right," Tim agrees. "Too bad nobody's ever figured out a way to make him bite his own tail."

"Dear Willie," Renny writes in response to Willie's note. "Thanks for the invitation to the reunion. I hope it will be better than the last one. I hope to attend. Sincerely, Renny."

About as sincere, Willie thinks, as a dead fish. But, oh, well. Timmy of course is right. There is no way that they are going to keep the reunion quiet, and if Renny were snubbed and decided to retaliate, there would be another public row of the kind Renny has flourished on all his professional life. More of his savage and self-righteous rhetoric would spill forth to inspire stories in the campus *Daily* and the ever-sycophantic pro-Renny newspapers of San Francisco, always ready to publicize anything that might embarrass the University, Duke and/or Willie.

Randy Carrero's prompt response in the next mail takes away much of the bad taste of Renny's response. Randy, twenty years a cardinal, writes from the Vatican, where he has been stationed in the Holy See's diplomatic office for the past decade.

"Imagine my surprise," he writes, "to open my mail today and find—guess who? Old Willie! Of course I've known that you were still very active—who could follow the news and not know that?—but I'd forgotten what a sentimental soul you are, at heart. Washington hasn't changed that, I'm glad to see. You can put me down as a positive, I think. It's been a while since the Holy See stroked the egos in the State Department; I need to come over and have an intimate chat with the Secretary. I'll arrange to be there four or five days before you leave for the Coast. Maybe we can fly out together. More on this when we get nearer the time."

That, Willie thinks, is more like it; and is pleased that Randy, whom he has not seen since an international conference on crime held in Rome ten years ago, is definitely planning to attend.

Guy Unruh, writing from Hawaii, is equally enthusiastic if, characteristically, a trifle caustic.

"Dear Statesman," he writes, "if you aren't the damnedest. Just as we were preparing to attend your state funeral in Washington, you leap off your (political) deathbed and surprise us all with a sentimental gesture like a reunion. I'm dubious you'll get much of a response from the guys, most of whom are beginning to drop by the trail as they head for the old corral in the sky, but you can count us in. Maggie wants to see a couple of sorority sisters and do some shopping in the City, and I want to make book on who's left and how soon they'll kick off. If nobody else comes, we can always drink a cyanide cocktail with Renny.

"Seriously, it will be great to see you again. It's been too long. I hope you still have your hair."

Two days later their other representative in Rome reports in.

Hack Haggerty discloses that he is well and flourishing, "at work on another symphony. *Still* working, at almost eighty-two!

"As are you, Willie," he goes on. "The whole country is going to miss you when you retire. But in your business, it's probably time—if you can bring yourself to let go of politics. With me, I can keep scribbling music 'til I drop, but I know your job demands a lot more than mine does. You not only have to stay alert mentally, about which no one has any doubts, but there's all the physical wear and tear of campaigning and keeping in touch with the constituency. I just sit on my terrace on the Janiculum and look out over Rome and follow the inspiration when it comes. (Well, maybe it's not *that* simple, but I must say the view of Rome is a great help. I've lived here forty years and I love it more every day.) I'm aided by the kids, both of whom are married and live nearby; they keep a close eye on me now that Flavia's gone; and four grandchildren. A long way from the University, Willie! I'll try my damnedest to get there. It's time to say hello again—most likely for the last time. Hope to see you soon."

Hack has put his finger on it, Willie thinks—"most likely for the last time"—though he himself has not expressed it that candidly in his invitation. The "old hype" has been there, as Guy said. Willie wrote:

"It will give us the chance to get caught up on everybody and find out what we all have planned for those famous 'golden years.' "

What he really meant was:

We're all going to drop dead tomorrow morning, so let's get the hell to it before it's too late.

But of course he didn't have to spell it out. They all knew it well enough, though few would be as forthright as Hack, who had always pretty much cut to the heart of things.

"Willie!" Diana Musavich writes from the comfortable old house she and Moose have occupied in the University's neighboring town for the past fifty years. "What a grand idea! Moose and I are agreed that it couldn't be more fun. He'd write you himself except that he's pretty busy over at school, acting as 'adviser' to the football team. He can't sit on the sidelines; even at eighty-plus, he still has to be in the thick of it! So he asked me to do the honors and say it will be grand to see you again. We can't wait!"

The thought crosses Willie's mind that this is a bit odd. There hasn't been any news about Moose in the alumni magazine since his retirement as head coach fifteen years ago, except that he would be acting as special adviser from time to time, "just to keep my hand in."

Willie wonders if something is wrong and then concludes that he won't press it, he'll find out soon enough. He sincerely hopes not. Old Mooser deserves better than to have life sneak up and land a haymaker just when he should be enjoying to the full his semi-retirement with his beloved team.

———

North McAllister is the last surviving member of the class of '39 to check in, writing from Salt Lake City, where he is long since retired from a very successful medical practice.

"Dear Willie," he writes, "your idea of a 'last reunion' strikes me as an excellent one. You catch me feeling a little sentimental anyway, and this puts the cap on it. I'm retired, surrounded by grandchildren. (Eileen's. Jason has never married, though he seems to be content.) The idea of one more trip back to campus is nice. I've tried to get there fairly often over the years, as Duke can attest, but lately my travels have been narrowing down a little, thanks to bad arthritis in both hips. It takes Willie, as always, to liven things up for us and get us off our duffs. I only wish B.J. were still with us, she would have enjoyed it so. Gone twenty years this October, but I still miss her as much every day as I did right then.

"It will be good to walk the Quad again, even though the rest of campus is almost unrecognizable, there are so many new buildings (as of course you know from being a trustee for so long). They've done a good job of keeping most of the new structures consistent and in proportion, I think. It's still beautiful. See you soon."

And below his signature, almost as an afterthought, though Willie didn't think so, "We'll have a good talk."

Yes, Willie thinks with a certain apprehension, that we will—if you really want to. North must have something on his mind, to volunteer the idea. Willie had thought all that must be over by now, but maybe it wasn't. He sighs and stares out his office window at the bare trees, whipped in the first heavy snowstorm of Washington winter. He wishes again, as he does so often, that his younger brother, Billy, were still around. He could perhaps reinforce Willie's determined belief that they had done the right thing in counseling North to marry Betty June Letterman so long, long ago.

Well, Billy wasn't. Nor Janie. "The perfect marriage" of house legend had ended on a two-lane country road near the ranch thirty years ago when a drunken Mexican in a battered old truck had roared out of nowhere on a Saturday night and caught them head-on just as they were almost home from a party in nearby Porterville. All three had been killed instantly. Willie still misses Billy and Janie as sharply today as he had when the phone rang at almost midnight and he had to drive headlong down the ranch road to confirm things, and then return to the house to bring the news to his parents and to Billy's kids, Leslie and Tom. Both were now grown and married long since, but still able to be unnerved, as he often was, by sudden memories of that awful night.

In the same mail with North's letter, brightening things as he always seemed to be able to do whatever his own problems, comes a cheery screed from Tony Andrade, still sitting atop his beautiful hill in Napa Valley and now a much-liked and much-respected elder statesman of the wine industry.

"Hey, Willie!" he writes, and Willie can hear his lively, still youthful, still upbeat voice behind the hastily scrawled words on a Collina Bella Winery letterhead. "You old son of a gun! You do pop up in one's life at the damnedest times!" (How like Tony, Willie thinks with a wry fondness, to fly right into the face of it and deliberately rouse memories.) "And always with something helpful and interesting to contribute!" (Not "supportive"? Willie thinks, and smiles. Not even Tony would go that far. But of course he would.) "And very supportive, too," he goes on cheerfully. "I can't think of anything that would take us into the twilight more happily than a reunion of whoever's left. Who is, by the way? I haven't counted lately, or heard from anybody except Lor, so I don't know.

"Lor's not doing very well, as you may have heard, or may have found out with your call to the troops. He won't be there, but I'll let Angie tell you about that if she wants to. It's all very sad, but that's life, I guess. *Life!*" (He underlines it heavily.) "God damned *life!* A guy's your best buddy forever, and then suddenly he just isn't— *there*—anymore. Only he is, which makes it all the more difficult.

"Well, anyway, enough of that. Louise joins in sending love. We'll both be happy to join you. Maybe we can have a party up here one afternoon, like we did last time. Or if the weather's bad, we'll plan to stay on or near campus, along with you and whoever does come. I'm sure we'll find plenty to do to pass the time. And talk about, right?"

And you, too, want to talk, Willie thinks. What's this all about, anyway? I hope this isn't going to turn into a confessional, you in one ear and North in the other.

From the office of Davis Oil in Long Beach, California, he receives a day or two later a note from Angelina D'Alessandro Davis, Lor's wife of fifty-five years. Although prepared by Tony's letter, he finds hers touching and a heavy burden. God damned *life* is right, he thinks with some bitterness; not eased when two similar letters arrive, one from Hollywood and the other, most hurtful of the three, from South Carolina.

"Dear, dear Willie," Angie writes. "Thank you so much for thinking of us in connection with your idea for a 'last reunion' of the house. I do so hope you get a good response, and that everybody who can possibly be there does come. This will not, alas, include Loren and me.

"As you may already have heard from Tony, Lor is with us but he isn't. He looks much the same, still handsome—beautiful, really, as he has always been—still gentle and good-hearted, as he has always been—but with nothing inside. He was diagnosed about three years ago with Alzheimer's, and since then it's been steadily downhill. Fortunately there's enough money so we can keep him at home with around-the-clock nurses, but he might as well be anywhere, for all he knows. I'm sure we're just unknown faces that come and go, and meaningless voices he can't recognize. It's really terrible, but what can you do? Just go on—keep him comfortable—pray, if that does any good—and just keep going. So that's what I do. How much longer, who knows?

"But, dear Willie, enough of that. I'll be thinking of you all. And you all think of us. I'll be with you in spirit. And so would he, if he could. Much love, Angie."

The day he receives her letter is another stormy day in Washington, D.C., but for a few minutes Willie does not see the trees bending in the wind or the sleet racing down. His eyes are filled with tears. Poor Lor! So handsome. So dumb. Such a nice guy. Belonging to Tony so faithfully for a half-century and more. And now—nothing. God damned *life,* indeed.

His mood rebounds, as moods do, particularly as one gets older and must accept with a sad philosophy the increasing acceleration with which old friends and family deteriorate and drop away. The next couple of letters dash him down again.

Mary Dell Barnett writes with equal courage and equal sadness. Bright and lively Jefferson Davis Barnett—"Jeff"—"Reb"—"Don't y'all go callin' me a damned Suthunnuh, you damned Yankees!"—

with his ever-ready smile and an endless fund of good nature—Jeff is gone into the same twilight, though as Mary Dell writes, "Once in a while there's a gleam of—something. But it isn't really Jeff, and it doesn't stay long enough to do more than tear your heart out for what was, and might have been."

Jeff's diagnosis had also come approximately three years ago and, as with Lor, family funds are more than sufficient to keep him at home. But that, as Mary Dell observes, is small comfort compared with the overall picture.

"Very docile," she writes. "Very placid. Very *gone*. Not the Jeff we knew at all. At *all*.

"All three kids live nearby. Jeff Jr. is head of the business. Bryant is second in command, and Mary Helen is married to a nice boy—'boy'! more like fifty now, with four kids, who is one of the top lawyers in the Carolinas and handles all our affairs. A real Southern clan operation. The only difference is, Big Daddy doesn't live here anymore. Or he does, but he doesn't know it.

"But we manage. And life goes on. I'll be thinking of you all, as I'm sure, in some dim recess nobody can reach, he perhaps will be too. Fond love to everybody and particularly to you, dear Willie, who has held us all together so gracefully over so many tumultuous years. Thanks for all you did for Jeff in the house. You helped him come to terms with By Johnson, and with his heritage, and made a fine and worthy citizen of him. I will always love you for that. Mary Dell."

And that, too, makes Willie cry.

Twenty-four hours later comes a letter bearing a Santa Monica postmark he does not recognize. It turns out to be not a constituent seeking help but a name of vague but nagging familiarity—a "Patti D'Arcy," who signs herself "Niece of Dr. Galen Bryce." She recites Gale's story tersely without much detail. But enough.

"Dear Senator Wilson," she writes, "With reference to your kind invitation to my uncle, Dr. Galen Bryce, to attend a reunion of your joint fraternity at the University in September 2000, I regret to inform you that Dr. Bryce suffered a series of severe strokes some six months ago and recently had another. His condition is deteriorating drastically. His permanent residence is now the Shady Oaks rest home in Hollywood. You may transmit messages to him through me at Miramax Studios, if you so desire. Sincerely, Patti D'Arcy." And a secretary's initials and a wandering childlike signature.

Then the name clicks. A new young star, appearing near-naked during the last year in a dozen publications, a rising white hope—(Ooops! Willie corrects himself. Just "rising," please! Strike that "white"! No racism, now!)—all right, then, a rising young star, already featured in three major films of the 3-G genre (grunt, groan, grunge) so beloved of present-day Hollywood, so deplored by stodgy old types like Tim Bates. One of Tim's "scum" and doing very nicely at it, thank you—apparently concerned for her uncle, which is worthy and for which she deserves credit.

So Gale is out of it, after all those years of arch, superior "fucking about with other people's lives," as Tony put it disgustedly back in undergraduate days when Gale was loudly and obnoxiously analyzing everyone in the house. How many personalities had he arranged, rearranged and deranged in all his famous years as "psychiatrist to the stars"! Enough to give him a very substantial reputation in the movie colony and a very substantial bachelor living—but never the lasting love of anyone except possibly Patti D'Arcy and other members of his family; and how disinterested are they? Willie tells himself this is a very ungenerous thought, but for the moment indulges it. Gale has always belonged to the "politically correct," insufferably smug Hollywood group that has opposed Willie throughout his public career. So why bother?

Later he thinks better of it, decides such a vengeful dismissal isn't worthy of him, calls the studio and speaks briefly to Patti. She sounds surprisingly young and shy for one so casual with her body and so crude and half-literate in her published statements on all the aspects of life and politics that a rising Hollywood hope is expected—and of course is fully qualified—to comment upon. She will carry his greetings to Gale, she promises; thanks him quite sincerely; and concludes, with a sudden nervous, self-conscious little laugh, "Come see my pictures, now!" He promises to do so, and they part with mutual, and politely suppressed, skepticism.

Rodge Leighton is still active as a senior adviser to the International Atomic Energy Agency in Vienna. His letter, as always, sounds calm, steady, judicious and reliable; concerned, as always, with his lifelong interest and obsession, the fearsome force whose potential for world destruction he grasped instantly in 1945 when he was flown over the ruins of Hiroshima two days after the first bomb fell. Rodge has always been a fine world citizen, even though as he reaches the final stages of his life he finds himself less and less optimistic about humanity's collective ability to save itself from suicide in some last, awful, insane cataclysm. To his constant worries about nuclear destruction have recently been added the awful potentials of biological and chemical weapons.

"Dear Willie," he writes, "how did you know I was planning to be at our house in Santa Barbara with the kids in September? It won't be difficult to join you and the others for the reunion. How many of us are still around, anyway? I've lost track, except when once in a while you surface in the media for some stroke of genius in the Senate (which needs a few, nowadays) or old Renny grabs the headlines with some scathing attack on you or Timmy or Duke or me, or some other of his endless string of hates. I guess spite is what fuels his perpetual-motion machine. It doesn't run on love for his fellowman, that's for sure. *He* certainly shows no signs of slowing down, does he?

"Neither do I, thank heaven. I manage to stay reasonably busy, too, though now about to hit seventy-eight, as you perhaps remember. I'm still active over here, and on the lecture trail over there. There's always a place for a cautionary voice, even though caution, while needed more than ever, no longer seems to have the audience that it did before the Soviet Union collapsed. That damnable trait of the American people, to dismiss a threat the moment there's the slightest hint of the relaxing of it! There's no relaxing, in reality. All the tensions and the terrible possibilities of nuclear war are still there—plus, now, biological and chemical horrors. All that's changed is the American sense of urgency. Who in America wants urgency? In America, it's so much more comfortable to forget all about it, and relax.

"Well, enough soapbox. No doubt I'll get on it again when we're all together. One last debate between Renny and me about my contributions to world disaster because of my continuing suspicions of many of our more noble and 'honest' world leaders. How can I be so suspicious and irresponsible? he'll ask. Easy! I'll reply.

———

"Take care, Willie. I'll see you in September."

And from Pittsburgh, Pennsylvania, from the hushed executive offices and humming plants of Taylorite Corporation, the one Willie thinks of as "our last functioning millionaire" also surfaces. He still sounds shy and reticent after all these years and all his great success in running the company his father left him. Marc Taylor is also pushing seventy-eight, and still sounds as tentative as he did when he tried to commit suicide in the house sixty years ago.

"Dear Willie," he writes, "imagine my surprise and delight when I got your very nice letter setting forth your ideas for a 'last reunion' of the house. It's been so long since I heard from any of you (although I've of course followed *your* career, and have supported it wholeheartedly, as you know, on the national scene) that I was quite startled, and greatly pleased, to receive your communication.

"Of course you can count me in. I usually get to the Coast four or five times a year (less, now that Marc III is moving into full control of the company). We have plants in Southern California, Oregon and Washington State. I'll just time my next trip to California to coincide with the reunion. This will probably be my last trip, anyway—last trip, for the last reunion! I'm almost seventy-eight, as you may recall; and while my children think it's great for me to keep busy, I think maybe I can keep busy with a few hobbies, some books and some civic activities, and leave the business in Marc's capable hands, where it's been for all practical purposes for almost the last ten years. *He'll* be pleased, I know!

"I don't know how many of our remaining brothers will be glad to see *me*, but I'll be glad to see *them*. Fond fraternal greetings, as always."

Oh, Marc, Willie thinks. For God's sake, stop humbling yourself! Of course we'll be glad to see you. Why wouldn't we be glad to see you?

But then he stops the argument in his mind. Marc has had a lifelong inferiority complex and nothing is going to change it now. Willie makes mental note to be extra cordial, extra welcoming, extra fraternal—the burden the shy put upon the sensitive and sympathetic. Willie sighs, but it is more a sigh of exasperated affection than one of real annoyance. When they took Marc into the house so long ago they took on a lifelong obligation, though they did not recognize it then, to protect a fragile personality. They had obviously succeeded, for Marc had succeeded; but it had apparently not changed the obligation, or the personality.

The last response, completing the roster, arrived next day from Dr. Alan Frederick Offenberg—Duke—at the University. It was exactly what Willie had expected—pleased, and offering to help.

"Willie!" Duke writes. "What a great idea! We only hope you get enough favorable answers to make it feasible. If so, don't hesitate to call on us for anything we can do that will contribute to its success. I still have enough (friendly) contacts in the school administration so I can arrange a lot of things, including a private dining room in the Faculty Club that we can use for a formal dinner, if you like.

"(You remember, of course, that the dear old Alpha Zeta house fell to the inexorable ax of 'progress' almost fifteen years ago—membership 'way down—no real interest in keeping it going aside from a few sentimental old alums like you and me—a prize piece of property five minutes' walk to the Quad, that the University wanted to turn into a cash cow. Now a much sought-after eight-suite rental property for thirty-five or younger faculty, limited to one child, after which they have to move on and make room for the next generation. Sentimentally bad for us, but a moneymaker for the University and a great convenience for young faculty, so I guess it's probably for the best.)

"Anyway, keep us involved in the planning. I checked with the alumni office the other day and find that we now have fifteen members remaining, not a bad record for century's end. The Delts have fifteen also, the Zetes ten, the Betas eleven. The Kappas are triumphantly outliving us all with seventeen—all, no doubt, gray-haired little old widowladies presently on a cruise ship somewhere in Antarctica. So we're holding our own pretty well.

"Some of us, like Rodge Leighton, are pretty remote unless he's planning to be in the country anyway. And maybe Renny won't get out of his perpetual snit long enough to join us, which would be a blessing. But we should have an almost complete turnout, I should think, travel being as easy as it is nowadays. If you like, I can line up some housing on campus. People are often in and out, there are various condos and apartments that can be rented. Let me know and I'll get on it.

"Meantime, take care of yourself and give 'em hell in your last days in the Senate. It's been a long run for you and you've done it, I think, magnificently. Of course Renny doesn't agree, but the hell with him! As ever, old friend—Duke."

At the bottom Shahna had scribbled a brief P.S.:

"Don't be too hard on old Renny, you guys. This is supposed to be a happy occasion. He's getting ancient, too, remember."

Shahna, Willie thinks, only someone of your infinite patience and compassion could be so Christian (if you'll forgive the word) toward someone like Renny. He is *not* a nice individual, damn it.

But, he reflects, how important has he made himself to some of our lives, and how much does he sum up in himself a certain dominant segment of the World War II generation—an "attitude," a "mind-set," an "establishment" of violent likes and dislikes, of wild, blindered enthusiasms and automatic, harsh, vindictive hatreds, still fighting old, tired "liberal" battles in a time-warped world that never changes? How ruthlessly have he and his fellows of "the interlocking direc-torate" tried to destroy everyone and everything that disagrees with their rigidly intolerant ideology!

How much has Renny, in and of himself, given body to Tim's argu-ment, some of whose most searing indictments Willie can still remem-ber to this day? How much has Renny, now and always, epitomized "the scum"?

And how determinedly, and with what unyielding character and determination, has he, Willie, withstood the scum's incessant and unrelenting attacks during his long, contentious public life.

It has indeed been "a long run," as Duke says, and while Willie would not himself describe it as "magnificent," he reflects with some satisfaction now that he has not done so badly with his public trust.

Offstage he can hear the mocking laughter of Renny and his think-alikes. He is sure they would consider such a statement fatuous, self-serving arrogance.

But he has never been deterred by their hoots and caterwauls.

And is not now.

3   He was almost sixty-two when he finally made a serious
run for the presidency; rather late in the game, as half a hundred arch
editorials informed him. Three other contenders, all younger, vied for
the nomination. Only the incumbent was older, and that by only a year.

"Willie for President?" inquired the editorial in New York's Mother
of All Newspapers. "Why now?"

"Willie for President?" rejoined its principal rival, Washington's
Daily Conscience of the Universe. "Why ever?"

The thesis of the first, of course, was that he was already too old to
make the run, "too set in his ideological ways, too enwrapped in the
past to be able to deal successfully either with the surging needs of
America in the closing quarter of the century, or the anguish of a troubled world crying out for peace."

The thrust of the second was less polite:

"Senator Wilson's announcement is a triumph of ego over common
sense, of which he once appeared to have a lot. It seems to be gone
now. The whole idea is quixotic and, indeed, rather pathetic, given his
years and relative lack of equipment for the job, to say nothing of his
rigidly ideological mind-set. It is a little late in the game for him to
participate effectively now. We suggest that he reconsider—speedily."

"That," he told the latter publication's proprietress (known to many
envious rivals as "the Ditzy Doyenne"), whom he saw that night at one
of Jimmy Van Rensselaer Burden's lavish Georgetown parties, "is what
you think."

"We'll see, Willie," the Ditzy Doyenne said crisply. "If I can possibly
stop you, I will." She was wearing the famous diamond that was part
of her carefully calculated image. He fancied that it twinkled at him
malevolently.

"Go ahead," he said, equally crisp. "It's a free country. Despite your best efforts to make it conform."

Which had earned him a glare and a thin-lipped dismissal. He couldn't have cared less. The paper had been his enemy since he first entered the House; the animosity had only increased when he moved to the Senate. He had never forgotten Tim's report after he had been seated next to the Doyenne at a White House state dinner for the military ruler of some spot of sand in Africa.

"Willie is a friend of yours, isn't he?" the Doyenne had demanded. When Tim had said yes, he too had received the glare and the thin-lipped response.

"He's a dreadful man!" Tim reported the rejoinder. "He's a *dreadful* man!"

"It was said absolutely without humor," he added. "With absolute, naked hatred for you." He shook his head in the manner of someone confronted by an individual genuinely unbalanced. "Even for this town, I thought that was a little extreme. Even in the climate she and her staff have done so much to create."

Well: Willie reciprocated heartily, and was one of the few to keep right on being true to his own convictions and beliefs in spite of the paper's frequent withering attacks ordered by its proprietor. It would take more than that, he thought contemptuously, to make him knuckle under. He promised himself, being then young and idealistic and a newly minted denizen of Capitol Hill full of dreams and vinegar, that he never had and never would. Since then his views and those of the paper had occasionally run side by side, but there had never been any real trust or collaboration.

His ultimate decision to run for President was not, in any case, a sudden thing. He had cherished it silently, as many did, for many years. It was not until after his return from the previous, twenty-fifth, reunion of the house that it became a fixed objective in his mind. For him, as for so many, it became a matter of intense thought and calculation and, above all, of timing.

Everyone from the Vice President to the head doorkeeper of the House of Representatives, it sometimes seemed, had in his or her head the idea of running for President, as one of Willie's colleagues had once remarked with wry amusement.

"So why not thee and me?" he had asked, giving Willie a sudden sharp, inquisitive glance.

But Willie at that point was not ready to say or do anything. It was far too early, in his estimation, and his lifelong habit of holding most things close to his chest prevented candor that might possibly turn out at some future date to have been ill-advised. He had simply shrugged and smiled—the all-purpose, all-weather, all-concealing smile he had very early found to be a very useful shield against prying eyes and prying minds. He had learned—about the time of his successful campaign for president of the student body at the University, in fact—the advantages of retreating behind an amicable and noncommittal exterior. His years in Washington had honed and refined this mechanism of secrecy and independence into one of the major weapons in his armory.

"Willie goes away, inside," Donna had once remarked; and added, with a certain bitterness that seemed to increase as their years together lengthened, "but he always leaves that damned Cheshire Cat smile outside on the doorstep to fool the passersby."

Others of course had run for President at the age of fifty-four, which he then was when his first tentative gestures surfaced; many, even younger. But the complex web of American politics had seemed at that time even more complex than usual; and, with the added increment of the Vietnam War, a sea of discontent he did not particularly wish to enter.

There had been what one of his harshest critics, a loyal follower of Renny's in the national media, described in his column as "a minor Wilson boomlet here and there, but very low on the political applause-meter"—some small stirrings in Iowa, New Hampshire, his native California, the upper Midwest, the deep South, but nothing anywhere to provide a viable foundation for a really serious campaign with all its organization, money, state and local chairmen, enthusiastic volunteers and enormously costly advertising. He had never encouraged such halfway movements; had, in fact, actively discouraged them whenever questioned by the media. He had finally issued a statement designed to put a stop to them once and for all—for that time:

"I deeply appreciate any efforts anyone would like to make on my behalf in this presidential year, but I must respectfully point out that we have in both parties men of distinction and experience far greater than mine.

"I shall wholeheartedly support the nominee of my party. I look forward to working with him enthusiastically for the good of the United States of America, both before and after his election."

But who he would prefer that nominee to be, he steadfastly refused to speculate publicly. He did not finally commit himself until after the convention had worked its will and the nominee was duly acclaimed. Then he went to work, crisscrossing the country with a vigor and a dedication—and a genuine response from audiences everywhere— that made him one of the stars of the party and "a man to be reckoned with most seriously in any assessment of future presidential possibilities," as the *New York Times* put it.

When the new administration took office he was barely fifty-five. And the future—"The future," as he liked to remark with a sardonic flourish when doing a takeoff of one of his speeches for the private amusement of Donna and Timmy and the kids, "the future—lies—*ahead!*"

And so it did, he often reflected wryly as the years drew on, and there had been a lot to fill it. And perhaps that accounted for what Donna and Timmy and the family and close political friends and supporters came to regard as a quite puzzling delay between his first direct contact with presidential politics and his formal announcement at age sixty-two.

There had been Latt—and Ti-Anna—and Maryetta Johnson . . . and Amos and Clayne, "the other two kids," as he and Donna always referred to them, automatically according to Latt his separate place as the eldest and in many ways the most dominant and gifted of their children . . . and Anne Greeley and Fran Magruder Haggerty, and all the happiness—and headaches—their reentry into his life occasioned—and Donna's ailment with all its attendant worries and crises—and the constant battles with the "scum" and all the forces allied with them who had attempted, so persistently and relentlessly over the years, to undercut, undermine and ultimately (they hoped) destroy his career . . . and all the endless, nonstop grind of legislating for a rapidly growing nation thrust in spite of itself into worldwide dominance, and a constituency whose demands for attention and help never seemed to stop . . .

4   He and Donna had left the original twenty-fifth-year reunion, and the beautiful campus that held so many memories for them, in an emotional turmoil over Latt and the Johnsons, which, though they could only dimly perceive the possibilities at that moment, smoothed out into a more comfortable acceptance than they could then conceive.

Latt's decisions had been controlling them. As his parents saw it, Ti-Anna was too young and Maryetta too ideologically skewed for any kind of objective judgment to prevail. Latt was conditioned largely, they felt, by the era in which he came to maturity. His life for a while became "very sixties," as his mother put it—that hectic decade that was described then, and in subsequent histories written by defensive participants and fawningly sympathetic observers, as something per- haps more lasting in its effect upon America than it actually was.

It was influential enough to twist many young lives out of shape, however. For a substantial period, Latt's was among them.

Strong and determined son of a strong and determined father and mother, he thought he knew what he wanted and swept all opposition aside to get it.

He had disappeared while they were on campus and had not shown up to say good-bye, which hurt them, Donna particularly, terribly. But the minute he felt fortified by distance and their consequent inability to confront him in person, he joined battle. They had been back in the comfortable old house in suburban Maryland scarcely half an hour when the phone rang.

"That's Latt," Donna said with absolute certainty. For a brief moment they looked at each other. Then Willie picked up the nearest of the five phones they had in the house and spoke in a voice he kept as level and unemotional as possible.

"This is Senator Wilson," he said. There was a slight hesitation and he thought for a moment that Donna's intuition was mistaken. He decided to push it.

"Is that you?" he inquired.

His son, obviously also fighting to sound unemotional, but not quite able to conceal the little tremor in his voice, said, "Dad?"

"There's only one Senator Wilson in this house," Willie said with a sudden chuckle that sounded more openly relieved than he would have liked. "Until you decide to run."

"That'll be the day," Latt said, sounding relieved himself. But his voice was still guarded and on the defensive. It would take more than a show of the old Wilson charm to bring this younger version to heel, Willie thought; and was amused at himself for his choice of metaphor.

"What's the matter?" Latt asked sharply. "Is something funny?"

"Hardly," Willie said. "You've put your mother and me through quite a bit in the past twenty-four hours. What can we do for you now?"

"I'm on the other line," Donna said.

"Hi, Mom," Latt said, sounding a little more relaxed. "Did you have a good flight home?"

"No problems," Donna said. "Except wondering about you. Why didn't you come and say good-bye?"

"I had to stay with Ti-Anna and Mrs. Johnson," Latt said; and added simply, "They need me."

"Perhaps we do too," Donna remarked.

"I was going to stay out here anyway, wasn't I?" Latt inquired. "I am starting college out here tomorrow, after all. It wouldn't make much sense to fly back there and then turn right around and—"

"No, of course not," Donna agreed. "We wouldn't have asked that, of course."

"Still, it would have been nice if you had decided to at least say good-bye," Willie observed. "Conventional, but nice."

"Yes, Dad," Latt said, all too familiar with his father's tendency to be ironic, if not sardonic, on occasion. His tone turned stubborn again. "I said, I'm needed here."

"That's not exactly responsive," Willie noted.

"Why are you needed there?" Donna inquired. "Ti-Anna has her mother with her. Maryetta's perfectly capable of taking care of both of them."

"They've had a terrible shock with Mr. Johnson's death," Latt said. "That isn't something easy to take, you know."

"We have some regrets, too," Willie remarked dryly. "The house and By go back a long way. Jeff Barnett and I, in particular, go back a long way with By. His death is a terrible tragedy."

"In a sense," Latt said, with the curiously detached objectivity he seemed able to marshal when beset by emotional stress, "his death was almost inevitable, wasn't it? After all, he was opposing many of the most progressive elements—"

"Do you have any concept of what it took for him to be a symbol at the University?" Willie inquired sharply. "The first black ever admitted? I've told you the battle we had over my attempt to get him into the house, Jeff's opposition and the close vote, and all. He was a very brave man. So was Jeff when he eventually came around and accepted what was going to happen and became a leader—with By—of some of the most progressive racial forces in the South. Who's 'progressive,' by the way? You kids don't have a monopoly on the word. Particularly since," he couldn't resist adding, "you may not know too much about it."

Latt, as his father expected, rose to that challenge with vigor.

"Oh, don't we?" he demanded. "You don't know what you're talking about, Dad. By and Maryetta Johnson were the real leaders. Mr. Barnett just went along for the ride because he couldn't stop the tide. Maryetta's going to stay right in there and fight now. She's going to be heard from."

"She's always been 'heard from,' " Donna remarked. "If there was ever a time when Maryetta wasn't 'heard from,' I don't know about it."

"And it isn't just publicity-seeking, either," Latt said earnestly. "She's genuine. She means it!"

"Oh, does she *ever*!" his father agreed. "Does she ever! She *has* been very active, and I'm sure will continue to be. And I'm sure a lot of people who want publicity will be riding By's coattails to the grave and far beyond. I don't know that you need to be one of them, however."

"How do you know what I 'need'? " Latt demanded.

"You don't need to get caught up in what I'm sure will swiftly become the new Johnson bandwagon," Willie said. "Now they've killed him they'll sanctify him. You don't need to let yourself become a pawn in that phony enterprise."

"Why, because it would upset your political plans?" Latt inquired with an insolence that would have been insufferable if it hadn't been so familiar: he had used that weapon since about age six, his mother estimated. She intervened with a sharpness of her own.

"Your father's political plans have nothing to do with it," she said. "We're just thinking of your future happiness and well-being—"

"I didn't say I was going to marry the girl," Latt interrupted with an air of bland disclaimer that instantly confirmed Donna's most uneasy imaginings.

"I certainly hope not!" she said.

"Of course if I did," Latt said in the same rather remote and dreamy tone, "it really wouldn't be anybody's business but my own, would it?"

"Oh, Latt!" his mother said. "Stop being disingenuous. It would affect us all and you know it."

"I could stand it if Dad could," Latt remarked with a wry little chuckle that revealed as much about generational ties as any other of the characteristics he had inherited from his father—which, Donna reflected, were many. She decided, as so often, that her most effective response would be to veer away from a subject whose potential diffi-culties she could already see looming around the head of her firstborn. Something Willie had said one time about his son flashed briefly through her mind.

"I love him," Willie said on some occasion when Latt was being particularly difficult. "But I don't always like him."

That, she supposed, was the price of producing a strong son. Hope-fully the end result would prove to have been worth the wear and tear.

"Are you going to come back with them for the funeral?" she asked.

"As I said," Latt responded thoughtfully, not answering directly, "school's beginning. I'd sure like to, though."

"It will be a great White House show," Willie remarked. "Very his-toric. It would be a shame to miss it. Perhaps you should get here if you can."

"Will you pay my way?" Latt asked quickly. "It would be nice if all of us could be there at the service."

"Borrow it from one of your new roommates," Willie suggested. "That's what we did in my day."

"They aren't very wealthy," Latt said. "And they don't really know me yet."

"Tell them who your father is," Willie urged, with a wink at Donna. "That may impress them."

"Well, I don't know," Latt said, for the first time sounding a little doubtful. "I could try."

Willie sighed, but humorously.

"No, don't try. I'll loan it to you if you feel you absolutely must. But you will sit with us at the White House and you will stay here at home with us while you're here. You won't stay with the Johnsons. We don't want to have to face the media with a lot of questions about you and Ti-Anna before we have to."

"I repeat," Latt said with a patience that wasn't quite convincing, "it isn't as though I'm going to marry the girl."

"You can if you like," Willie said with an indifference he didn't feel but managed to carry off with a fair reasonableness. "We'll support you in whatever you want to do."

"I do appreciate that," Latt said, sounding genuinely grateful for the moment. "But you don't need to worry. I'm a long way from that . . . Well, guess I'd better run. Don't bother to meet me at the airport. Mrs. Johnson has already arranged with Ti-Anna's younger brother, Melrick, to pick us up. They'll drop me off at the house. We're going to catch the red-eye. I should be there around nine A.M."

"Good," Donna said, shaking her head in wry disbelief as she looked at Willie. "We'll be expecting you."

"You folks are really nice, you know?" Latt said in a tone that sounded more impressed than he probably intended. "You really support me."

"It's known as love, I believe," Willie said. "It's an obligation some parents feel. In spite of everything. But don't push it."

"You, either," Latt said, sounding amicable now that everything was arranged as he had planned. "See you tomorrow morning."

"Have a good flight," his mother said. There was a click and their son was off the line. She smiled at Willie as they put down their receivers. "Well, I guess we're going to have some fun in the Wilson family before this is over. He's going to marry that girl."

"Are you sure?"

"Positive," Donna said.

"Too bad By isn't here," Willie remarked, his tone first amused, then regretful, then genuinely sad. "We could certainly use his judgment now."

"I think he would have been pleased," Donna said. "Are you?"

He shrugged and, characteristically, avoided a direct answer.

"I really don't know. It's all just your hunch so far."

"Trust me," Donna said. "Mother knows."

He smiled a rather rueful smile.

"That boy is a force of nature," he remarked. "He's been trying to raise me properly for eighteen years. I only hope I can mature fast enough to keep up with him."

"By would have been fair in his judgment," Donna said, "which Maryetta never could be. It's a great loss for everybody. Us—the country—everybody."

"Tremendous," Willie agreed. "And so unnecessary."

"Latt and Ti-Anna were part of it," Donna said. "I wonder if they fully realize that?"

"Probably not," Willie said. "Perception at that age rarely cuts much below the surface. The full impact will hit them a little later." His tone turned bitter. "I hope Renny's happy."

"I can't stand him," Donna said as she resumed the unpacking interrupted by Latt's call. "I've never liked him from the first minute I laid eyes on him at school. I can't *stand* him."

"You're not alone," Willie said. "Dr. Suratt has never won many popularity contests among those who know him best."

And thinking back over their first reunion, he reflected sadly on how egregiously Renny had injected himself into what would otherwise have been a genuinely happy time, and how terribly his intervention had twisted a sentimental occasion into a national tragedy.

He thought of By and his sadness deepened.

What an ending, for the dream that had begun in Willie's senior year when he and Bill Lattimer had witnessed By's arrival as a transfer student on fall registration day—the first black to be accepted by the University, who very swiftly became the symbol for contending forces that now, a quarter-century later, had caused his death.

First had come Willie's attempt to get him into the fraternity . . . the pitched battle with Jeff Barnett, at that time the most set-in-his-ways little Southern rebel imaginable, the battle that Jeff won when he persuaded a sufficient number of their fellow members to blackball By . . . By's virtual kidnapping (as Willie sometimes thought of it) by Maryetta Bradford, that fierce, utterly humorless little campus radical who all of their married life had tried to push By into the more extreme areas of the civil rights movement . . . By's rise to national prominence, aided by Jeff, who, back home on the family holdings after graduation, had amazingly (but willingly) bowed to the forces of change—and changed himself—to become a major leader, along with By, of the more peaceable, less emotional middle ground of protest . . . By's appointment just days ago to be assistant director of the Equal Employment Opportunity Commission . . . his selection to give the first of the memorial lectures funded by their sometime housemate Rudy Krohl, that pseudo-Nazi, who during the war and after had sailed very close to the law and profited enormously from his family's trucking and moving-van business and his commercial contacts in a resurgent Germany . . . and the riot on campus two nights ago when a crowd inflamed by Renny and his followers had screamed "Nazi!" at Rudy and "Uncle Tom!" at By until finally some person unknown had hurled a brick that, either deliberately or by sheer insane fluke, followed a deadly trajectory straight to By's head and shattered forever that amiable, well-meaning brain.

So ended one of the most constructive forces in the struggle that agitated, and perhaps would always agitate, American society.

And now Latt, named for gentle Bill Lattimer, who was officially listed in the grade records of his time as being literally the brightest student in the entire University, dead at twenty-one in the car driven by Randy Carrero (who even now, cardinal and high official in the Vatican almost sixty years later, still remembered with anguish that other terrible night in house history) . . . and By and Maryetta's daughter, Ti-Anna, whom Willie thought of as "a cute little thing . . ."

But—his son's wife? *His* daughter-in-law? "Mrs. Latt Wilson," inheritor perhaps of her father's (and particularly her mother's) sense of missionary zeal, certain to be a constant target for media attention as the black daughter-in-law of one of the Senate's most prominent members?

"What's the matter?" Donna inquired, pausing to give him a shrewd glance. He realized he had stopped in the middle of his unpacking to stare vacantly out the window.

"What's the matter?" she repeated. "The happy nuptials?"

"I would pray that they might be," he responded. "If they come about."

"So would I, of course," she agreed. "But it won't be easy."

"No," he said. "Everybody involved will have to call on a lot of reserves."

"Well, one thing at least," she said, characteristically Donna-looking-on-the-best-side-of-things, "it won't happen tomorrow. And they're only eighteen."

"I don't place any bets on Latt's discretion at any age," he said. He added, sounding almost wistful, "Are you sure he's really interested in her? It isn't just a fashionable passing fancy?"

She smiled.

"You can ask him. He'll be here tomorrow morning."

Next morning he was, arriving shortly after 9 A.M. as he had promised.

With the morning mail, delivered as usual around eleven, something else arrived. His life, and all their lives, were abruptly rearranged by the local draft board. In late 1964 the junior Senator from California, who had successfully managed to finesse the Vietnam War for three years, was forced to meet it head-on in his own house.

The collision was made more disturbing by something he had never seriously contemplated, and indeed had always rejected out of hand as a stupid, self-defeating indulgence that had ruined all too many political careers. He had always told himself, with a certain smugness that was almost guaranteed to self-destruct, that he would never get involved in Anything Like That.

Then Anne Greeley came to Washington, as she had told him she might when they first met as fellow trustees of the University—highly intelligent, perceptive, decisive, a first-class political mind, comparatively young, not beautiful exactly but very attractive; treating him as an equal in a way that was far more appealing—and flattering—than the antics (as he described them to himself) of some ambitious simpering young intern sleeping her way around the Hill. There were plenty of those, and none had ever managed to intrigue him, though some had tried.

Within a few months after that, Fran Magruder Haggerty arrived, elected to the House just as he had told her she could be if she wanted it; sharing with Anne most of the same attractive qualities, plus sharing with him memories of attending college together, of old times and old friendship begun back when the world was young and she and Hack, now the famous composer far away in Rome, had seemed to be settling in for the long haul.

But Donna shared those qualities, too, he kept telling himself in a running argument he could never seem to resolve. So why stray? He didn't really know. ("Does anybody?" Tim inquired dryly from the lofty height of his bachelor perspective when Willie finally unburdened himself, as he did sooner or later to Tim about most things.)

It just happened, in both cases, seeming to catch him on the edge of something, perhaps prompted by Donna's sad crisis, though he was never quite sure. Perhaps it was just one of those cusps in life that hide just below the surface of things to trip up the unwary. And the wary. God knew he thought he had always been wary enough.

He never entirely understood it. The increasing pressures of Donna's illness formed as good an excuse as any.

Meantime Vietnam, the country, legislation, the concerns of his constituents, his family, hopes, plans, dreams and ambitions, went right along having to be met, faced up to, coped with. Reflecting in old age as the last reunion neared, he wondered how he had done it. The answer was the universal one, he supposed: if one was strong enough—and determined enough—and above all, lucky enough—one survived. Without these things—particularly the luck—one went under.

5   First came Vietnam and his son. At the time, they seemed to him a combination quite challenging enough.

The war, building ever more rapidly, was beginning to weigh ever more heavily on the country by the time Latt received his notice from the draft board.

His generation, most at risk, bore the heaviest burden.

Some of its members were genuinely and philosophically against the whole idea of war, any war.

Some were ideologically opposed to their own government and welcomed any excuse to subvert it and if possible bring it down.

Some were happy hedonists eager to ride the wave of protest, with all that it offered in the way of unrestricted license and uninhibited sex.

And some were desperately anxious to save their own skins.

Latt, like many, went through several stages of mind and attitude. None agreed with his father's basic thesis, which was simply: the Communists are using the war as a weapon against us and as a major means to achieve the long-range domination of Asia.

As it turned out, they did not achieve the second objective, the domination of Asia, despite the heavy investment by the Soviet Union and its satellites and allies in the North Vietnamese cause.

The first objective, the thwarting, destabilizing and weakening of the American will and purpose, was triumphantly achieved. It created the "Vietnam syndrome," which continued to haunt American policy-makers and the American military for a quarter of a century and at the start of the millennium was still going strong, despite the desperate claims by some American Presidents that it was not so. A couple of them gave ample proof that it was, with their gingerly approach to the exercise of American power in the post-Vietnam era.

It was only after the war had dragged on into the seventies under the tortuous tutelage of its third presidential micro-manager in the White House, and his Secretary of State, that Willie became as opposed to it as his son. All the three war Presidents were driven by one overwhelming gut reaction: the United States was not going to be defeated on *their* watch, by God. But in time—as an increasing number of the war's opponents, operating without much knowledge but always with great fervor, predicted—it was.

Eventually Willie, and the many like him in the World War II generation who were only reluctantly convinced, gave way.

Before that occurred, and before he joined the all-out opposition in Congress that finally moved to cut off all further financial support for the war, many battles royal took place inside the family. Donna remarked unhappily that they demonstrated "what happens when Wilson meets Wilson." Latt spoke with more genuine authority than most of his generation because he had been there and within six months suffered a major injury that sent him home early and marked him for life. This increased a natural dogmatism, largely inherited from his father, that made him a formidable opponent in argument. It also gave ammunition to those like Renny Suratt who bitterly resented Willie's success as a Senator and potential presidential candidate, and saw in his elder son a fortuitous and effective weapon to use against him.

Willie often remembered that he had warned Latt against Renny when he and Donna were flying out to the University to attend the first reunion and simultaneously see Latt launched on his freshman year. Latt remarked that he had heard about "some really neat professor" who was "quite a popular guy," whose classes he wanted to take. Hunch told Willie who it was, a question or two confirmed the identity. Renny had already published a couple of books, appeared on a number of television programs and begun to acquire a rapidly rising national reputation. By the time Latt arrived at the University, Professor Suratt was one of the great academic magnets who easily attract students and disciples. Every campus has a handful but not all ascend to national notice quite so swiftly and easily as Renny. He said all the right things, espoused all the right causes; the "great interlocking directorate," as Tim would later call it, spotted him early as a welcome

ALLEN DRURY

addition, took him to its politically correct bosom, guaranteed immediate prominence and lifelong success.

Willie's warning, as he realized as soon as he said it, had only served to send Latt even more eagerly into Renny's orbit. Renny of course was opposed to the Vietnam War from the beginning. Latt had barely met him the night of the disturbance that cost By Johnson his life, but Latt was more than ready to embrace the gospel and become a fervent follower.

Renny's influence increased steadily during the uneasy freshman year when Latt was expecting to be called up at any moment. When he finally went to Southeast Asia it was with Renny's ostentatious sympathy and unctuously regretful blessing. Renny made a great point of corresponding regularly with Latt, read to his classes Latt's increasingly anti-war responses and arranged for the publication of several of them in the University *Daily*. The situation was ideally tailored for opposition to Latt's father. Renny made the most of it, as did Willie's many other political enemies. The father-son conflict, set against the larger conflict of the war, was too good an opportunity to miss.

Willie's first election to the Senate after three successful terms in the House had been by a margin so narrow that Renny had successfully tagged him with the epithet "Senator Squeak-In." The media took it up happily; it was thrown at him constantly. Only a comfortable majority in his second race finally put it to rest, as much as it would ever be. He suspected he would never shake it entirely.

What he had done to ensure Renny's lifelong animosity, he and their other fraternity brothers could never quite figure out. Why Renny, only scion of one of the largest mansions and largest fortunes in Hillsborough, a short distance north of campus on the peninsula, should have zeroed in on Willie as a permanent target—why he should have been so generally embittered about life—who knew?

"It's just the way he is," Guy Unruh had remarked sixty years ago after one particularly acrid house bull session. "Smarmy, sarcastic, unpleasant son of a bitch."

And so he was. In a society engaged upon a relentless and endless search for The Reasons Why in everybody's character, Renny was one of those classic enigmas that just *is*. His childhood had been loving and well cared for, his adolescence spoiled and indulged; a single child in a

52

relatively elderly household (his father forty-five when he was born, his mother thirty-seven), he had always been heir-to-the-manor, unchallenged, undisciplined, free to be, first, an obnoxious brat, second, a sour and suspicious adolescent, and, third and from then on, a superior, unpleasant, critical, hostile human being. Fortunately he did not kill his parents, bomb a supermall or shoot up a fast-food outlet. He had been gifted from somewhere with a flair for words and a facile pen and they seemed to give him sufficient outlet. His targets were numerous. None did he seem to relish more than Willie Wilson.

His relationship with Willie had been difficult from the first. Willie's initial instinct with people was to be open, friendly and outgoing until given cause to be otherwise. This did not succeed with Renny.

Renny confided to one of his few friends in the house, Galen Bryce, the putative psychiatrist, that "there's something about Willie that I just don't like."

Gale didn't like Willie either, but was sufficiently astute to recognize his feeling for what it was: Willie was just too much the golden boy, the Big Man on Campus, the glamorous and seemingly always successful student body president and perfect natural leader. Renny, like Gale, was simply jealous of all these attributes. Sometimes that kind of resentment could carry over for a lifetime. With Renny, it apparently did. Put this together with Renny's influence in the intellectual and political segment of society that dominated American opinion on so many subjects, and Renny's fixation became one of Willie's most difficult and lasting burdens.

"My maggot," he called him sometimes. "He's always there, eating away, eating away."

Into this exasperating but apparently indissoluble relationship, Latt for quite a while fitted as perfectly as though Renny had invented him.

"If you didn't exist, he would have had to create you," Willie once told his son when some particularly bitter Vietnam argument flared.

"You did," Latt snapped, "and look what it's got you."

At which point Donna, alarmed as always by their vehemence, intervened sharply and told them to stop it. They obeyed grudgingly, as they usually did when she became really upset; and later Latt apologized when he and Willie were alone, which was something he rarely did.

"That's all right," Willie said; and with a sudden, rather rueful smile, "I guess I really have only myself to blame for what I did to your mother that night."

At which Latt had the grace to blush, and laugh, and tensions temporarily eased.

But not for long. The tensions and the arguments returned, increased by Latt's not very subtle attempt to escape from what his father regarded as his inescapable duty.

Duty to America was not a concept that many of Latt's American generation seemed to put much store by.

"I have a larger duty," he announced at Christmas break with the enormous pomposity of eighteen-going-on-nineteen. "My duty is to humanity."

"Well, bless *you!*" his father said, with the kind of elder's laugh that infuriates the young. "I wish I had such an awesome calling."

"You do," Latt said, "but you're afraid to exercise it."

Willie looked at him with exaggerated surprise.

"Really? That's one thing I've never been accused of—being afraid. Almost anything else, you name it, but not being afraid. My colleagues in the Senate don't think so, California doesn't think so, the President doesn't think so. Who does? Only my son. That's nice."

"I'm sorry if that offends you," Latt said, "but I have to be honest."

"You don't necessarily have to be honest," Willie said, "but I can see you do have to express your opinion. I suppose that's worthwhile, though I don't see how it helps the situation."

"The 'situation,' as you call it," Latt said, "is only killing a lot of good young men of my generation, and may kill me. But I suppose that doesn't matter."

"Oh, Latt," Willie said, "for *heaven's* sake, relax. I'm not in favor of killing the good young men of your generation. I'm not in favor of killing you."

Latt gave him an agonized but unyielding look.

"You would be if it came to a choice between me and supporting this God-awful war. You know it."

"I don't know any such thing," Willie said angrily. "I know you're a spoiled, arrogant, intolerant youngster who's been indulged far too much by your mother and me. I also know your life is as precious to us as any son's life to any parents. I also know there are times when the vital interests of the United States have to assume an equal importance in the minds of those elected to protect them. That's when things get difficult for us beyond your wildest young dreams."

" 'Vital interests of the United States!' " Latt echoed with an almost desperate scorn. "A typical Senate cliché you guys on that side of the issue always use. Who says 'the vital interests of the United States' are so tied in to Vietnam? That's a hell of a long reach, it seems to me."

"That's the worst-case scenario, I'll admit," Willie conceded somewhat lamely. "But it's among the major things that have to be considered. By me as a United States Senator. And as a father, which I was before I became a Senator."

"Well, as a *father*," Latt said with an angry emphasis, "you can think about me for a change. I don't want to go. And not," he added, "because I'm afraid of anything. I hope you'll concede me that."

"You've never hesitated to sail right into things," Willie agreed wryly. "A characteristic your mother would say comes straight from me. And always in the conviction that things are going to work out all right for you."

"So far they usually have," Latt said in a smug tone he would have rejected had he been aware of how it sounded. "And I think they will this time. But I sure as hell don't believe in it, any more than most of my generation do."

"Yes," Willie said. "We in Washington are being given lots of opportunities to note how your generation feels. At least you're not out there demonstrating and rioting with the rest of them."

Latt scowled.

"I should be. If I weren't a Senator's son—"

"That would make you even more precious to them," Willie said. "Why don't you join them? You and I could have a big public confrontation. They'd love that."

"I don't want to embarrass you," Latt said.

"No!" Willie exclaimed. "I can't believe such consideration from my own son!"

"Keep on riding me," Latt said with a sudden coldness Willie had seen in him from childhood when something really got to him, "and I may forget the consideration and do what *I* want to do."

Willie hesitated for a moment, then made the decision he would come to regret as the war meandered hopelessly on and Latt came home from it the wounded hero of the dissenters. But, he reflected, he too could be cold and stubborn and sometimes unheeding and unyielding; his son got it from somewhere, and it obviously wasn't from Donna.

"Go ahead," he said in a voice as adamant as Latt's. "I can stand it. Although I do appreciate your attempt at thoughtfulness and consideration."

"It isn't thoughtfulness and consideration," Latt said in a bleak voice. "It's love for you, but of course you wouldn't understand that, you have so little love for anybody but yourself. All right, then, I *will* do what I want to do. I will protest. I will demonstrate. I will do all I can to stay out. I may even go to Canada. But don't make any mistake about it, Dad. I will never ask *you* to help me. Never."

Willie gave him a long, thoughtful look.

"Well," he said finally, "that's telling me."

Latt returned his look somberly.

"That's telling you," he agreed. "Now what are we going to do?"

What they did, then and for several years thereafter, was to maintain an armed truce within the family and a very sharp disagreement in public. The public clash was inevitable, given their prominence and very similar personalities; the private truce was made both easier and more difficult by the underlying love that bound the tall, handsome, difficult son to the tall, handsome, difficult father; compounded, that first year, by all the tensions, also public, aroused by Latt's defiant marriage.

It was not, as Donna had foreseen, an easy time for the Wilsons; made even more difficult when, at age forty-nine, she suddenly "felt a little dizzy," tripped and fell headlong on the sidewalk in front of the east gate of the White House, where she was accompanying a group of California constituents on the morning tour. Recovering quickly, seemingly unharmed save for scratched knees and elbows, she said it was "nothing" and proceeded on her way.

A medical checkup at Walter Reed Army Hospital in northwest Washington also discovered "nothing."

But in her mind, and in those of her husband and children, a little alarm bell rang—and now and again from then on, with increasing insistence, rang softly again.

As with any public man and family, the headlines and news programs told the superficial story of Latt's marriage, Donna's decline, Willie's political journey in the Vietnam years. The trials and tribulations of the Wilson family, rendered in the surface shorthand of the media, provided a minor but recurring counterpoint to the war, rising on several occasions to the status of major news events, not only in the newspapers but in the ever more ubiquitous, ever more dominating world of television. What Willie referred to as "the incessant, infernal damned spotlight" seldom left them and only seemed to grow brighter as time passed. Everyone in public life, and, increasingly, anyone of any prominence in what was coming to be called "the public sector," was subject to it.

"Grin and bear it," he advised Latt when Latt complained about its intrusions at the time of the draft. Six months later, returning wounded from Vietnam to face hovering reporters eager to stir up trouble for a then pro-war Senator, Latt suddenly perceived what an ally the media could be for anyone smart enough to manipulate it—no hard task for anyone critical of the administration's policies.

"The media was waiting to be raped," his father remarked dryly later, "and Latt took advantage with every atom of his rambunctious being."

What the family referred to as "the draft stories" were prompted by an accidental, but lucky, at-random question by a Senate staffer of the *Washington Post.* At the end of a routine interview on pending legislation she had inquired, almost as an afterthought, "I don't suppose your boy has been bothered by the draft, has he?"

The implication that in some way he was too special or privileged to be "bothered" annoyed his father.

"He's heard from them," he responded, for once failing to keep his guard up with that particular hostile publication. Instantly her eyes lit up.

"Are they going to call him?" she asked. "Any indication when?"

"Nothing definite," he said, making his tone deliberately casual and offhand. "Eventually, I suppose."

"I think I'll ask them," she said; and being a good reporter, did. After that, everything fell into place.

**Senator Wilson's Son Gets
Draft Notice, May Face
Early Vietnam Call-Up**

**Colleagues Question
Wilson Draft Board
Pressure for Son**

**Sen. Wilson Denies Pressure
on Draft Board, Says Latt
"Should Be Treated Equally"**

**Draft Board Confirms "No
Go-Easy" on Latt Wilson**

**Colleagues Continue to
Attack Wilson on Alleged
Draft Board Pressure**

**Senator Wilson Again Denies
Putting Pressure on Draft
Board for Viet-tagged Son**

**Draft Board Confirms Wilson
Denial but Opponents in
Senate Remain Skeptical**

**Latt Wilson Denounces
War, Says "I'll Take
My Chances." Suggests
Pro-War Dad "Relax"**

**Sen. Wilson Joins Latt in
Appeal to Draft Board:
"He Wants to Go. Let Him!"**

**Donna Wilson Faints as
Son Leaves for Vietnam.
Senator Confident Latt
"Will Come Home Safely"**

And that, for six months, was that. The phony draft uproar, created by Willie's Senate opponents on the war issue and nurtured by major media beating the same drum, died down for lack of fuel once Latt was on his way. Relative peace and quiet descended on Capitol Hill where that particular minor sideshow was concerned.

Then Latt stepped on a primitive but effective Viet Cong land mine and came home minus his right leg below the knee.

He also came home with an absorbing and virulent contempt for the administration and all who supported it, which at that time included a large majority of the American people and his own father. Family tensions recurred and were sharply increased when Donna, thankful to have him back alive but appalled by his injury, sided with him in his increasingly bitter arguments with Willie. Amos, at that time almost seventeen and a lifelong worshiper of his big brother, began to side with him too; and presently Clayne, at fifteen turning into a beautiful and very intelligent girl, who, her father thought, shouldn't have to think about serious subjects at all, became equally vocal in Latt's support.

"I guess I'm alone in this household," Willie remarked, sounding less cheerful and more wistful than he had intended; and it often seemed so.

When it came time for Latt to return to the University to resume his interrupted education, it was quite obvious that he intended to return as an agitator, protester and determined and effective organizer. Two weeks after he got there he had a major hand in the first big anti-war protest to shatter the traditional serenity of the University.

He was already quite adept with his new artificial leg, but with a political shrewdness his father could only admire, he still used his crutches to maximum effect whenever opportunity arose. Because he was who he was, and because major media were zeroing in ever more relentlessly on legislators who supported the increasingly embattled President as he sought desperately and futilely to find a way out, it was inevitable that a picture of Latt on crutches should appear on a great many front pages and television news clips. He was also interviewed extensively. Since he was Willie's son, handsome, highly intelligent, fluently vocal and carrying the aura and authority of the wounded veteran, he became an instant hero and spokesman for the national anti-war movement.

"We've spawned a monster," Willie told Donna with an attempt at wry humor.

"I don't think so," she said flatly. "I agree with him one hundred percent."

"You would," he said. "You're his mother."

"You should," she retorted. "You're his father."

But of course it wasn't that simple. The President was stretching the claimed permissions of the Tonkin Gulf resolution to their limits, bombs were falling on North Vietnam, American troop strength was already over two hundred thousand, the President was anxiously trying one tactic after another as he sought compromise with little brown men who had no intention whatsoever of compromising. This was contrary to all his experience in his previous incarnation as supreme political genius.

"Why, shit!" he exclaimed in frequent frustration. "There isn't a son of a bitch on this planet who can't be persuaded to compromise!"

But there were plenty of them in North Vietnam; and aided by a constant drumbeat of anti-war media coverage, they were having an increasing impact on the Congress, where debate was becoming increasingly contentious.

Willie, still with the majority that continued to follow the President despite grave and growing misgivings, found it hard to keep the annoyance out of his voice when he was finally confronted by the same bright young woman from the *Post* who had stirred up the original rumpus about Latt and the draft.

"Senator!" she hailed him as he came off the floor from the latest bitter war debate. "What do you think of Latt's role in the anti-war movement?"

"Why do you want to know?" he inquired. She looked abashed by his tone for a moment, but her expression quickly changed to what he referred to, in private conversations with Tim, as "the media smirk."

"Everyone is interested in your son, Senator," she said. "He's becoming one of the bright hopes of his generation."

"A bright hope of your newspaper and everyone else who wants to subvert the war," he retorted with some asperity.

Again she blinked but again the armor of a self-righteous smugness came to her aid.

"I'm sorry you feel that way, Senator," she said, "but my paper and I feel the war to be an ill-conceived, ill-advised, inexcusable adventure. If we can stop it, we intend to."

"Don't you think I want to?" he asked, lowering his voice as the ever-alert Senate correspondent of the *Wall Street Journal* began to move toward them, obviously intending to force his way into their conversation. "Don't you think the President wants to? My God, Susan, you must think everyone who supports the war enjoys it. Well, I don't."

"Then why do you keep supporting it, Senator?" she inquired; and the *Wall Street Journal* chimed in with the blunt comment, "Your son certainly doesn't."

"That's right," Willie agreed. "He certainly doesn't."

"Do you try to argue with him?" she inquired.

"Constantly."

"Do you ever try to convince him he should change his position?"

Willie smiled.

"Constantly."

"Does *he* try to convince *you* that *you* should change *your* position?" the *Journal* pressed; and again he smiled.

"Constantly."

"Aren't his anti-war activities a considerable embarrassment to you, Senator?" the *Post* wondered. "I should think they would be, as it only serves to emphasize your own pro-war position."

"Which must not go down too well in California," suggested the *Journal*.

And again he smiled.

"I have my critics. But, then, I always have."

"Are they going to beat you in the next election?" the *Journal* asked. He shrugged.

"Maybe. Maybe not. Who knows? The war may be over by then."

"I'd like to hear Latt on that one," the *Post* remarked as the *Journal* started to turn away. "It sure doesn't look like it from here."

"No," he said, suddenly impatient with their constant carping; and deeply impatient, though he never said so in public, with Latt's. "It doesn't look like it to me, either. If you have any solution besides complete surrender, let me have it. I'll pass it along to the President. I'm sure he'd be grateful. He needs all the help he can get."

"Can we quote you on that, Senator?" the *Journal* asked quickly. Willie gave him a look of weary scorn.

"Oh, for God's sake," he said in a tired tone. "No, you may not. Now you'll excuse me. I have to go to a special meeting of the Foreign Relations Committee."

"About the war?" the *Journal* inquired, undaunted. Willie smiled, reverting to customary amicability.

"Is there ever anything else?"

So it seemed, all through those hectic years. And through them all, Latt clung stubbornly to his angry and embittered position. The consequences for his father, and for the anti-war movement, continued to swirl around Latt's discontented and forceful personality.

"Constantly" they argued, as Willie had acknowledged; and never with any very constructive result. For a time Latt—interrupted only by his highly publicized marriage to Ti-Anna Johnson, which provoked another media circus for a while—became one of the major figures of "the movement," as its self-important proprietors took to calling it—that hurly-burly, helter-skelter amalgam of genuinely idealistic protesters, shrewdly cynical manipulators and gleefully irresponsible hedonists who came along for the ride. Now and then decisive figures cut through the often violent miasma and pursued a clear and consistent agenda. Latt was such a one.

For Willie, repeatedly asked to comment on his son, challenged in his own family and under constant political fire in California, there was little so clear-cut and easy about it. No matter how often he carefully analyzed the situation and concluded that his own course was the right one—as he gradually and cautiously changed it—there remained the inner acknowledgment that Latt and his fellow leaders, much as Willie despised and abhorred some of their methods, might in the long run prove to have been on the right side of it all along.

They were inevitably having an effect upon a vote-conscious government. Willie did not like the preening pomposities whose pictures, actions and juvenile statements were so fawningly recorded on tube and news page; but he was able to satisfy himself that Latt was of sounder substance and more worthy purpose. Certainly he fully understood, and seemed to have Willie's instinctive flair for, politics.

His son, he reflected wryly, was indubitably his. There was a more than passing political resemblance, as Donna, growing increasingly uncertain about her own health, told him on several occasions.

"Then maybe I'm too harsh on him," Willie said in the aftermath of one of the demonstrations at the University that were shrewdly organized and orchestrated by Latt and his ubiquitous faculty friend. "Maybe he and Renny are just innocent, idealistic protesters, after all."

"Don't be sarcastic," she said. "Latt is. Renny is the one element I worry about. I wish Latt didn't have to associate with him, but he seems to stick like glue. Latt's too big a prize for Renny to let him get away. He'll keep on using him any way he can, you being who you are."

Being who he was, his son's marriage, which occurred within a year after Latt returned from Vietnam, was also of major media interest. The racial aspect was too good to pass up—also "very sixties," as Donna put it when her first instinctive intimations were proven correct.

Again the headlines erupted. Latt, already an old hand at the game of manipulating the media for his own purposes, invited their attention and got it.

**Latt Wilson Announces
Engagement to Daughter
of Slain Rights Leader**

**Bayard Johnson's Daughter
to Wed Viet War Hero, Now
Protest Movement Leader**

**Senator Supports Son's
Wedding to Black Girl,
Tells Talk Show She's
"A Fine Young Lady. We
Want Her in Our Family."**

**Maryetta Johnson Scorns
Wilson's "Tolerance,"
Says, "He Never Knew Her,
It's All Just Politics"**

**Senator Wilson Reaffirms
Approval of Latt's Bid
to Wed Johnson Daughter**

**Maryetta Johnson Says
"Wilsons Should Be
Honored" by Marriage**

**Senator Wilson, Eye on Voters,
Claims He's "Delighted"
With Latt, Ti-Anna Betrothal**

**Latt, Ti-Anna Elope to
Nevada: "If We Wait
for Parents to Agree,
We'll Be Old and Gray"**

So ran a cursory sampling of headlines. Behind them, an abrasive talk with Maryetta, whom he had not seen or heard from since the morning he had stood at the dying By's bedside in University Hospital. That had not been a pleasant confrontation and this wasn't either.

On a warm Indian-summer October morning about a week before the elopement, the phone rang in his study. Donna, seated in his big leather armchair reading a medical encyclopedia she had purchased recently, reached over and took it just as he picked up the extension in their bedroom upstairs.

"Yes?" she said.

"It's me," Maryetta said. "Is this Donna?"

"It is," Donna said. "Who is this?"

"Don't you recognize my voice?" Maryetta demanded with the little undernote of sarcasm that so often ran through her words. "The other mother-in-law . . . to be. If we can persuade the distinguished Senator to get over his conniption fits and stop blocking the marriage."

"Hello, Maryetta," Willie said. "I'm on an extension. What can we do for you?"

"What do *you* want to do for *us*?" Maryetta inquired dryly. "And what do you think you would be able to do? Except, as I say, get out of the way and stop interfering with the kids and their plans."

"We don't want to play games," Donna said sharply. "That's the thing we don't want to do. Where are you? If you're here in D.C., why don't you come and talk to us in person? If it's important."

"It wouldn't be any more comfortable than on the phone," Maryetta said. "Probably less so, in fact. Anyway, this marriage is very important. And I want you to stop opposing it."

"I'm not opposing it," Willie said, keeping his voice down though with difficulty. "The media has me on record in a dozen places in the past week as saying that I think it will be a fine thing. What more do you want?"

"You don't mean it," she said. "The media knows that. We all know it."

"How do I convince you of a negative?" he retorted. "You never did believe in my good faith, particularly when it came to By and me."

"I wouldn't accept this marriage myself," Maryetta said, "if I didn't admire Latt's stand against the war. Other than that, I have my doubts when I contemplate your lightweight little boy and my very solid and worthwhile little girl."

"Latt's no lightweight," Donna said firmly. "He is a thoroughly genuine and responsible individual."

"He is with regard to the war," Maryetta agreed. "Not in other aspects. Renny Suratt tells me he's bedded half the girls on campus."

"How would Renny know about that?" Donna demanded.

"He beds the other half," Willie suggested. "I just hope they haven't done it together."

"Renny Suratt is one of the great minds of our generation," Maryetta said sharply, and memory instantly brought a mental picture of her fox-featured little face, bun of hair, once brown now gray, drawn severely back to frame her customarily disapproving expression toward a world that never quite lived up to her demanding expectations. "It's typical of you to attack him personally, Willie. You should talk."

"Maryetta, darling," Willie said, "you haven't changed a bit. Always go for the jugular, to hell with any kind of reasoned argument. How did By stand it?"

Maryetta uttered a sudden sob but conquered it immediately.

"That," she said coldly, "is entirely typical of you, Willie. Completely unfair, completely vicious. That's the way you've always argued ever since I've known you. And you get away with it, with that pious, holier-than-thou air of yours. By and I had a wonderful marriage. At least *we* believed in something."

"So do I," Willie said calmly, "and I apologize if I was unfair. You've always been able to provoke me that way, Maryetta, I should be old enough to ignore it, after all these years. Anyway, I'm for this marriage, I'll say again . . . even if," he added carefully, "I do have a few misgivings—in some respects."

"Why?" she demanded. "Because she's half-black and he's pearly white? It won't be the first time it's happened."

"Or the last," he agreed. "But—"

"But what?" Maryetta responded. "Are you afraid Ti-Anna won't be able to hold her own in D.C. society? They may not even want to live here. I wouldn't, if I had you for a father-in-law."

Willie uttered a startled laugh, Donna a disapproving sound.

"With you for a father-in-law," Maryetta repeated firmly.

"Well, thank you, Maryetta," he said. "For that overwhelming expression of faith and support. I know having you for a mother must compensate for almost anything. I'm sure Ti-Anna can hold her own, wherever she is. She seems to be a very self-possessed little lady."

"We brought her up that way," Maryetta remarked with some complacency. Her tone sharpened again. "Are *you* afraid you can't afford a black daughter-in-law, politically? Maybe you're the one who might be at a disadvantage."

"That has occurred to me," he said dryly. "But I agree with you, it's coming, our kids soon won't be the only ones by a long shot. But certainly Donna and I don't need to worry about it. It won't affect me politically, certainly not in California. And we can be a buffer for them, here in D.C."

"You sound smug, Willie," Donna observed, surprising him. "What I worry about are the children. What sort of life is in store for them?"

"The same sort that Ti-Anna and Melrick have," Maryetta said. "They're not under any pressure. They're popular and respected."

"They're also the children of Bayard Johnson," Donna said. "The same sort of 'buffer' Willie and I could give Latt and Ti-Anna. When it passes down to the next generation, then what?"

"You're certainly jumping way ahead," Willie noted with some amusement. "Latt and Ti-Anna aren't even married yet. By the time our grandchildren are grown, things may be considerably different."

"They'll always be black," Donna said. "They'll always be automatically shut off from half their inheritance. They'll always be subject to challenge by people who won't be friendly just *because* they're black."

"You're projecting probably twenty years ahead, at least," Willie objected. "Do you really think the country will still be that prejudiced, then?"

"Yes," Donna said bluntly.

"But now we have the Civil Rights Act," he objected. "Now there are laws on the books—"

"We can have laws," Donna said, "but it's people who are going to have to change. Inside. Laws may help, but where it counts will be inside."

"I agree with you," Maryetta said. "But if you've talked to your son, you know he won't listen to arguments like that. He's bound and determined."

"We've talked to him," Donna said wistfully. "As always, he won't listen to us."

"You *are* against it, then," Maryetta said. "You did try to dissuade him."

"He's a hardheaded, stubborn boy," Willie said, ignoring both her assertion and her triumphant tone. "Surely you've seen that, Maryetta. I only hope Ti-Anna can cope."

"She's tough, too," her mother said, again with some complacency. "He won't push her very far. And now that he's going to be more involved with the civil rights movement—"

"Yes," Willie agreed. "I suppose marriage to By's daughter will have some moderating effect."

"Not just the marriage," Maryetta observed, "but what he's planning to do."

"Oh?" Willie said sharply. "What's that?"

Maryetta made no attempt to keep the triumph out of her voice.

"He thinks, and I agree with him, that the logical next step for him once the war is out of the way is to join the racial equality movement in some capacity where he can be a leader."

"He'll be a leader wherever he goes," Donna remarked with a complacency of her own. "But"—her voice became thoughtful and troubled—"whether it should be in that area or some other—"

"What better area?" Maryetta inquired. "Where could he be of more use to his country? Anyway, you're not going to be able to stop him."

"Not if you've gotten there first," Willie said. She snorted.

"Would it matter who 'got there first' with Latt? He makes up his own mind."

"I'm sure it's helped to have you there pushing him along," Willie said.

"If he hasn't raised the subject with you already, it shows he's made up his mind," Maryetta said.

"No, it doesn't," Donna said, sounding sad. "All it means is that he doesn't want a fight."

"After Vietnam," Maryetta said, "I don't think he's afraid of anybody. And certainly he isn't afraid of a fight. He isn't going to change, and why should he? It's a good cause."

"The best," Willie agreed. "It won't be a fight, anyway. I don't disapprove. I just want him to go in with his eyes open. He ought to know what he's getting into."

"He's not stupid," Donna observed rather bleakly. "He knows what he's getting into. I guess you've won, Maryetta."

"I haven't 'won' anything," Maryetta said. Her tone became dry, the customary sarcasm returned. "I'm not converting anybody. Renny Suratt was the one who really persuaded him. Talk to Renny, he'll tell you how determined Latt is."

"Renny!" Willie exclaimed, sounding as bleak as Donna. "I am wholeheartedly sick of God damned Renny."

"One of the great forces for good in our generation," Maryetta said flatly. Willie snorted.

"You're forgetting who started the riot that killed your husband."

"He didn't mean for it to get out of hand," Maryetta said, unmoved. "We've talked about it. I understand what he was trying to do. He didn't mean for it to get violent."

"If it had been me instead of By who took that hit," Willie said, "you'd be singing hosannahs and dancing in the street. You wouldn't be rationalizing it then. You wouldn't have to. It would have been a kindly fate, and a blessing for America, and just fine. Right? Too bad it turned out so you have to go through contortions to swallow the evidence and justify it. You have a good mind, Maryetta—a brilliant one, I've always thought. Too bad you parked it way out there in left field when you were at the University. You could have contributed so much, yourself."

"Thank you for nothing, Willie!" she snapped. "You're so flattering. I *have* contributed. And I'm going to go right on contributing. And with Latt and Ti-Anna to help me, we're going to do a lot more in the continuing battle for racial justice in the United States!"

"Now you're sounding like a pamphlet," Willie remarked. "Time to stop the clichés. Why did you call us, anyway?"

"I want you to issue a statement expressing your enthusiastic support for this marriage," Maryetta said.

"How many statements do I have to issue?" he demanded, exasperated. "And what good does it do? Every time I say something you come out with a statement undercutting me and saying I don't mean it. Why should I bother? Latt knows we'll support him in whatever he wants."

"That's very grudging," Maryetta said. "I'll bet you haven't told Ti-Anna that. How is she supposed to feel?"

"Why doesn't she come around and see us?" Donna inquired.

"Why doesn't he bring her?" Maryetta said.

"Ask him," Willie suggested bluntly.

"They're both afraid of you," Maryetta said.

Donna laughed, not sounding very amused.

"I doubt that."

"Well, she is," Maryetta said.

"They're always welcome here," Donna said. "They know where we are. Send her around."

"You'll have to ask her direct," Maryetta said. "She's too shy to impose herself when she thinks you don't want her."

"Any daughter of Maryetta's," Willie remarked, "cannot be shy. It just isn't in the genes. All right, we'll invite them formally. Want to come too?"

"No," Maryetta said. She chuckled suddenly, as unamused as Donna. "I'm not among those you can convert with the old Wilson charm, Willie. That ended about ten minutes after I met you at school. But try Ti-Anna. She's still up for grabs."

———

"That I doubt," Willie said.

When "the kids," as he and Donna thought of them, did finally come over a couple of days later to seek their blessing, Ti-Anna was so tense and Latt so defensive in her behalf that the visit ended in near-disaster. He and Donna were not at all surprised when the elopement came, even though its abruptness did embarrass them a little among friends and his Senate colleagues. But they made the best of it, bland in public, trying with moderate and fluctuating success to get every-one in both families on a plane of reasonably cordial acceptance.

After seven months of the marriage little Bayard Latt Wilson came along and everyone relaxed in his dusky, gurgling, endlessly cheerful presence—except Donna, increasingly centered on her own health and its noticeably downward trend. Many certainties went out the window. Uncertainties came in.

6   It was the third visit to Walter Reed Hospital, the last in an increasingly tense series of confrontations with doctors who either did not know what they were dealing with or were reluctant to say.

It was also the day when he found out that Anne Greeley, whom he had last seen three months ago at the regular meeting of the University board of trustees, had finally made up her mind to come to Washington.

The decision had been a long time in the making. Whenever the subject came up—as it seemed to do with increasing frequency when they were together, as they had been that day for a quick lunch at the Faculty Club—she had professed to be very uncertain about it.

"It would mean uprooting the kids," she said thoughtfully. "And David of course has regular visitation rights. It would mean quite an inconvenience for him if he had to go to D.C. or they had to come out here every time he wanted to see them."

"How old are they now?" he inquired.

"Deb's sixteen, Sally's twelve. They could handle the travel all right."

"And he's forty-five," he said, sounding a trifle dry. "He probably could too. I'm sure Bank of America could use another good lobbyist on the Hill. Why doesn't he go for it? Then you could all be together back here."

"That's the point," she said, not responding with much humor. "We're too together as it is. I don't want to just transfer it all to Washington. That would defeat the whole purpose."

"Which is?" he inquired. Across the room he could see their fellow trustees, Walter Emerson, president of the board, and Bill Nagatani of Nagatani Farms near Fresno, the board's newest member, obviously watching their conversation with some interest. He saw her note this, and noted her quizzical expression in response. He uttered a wry little laugh.

"We've got to stop meeting like this," he said wryly. "We'll be the scandal of the board."

"If ladies snorted," she said, equally wry, "I'd snort. That would be the day."

"It could be," he said, feeling suddenly rather reckless; but it was really, as he reminded himself sternly, just two board members relaxing over lunch in the midst of a hectic session enlivened by the increasing tensions of the war. New demonstrations were keeping the campus in turmoil. Latt, his wife, his artificial leg, his cane and his child seemed to be everywhere, although up to that moment in this particular board meeting he and his father had not seen each other, even though Willie had been on campus since yesterday.

"So," he said, more matter-of-factly. "So: your firm wants you to go to Washington, right?"

"They do," she said. "I'd be in charge of the office. Meantime," she added, with an enforced calmness that didn't escape him, "Covington, Burling called me yesterday."

"What a self-possessed young lady!" he exclaimed. "If I were still in the law and the capital's most famous law firm called *me*, I'd be jumping over the moon. Might do it anyway, even if I were still in the Senate at the time. That's a real honor, to have *them* call *you*."

"I assume they consider me worth it," she remarked, sounding more matter-of-fact than she looked: she couldn't quite conceal the little smile of satisfaction that threatened to break through.

"Go ahead!" he urged. "Give it a shout! Stand up and yell! This old dining room needs some pepping up."

At this, she did the thing that he found, rather disturbingly but also quite endearingly, was beginning to please him a lot. She threw back her head and collapsed into a genuine, delighted laugh that rang out over the plate-clashing, silver-rattling, academic-world-in-full-voice noises of the crowded room. Across the way Walter and Nagatani glanced their way with pleased, approving smiles.

"Now it will be all over the board," he said. " 'What are those two cooking up together? What's with them, anyway?' "

"Well," she said, suddenly serious again (or semi-serious, he couldn't tell which), "what is?"

"I don't know," he said, retreating. "What is?"

"Senator," she said with mock sternness, "don't duck, dodge, defend or equivocate. Just tell me. I asked you first."

"Hunh!" he said, getting busy with the rather overwhelming vegetarian salad he had ordered in deference to what he knew were her active dietary convictions. "There goes that typical lawyer's trick, answer a question with a question."

"Skillfully and shrewdly rebuffed by another lawyer," she said. "What a standoff of equal legal brilliance! I can't believe it."

"Believe it," he said. "I'm not confessing anything until you do."

"I have nothing to confess," she said firmly—and then, at the momentary look of chagrin that flashed across his face in spite of himself—"There, there, Willie," she said, patting his hand with mock compassion. "Don't take life so seriously. It will all work out."

"The most hopelessly hopeful, utterly vacuous assumption there is," he remarked, but smiling. "Often uttered by people who have nothing better or more realistic to say. 'It may work out—or it may not.' What a vast choice of alternatives! Talk about legal brilliance! Anyway, what are we talking about?"

"You tell me," she said cheerfully, attacking a large slice of cantaloupe with commendable vigor. "I'm completely mystified."

"That will be the day," he said. "The last time you were completely mystified was at the age of one year, three months and fifteen days."

"And six hours, two minutes and thirty-three seconds," she said. "What a revelation that was!"

"I think," he said with mock severity, "that we had better stop this and concentrate on eating. We're due back at the meeting in about twenty minutes."

"Right," she agreed. "Walter and Bill Nagatani will soon be coming along to collect us."

"You go along with them," he said. "I'll see you back there. I have to stop by the bookstore and pick up something for Donna on the way."

"How is she?"

He frowned.

"Not too good."

"And they still haven't found anything specific."

74

"Not yet. They're still working on it." ·

"Nerve-racking," she observed. "We've never met but I feel I know her. Give her my best."

"I will," he said, pleased. "Thank you."

"Willie," Walter Emerson said, suddenly materializing over his shoulder. "What is that boy of yours up to, anyway?"

"God knows, Walter," he said. "He's about as predictable and controllable as Marian and I were, back when *you* were the worried parent."

"She's done all right," Walter said in a musing tone. "Not so happy marriage, but three great kids and a reasonably stable life. And as for you, you've hit it. Too bad the two of you never quite—"

"That was a long time ago, Walter," Willie said firmly. "A *long* time ago. Anyway, looking back makes me a little more tolerant of Latt."

"They're much worse nowadays," Walter said gloomily. "Much worse. It's a whole different ball game. You kids were nothing compared to the foul-mouthed brats we have to deal with on campus now."

"I'll tell him you think so," Willie said. "He'll be pleased. He fancies himself as the rebel."

"Mine, too," Bill Nagatani said unhappily, a rare show of candor about his true feelings. His expression became wry. "We think Hiro's experimenting with drugs. And Mary Ibu wants to marry a Latino."

"Adjust," Willie advised dryly. "She will."

"I'll have to talk to you privately about how to adjust to a mixed marriage," Bill said. "You're the expert there."

"No mystery," Willie said. "You just accept and hope your training has equipped them for it. If they're good kids, which yours and mine are, basically, they get along with each other—and with you—and all's well. So, Walter, what's on the agenda for this afternoon?"

"You know perfectly well," Walter said, "since it's been your long-term project for years. We're going to start the ball rolling to make your fraternity brother, Alan Offenberg, president of the University."

"Over my dead body," Anne said, finishing her salad and placing her neatly folded napkin beside her plate.

"Maybe," Walter said with a fatherly chuckle. "But it's going to be done, so get used to it. Adjust, as Willie says."

"Brutal male domination," she remarked, humorously but not so humorously.

"You're welcome to beat it if you can," Walter said in the same there-there-little-girl manner. "It won't do you any good, but have fun."

"It will give you a chance to vote with Rudy Krohl," Nagatani said with a mischievous smile. "You'll love that."

"So will he," Willie said. "I think he has his eye on you, Anne."

"Hmph!" she said tartly as she stood up to join them and they all began to move toward the door. "Let's go, Walter, before this man thinks of any other great jokes to offer."

"I'll be right along," Willie said, joining in their laughter. "Save a seat for me."

Outside they found the afternoon golden in October's Indian summer. No lovelier time on campus, he thought wistfully, as he started for the bookstore and many happy young ghosts walked suddenly into his mind to accompany him . . . no lovelier time.

"Dad!"

The voice was young and vigorous and (he thought wistfully) perhaps genuinely welcoming, though one could not always be sure. He stopped and turned around, gave a start of recognition and almost turned back and plowed ahead with deliberate rejection. But the impulse died stillborn. He could treat his son's companion that way, but in spite of everything, not his son.

"Willie!" Renny Suratt said, his tone as always holding a subtle but never absent jeering note, his usual secret and self-satisfied little smile implying, as always, that he had just won whatever private battle with the world he thought he was waging at the moment. "What a wonderful surprise."

"It's made my day," Willie assured him, managing a barely polite handshake. "What are you two cooking up now?"

"Take a seat," Latt suggested as they threaded their way among the Student Union's busy outdoor tables. "Let's talk a bit."

Willie hesitated.

"I've just had lunch."

"Have some coffee," Renny suggested. His smile turned sardonic. "On me."

"All over you," Latt suggested with a lighthearted laugh as they found a table and sat down. "If he had his way. How are you, Dad? And how's Mom?"

Willie shook his head unhappily.

"About the same as she was last week when you phoned us. They're still giving her tests. They don't know."

"Are they making any progress at all?" Latt inquired with a characteristic sudden sharp impatience. "Haven't the damned doctors got the slightest idea?"

"Something neurological," he said. "They claim they're narrowing it down."

"But they haven't yet found the agreed-upon doctors' cliché," Renny remarked sourly. "That's the story of modern medicine, you know: nobody has the time or the patience—or the interest and ability—to do any real diagnosing. They all find the agreed-upon cliché. They read the book and decided that it's A-B-C and then they can treat it by the book, A-B-C. Nobody has to think, nobody has to really pay attention, nobody has to *really* find out what's wrong; that would be too much bother. The cliché is so much easier."

"I didn't know you had taken on the medical profession, too, Renny," Willie remarked as an obsequious student waiter appeared and showered Renny with a lot of unnecessary "Professor Suratts" as he took their simple order.

"Why, don't you think they need it?" Renny demanded sharply, defensive at once.

"Oh, yes," Willie said, suddenly feeling tired in the warm, singing day: Renny was always so predictable. Renny had been predictable almost thirty years, at that point. Willie wondered if putting up with him was worth it—if anything was worth it. "I'm feeling tired," he announced. "And old. Don't press me too much, Renny. I might let you have it, right here at the Union."

"Another sensation for the *Daily* and the city papers," Renny said with a pleased little laugh. "You will never cease to provide them with colorful copy, will you, Willie? They'd be delighted!"

"And so would you, I suspect," Willie said. "Anything for a headline, eh, Dr. Suratt?"

"The same applies to you," Renny said. "We're in the same business, essentially. Publicity. That's all it is, publicity. And," he gave Latt's bronzed arm a familiar squeeze, "the same with this one here, right?"

"Why don't you two stop spitting at each other like a couple of cats?" Latt suggested, removing the arm, but gently. "When do they expect to give you a firm answer, Dad?"

"Any day," he said, as their waiter, so obliging he almost seemed to be wagging his tail, deposited their coffee cups with a flourish and wafted away. "We should know something by the end of the week. Maybe before I go back."

"Which will be when?" Latt inquired.

"Probably tomorrow," Willie said, a certain defensiveness coming into his voice as he anticipated the rejection he was sure he would get. "Unless you and Ti-Anna would like me to stay over for a day or two."

"That would be fine," Latt said promptly, thereby making the world suddenly quite a bit brighter. "Give you a chance to visit with her and little By, who's getting to be quite a big boy now."

"That would be great," he said, trying not to sound relieved. "Your mother will want a firsthand report."

"I think you'll be able to give her a good one," Latt said comfortably. "Everybody's in good shape at this end of the line."

"Including you, obviously," his father said, giving him an appraising look. "Life on the barricades seems to be agreeing with you."

"That isn't funny," Latt said, suddenly scowling and looking disapproving. "This war is serious business. Even if you don't think so."

"That remark is so silly," Willie said tartly, "that I won't even dignify it with comment. And don't you, either," he added, swinging around so suddenly toward Renny that he visibly jumped, which made Willie and Latt laugh. Renny, not accustomed to having his dignity assaulted in the worshipful aura of student adulation in which he passed his busy days, flushed and looked quite insulted.

"Relax," Latt ordered. "The Senator really won't hit you."

"I've never known," Renny said, recovering his poise sufficiently to look around furtively to see whether anyone had noticed. No one had.

"He always had such a temper, in the house. He was always so formidable. Or liked to think he was."

"Oh, the hell," Willie said, again feeling tired. "I never said boo to a mouse. You live in such a dream world, Renny. I only hope Latt gets out of it alive."

"Latt," Renny said with relish, "does very well, thank you. You know his reputation, here and nationally. He's one of the major leaders in the student anti-war movement. We couldn't get along without him."

"I'm sure," Willie said dryly. "You always were adept at mesmerizing your juniors, Renny. Hopefully Latt will come out of it intact one of these days."

"But not with his views any different, I hope," Renny said; and for a moment they both looked expectantly at Latt, who seemed to be, momentarily, completely preoccupied and far away. He shook his head as if to clear it and gave them a rather vague smile.

"I don't intend to change," he said. "Why should I? The war is still inexcusable." He gave Willie a sudden challenging look. "When are you going to get smart and stop supporting that jug-eared jerk in the White House, Dad?"

"He knows what I think," Willie said, more ruefully than he would have liked: but suddenly it did seem that his own position was quite shaky. "I tell him what I think, often enough."

"But you won't break with him publicly," Latt said.

"Not yet," his father said. "Maybe when the time is right—"

"You're going to lose California next time," Renny predicted, again with relish.

"You'll be there trying to help me out the door, I know," Willie retorted. "Once a pal, always a pal."

"Never a pal," Renny said, suddenly sounding bleak and completely serious. "Never that. And never one, I might add, to be dazzled and besotted by the handsome, dashing, all-knowing, all-perfect Willie Wilson of California. Not on this campus in the beginning, and not now."

"Well," Latt said, standing up abruptly. "I've got a class this afternoon and"—his tone turned wry—"another demonstration to plan for the weekend. Right, Dr. Suratt? Dad, when will your trustees' meeting end?"

"Some time this afternoon or evening, I hope. We're going to begin the process of appointing Duke Offenberg president of the University."

"You will find the faculty overwhelmingly opposed," Renny said flatly.

"And two thirds of the student body with them," Latt agreed. "Isn't it time to cut the old fraternity bond? There are several hundred educators in the country better qualified."

"By ideology, maybe," Willie said crisply. "Not by character."

"Oh, character!" Latt said. And Renny chimed in wryly: "What's that?"

"Yes, character!" Willie said. "And what it is, you wouldn't know, Renny." He too stood up, Renny did the same. "I've got to get going or I'll miss half the debate, which is going to be fun. I congratulate you two for being on the same side as Rudy Krohl. No more worthy colleague than that two-bit leftover Nazi, I imagine. Thank you for the coffee, Renny. I'm overwhelmed by your generosity, as always. Take care of my boy. He seems to be in your hands, at the moment."

"Not in anybody's," Latt said firmly. "We do agree on a lot of things, though."

"I'm honored to have him working with me on issues so gravely important to the country," Renny said with a solemn smugness.

"I'll check with you in the morning about coming to the house, Latt," Willie said. "Should I plan on staying overnight?"

"If you can stand little By," Latt said with the quick, engaging grin he had inherited from his father, "count on it."

"Thanks," Willie said with genuine gratitude. "Maybe by then we'll know more about your mother."

"Give her my best," Renny said with the customary mocking undertone he adopted when dealing with people he knew didn't like him. "Always one of my favorite people."

Willie snorted.

"Oh, hell," he said. "Do you ever stop posing, Renny? Just stop it for once, O.K.? Just the hell stop it. Donna doesn't need your insincere sympathy."

"I couldn't be more sincere," Renny said blandly. "After all, she *is* a sick lady, I gather."

"Yes," Willie said, abruptly sobered as he turned away and started down the Quad toward the bookstore. "That she is."

But for a little while he was able to put that reality out of his conscious thinking, though it kept right on silently accompanying him as he walked along. He supposed it would be this way until—what? He backed away hastily from the void that opened before him then. Life without Donna? He could not conceive of it, so inextricably had she been intertwined with his life for thirty years.

Donnamaria Van Dyke! What an image that aroused, of all the perfect Activity Girls of a thousand campuses, all bright, all sparkling, all attractive, all overwhelmingly *involved* in every possible aspect of college life. They were born to participate, and they did; they were born to lead, and they did; they were born to show up their male competitors by sheer weight of brains and personality, and—to the annoyance of many of their male competitors—they often did. Big Men on Campus found their footsteps dogged and often overtaken by Big Women on Campus—always there, always eager to participate, always ready to run for office, chair committees, organize rallies, lead charity drives, plan dances, manage class affairs. Be Part of It.

A major aspect of growing up in college was finding out how large a part women played in life. Many a macho masculine career was devoted subconsciously thereafter to trying to prove that this wasn't so.

It was a lost cause. Sooner or later, Willie thought dryly, the Great Female Juggernaut swept over them all.

Not that it had been a bad marriage, far from it, or that he objected to Donna's major part in his own career. The senior year when he had been president of the student body and she vice president had been one of pleasant and harmonious cooperation, culminating in what most of their fellow students and the faculty seemed to feel was an inevitability.

Marriage had brought with it at one time or another all the tensions, difficulties, strains, hesitations, irritations and dependencies that marriage does. It also brought a reasonable amount of the ecstasies, comforts, satisfactions and solidities that a good marriage can. Particularly in these past couple of years when they were drawn closer by uneasiness about Latt's activities (which Donna, though maternally defensive, basically viewed with as much concern as he did), the marriage had been a source of strength and comfort. And Donna's presence had always been a great asset to his political career. All the helpful aspects of her years on campus had been carried forward and developed on a statewide, nationwide, basis. He had told her early in his career, and firmly believed it always, that "if I were to drop dead tomorrow, you'd be elected overwhelmingly to take my place. You're more popular than I am," he added with a humor that sounded just a bit rueful.

"I'm just here to tend to the details," she said with a smile; and he reflected how far she had come from the wide-eyed, eager, rather naive coed who had been at his side during their joint year of heading the student body. Her presence in his life had swiftly become quite indispensable.

Why, then, had she become boring to him in recent years? He recognized somewhat ruefully that after the usual traditional interval they had never been exactly the world's most passionate lovers; but they had enjoyed each other's company and had found many companionable satisfactions in his career and in the rearing of Latt, Amos and Clayne. Both areas of activity had their problems, but that was life—capital "L," he thought wryly—Life. Nothing insurmountable and usually taken care of in partnership and understanding.

There was no reason, then, for boredom; and no reason to be even remotely interested in Anne Greeley or in that other, much more familiar figure in his life, going all the way back to campus days, Fran Magruder Haggerty.

Particularly now that Donna was in the grip of something mysterious that was increasingly incapacitating, making her increasingly incapable of "defending herself and fighting back," as he put it to himself when the pain of the whole situation became inescapable and pressed inexorably upon him.

This it did increasingly. Was it Alzheimer's? Parkinson's? Multiple sclerosis? Or something even more elusive, hidden in the haunted, mysterious reaches of the brain?

Neurological it almost certainly was, the doctors agreed. Other than that, so far, they professed to be unable to specify. Moved by a desperate impatience, he was almost inclined to say with Renny Suratt: they hadn't found the "agreed-upon cliché" yet, and so were powerless to diagnose, react, treat, cure.

Hopefully, cure. He was increasingly less certain of that. An ominous sense of doom depressed him with increasing frequency nowadays. Behind Latt's impatience and the solemn-eyed earnestness of Amos and Clayne he could see it rising in them, too. And Donna was beginning to get something of that desolate look so many cancer patients projected, even though the one thing the doctors did agree upon—including Guy Unruh, who had flown in from Hawaii for two days of consultations, gratis, and then gone home, baffled—was that it wasn't cancer.

Anyway, anywhere he looked the prospects were not bright. The thought shadowed the drowsily peaceful afternoon as he almost automatically went to the bookstore, bought a copy of a new book on the University's founders and made his way back to the board meeting in the president's office.

Many students recognized him as he walked along. Many gave him polite greetings; a few, obviously war-inspired, did not. The former he thanked, the latter he ignored save for one ostentatiously scruffy boy who snarled, "Looking for corpses for Vietnam, Senator?" as he passed.

Willie, not looking around, tossed over his shoulder without missing a beat, "Fuck off, half-ass."

The boy's companions broke into startled hoots of laughter. The boy's riposte, if any, was lost.

Willie walked on, worried, brooding, embittered. It had been many years since he had walked the campus in that kind of mood. He tried to shake it as he entered the room to find Anne and Walter, as he had expected, going at it hot and heavy. He slid into his seat and prepared to resume his public role as United States Senator, member of the board.

Later, angry debate was concluded and the resolution to notify Dr. Alan Frederick Offenberg of his selection as the next president of the University, as of the start of the coming academic year, was passed by a narrow but decisive margin. Anne waited for him at the door.

"My, you looked mad when you came in," she said, falling into step as he strode along, head down, pace determined. "Are you feeling better now? After all, your fraternity brother won. We're going to have Duke Offenberg for the next few years, apparently. God knows how he and the anti-war movement are going to get along."

"Tensely, I imagine," he said. "But knowing Duke, fairly, I think." He stopped, on a sudden inspiration—but maybe not so sudden, maybe he had been planning it, subconsciously, all along. "Are you going back to the city? How about letting me drive you back and take you to dinner tonight?"

"Why, Senator!" she said, looking pleased but also, he noted with some relief, a little humorous, too: it wasn't an end-of-the-world thing for either of them (he congratulated himself comfortably then). "I don't know what I've done to deserve this, but it would be very nice."

"Good," he said, feeling suddenly very pleased with himself. "It's a deal."

"Where shall I meet you? Walter was going to drop me off on his way to the East Bay. I'll have to go back and tell him I've made other arrangements."

"I'm parked over behind the library."

"I'll see you there in fifteen minutes," she said.

"Fine," he said.

From that point the evening developed as he had hoped it would. He did not realize until he had delivered her to her apartment door, and she had invited him in, how much he had hoped that.

Once begun, everything seemed to become, quite rapidly, inevitable— at first, exciting—then calm—comfortable—free from awkwardnesses and uncertainties—a relaxed and enjoyable union, a meeting of equals, a happily accepted meant-to-be. He congratulated himself again on its feeling of rightness, its sure inevitability.

The episode was not a characteristic part of his life, as it would have been with some of his more free-swinging, risk-taking colleagues on the Hill. He was too innately cautious, too careful, too self-protective; and, he liked to think, too honorable. He was pleased with how sagaciously he had handled it; how skillfully, gently but firmly, he managed to avoid being trapped by what he interpreted as her attempts to make it more meaningful and more binding. Once again, he congratulated himself.

All of this smug male rationalization lasted approximately an hour. He was again on the Bayshore freeway, driving back south to his hotel near the University, when he suddenly found himself, as he thought of it ruefully, "sandbagged by guilt."

How could he do such a thing to Donna, facing who knew what demons? How could he betray his constituency and a national following accustomed to thinking of him as a staunch and unshakable pillar of society? How could he betray his own concept of Willie Wilson, to which he had tried to adhere, with reasonable success, all of his life both public and private?

It was easy, he told himself with an ironic regret as he relaxed into bed and memory came surging back: it was easy.

Only it wasn't, nor would it ever really be, even when Donna and Anne and Fran were long gone and Willie Wilson a figure protected by legend, whom scandal could not touch.

His stay the next night with Latt, Ti-Anna and the baby, whose nickname, "Little By," was almost becoming a title, went about as he had anticipated. There was a certain inevitability about that, too, though he did his best to keep it as light and pleasant as possible. A call from Maryetta, obviously deliberately timed to coincide with his arrival, did not help matters; but they all seemed to survive it fairly well. It was only after, freed from what they all seemed tacitly to agree was her domineering, overbearing personality, that the strains and stresses showed.

First, though, the baby had to be chin-chucked, tickled, bounced, cuddled and coddled; a squirming, laughing, lively armful, then almost a year old; an amiable, easygoing infant who, as Willie remarked, seemed to have come from some happy spot in space rather than from his two strong families; a uniting element in whose presence, for the time being, arguments could be subdued and differences submerged. It was only after he had been put to bed and they had consumed the meal prepared by Ti-Anna, a surprisingly good cook, that the world rushed in again. With a forcefulness like her mother's that surprised Willie but with which Latt was obviously fully familiar by now, Ti-Anna did her best to hold argument down. She seemed to be fully adjusted to her husband. All trace of self-conscious deference appeared to be gone. Maryetta's daughter was in control.

"Latt," she said firmly, "your father is here so briefly that I think we ought to just visit and not talk politics."

"Talking politics," Latt said with a smile, "is how we visit. Right, Dad?"

"That's right," Willie said. "But I think Ti-Anna has a point." He grinned mischievously. "After I make one more point. Have you changed your mind since yesterday, or do you still belong to Renny Suratt?"

"I don't 'belong' to Renny Suratt," Latt said in a tone that threatened instant flare-up but stayed relatively calm. "I do think his ideas are generally good, particularly about this God-awful war. And he is a very effective teacher. And his classes are fun and everybody enjoys them. I guess I'm no different from most of the guys and gals on campus. We like him."

"I know," Willie said. "You didn't grow up with him."

"Nope," Latt said decisively, "so we don't start from the same point that you do, at all."

"And you and your friends don't like me," Willie said, "so that puts us even further apart."

"They like you," Latt said. "I'd say most of them respect you, because you always seem to have a pretty sane balance on things. But they sure don't go along with you on the war. I think if you're ever going to change your position you'd better do it fast. Otherwise Professor Suratt may be right. You may lose."

"Would you mind?"

Latt gave him a look impatient and exasperated.

"Are you kidding? You're my father, of course I'd mind. I think you've done a lot of good things in the Senate so far, and I think there's a lot more you want to do, and can do. But you have to be reelected; and you won't be, if you stay on this course."

His father looked thoughtful.

"You may be right."

Latt gave him a look of mock astonishment.

"Am I hearing correctly?"

"I'm thinking," Willie said slowly. "I'm thinking. The issue isn't easy—it never has been, even in the first few months when it seemed so certain we'd win once we set our minds to it. It's become increasingly difficult for everybody."

"Tell me about it," his son suggested dryly.

He smiled.

"I tell you what, Latt. If you stop these near-subversive activities you're involved in and get out of the group you're running with and become your own man again and not Renny Suratt's"—Latt made an impatient gesture but Willie continued calmly—"then I'll make a speech in the Senate, breaking with the President and urging that we get out. I'll even join you in an anti-war statement in which I'll condemn the war—and you'll condemn the disruptive, lawless, self-defeating tactics used by your friends and supporters in the so-called 'movement.' How about that?"

Latt studied him quizzically for a moment.

"Why should I betray the people who believe in me?"

Willie shrugged.

"Why should I?"

"If I had to bet," Latt said, "I'd say your supporters are decreasing by the day—maybe by the minute. Mine are growing all the time."

"Maybe you should run for Senator," Willie suggested wryly. Latt smiled, but with an edge.

"I'm not old enough. Anyway, California has a good Senator. Why should I compete? I couldn't anyway. You'd lick me hands down."

"Hopefully," Willie said, sounding a bit grimmer than he had intended, "we'll never have to put it to the test. I don't see why you don't run for the House, though. Seriously."

"Not quite old enough there, either," Latt said. "But maybe one of these days . . . Your old seat will be open before long," he added, indicating that he had been paying attention, because very few people knew that the incumbent, a rancher from Tulare, had serious health problems and was thinking about retiring. "That would be a good little referendum, wouldn't it?"

Willie nodded.

"If we continue on opposite sides."

"I suspect we will for a while longer," Latt said. Willie nodded again, reluctantly.

"Yes, I guess we're going to. I think I've made you a pretty good offer, though. You'd better think it over more thoroughly before you turn it down."

"Oh, I will," Latt said, "but I doubt it will look any better."

Willie uttered a sound of mock frustration and regret.

"Damn! And here I thought I was giving you an easy out from the dead-end you've worked yourself into. But your mother always said we were equally stubborn and impossible to dislodge once we've taken a position."

"Not true of you," Latt said. "And not true of me. Except for a few little things like Vietnam. There's too much at stake there." His voice trailed away into sober thought for a moment. "Too much," he said again; and once again, coming back strongly: *"Too much."*

"So let's drop it, O.K.?" Ti-Anna suggested. "I made a good apple pie this afternoon, Dad. Want some?"

"It's the best," Latt assured him with a smile. "Better have it, Dad. Guaranteed to soften up the most curmudgeonly of Senators."

"Which I'm definitely not," Willie said. "Sure, I'll have some. With ice cream, if you have it."

"I just happen to," Ti-Anna said, with the flashing little smile that always made him add the adjectives "cute little" to her name when describing her to others, as in "that cute little Ti-Anna my son married." She had quite swept away earlier misgivings with her bright and attractive personality—except that Willie always felt as though he were inside the barricades when he came to their house. It wasn't like Vietnam—he could handle that. It was the angry legions of prejudice that always seemed to him to be waiting just outside the walls threatening to crash in upon the fragile citadel of their mixed marriage. He could never adjust comfortably to the thought, though Latt and Ti-Anna somehow seemed to be able to.

She was just returning from the kitchen when the phone rang. Almost midnight in D.C., he thought automatically, tensing as they all did. They had called Donna earlier and she had seemed steady and untroubled then; but knowing Donna, she would, regardless. Perhaps this wasn't Donna, or anything to do with Donna—

"Oh, hi," Latt said, in what Willie thought of as his "family" voice. "Yeah, Ti-Anna cooked us a great meal and now we're just sitting around. What's up?" He turned to them and mouthed: "The kids." He listened intently, face increasingly somber. "I see . . . I see . . . That's the damnedest thing. Hang on, Dad's right here."

"Well, hello!" Willie said cheerfully, trying to project a casualness he did not feel, using the humorous chiding they all used when something major came along that needed to be kept under control. "You two ought to be in bed by now. How come your mother isn't on the phone?"

His face became grave. Ti-Anna, standing next to Latt, instinctively placed her hand on his shoulder. He grasped it, hard, and pressed it against his cheek.

"I see," Willie said finally. "I'm scheduled to get out of here early tomorrow morning, into D.C. around five P.M. your time. Can you hang on until then, or—"

"You still have time to catch the red-eye," Latt said. "I'll run you to the airport."

Willie nodded.

"Scratch that. Latt's going to take me to the airport right now and I'll hop the red-eye and be there around seven A.M. Don't try to meet me, I'll catch a cab out. You sit tight and try to get some sleep. She's in good hands at Walter Reed and I know she'd want you to get a good night's rest"—*in case you need all your energies tomorrow,* as they all understood him to mean—"so lock everything up and go to bed and go to sleep and I'll see you first thing in the morning. Try not to worry. I love you."

He listened for a moment, face tender as they told him he too was loved. He hung up slowly and looked around at his son and daughter-in-law.

"Well, guys," he said slowly. "Here we go."

"But of course she'll come through all right," Latt said firmly. Willie nodded.

"Oh, yes. I'm sure of that. But in what shape, or how long—"

"Be hopeful!" Latt ordered sharply. "It's all we can do for her."

"Yes," Willie said, starting for his room to get his things. "Call the airport and get me on a plane."

"Yes, sir," Latt said soberly. As Willie went down the hall to grab his shaving articles from the bathroom and toss them in his bag he could hear Latt's voice assume the imperious tone he could use when he felt he had to.

"My father is United States Senator Richard Emmett Wilson of California," he said sharply. "My mother is very ill and he *must* return to Washington tonight. *Now please get him on that plane* . . . Thank you! Thank you so much."

He slept hardly at all across the continent. The plane was barely half-full (why Latt had to raise his voice to get him a reservation, he couldn't understand—except that sometimes Latt enjoyed doing that). The attempts at service were routine and perfunctory, just enough to interfere with his rest every time his fitful dozing was about to spill over into genuine sleep.

The scene at home kept repeating itself endlessly in his mind. He could imagine it so well: Amos and Clayne in the television room watching their favorite after-dinner program, Donna in the library reading, house and neighborhood quiet as always at that hour, no cars passing, everything peaceful and untroubled . . . and then suddenly a quiet little sound, not loud, not harsh, not demanding, barely registering on the kids' minds—but just enough so that after a moment Clayne asked sharply, "Was that Mom?" And Amos said, "I don't know. It was something."

And they had jumped up and headed for the library, to find her slumped halfway out of her chair, sprawled halfway on the floor, eyes closed, breathing heavily—unreachable.

They had reacted as the troopers they were raised to be, he thought with a surge of emotion; bless their hearts, they had taken over. They had gently eased Donna to the floor, put a pillow under her head, a blanket over her. Amos had called her principal doctor and an ambulance. It had been there in ten minutes; in twenty she was being rolled up to a room in Walter Reed. In less than an hour, dazed and terribly frightened but still functioning like the responsible young citizens they were, they were back home at the doctor's orders, about to take the sleeping pills he had given them, but before that, of course, determined to reach him and Latt in California and pass on the news, as the doctor had requested.

"What caused it, do you know?" he had asked, while Latt and Ti-Anna listened intently.

"We don't know," Amos said.

"The doctors don't know either," Clayne offered. "We just heard this sound."

"You did the right thing," he said. "I'm proud of both of you. Could you call the hospital and tell the doctor I'm on my way? And try not to worry too much. They're doing everything they can. Did she recognize you at all?"

"No," Amos said, voice thin and threatening to break.

"I think she tried," Clayne said, also on the verge of tears, "but she—she couldn't. She didn't even open her eyes."

"All right," he said gently. "Now, you take it easy and try to sleep. I'll be there before you know it."

"It can't be fast enough," Amos said with a shaky little attempt at a laugh.

"Like right now," Clayne chimed in, also bravely attempting lightness but not quite bringing it off. "Oh, *Daddy!*"

"Now, there's my brave boy and brave girl," he said quickly, his own voice unsteady. "Hang in there, I'm coming. Oh," he added on a sudden inspiration, "why don't you call Uncle Tim and ask him to come and be with you?"

"We're not afraid," Amos said stoutly.

"We're *not,*" Clayne agreed.

"I know," he said reassuringly. "But he won't mind. And I'd feel better. And so would Mommy if she knew about it. So do it for us, O.K.?"

"O.K.," Amos said, sounding relieved.

"He's so nice," Clayne said. "We can always count on Uncle Tim."

"That you can," he said. "Now I've got to run, Latt's waiting. Love from all of us. Be brave a little while longer."

"We will," they promised together, sounding so determined that his eyes filled with tears and he could barely see as he put down the phone and turned to Latt waiting at the door.

"On your horse, buster," he said to his oldest child, rallying for a passable attempt at humor. "Let's roll."

They said very little on their way to the airport. Latt drove too fast but no one stopped him. If anyone had, Willie would have pulled rank and probably received an escort in return. But it wasn't necessary, there was time. He could only hope, so repeatedly that it became a stupid chant in his head, that there would be time on the other end.

Somewhere over mid-continent, where he would someday range far and wide in his quest for the White House, often remembering then his anguished passage on this frightful night, Anne came into his mind.

He rejected the thought of her angrily, ashamed of himself. He ended up almost wishing she were there. She was a loving and helpful person, all else left aside.

7　They were waiting for him at the airport when he reached Washington. Obviously no one had managed much sleep, but though tense and tired they looked determined and ready to support him in whatever the day might bring.

He threw his arms around Amos and Clayne, drew them close for hugs and kisses, managed to free a hand simultaneously to hold it out to Tim. The kids were trembling on the edge of tears but Tim was, as always, steady and unflappable, thirty years of friendship summed up in his firm and reassuring grasp. There flashed through Willie's mind the thought, brief tribute to the endless complexities of human nature, Is this dignified gentleman the raging flamethrower of the media? Then the present moment resumed as Amos demanded his baggage checks and he and Clayne hurried off to get his suit bag and overnight.

"Well, buddy," he said, "thanks for babysitting."

"Not at all," Tim said quietly. "You know it was no burden." He smiled. "A little surprising, to one sleeping the sleep of the just shortly before midnight, but otherwise no problem."

"Thanks. Have you checked with the hospital this morning?"

Tim nodded.

"She's out of the coma and appears to be O.K.—so far."

"Was it a stroke?"

"Stroke-*like,* the doctor said. But they aren't sure. No paralysis. Mobility and speech O.K."

"God *damn* it," he said in a hopeless tone. "What *is* it?"

"They don't know," Tim said soberly. "They just do not know."

"Renny says they haven't found the right cliché in their medical books," he said; and in response to Tim's surprised look, "Yes, I saw

Renny. He's moved in on Latt's life pretty heavily but we managed to remain moderately civil over a cup of coffee at the Union."

"Still the flaming radical," Tim noted. He uttered a short, unamused laugh. "As I realize every time he attacks me as 'the leader of the deliberately blind conservative wing of the media.' Which usually," he acknowledged wryly, "follows an attack by me on him as 'probably the leading practitioner of fashionable far-left stupidity.' But of course he isn't stupid."

"Not at all."

"And he's got Latt mesmerized?"

"Not mesmerized, but they do see eye to eye on a lot of things, particularly the war, and they're both running with the radical wing of 'the movement,' as they call it. Hopefully Latt will outgrow it eventually. Renny never will."

"Arrested development," Tim suggested dryly as Amos and Clayne came hurrying back with the luggage. "I brought my car. I assume you want to go directly to the hospital."

"Yep," he said and uttered a sudden, spontaneous deep yawn. "God, I am tired."

But, of course, so were they all, except for Donna, who, though still a little groggy from the "neurological episode" and medication, still somehow managed to look reasonably bright and alert. Amos and Clayne led the way, hesitantly at first then almost throwing themselves on the bed as they embraced her. He followed with a kiss and protracted hug. Tim stood back a little until she raised a hand that shook noticeably and said in a weak but determined voice, "And dear Timmy. How kind of you to take care of them."

"It wasn't much," Tim said as he too leaned down and kissed her lightly on the forehead. "They're big guys now. Clayne made us all some hot chocolate and then I just crawled into bed and went to sleep until the alarm went off at six. Then juice—toast—coffee—off to pick up our gallant Senator—and here we are."

"He is gallant," she said, turning to Willie with a self-deprecating little smile. "I'm so sorry to mess everything up like this."

"For heaven's sake, Donn," he protested with affectionate exasperation, "as if you had anything to do with it."

"Well, it's my body that isn't behaving," she said with an almost shy attempt at humor that touched them all. "I ought to be able to do something to control it."

"That will come," he said, more confidently than he felt. "It will come. When do they say you can come home?"

"Another day or two. They want to run a few more tests—"

"Tests!" he exclaimed. "How many more tests are there in the world, anyway?"

She managed a wry little smile as her principal doctor, young, bright-eyed, humorlessly efficient and bushy-tailed, came in.

"I don't know," she said, "but I'm sure I will have had them all by the time they let me go home."

"We won't keep her very long," the doctor promised. "There are a couple more we want to do, particularly after this little neurological episode, but I think we're about to come to some conclusions. She will probably have to have a nurse at home for a little while, just to make sure she's navigating all right. But in a week or two she ought to be in good shape and raising hell with you all."

"That's me," Donna said with a weak but genuinely amused little laugh. "I'm a real hell-raiser, I am."

"You raise as much hell as you like," Willie said with a shaky little laugh of his own. "Just so we get you home in one piece."

"*You* go home and get some sleep," she told him. "You look exhausted. And you too, kids. And, Timmy, I hope you have your next column written so you can take a nap, too. And thanks again for everything. All you've done for the kids and for the Wilson family. You never fail us."

"I hope not," he said, leaning down to kiss her again. "You're my family."

"We're lucky," she said.

"I'll be in this afternoon," Willie said. "I'll tell you about my visits with Latt and Ti-Anna."

"Don't forget Renny," Tim suggested dryly.

"*Renny?*" Donna demanded, voice strengthened by distaste. "Don't tell me you saw Renny!"

"It's still not a very big campus," Willie pointed out. "Particularly when he and Latt are palling around together."

"I've got to get well and talk to that boy!" she said, not altogether in jest. "He's in bad company."

"There are millions of the faithful who would be flattered to death to be hobnobbing with the famous Professor Suratt," Tim remarked.

"I think even Latt is, a little," his father said. "But he has a way of seeing through people. Ultimately."

"Not too soon for me," his mother said, cheeks flushing at the thought of it.

"Getting mad at Renny is good for you," Willie said with a smile. "Get some more rest. I have to go to the Hill and check the office before I go home, but I'll try to get a few winks before I come in again. Around four, I imagine."

"Good," she said, turning on her side, suddenly drowsy and dismissive as the doctor checked her pulse and nodded reassuringly to Willie. "I'm not going anywhere."

Tim dropped Amos and Clayne off at the house, swung back and took Willie to the Russell Senate Office Building, where Willie invited him to come in and watch him set the wheels in motion, "if you'd care to." Tim said he often had, "but I think you need the company right now. And maybe I can contribute some sage advice to California's brightest."

"You often do," Willie acknowledged with a smile.

In the office building the high-ceilinged marble corridors were beginning to stir with life. Eight-thirty found many offices already cranking up for the endless routines of legislation, constituency problems, public appearances, speeches, interviews, functions, groups of visitors from back home who had to be shepherded around the Hill—all the thousand and one interminable, exhausting, monotonous details that lay behind, and exacted their price for, the formal titles of "Representative" and "Senator."

Next door, the office of Willie's neighbor, Ranulf White Cloud Petersen of North Dakota, was already bustling. His own was gradually taking shape: a couple of secretaries, a clerk or two, his public relations man, his administrative assistant. His desk was half-obscured by documents, letters, proposed bills and committee reports. He sighed. He had been gone only four days, but the accumulation, as always, was staggering if one tried to keep an eye on everything that needed it. He always made the attempt, was not always successful but thanks to a good staff was able to keep reasonable control of the things he had to know and do.

One of the secretaries brought them coffee, and he settled into the big leather armchair he had purchased years ago when he first came to the House; Tim sank into another on the other side of his massive desk. He began skimming aloud through his mail.

Tim offered flippant comments from time to time. The mail, Willie noted, was perhaps 70 percent Vietnam, the rest constituents needing help to meet the burdens of life in their enormous nation-state.

"Is that a normal percentage on Vietnam?" Tim inquired.

Willie frowned.

"These days."

"And it's running against the administration's position."

"Not entirely," he said. "Surprisingly, there's still a lot more support, even in California, than the anti-war movement and the major media would have us believe."

"The general perception, though," Tim said thoughtfully, "is that we ought to get out."

"Oh, yes." He sighed again. "Renny and Latt and company are making a lot of headway."

"How much longer can you withstand the pressure?"

"Not much," he said. "How about you? You must be getting a lot, too."

"Including Anna," Tim admitted rather gloomily. "She's beginning to waver. You'll soon find the *Washington Inquirer* beating the drums for withdrawal, unless I miss my guess. As for me, I'll hang in there a little longer, but the day's coming. And not because of pressure; you know me better than that. I'm not as convinced as I was. And you'd better not be, either. I'm beginning to think you may have to kiss California good-bye."

"I will never kiss California good-bye!" Willie exclaimed, slapping his desk with his palm in a gesture so uncharacteristic that it made Tim jump and blink and smile at his own reaction.

"My goodness, Senator!" he said. "No need to get violent . . . Seriously, I think you're going to have to give the matter 'most earnest thought,' as they say in this distinguished body."

"You sound just like Renny," Willie said. "And my son. They agree on that. Renny says flatly that, 'You're going to lose California next time.' And Latt says I must change my position 'fast' if I'm not to. Well, I'm thinking, as I told them: I'm thinking."

"Funny how the world of politics seems to be boiling down to that one issue, isn't it?" Tim mused. "It isn't as though you've been exactly inactive in the Senate. Or that you'll take an inactive record into the race for the presidency. You've taken plenty of positions on things, been in all the major battles. Not exactly an inactive Senator."

Willie smiled and shook his head.

"I'm not racing for the presidency."

"Yet."

"Maybe not ever."

"Oh, come," Tim said. "Knock it off. The only question is, when? Can I write another column about it?"

"When did you ever ask anybody if you could write a column about anything? If you want to, go ahead. It may be a little premature, though."

"Ah, ha!" Tim said, amused. " 'A little premature' but not mistaken, I take it. I gather it's about time to float the balloon again."

"Go ahead," Willie repeated. "I can't stop you."

After Tim left, having refused another cup of coffee and saying he was going home to take the nap Donna had recommended, Willie sat at his desk awhile longer before he too departed for home and a brief rest before returning to the hospital. His mind was operating, as it had learned to do over many years in Congress, on two levels. On the one, he was automatically jotting down brief answers to be transcribed by his secretaries into formal letters of reply to constituents; scanning committee reports and transcripts of hearings; reviewing upcoming legislation. On the other, he was reviewing a record that was not, as Tim said, "exactly inactive."

It was, in fact, a damned good and constructive one if he did say so himself—which he did not, as a general rule, except when running for office.

The only trouble with it, he reflected wryly, was that it was hardly the all-out, partisan, black-and-white, one-thing-or-the-other record that seemed to be demanded increasingly of presidential candidates in the latter decades of the twentieth century. He was often accused of being "hard to pinpoint . . . difficult to classify . . . doesn't lend himself easily to categories . . . independent, yes, but independent in so many directions that it is almost impossible to say at any given moment what he is independent *for*."

In his mind all of the characteristics that prompted these hostile scribblings and pontificatings translated into: fair, balanced, steady, objective, judicious, moderate, middle of the road—"so middle of the road," Renny had written in a sour article for a recent Sunday edition of Washington's most ubiquitous publication, "that he is in real danger of being run over and squashed out of public life by more well-defined characters in their rush for the nomination. Which would probably be a good thing."

The quote, minus the last sentence (due to some delicacy on the part of the publication's editors, who loved to be partisan but not *nakedly* so), was repeated in larger type in a black-bordered box inset in the main body of text.

As often happened with Renny's dicta when they appeared in the major national outlets that always gladly gave him space, a spate of similar articles from dutiful think-alikes followed in many wanna-be publications around the country. Willie did not particularly mind, since he had already decided not to pursue in that particular year the nomination Renny and his friends were so obviously working hard to deny him.

When called upon to characterize his own view of himself, as he fairly often was by the same publications, programs and commentaries that led the pack against him, he referred back to the middle-of-the-road cliché:

"I think that would be a reasonable appraisal," he would say thoughtfully. "Pro-choice, for one thing . . . For heavy taxes on those most able to pay, more moderate taxes on those less able to pay . . . For as much public education as we can possibly afford . . . For some sort of national health insurance, probably government-subsidized, since government is the only agency broad enough and big enough to handle it for the whole country . . . For reasonable controls on doctors' fees, drastic controls on the price of pharmaceuticals to stop unconscionable price-gouging of millions of people trapped by medical necessity into a constantly rising spiral of drug prices . . . some sort of advisory board or boards to maintain a constant review of hospital charges, with the power to force them down when they become too ridiculous and exorbitant—the bedpan charges, so to speak, the penny-cheap little touches hospitals love to add to the bill, as absurd and inexcusable in their way as any high-priced wrench or toilet seat in the military. . . .

"I am for the most stringent gun controls, even to the point of banning all weapons in private hands. Our permissiveness in this area is insane . . .

"I am for complete abolition of atomic weaponry in all its forms, and of the missile systems that can deliver it. The same goes for biological and chemical weapons. . . .

"I am for equality—genuine, not artificial—in all areas of our national life, from private business to academia to government agency. . . .

"I'm for an America that always tries to help all its citizens and bring them closer to the goal of a safe, secure, comfortable present and a hopeful, peaceful, promising future . . . an America that always tries to blend, rather than separate, all of its peoples of so many diverse racial and national backgrounds into one unified nation—a nation which, to use the old oath-of-allegiance clichés, is truly 'one nation, indivisible, with liberty and justice for all' . . .

"And in its relations with others, an America that has a strong, consistent, responsible foreign policy, without the constant arrogant posturing of Presidents who lecture everybody in the world and try to interfere in every crisis around the globe—Presidents who issue threats and warnings and ultimatums and then hastily turn tail and run away from them when any hostile power, even the most minimal like Somalia and North Korea, shows signs of defiance. I am against a policy of bluff, bluster and back-down. . . . I am for a President who puts America's word on the line only when he intends to keep it, and keeps it when events call on him to put up or shut up . . . a President with some minimal maturity and sophistication who realizes that he is being judged by some very cynical and world-weary minds around the globe; who is constantly skeptical and alert when confronted by their smiles and handshakes for the cameras at international conferences or in the heat of international crisis; a President as tough and realistic as they are—one who realizes that the world's loss of respect for him, if he permits it with empty words and timorous actions, or pathetic and almost laughable personal weaknesses, can only result in a steady decline of respect and support for the United States he embodies and speaks for . . .

"Essentially, I suppose, you can call me a pragmatic idealist. I believe enormous waste and sloppiness cripple all our purposes, domestic and foreign.

"I like most of the things my most rabid critics like, but I believe they can be done more skillfully, efficiently, effectively. If you have to sum it up, I guess you can say I'm a middle-of-the-road, want-to-do-it-better kind of guy. Not 'conservative.' Not 'liberal.' Just *here,* hoping the country and the world will get better, and trying to make them so."

The media, whose preachers, pundits and pontificators always hate independent minds they cannot control, never forgave him. He did not fit their stereotypes, he was often openly contemptuous of their vain posturings and insufferably arrogant pomposities, and they did not forgive him.

As he often told Tim, "I can't run for President, I'm too independent minded—*for me.* I value too much my right to think my own thoughts and make my own decisions without regard to the latest fashions in Group-Think."

And of course it was not only the media whom this attitude alienated. For many on the Hill, particularly among the younger, blow-dried generation whose smiling faces, perfect hair, glittering teeth and noble, ringing sound bites were more and more guaranteeing their success at the polls, he was equally anathema. He had a knack for making friends, and in the generally tolerant atmosphere of the Hill, still there though fraying under the pressures of increasingly personalized politics, he had quite a few he could call genuine friends. But they were certainly not followers or supporters.

In spite of that, Senate seniority, often complained about and challenged but never really successfully defied, saw to it that he rose inexorably through the ranks. Before Vietnam ended he was second-ranking man on the Senate Foreign Relations Committee, third in line on Armed Services. Between him and the chairmanships were three members, two at least in shaky health. He would get there yet, he sometimes thought rather ruefully. He only hoped the chairmanships would not fall open simultaneously. He would enjoy a couple of years heading Armed Services before he went on to Foreign Relations, his major heart's desire.

Except for the White House. He was always honest with himself about that—and with Donna and with Timmy, even though he and Tim kept up a running teasing game about it in which he never really admitted his final ambition.

He decided now, as he concluded his hurried skim-through of accumulated mail and prepared to go home for a few hours' rest before returning to the hospital, that he would put his ultimate ambition on the back burner until Vietnam was out of the way. He didn't want to get caught in the middle of that; for the time being he had to concentrate on getting reelected to the Senate. For that, he found himself more and more in a frame of mind in which he could contemplate seriously a sudden shift in position—so sudden that it would both shock, and get shock out of the way in a hurry. It would be something of a sensation, no doubt. Latt would be pleased. And Renny, he thought with some satisfaction going all the way back to the fraternity house and many insults since, would wet his pants. Hopefully.

Two days later the doctors came up with "something," as he thought of it.

"Something," presented with a suave assurance that attempted to put the gloss of a smooth professional manner on basic uncertainties.

" 'Organic brain syndrome' or 'organic mental disorders' is what we call it," the chief neurologist said.

"Even though in this case it takes the form of the physical," Willie noted.

The doctor acknowledged his point with a quizzical little smile and nod.

"Yes," he said. "The term does cover a multitude of things, and unfortunately we still don't know much about it."

"So when in doubt—" Willie said. Again the doctor nodded.

"When in doubt we do all we can. You will have to trust us."

"Oh, I do," Willie said. "Can she remain at home?"

"For as long as possible," the doctor said. "Home surroundings are always best, where possible."

"They will be," Willie promised with a sudden grimness, "as long as it can possibly be managed."

"A lot of 'possibles,' " the doctor observed. "We will all work together. And don't let it get either of you down too much. If we can find the right combination of medications it can quite conceivably go on for a number of years."

"With mental capability undamaged?"

"Hopefully," the doctor said. "It varies from case to case. Like many things affecting the brain and through that the human body, it can veer off in any direction, wind up in a number of different things."

"All unhappy," Willie said.

The doctor studied him for a moment, remembered who Willie was, and what he knew of Willie's long public record.

"You're a survivor," he said. "You'll manage."

"So is she," Willie said. "Except"— his voice broke a little—"when the odds are completely stacked against her."

"I can only reiterate," the doctor said. "We will do all we can."

"I know," Willie said. "We both thank you for that."

Home from that unhappy interview, eating Chinese takeout at a gloomy emotional dinner with Amos and Clayne, he received a call from Anne and life became more complicated. Particularly after his talk with Donna following his conference with the neurologist, which revealed her to be much more reconciled to her own mortality than he had suspected; and more than ever the fine woman he had married and could not now really contemplate betraying again.

Or so he told himself firmly then . . . not knowing how soon or how surprisingly he would be given the option.

8　He telephoned love and reassurances next morning but was not able to get back to the hospital until almost midnight, following another bruising session of the Senate that revolved around the President's latest troop escalation in Vietnam. He did not know whether the neurologist had spoken to her; he had not inquired and the doctor had not volunteered. He had continued to defend the administration's policies, for which he received a presidential call of thanks just before he left the floor around 11 P.M. There were follow-up questions from the media, the likelihood that he would probably loom large in tomorrow's headlines. He decided he would have to renew his offer to Latt as soon as possible. He knew he would soon have to say something definitive. As he left the floor he told the majority leader tentatively that he hoped to make a major speech on Vietnam, probably the following Monday.

"For us or against us?" that canny gentleman inquired.

"You may have to guess," he responded with a smile.

"I'll bet we'll still be guessing when you're finished, Willie," the majority leader said wryly. "But we'll all be looking forward to it, anyway."

Willie's expression also became wry, and a bit rueful, too.

"Good," he said. "So will I."

The hospital, never entirely quiet, was at its most hushed and subdued when he arrived just before midnight. He told the nurse on duty at the desk that he just wanted to peek.

"Go ahead, Senator," she said cordially. "I think she's asleep, so"—her large black frame quaked with coy admonition and quiet laughter—"tippy-toes! Tippy-toes!"

"You've never seen such tippy-toes!" he promised, and went off down the hall leaving her still jiggling slightly like an amiable bowl of blueberry Jell-O.

At Donna's door, he did "just peek." She sensed his presence immediately.

"Hello," she said, rolling over and gesturing him in. He approached with customary visitor's hesitation, pulled up a chair, took her hand, leaned over and kissed her gently. She responded with a sleepy smile that rapidly became more alert as she focused on his troubled face.

"You've talked to the neurologist," she said. He nodded. "Did he scare you?"

He smiled a little and relaxed a little; whatever Donna had to face, she was obviously going to do it undaunted, as always.

"Yes. What did he do to you?"

"Scared me too." She smiled ruefully. "I never thought I'd wind up as a medical mystery woman."

He tried to be humorous.

"It's a whole new career."

"One I could do without," she observed, also trying to keep her tone light. "However——"

"However," he agreed, "it does seem to be the consensus. So— where do we go from here?"

"We endure," she said. "What does anybody do, with something like this? What can't be cured—"

"I took occasion today to do a little research," he said. "I asked the Library of Congress to send a couple of books over to the floor and sat there reading while the flames of Vietnam swirled once more around our senatorial heads."

"At least it was a diversion," she said. "Did you learn anything?"

He sighed.

"Not really. All very mysterious, as the doctor said. A generic name for the unknown and inexplicable. Something. Except that nobody knows what it is."

"Except that it's unpleasant."

"Yes," he said gravely. "And may have dire consequences."

"Yes," she agreed. "It's beginning to."

They were silent for a moment. Down the hall someone moaned.

There was a brief scurry of nurses. The moaning stopped. The hall became silent again. She sighed suddenly.

"I wish—" she said; and began, very quietly, to cry. "I wish—"

"I know," he said, squeezing her hand again with the healthy visitor's frustrated urge to ease burdens. "Dear, dear Donna. I know . . ."

After a moment she mastered the emotion, dabbed at her eyes, blew her nose, looked apologetic.

"I'm sorry," she said.

"For *heaven's* sake," he said, close to tears himself. "You don't have anything to apologize for."

"I know," she said, "but it's such a burden on you and the kids. Have you told them?"

"Oh, yes. They wanted to come in again tonight but I told them you'd be home very soon. Latt offered to come back from California right away, but I told him the same thing, and to wait a bit."

"So did I," she said. "They all called earlier this afternoon. They all sounded determinedly brave. And cheerful. How are they all taking it, really?"

"Staunchly," he said. "Like their mother. Character tells."

"It's a mutual inheritance," she said. She shifted position with a sudden grimace.

"What's the matter?" he asked sharply. "Does it hurt?"

She nodded.

"Yes. Somewhat. I can't describe it exactly."

"Not your head?"

"Just general," she said. "I've begun noticing little things, from time to time. They're increasing. My tongue got tied up this afternoon when I was talking to one of the nurses. A little vague pain in the back of my head, which isn't like me, you know I've never had headaches. A sudden flickering at the edges of my eyes, a feeling of weakness in the limbs. This growing tendency to faint. The momentary blackouts, which are coming more often." She smiled another grim little smile. "It's coming after me," she said. "It's coming after me."

He couldn't think of anything to say to that except to shake his head—wasn't able to, anyway, so powerful was the sudden wave of sadness that swept over him.

"We'll have you home in another couple of days," he said presently.

"I'll be glad of that," she said softly. Then she gave him a sudden long, earnest look. Her tone when she spoke was equally earnest, commanding attention.

"Willie—"

"Yes?" he said, instinctively bracing himself.

She spoke gravely; this was obviously the result of long cogitation.

"If this—gets worse, as they indicate it will, and if there really is no way out except—except one . . . then I want you to know that you should lead your own life as much as you can and not restrict yourself arbitrarily on my account."

"What do you mean?" he asked, sounding stupid because he was so surprised.

"I mean what you think I mean," she said. "I think you should run for President, as I think you will eventually, and I think in your private life you should"—she paused but then went on, a little unevenly, but firmly—"you should be happy."

"What do you mean?" he asked again, unable to believe what he was hearing, it was so at variance with the whole concept of what he thought of as "Donna."

"I'm not going to draw you a diagram," she said with a sudden little chuckle that sounded for a moment quite like the old Donna. "You're not even fifty yet and if I know my Big Man on Campus it will be a long time before you bow to age, or even conceive that you might someday have to. So don't argue. Do whatever is necessary for your own happiness and don't worry about me."

He started to protest but she looked at him with the absolute candor of thirty years of marriage.

"I don't want to argue about it," she said with an expression somewhere between amusement and tears. "I'm not happy about it, but there it is. Just don't tell me, that's all I ask. Just don't tell me."

"I wouldn't," he said earnestly. "And of course I wouldn't—"

"Maybe yes, maybe no," she said. "You're only human, Willie. *That* I discovered a long time ago. Don't tie yourself up in knots making promises. I'm not going to talk about it anymore. Or mention it, ever again." A sudden bitterness swept across her face for a moment. "Do you think I *enjoy* the idea?"

"No, no," he said hastily, "of course not. But—"

"Better drop it, Willie," she said, still half-amused but basically still bitter. "I might change my mind."

He smiled, a smile almost pitying except that he knew he must never do that; or be too upbeat, either. His expression finally became sad—a sad smile, he guessed it could be called, which she returned in kind for a long, sad moment. He took her hand again.

"I love you," he said.

"And I love you," she said. "And always will."

"And always will," he agreed.

Silence lengthened, the hall was still. Thirty years and more sped by, a hundred snapshots of youth and marriage.

He could never betray her again.

Yet now he had been given the option. It was all right—she wouldn't object—she just didn't want to know.

Willie, he told himself as her eyes closed at last and she drifted gently off to sleep, now you must really be strong.

Next morning he called Anne at Covington, Burling and suggested they meet for lunch.

They met at the latest fashionable restaurant on Capitol Hill, one of the many that come and go—or stay and become temporarily favorite haunts of the Importantly See and Be Seen. Quite often the Speaker, the majority and minority leaders of Senate and House, sometimes even the Vice President with some O.V.I.G.s (Obviously Very Important Guests) could be observed being ushered with lavish deference into the small, private, much sought after Seniority Room, named in honor of the Hill's oft-attacked but most tenacious tradition, where many a legislative deal was hatched and many a legislative apple polished.

He chose it because it was one of the most conspicuous watering holes in Washington, where patrons went to be noticed and where few could imagine that things flaunted were sometimes really things to be concealed, and where most were automatically absolved of any purpose other than power and politics.

Characteristically she went straight to the heart of it the moment they were seated.

"You look tired," she said. "Is it Donna?"

His look was grave.

"We got a diagnosis," he said. "Finally."

"Good or bad?"

He sighed.

"Complicated. Obscure. But not good."

"I've heard of that," she said when he finished describing it. "Not encouraging."

"No."

She studied him with the sudden, intently close scrutiny he had observed when they were discussing some complicated problem in trustees' meetings.

"How is she taking it? How are *you* taking it?"

"Both well," he said. "As well as can be expected."

"She's a brave lady, I imagine. I know you're a brave man. What's the prognosis?"

"Treatment uncertain," he said. "Ultimate conclusion, probably inevitable. Time frame, who knows?"

"Soon?"

He shook his head and repeated: "Who knows?"

"I'm sorry," she said. "I really am. I wish I could do something to help."

Various clichés sprang to mind—"You help just by being you. . . . Your sympathy and support mean more to me than I can say. . . ." and finally the lay-it-on-the-line "Just hold me and let me cry." He dismissed them all.

"Let's order," he suggested, taking refuge behind the Seniority Room's lengthy menu, designed, with excruciating cleverness, to represent a page from the *Congressional Record*. "Want a drink?"

"Chardonnay will be fine," she said.

"I, too," he said, giving the order. "How's life at Covington, Burling?"

"I haven't been there long enough to find out," she said. "I'm still in a daze from just being here."

"How are the girls? Standing the transition all right?"

"New for them, too," she said with a smile. "But they'll manage."

"Tough mom," he said with an answering smile. "Tough kids."

"I'd prefer 'forceful,' " she said, and, suddenly grave again, "with a forceful friend. And thank God for that."

"Why?" he inquired, and couldn't resist a wry joke. "You don't need help. Everything always works out for Anne Greeley. I've noticed that at the University."

"Everybody needs friends," she said. "Even Anne Greeley. When am I going to see you again?"

"I don't know," he said, so truthfully that a sudden bleak look crossed her face for a second.

"I suppose I deserved that."

He smiled more warmly, and looked contrite.

"I'm sorry. I didn't mean to sound harsh."

"You didn't," she said. "Just—remote, somehow." The sudden concentration zeroed in upon him again. "*Are* you remote?"

"All my life," he said in a tone that sounded, not remote, but curiously lonely, "going way back to college days, people have accused me of that. 'Willie's wall,' Donna calls it, 'when he just goes away, inside, and nobody can get through.' I never mean it that way, though, it just seems to happen—either in me, or in them, I've never quite decided which. Maybe both, I suppose. Very confusing, to me, and I suppose to them . . . and now I'm even more confused. Do you know what she said to me?"

" 'Go your own way and be happy,' " she said crisply. " 'With my blessings.' "

He looked at her, startled, as their waiter appeared at his elbow, pencil poised, prepared to rattle off the day's specials. "How did you know that?"

"It's what I would do in the same circumstances," she said. "I was just guessing."

"Too good a guesser," he remarked. "It's frightening . . ."

After the waiter had jotted down their selections and briskly departed, he returned to it.

"You're too good a guesser. What do you guess that I replied?"

"You didn't," she said, with a smile that was suddenly, he felt, too

———

111

tender for public consumption. "You went away with your head whirling and called me. And now what?"

"You tell me," he suggested, with an expression at once amused, quizzical and uncertain.

"We shouldn't discuss it here," she said. And added, mocking a popular song, "Better come on-a my place."

"That really would destroy my ability to think," he said. "I've got to figure this out for myself."

"I can help if you'll let me."

He grinned ruefully.

"Indeed you can. And what would that do to all my brave resolutions then?"

"Why don't we find out?" she suggested. "If they're strong enough, you won't have anything to worry about."

He tried to look serious, but failed. And took refuge in light humor.

"You have to go back to Covington, Burling and be a big legal eagle after lunch," he pointed out.

"I'm beyond punching a time clock," she said. "At least for checking-in purposes. But if you're really worried for me, you're having another night session tonight: skip it. I'll be home."

"Don't wait up," he suggested dryly. "I may not be there."

"You'll be there," she said with a smile that would have been smug were it not so relaxed and friendly.

"Sitting at the far end of the sofa," he said.

They laughed and finished lunch in an amicable glow that stayed with him through afternoon session, dinner and acceleration of evening debate.

At 9 P.M. he called his office and told his secretary that he would see them all in the morning.

And so it began again, and went on, despite his best intentions. They had been genuine enough as he approached her new apartment in Georgetown: an intimate talk, a reluctant parting, a bittersweet farewell. It is a far, far better thing I do—and then there would be noble ships that would pass in the night at many a Washington cocktail party and diplomatic reception, clutching to themselves the high, secret intoxication of righteous self-denial.

Except, of course, that it didn't work out that way. The spirit was willing if shaky. The flesh enjoyed it all too much, and after it ended that time there came an insidious surge of satisfaction: he had been willingly seduced, not by some eager little Hill camp follower on the make, but by a highly intelligent, very attractive gentlewoman in an expensive gray business suit, quickly discarded. It was not only flattering from the standpoint of age, but because it was a union of equals. He liked that. In some curious way he could not define and did not want to analyze too closely, it made it all the more acceptable where Donna was concerned.

A lifelong habit of introspection caused him to reflect with some irony that this was typical: things had to be rationalized on a basis that would fit all his many imperatives and circumstances. Fortunately Anne seemed to feel the same way. They slipped quickly into a relationship as comfortable and reliable as though it had been there for years.

He never told Donna about it, of course, but he often thought that it was just the sort of solution she would have selected for him had she been able. This made the rationalization even easier, and to some extent eased the moral pressures he could never entirely forget or escape.

9

From that time until his first public pronouncement on the presidency, life flowed on in predictable channels. His public career continued to flourish, his vigorous participation in major legislation made him increasingly influential in the Senate, increasingly prominent on television, in major news stories, columns and editorials. He was consistently referred to as "one of the major leaders of the Congress," and indeed he was.

Donna grew progressively weaker, responding only fitfully to various combinations of medication devised by increasingly frustrated doctors. Anne flourished and prospered at Covington, Burling, soon becoming one of its most visible and effective advocates for various wealthy clients appearing before congressional committees, departmental review boards, administrative law panels. Her name appeared with increasing frequency in society pages, gossip columns, political commentary; it was tossed about in speculation concerning various lower-ranking judgeships. She was becoming, she remarked to him wryly after she had been in Washington four years, "the most prominent legal almost-was in town."

"It's going to happen," he assured her. "It may take a little longer, but you'll get there."

"I hope so," she said; and echoed the frustrated plaint of many idealistic thousands coming wide-eyed and eager to their nation's capital: "I want to get somewhere where I can *do* something!"

Fran Magruder Haggerty also wanted to *do* something, she told him on one of the occasions when, at Donna's urging, he asked her to accompany him to some official function. Her initial election to the House had resulted in a very successful first term in which she rapidly became one of the most media-favored members of the California delegation. That was followed by two more terms equally successful. In no time at all, it seemed to him, she was in her fourth term and consistently referred to as "one of the most prominent and effective women in the House," in a time when there weren't very many either prominent or effective.

She *was* "doing something," he told her on one of her visits to see Donna, which she did faithfully at least once a month. She gave him her characteristic quick smile, a businesslike, largely impersonal gesture that went with her trim brunette handsomeness and general air of shrewd competence. Anne had certain soft edges, he sometimes reflected. Fran had none.

"A very shrewd, very sharp, very political lady," he described her to the University's alumni magazine when it interviewed him for a roundup on "Graduates in Government: Our Men and Women on Capitol Hill."

He could understand her divorce from Hack Haggerty after their long and determined wooing in undergraduate days: Fran was going places. Hack was, too, but they turned out to be different places. Hack was quite content, his talent comfortably swathed in domesticity, to sit in his beautiful house on the Janiculum overlooking Rome and produce the many musical compositions that were received so respectfully around the world. Fran, Willie felt, was just beginning.

"You'll join me in the Senate one of these days," he predicted. Again came the quick-flashing, businesslike smile.

"Over several thousand dead bodies of ambitious male politicians in California," she said with a dismissive laugh.

"You can do it," he said; and Donna, though now very weak and barely able to move her head on the pillow, agreed with a ghostly chuckle in the high, husky voice that was all that was left, "Yeay, Fran! Go for it, girl!"

Briefly he considered—and knew Fran had considered—something more than just their close but casual friendship going back to campus days. She was, in a career-dominated way, a very attractive woman; all the intelligent things that Anne was, plus her own wry, perceptive, incisive view of life and politics. By mutual unspoken agreement they had reached the same conclusion: No. And had stuck to it, even though on a couple of occasions when he had brought her back to her apartment in the Watergate from some glamorous private party or state dinner at the White House, they had come very close.

Along the way he had told her what Donna had said to him that night at the hospital, which now seemed very long ago, so slow, tortuous and exhausting for them all had been the days and weeks and months and years between.

"That sounds like Donna," she said, obviously touched. "What a loving heart! And have you done anything about it?"

He hesitated, but in the face of her matter-of-fact, honest scrutiny thought: what the hell; and knowing her confidence was absolute, told her enough about Anne.

"I know her, I think," she said. "I met her at some trustees' dinner at Duke and Shahna's when you and Donna were in Europe someplace. A very *nice* person. But of course Donna doesn't know."

"No," he said, "but I like to think she would approve."

"Oh, she would," Fran agreed. Her gaze narrowed, became concentrated and alert: the political mind at work. "Are you going to run for President?"

Again the thought: what the hell.

"Sometime, yes. I've always sidestepped the question, but—"

"Yes, I know," she said, and smiled; briefly, but concerned. "You've been very smart about that. Of course you know, though, that when you do, you and Anne—and Donna—will be at risk. The media are beginning to lose all respect for personal privacy: They're beginning to thrive on its ruins. It's a downward slope from here on in. I'm sure you've been completely discreet, but somebody will know. Somebody, somewhere, will know. Somebody always does. And inevitably, somebody tells."

"We're very aware of that," he said. "We've always been very careful."

"I hope for your sakes it's been careful enough. I see now that I must worry about you."

"Don't," he said with a smile.

"Too bad it's never been us," she said, putting a hand on his arm as she walked him to the door. "You have a mind like mine, very political, very—*aware*. We would have made a great pair."

"Anne has that kind of mind, too," he said; thinking: what other kind would ever really appeal to me?

"Then marry her, when—when the time comes. I don't mean to be cruel to Donna, you know that, but—don't hesitate."

"We'll see," he said.

"And meantime," she added earnestly, "don't let anybody else know. Not *anybody*. It would just be asking for trouble. And trouble would be inevitable."

"Thank you, dear Fran," he said, kissing her lightly on the cheek. "One thing I've got here, anyway, is an absolute friend. And that means a lot."

"Absolute," she agreed. *"Be careful."*

But of course someone did know. He was positive there were no others, but as always with public men, he could never be entirely sure. A small uneasiness was always there, no matter how mitigating the circumstances. He knew that in a society still basically moralistic despite all the spoiled, ubiquitous, self-promoting narcissists of the unbuttoned sixties, it would be held against him by many of the older generation conditioned by the strictures of the earlier era in which they had been reared.

He had never discussed it with his Number 1 son, assuming that Latt, a psychological product of later days and also possessed of the political instinct of his heritage that told him what would and wouldn't play in Peoria, would be unsurprised by many things. In due course Willie found that this conditioned not only Latt's acceptance of Anne but his reaction to the speech in which his father had finally broken with the administration and announced his opposition to the official policy in Vietnam.

On that memorable afternoon, which Willie and all astute commentators regarded as the one indispensable step if he was ever going to run for the presidency, he congratulated himself that the event was going to receive full media coverage and complete national attention.

It was one of those days that unfold in the Senate with a sort of stately pageantry as they have for two hundred years and more—"one of the great days," as described by Latt, who flew in from California especially to be part of what he regarded as something of major significance, not only to him and his anti-war cause, but to his relationship with his father. His father, he felt, was finally reinstating the integrity Latt had always depended upon up to the time when Willie, as Latt put it, "waffled on Vietnam." Now that Willie was finally changing to embrace Latt's position, Latt was satisfied that the integrity was back.

"I don't mean to be smug about it," he remarked as they entered the chamber, "but I'm glad I kept after you. I'm pleased as hell."

"I'm glad I'm finally going to live up to your high standards," Willie responded dryly. "I never thought I'd survive your attacks to see the day."

"God!" Latt exclaimed with an amicable grin. "Neither did I."

They stood together at the back of the chamber for a few moments before Latt departed for his seat in the family gallery and Willie went to his desk on the floor: two tall, handsome, distinguished men, the one graying, the other youthful, on a cane, obviously father and son. The public galleries were filling rapidly with excited tourists; the press, radio, TV and periodical galleries were already standing room only. From every door the members of what Willie called "the Senate's unique one hundred" were streaming in to take their seats.

Watching all this, Willie became aware that Latt was quite ostentatiously searching the galleries. He decided he was supposed to acknowledge this, and did.

"What are you doing?" he asked.

"Looking for Anne," Latt said matter-of-factly, not desisting from his search. "I assume you invited her."

For just a second Willie froze. Than he took the only course open.

"Not especially," he said, equally matter-of-fact. "But she knew I was going to speak today."

"Nice lady," Latt remarked; and suddenly, "Ah-*ha*! There she is."

And he waved, and Willie looked, and indeed there she was, waving back. He waved too and could not keep a small ironic smile from his face, which he knew she would interpret correctly: so much for secrecy. "Somebody, somewhere, will know," Fran had said. "Somebody always does."

He must find out now, he thought, whether somebody was going to tell. He didn't think that of his son, but you never knew. He finished waving and returned his gaze to the rapidly filling Senate.

It did indeed promise to be "one of the great days," one of those days when Willie, looking around the floor, visualized stretching out behind each of his colleagues the cities, towns and villages, the farms and businesses, the roads and highways, the mountains, rivers, deserts, forests or shores from which each came. All America, he thought with a profound emotion that still gripped him after all these years, was spread out before him in this relatively small, old-fashioned room: the Senators and States of the United States, in panoply assembled.

"Mr. President!" he began. Guildford Dudley of Rhode Island, in the chair, responded with ritual recognition: "The Senator from California!"

The buzzing chamber abruptly hushed and prepared to give him full attention.

"Mr. President," he said, "let me say at once that I have a confession to make. I have been in error in these recent years and I rise today to correct it."

The last vestige of stirring, the last whisper of irrelevant sound, ceased. They were with him entirely.

"I have supported a war which I am now convinced America cannot win. I see some of my colleagues nodding with satisfaction, others shaking their heads in dismay. Some want to hail me for joining their ranks, others regard me sadly as they witness one who seems to them a renegade about to abandon their drifting ship. I must remove myself from these arbitrary categories. I am just one Senator, sincere then in supporting the official position, sincere now in leaving it. Circumstances change and with them the convictions of honorable men can also change. I would like to think I fall in that category."

He paused and took a sip of water. Across the aisle Ranulf White Cloud Petersen of North Dakota and Rupert Delancy Jimson of South Carolina, both hawks, murmured to each other in hawks' dismay. Closer by, Gavin Mullvaney of Massachusetts and Jeanette Gerson of Minnesota, both anti-war, exchanged approving whispers.

"I began by believing, as a great many of our countrymen did—

along with many on this floor, as well—that a line must indeed be drawn in Asia, that we were confronted by one more attempt to extend the physical, political and military reach of aggressive Communism in a way that would inevitably, in time, challenge us directly. Therefore, why not stop it now, before it reached uncontrollable proportions and acquired a strategic dominance that would only be corrected, if allowed to run on too long, by enormous effort and an expenditure of blood and treasure that might not, even then, achieve the goal of turning back the tide?

"Mr. President, we have expended enormous blood and treasure already, and we have not achieved a favorable outcome yet. And we may continue to do so, and still not achieve it. And so what, really, have we accomplished, what are we accomplishing right now, and what can we hope to accomplish in the future that will change the equation?

"I'm afraid the answer, Mr. President, is: nothing that can possibly justify the many thousands of young Americans dead and the many millions of American dollars wasted, being wasted, and yet to be wasted, if this goes on—nothing to date or in the foreseeable future that has noticeably deterred Communism—nothing that has strengthened our own strategic position in Asia.

"And what does the administration offer in the face of this, Mr. President? Why, more of the same. More of the same ghastly merry-go-round of more dead, more money, more war. It has long been sad and disturbing, Mr. President. For myself, and for many millions who are, like me, changing day by day, it is now insufferable, and impossible to support.

"I regret exceedingly that we ever got into this tangle-foot morass. I regret that I supported it as steadily as I have, and that I did not earlier listen to my common sense and say simply: No.

"I think the issue was sound, the issue one that we have faced and will continue to face all around the globe as long as the Soviet Union and Chinese Communism exist as major aggressive elements in the world; but I think the execution of the objective of pushing back and containing them has been abysmally and bloodily inept, costing us the lives of many thousands of young Americans who have been flung into war without clearly defined limits or a clear-cut goal. It is the lives that are most important, Mr. President. Always the lives.

"It is time to stop, Mr. President. Time to stop.

"I call on the administration to speed up these efforts at negotiation which are dragging on and dragging on and dragging on. I see where our Secretary of State meets with his Vietnam counterpart—and then they recess for a week—and the war goes on. I see where they are claimed to have made some minuscule progress—and then they recess for a month—and the war goes on. It is all very gentlemanly and casual, and, I am sure, very pleasant in Paris—the Tea Party of the Foreign Ministers. And the war goes on. And the young men die. And the war goes on. And it is time to stop. And the endless war goes on. And it must stop, Mr. President. It must.

"So, I was wrong to begin with, and in the minds of my pro-war friends and colleagues, I may be wrong now. But I think not, Mr. President. I think the logic is now overwhelmingly on the side of declaring peace and getting out as fast as we can.

"It was early decided to have a patty-cake approach to this conflict at the highest levels, because the President then in office prided himself that he had never met a man he couldn't reason with and talk into compromise. Well, he met them in Vietnam. And they don't compromise. His successor possesses an ego equally big and a delusion of infallibility equally great. It is now up to us in the Congress to rescue the situation from complete disaster. We can do it, Mr. President, and we must.

"There are many who will say: but we cannot abandon the South Vietnamese who have fought beside us so long and so valiantly for their own freedom; we cannot abandon gallant allies who have sacrificed so much in our cause as well as theirs. To those who say this I can only respond: we have done our best to help them; we cannot afford to do more, either in terms of matériel and resources or, much more importantly, in terms of American lives. If they lose in spite of our help, well, then, Mr. President, that may simply be the verdict of history which we have succeeded only in delaying, not denying. It is tragic for many of them, as it has been tragic for us, but we can only do so much. If the tides of history in that distant part of the world are against them, and us, then it may be that we, like they, will have to bow to them. We have done our best; our brave men have done their best. It is, I say again, time to stop, and to reappraise what we can and cannot do in terms of the world's problems and our ability to solve them for the world.

"It may be that even the United States of America cannot do everything, Mr. President. It may be that we have reached a defining moment in determining just how much we can do. It may be that history, which sometimes moves in even more mysterious ways than the gods do its wonders to perform, is telling us something we should not forget: that we cannot do it all, and that there comes a time when we must recognize the fact and moderate our conduct accordingly.

"Mr. President, speaking as one who has long supported the policies of the government in this tragic situation—and one who has himself, as the world is aware, had a son deeply and seriously involved in it, who, I am proud to say, is with me today"—he paused and there was applause and a craning in the galleries as Latt stood up with easy grace and, cane in one hand, waved with the other—"as one whose son has been in the crucible of Vietnam and thank God has survived it, I am serving notice that from now on I shall be in opposition to the Vietnam War; perhaps very late in the minds of many, including my own son, but nonetheless, here at last.

"It is time to stop, Mr. President. It is time to stop. Let us end this fatal—and fateful—exercise in futility and leave it to the ultimate judgments of history to decide. We have done all we can. We have done enough. Let us honestly admit it, and let us, as swiftly as we possibly can, get out."

And he sat down to first scattered, then vigorous applause that broke out across the floor and in the galleries, whose occupants were promptly admonished by Guil Dudley, still in the chair, that they were breaking the rules of the Senate and were subject to expulsion if they did not immediately desist. But the applause only rose defiantly, and only gradually, despite his heavy gaveling, subsided.

Later Willie reiterated his position in an informal press conference held in the ornate old President's Room just off the floor, where chief executives of the past used to come on the final night of a session to sign last-minute bills before final recess. He was informed by his young critic from the *Post,* among others, that die-hard supporters of the administration were already out with denunciatory comments: she and her colleagues could not resist needling one who had long and sharply criticized them, even though he was now on their side. His response was tart and unrelenting. He did not apologize or retreat:

"I still think many of you are doing a lousy, one-sided, inexcusably biased job. I still think you ought to be ashamed of yourselves. I still think many in the media are largely responsible for destroying American support for the war, which according to many polls still remains high despite your best efforts. So don't think you're out of the woods. History has a verdict to render on you, too. It will get around to you in its own good time."

Of course these comments appeared nowhere; he had long ago discovered that none censor more consistently or with greater ruthlessness than those who loudly and self-righteously wave the banner of the First Amendment. But it made him feel good, anyway. A little of the characteristic holier-than-thou smugness was removed, at least momentarily, from some of the more famous faces hovering around him.

For his critical Senate colleagues he had a kinder word: "They have their opinion, I have mine." And said the same for those being quoted in support of him, adding only, for them, "I thank them for their endorsement."

TV commentaries buzzed with sententious approval; headlines ranged from WILSON BREAKS WITH VIET SUPPORTERS, SAYS "WE HAVE DONE ENOUGH" to WILLIE SEES LIGHT, CANCELS PRO-WAR PAST to (in far fewer publications) WILSON TURNS TAIL, CAVES IN TO ANTI-WAR PROTESTERS.

This time he did not receive a grateful phone call from the current incumbent of the White House. Years later when certain tapes became public, he found on that date a bitter reference to "that c—s—ing c—s——r Willie Wilson and all the other fools like him who chicken out to these God damned fucking asshole protesters."

He cherished this example of dignified, statesmanly presidential prose and ratiocination, considering it to be among the most genuine—and certainly the most heartfelt—of the many comments he received on that significant day.

*   *   *

That night as he and Latt sat for a few contemplative moments in the den after a gentle good night to a Donna who drifted in and out of near-comas a good deal of the time these days, he decided to meet head-on the matter he knew was troubling them both:

"How did you know about Anne?"

"She called one day when I was here about a year ago," Latt said. "Mistook my voice for yours and began on a rather—rather intimate note." He hesitated and looked very young for a moment, which was not characteristic of the son Willie once described to Tim as "forty years old in his cradle."

"When I interrupted hastily, she became very flustered—not like you"—he smiled a little—"so much so that she actually gave her name when I asked for it. After that it was easy. I didn't pass along the message because I didn't know what Mom would think if she heard about it. And I felt it was your business, after all. I was quite surprised that she would call here. I thought your security would be better than that."

"It's one of the few times she ever did," Willie said. "She never told me about it. I suspect it was one of the times when her ex-husband was trying to get her back and was raising hell about not being able to spend more time with their two daughters. It happens now and then. She wants my help, though I can't do much except be sympathetic. I've never even met the individual."

"And in return," Latt said, "she is able to help you—more directly and often, right? And it's still going on, right? What does Mom think of this? Does she know?"

Willie sighed.

"No, she doesn't know. But let me tell you about your mother. . . ."

And related the long-ago conversation whose every word was permanently embedded in his mind.

When he finished, Latt's eyes (not surprisingly, for there were "depths beneath depths there," as Willie had also told Tim long ago) filled with tears.

"Mom," he said in a choked voice, "is a wonderful person."

"She is that," Willie agreed; and for several moments they were silent, contemplating what they had both received in the way of love and unhesitating support over so many years, and what they were so inexorably losing now.

"I wish," Latt said finally, blowing his nose vigorously, clearing his throat and speaking in a husky voice, "I wish—I wish she could just *go*. I wish God would just *let her go*. She never did anything to deserve what she's had to go through."

"No, she never has," Willie said. "And the reason why she has had to suffer so will never be clear to me, I'm sure. It's the greatest waste of my life—and I hope for your sake that it's the worst for you, too. I hope you never have to face anything like this again."

"I hope not," Latt said, and shivered as though suddenly cold. He started to say something—stopped—resumed.

"I don't mean to sound coarse and uncaring and political," he said with a bleak little smile, "but people in our position have to think this way sometimes—*could* you run, as long as Mom is—is dying?"

Willie too looked bleak.

"I know, I've thought about that. It can't be very much longer; the doctors are amazed it's lasted this long. Politically, I probably have about a year before I'll have to announce, if I'm going to; and you'll need at least that long to even begin to pull together the framework of a campaign. Within that time frame there should be some—culmination."

"I hope so," Latt said. "For her sake." He stood up. "Well, I'm going to bed. It was a great speech." He concluded with a cliché whose triteness but relevance he recognized with a wan little smile: "I suppose everything will work out."

He held out his hand and Willie took it, much moved.

"It will," he said. "Thank you for everything. Sleep well."

"I will," Latt said, returning a firm grip. "And you, too."

"I will," Willie said. And turned out the lights and went upstairs to bed, though he did not fall asleep for quite some time.

In the room next to his, which for many months now had been hers alone, Donna slept on.

*　　　　*　　　　*

125

A year later, two months after she was at last granted the release she had begun openly to desire—and after he and Latt had made a stone-cold sober appraisal of exactly where he stood in the current political situation—he issued his statement of declination:

"I deeply appreciate any efforts anyone would like to make on my behalf in this presidential year, but I must respectfully point out that we have in both parties men of distinction and experience far greater than mine.

"I shall wholeheartedly support the nominee of my party. I look forward to working with him enthusiastically for the good of the United States, both before and after his election."

Which, as New York's Mother of All Newspapers pointed out with some sarcasm, "leaves us exactly—where?"

And of which, Washington's Daily Conscience of the Universe remarked with obvious frustration, "Senator Wilson may know what he means by his so-called 'withdrawal statement,' but he has lost *us*. We must confess that, for us, he has only muddied even further waters already muddied. Which, we suspect, was exactly his intention."

Nonetheless, they had to take it. He promptly canceled all preconvention activities, later devoted himself wholeheartedly to the nominee's cause; and lived to fight again another day.

That the day would come, he was absolutely certain. The conviction seized upon him suddenly within hours of issuing his statement.

The revelation did not come on the road to Damascus, he told Latt with the self-humor that sometimes startled even those closest to him, but while he was trying to catch a cab at the corner of the Russell Senate Office Building, on a freezing Washington winter afternoon, with a devastatingly cold wind blowing up from downtown under a glowering gray-black sky that promised heavy snow.

To the success of that day he now devoted himself. Its imperatives underlay everything he did, dominated in one way or another his public acts, established its own inevitability, cast its decisive influence on his private life. He thought, with the inner irony that had characterized him all his life, going far back to his first taste of politics on a beautiful western campus, that Phase Two of the Remarkable Life of Richard Emmett Wilson was about to begin.

"I can't *wait* to find out what will happen," he remarked to the family with a wry smile.

"Don't push it," Latt advised. "It will all fall into place soon enough."

And so it did.

———

2

The Very Occasional Newsletter, Vol. 2

1 Prompted by the major flurry of national interest that greeted Willie's announcement (and prompted by Willie), Johnny Herbert, who had become one of the fixtures of the University and one of its outstanding (and outstandingly nice) characters, revived what he referred to as his *Very Occasional Newsletter,* the purpose being "to bring the boys (!) of Alpha Zeta up to date on all their by now far-flung and doubtless decrepit brethren."

"You remember the first edition," he wrote cheerfully, "about thirty years ago. I don't know quite why I'm reviving it now, except that Willie called me and said I should; and you know Willie. To this day, his wish is our command, so heavily does the weight of youthful obedience to superior intellect, wisdom and downright domineering (sorry, Willie, but sometimes you used to be) still weigh upon us.

"He also offered me the help of his staff in running you all down so I could call you for an update. I didn't really have much excuse to say no, with most of the work done for me. So here goes.

"I'm going to take us class by class, starting with the Class of '39. Leading all the rest like Abou Ben Adhem comes:

"*Timothy Bates.* Tim is still in Washington, still writing for the *Washington Inquirer* and many other publications, most of them—dare we say it—of a more restrained (his critics cry 'conservative!') sort than the great majority of the media. Tim is still unmarried and apparently still relaxed about it (as, I might add, is yours truly—still in place at the University, having gravitated to the history department where I seem to have found a compatible home). Timmy still swings a mean pen and gets mean responses in reply, which is the way the game seems to be played these days by our great thinkers in high places. He says he's having more fun than when he was editor of the *Daily,* so more power to him.

"At this point I hate to inject an unhappy note right off the bat, but the easiest way to do this is alphabetically—and life doesn't soften things—and so—

"*Dr. Gil Gulbransen,* whose striking blond good looks and happily randy ways once caused Willie to describe him as 'walking down the Quad followed by panting females, like a Lady Godiva in pants,' and his lovely Karen Ann (Waterhouse), whom I'm sure we all remember as one of our great campus beauties, are no longer with us. They were driving down from a stay in Carmel to their home in La Jolla when they met an oncoming car straying too far on the wrong side of the line on one of those killer curves on Highway 1 south of Big Sur. Gil swung wide to miss him, swung too far, and they went over the cliff and that was it. They left two fine kids, Grant and Gracia, and an adopted son, Placido Ramos, whose mother Gil met in the Philippines during the war. A terrible tragedy for the family and for the house. He was always a lively brother and great friend. We all remember him fondly.

"*Edward Paul Haggerty*—Hack—is still grinding out those tunes in Rome—sorry, Hack, we know they're a lot more than 'tunes,' in fact some of them are world-recognized major symphonies and concert pieces. We think it's wonderful how successful you've been. He tells me his gracious Flavia (Lampadini) died of cardiac arrest at age forty-seven (don't mean to inject more unhappiness here, but thought you'd like to know as much as possible what's happened to everybody). His ex, the very capable Francine Magruder Haggerty, is now serving in the House of Representatives from California after a very successful legal career in San Francisco. We count on Fran and Willie to keep the nation on an even keel.

"*Dr. North McAllister,* another of our great doctors, is continuing his highly successful career as an internist in Salt Lake City. His wife, the delightful Betty June Letterman, whom we all remember as one of the brightest little crickets on campus, died at forty-four of lymphoma (there I go again—or there goes God again—if you can conceive of a God who brings so much misery on the world. I see Him as a major force, but beneficent? Ha! Which will probably bring down the wrath of true believers. Good luck to *them,* say I). North's two kids seem to be doing fine. He has never remarried but sounds adjusted and reasonably happy, as are most folks, I suspect—stressing the 'reasonably,' which you may interpret according to your own lights and circumstances.

"But I'm editorializing as freely as Timmy, pontificating as egregiously as Renny (I'll get to him in a minute). On with the roll!

"And with it, more tragedy. But don't give up. We'll hit a patch of happy campers pretty soon, here. First, though:

"*Francis Allen Miller.* Franky, whom we all remember as one of the bright wits and balance wheels of the house, took his own life at age fifty at his home in Medford, Oregon. No one knows the reason for this sad event. Somehow Franky never quite seemed to live up to the promise of those happy days in the house—always joking, always disrespectful of pomposity and b.s., always a sly and sometimes rather unsettling sense of humor—'a laugher at the world,' as dear Bill Lattimer once described him. He and Katie (Sullivan) were always such a bright and sunny fun pair at school. (She's still doing well, she tells me, though 'I do miss Franky a whole lot.' As do we all.) He stayed with his brother-in-law's auto dealership, eventually took it over when the brother-in-law died, and had a good success with it. But Franky selling autos? One wonders what the laughter cost him then—or if the laughter even continued.

"But again I'm editorializing. So on to:

"*Moose.* The distinguished Theodore Krasnik Musavich, who has led our gallant University varsity footballers to victory after victory during his long tenure as head coach, is still at it, as witness the current season. Teams come and teams go, but ole Mooser seems to go on forever. He has a lock on the trustees, we suspect, and they're very wise to keep him on. Once in a while he's stumbled, but you know Moose—he's never placed the blame on anybody else, always shielded the kids, always said it was his fault when things went wrong. It's no wonder they've always loved him, just as most of his fraternity brothers, it seems safe to say, have done since our happy days back when. He and delightful Diana (Sorenson) still have their big house in town, where so many of us have been happily entertained over the years.

"*Dr. Clyde Gaius Unruh*—Guy—our third distinguished medico, is one of the nation's greatest oncologists. He has, as you all know, received international recognition as a co-winner of the Nobel Prize for medicine for his experimental work with recovering patients in Third World countries. When he is not wandering the globe searching for new applications of ancient remedies, he and jolly Maggie (Marguerite Johnson) preside over their fabulous home on the Pali overlooking Honolulu, where, again, a lot of us have had the privilege and pleasure of visiting them over the years. Guy's occasionally somewhat acid humor survives untouched by the many grim things he has witnessed in the field in his search for a cure for one of humanity's greatest scourges. A good man who can be counted on to see the ironic side of most anything. Fortunately Maggie, too, has a great sense of humor.

"*Willie*—the Honorable Richard Emmett Wilson, U.S. Senator from California—can scarcely be accused of hiding his light under a bushel. Willie, in fact, is one of the most-publicized people anywhere, and is certainly *our* most notable contribution to this dizzy world. Millions of supporters in this state and throughout this country and the world consider him to be one of the best Senators in many a year. Always active, always controversial, always at the center of major issues, Willie seems to arouse strong opinions pro and con whatever he does. You are all aware that he recently withdrew from the race for President, but as I said at the start, we all know Willie. He'll be back, we're sure of it, and next time maybe we'll be able to pitch in and help him go over the top.

"It wouldn't be surprising if that's his destiny. Most of us—(I'm always conscious of Renny over my shoulder, because we all know what he thinks of Willie)—but *most* of us who grew up with him in the house have never discounted Willie and his dreams. He makes things happen. And he ain't done yet! Only one tragic note (again)— wife Donnamaria Van Dyke, that campus dynamo who did so much as an Activity Girl at school and then contributed so greatly to Willie's public career, passed away last year, as I'm sure you all know, of brain disease. A great loss to Willie and a great loss to the country. A wonderful girl, who will always live in our memories of all those happy days, and her years with Willie since.

"That concludes the surviving seniors, most doing quite well, I'd say. Juniors, Class of '40, lead off with that amiable little ole wine-maker *Tony Andrade,* who still presides with great aplomb and efficiency as part owner and general manager of Collina Bella Winery in Rutherford, California, in the beautiful Napa Valley. All of us who were there can recall our first (and so far only) reunion and the great picnic that followed at his spectacular house overlooking the valley. One of the great views of all time, which many of us have been privileged to see many times since, thanks to Tony's great hospitality and that of his shrewd and lovely wife Louise (Gianfalco), whose father founded the winery many years ago. Tony is now one of the major figures of the Napa Valley wine industry. He says Louise 'has all the brains in the family,' but remembering our shrewd little operator Tony in the house, we must all discount this disclaimer. He remains, as always, his friendly and very astute self.

"*Dr. Galen Bryce* has gone on from studying psychiatry at the University and at Harvard to become one of the most famous and successful practitioners of his unusual craft, in Hollywood. We've all seen him hailed in *Time, Newsweek* and other entertainment magazines as 'psychiatrist to the stars,' and he deserves the title. He says his clientele is 'always interesting and stimulating—never a dull moment.' We can bet on that, and we can bet on Gale to make the most of it and well deserve whatever they call him down there. Some of us can remember times in the house when we called him other things, when his questions about our private lives became too probing. But, that's how it's done, and if you do it to movie stars, you flourish accordingly. Nice going, Gale, O insightful keeper of insights and perceptions! How interesting it would be if you could psychoanalyze us all now. Fat chance!

"*Loren Davis* is still his stunningly handsome, likable, easygoing self (Remember what a pair he and Tony used to be? And still are, from what Lor tells us about their frequent family visits). Lor is now owner and CEO of Davis Oil in Long Beach, California, which has become one of the top petroleum corporations in the world. You see his name mentioned often in the business pages and he's apparently well on his way to becoming one of the Forbes 500. It goes to show you what a great personality and a great liking for people—and having your dad found the company!—can do for a guy. He and Tony have probably kept in touch with each other much more than any of the rest of us. We envy them that continuation of close friendship, which is rather rare in our hurrying world. Who says oil and wine don't mix!

"I've already told you about me, so we move on briskly to the new president of our beloved alma mater, that great scholar, distinguished administrator and skillful molder of youth, *Dr. Alan Frederick Offenberg.* Good old Duke always wanted to be president of the University someday and now, by George, he is. (Or maybe by Willie and a few other powerful backers on the board of trustees.) He comes in at a tough time, what with Vietnam, racial problems and student unrest at probably a near-record high, but if anybody can handle it, I think it's safe to say that most of us in the house think Duke can. Delightful little Shahna is still at his side, loving and strong—a wonderful support for a man in these tough times. Duke will probably need much luck and support in handling his difficult new assignment, but here's to him. A great guy for a great university. We wish him a most successful time as president and we know he's going to have it. In spite of:

"*Dr. René Suratt,* who, along with Duke and Mooser and me, is the fourth man from the house to have remained at the University and to have achieved a position of great influence in deciding its future (and in Renny's case, of course, that of the whole wide world as well). Or at least, Duke and Renny and Moose can influence it. I'm just along for the ride, though I do help to keep the history department in order, and I suppose that's important. Renny, as you all know, has become one of the great gadflies of our era and has achieved not only a national but a world reputation for it. A prolific and powerful writer, he has published many books on the social and political issues of our time, all of them favorably reviewed by such publications as the *New York Times* and the *Washington Post.* Not so often—or anyway, not so uncritically—by Tim and other political—opponents, shall we say? But Renny doesn't think much of Timmy, either, or of Willie, or of Duke, or of Rodge or Jeff or Moose or me or any one of a long list of pet hates whom he regularly categorizes and castigates in his writings. Renny tells me that the *New York Times* recently remarked about him (I missed this, though I usually try to read the *Times* regularly, as it leads and speaks for a whole pack of opinion-makers on that side of things), 'We *need* Dr. Suratt. It seems safe to say that he would have had to be invented if he did not already exist.' It's nice for the *Times* to feel that way. We lesser mortals in the house remember Renny. He hasn't changed, doesn't want to, doesn't intend to, won't. And with such backing, why should he? You can't be a successful pundit, or a successful writer, or a successful most anything, without it. Or so we are all hyped to believe. Right, Renny?

"And so to the Class of '41:

"*Jefferson Davis Barnett,* our rebel, continues to do very well as owner and manager of Barnett Plantations, working out of Charleston, South Carolina. From being an absolute rigid Southerner when he first came to us, Jeff over the years has changed to become one of the major white leaders of the moderate wing of the civil rights movement. This was a great transition for him, as we can all remember from his early days in the house. Nobody ever waved the Confederate flag more vigorously—and nobody has been more generous and more kind and more genuinely helpful to people such as the late By Johnson in working to achieve a viable solution for the racial situation. It's a tough job and we wish Jeff all the luck in the world in his continuing endeavors to help set things right in a way that will be just to both races. We know he will always bring to it his very likable character, his great talent for getting along with people and his quiet, determined but always nonabrasive way of getting where he wants to go. More power to you, Jeff. It is people like you who will find the middle ground, if middle ground there be. And there has to be, or we will all suffer.

"And so to tragedy again—or mystery—or who knows exactly what? A disturbing note in our otherwise relatively orderly and predictable roll call. *Smith Carriger* vanished about six months ago 'somewhere in Asia,' according to Annelle (Chabot), who is still, understandably, very broken up about it. She says Smitty always had a way of going on vaguely defined 'business trips' to the Orient; she usually had only the sketchiest idea where he was going or what he was going to do. 'He always said it was business, so I didn't pry,' she told me. His latest trip was to Thailand, she thinks somewhere in northern Thailand, which of course is right on the border of warring Vietnam. She thinks he was working on contacts for Carrigcorp, which has now become a worldwide enterprise—another case, like Lor, where son succeeded father and has done very well indeed with it. Smitty, bright, bubbly, determined, very smart, very shrewd, was always a go-getter. We can only hope that he didn't make one too many trips this time, and that sooner or later he will come home safely. Annelle says he often has before, after protracted absences, and we hope and pray this will be the same. If you want to write her words of encouragement, which she needs, you can address her care of Carrigcorp, Philadelphia. And say a quiet prayer for Smitty, a great guy. It's hard to believe anyone so self-assured and self-reliant could have come to any harm, but you never know these days. You just never know.

"Randy Carrero—*Bishop Randolph Ramirez Carrero*—tells me he is now back in his native New Mexico as one of the kingpins of the southwest hierarchy. Randy wouldn't say that about himself, but knowing Randy, if he's really into something, he's a kingpin; that's his nature and his happy fate. He says he's being called into Rome more and more frequently and that there are some signs he may sooner or later receive a major assignment there. This would be great for him, and perhaps a little surprising, as you know he has often been a well-publicized leader in American movements to bring some changes and a broader social outlook into the workings of the Church. He tends to scoff at the idea that Rome may want to absorb him into the Vatican, on the theory that, 'If you can't lick 'em, have 'em join you,' as I put it to him. 'I'm not absorbable,' he says, and you can hear the old grin, even on the telephone; but—well, good luck, Randy. We know you'll have an impact, wherever you are.

"*Dr. Roger Leighton.* Rodge Leighton is still with the International Atomic Energy Agency in Vienna, apparently a lifetime dedication for which he is supremely well qualified and, by now, deeply experienced. He says he sometimes thinks of himself as Sisyphus, 'always pushing that old rock of Soviet resistance to nuclear control up the hill, only to have it roll back on me just when we think we have it finally locked into place.' Rodge has become a real international spokesman for atomic control and many of you may have heard him lecture in your area, because he often hits the lecture trail to push his very worthwhile and desperately needed objective. Someone the house can be proud of, like Jeff a genuinely constructive force in our chaotic twentieth-century world. Unhappily here, again, a note of sadness, as he recently lost his charming wife Juliette (Cambron) to heart disease. But, life goes on, he says, and what he calls 'the great task of disarmament' continues to need 'people like me to work for it.' Most of us (not including Renny, but there's an ideological problem there, or something, eh, Renny?) wish you every success in your often frustrating endeavors, Rodge. There's got to be some way out of this insane tangle that threatens the very world itself, and if anybody can help to find it, it's good-hearted, tenacious people like you. We are very grateful.

"*Marcus Andrew Taylor* is our third son-succeeding-father and building an already great heritage into something even greater. Taylorite Corporation of Pittsburgh, Pennsylvania, is, like Lor's Davis Oil and Smitty's Carrigcorp, the very successful story of a founding father passing on his achievement to a very able and worthy son.

"We all remember Marc in the house as a rather retiring young guy who was always quietly among us but rarely one to step forward and take the limelight. But when he finally had the limelight handed to him by inheritance, he took it and made a real success of it. He still shuns the limelight, and almost wouldn't talk to me when I called, but then he relented and said how much he always appreciates his membership in the house, and how he often looks back fondly to it and considers its treatment of him after his little episode freshman year (which he brought up, I didn't) to be 'always one of the strengthening factors of my life.' 'You helped turn me from a wimp into a man,' he says, and when I told him not to be so harsh on himself, he said (true Marc), 'I know my own limitations. They were even worse then.' They weren't worse than most people carry around, Marc, so stop saying so, or even thinking it. We like you and are very pleased with your great success in life.

"I end on another sad note, which most of you know, as it was widely publicized in the national media at the time, since it concerned the kid brother and sister-in-law of our Senator. Bright and happy Billy Wilson, whom everybody was so fond of, and his cute little Janie (Elizabeth Jane Montgomery) were killed several years ago in a terrible auto accident near the family ranch in the San Joaquin Valley. Billy had taken over the running of the ranch when their father died and Willie was unable to come home because of the demands of his public career. Billy had toyed briefly with the idea of leaving the ranch—he had always been interested in music and he was going to go to Rome and collaborate with Hack on some musical comedy ideas they had. But when Mr. Wilson died, Billy put that dream on the shelf to meet the demands of the family heritage. Willie tells me he did so without protest and with a contented heart, but you know Billy: he would have knocked himself out not to inconvenience or trouble anyone by making them feel sorry for him, so we will have to give him even more credit for pitching in and taking over when the time came. A great tragedy and a great loss to the world in general. One Wilson brother has achieved great fame but I know he would be the first to agree when I say that the other also contributed greatly to all of us—just by being Billy. Two kids, Leslie and Tom, both now married, carry on at the ranch.

"And so ends *The Very Occasional Newsletter,* Vol. 2, which I hope brings you up to date satisfactorily as to what's happened to everybody. Maybe someday we'll have another reunion (of whoever's left by then!) and exchange more detailed news on what we've been and what we've done—and what we *are,* so many years after our days together on this beautiful campus, which has grown so enormously but is still beautiful. Let's hope we do. Until then, if you want anybody's address, you can get it either from Willie's office at the Senate, or from me here at school. Affectionate greetings and continued good luck to you all.

"As ever, Johnny Herbert. P.S. And to Willie: Sound the bugle, beat the drum, toot the trumpet, lead the charge! Most of us will be there to rally 'round your flag. Say when."

In the next few days some omnipotent and all-hearing Ear might have heard, from various points around the country and a few overseas, a chorus of groans and outcries such as, "Oh, for *Christ's* sake!" and "What the *hell*—?" and (from the one most given to the occasional ripe profanity, Guy Unruh) "Oh, shit! What a *tiresome shit!*"

An equally omnipotent and all-observing Eye, peering over the shoulders of those originating these raucous and unseemly sounds, might have seen them holding in one hand Johnny Herbert's *Very Occasional Newsletter,* Vol. 2, and in the other a

MEMO

To: All members of Alpha Zeta Fraternity, Alpha Chapter
From: Dr. René Suratt

With reference to the so-called "newsletter" compiled and distributed by John Herbert, this is to protest most vigorously his very personal and derogatory remarks about myself and his egregious and uncalled-for attempt to arouse sympathy and support for the political ambitions of Senator Richard Wilson.

For myself, I must go on record resenting most strongly, and objecting to most vigorously, his intemperate, disrespectful language concerning myself. It is my constant attempt to serve my country and improve it. In this endeavor I have been fortunate to have the support and acclaim of many people, publications and institutions so far superior to John Herbert that they do not even know he exists. I have also received many awards, which contrast starkly with the lack of national recognition given to John Herbert. I would suggest that in future when mentioning my name he treat it with the respect accorded it by those much more famous and accomplished than he.

With reference to his call on Senator Wilson to run for President (which I assume his coy reference means), and his confident assertion that "most of us" would support Senator Wilson in such a futile enterprise, I wish it to be known that I completely reject his egregious attempt to associate me with any such foredoomed effort. I am not a supporter of the political ambitions of Senator Wilson, nor do I admire or endorse his so far quite lackluster and undistinguished public career. I would appreciate it if this fact is recorded in your minds, in Senator Wilson's, and in John Herbert's. His presumption in associating me, without my permission and certainly without my agreement, with the ambitions of Senator Wilson is, simply, inexcusable.

René Suratt

Having sent this out, and having a pretty good idea of what his fraternity brothers' reactions would be, Renny could not suppress a contented little smile as he walked along the Quad the next day.

He did not believe in the old political admonition "Never acknowledge, never defend." He was a great believer in nailing immediately anything remotely resembling an attack upon himself, his writings or his beliefs. His basic principle was never to let a single attack go unanswered, a single slur go unchallenged, a single hostile critical mention go uncorrected.

"The record is always important," he frequently told his students. "Your record may be the most important thing in your lives. Whatever you do, protect your record."

His pursuit of this principle had generated some of the most enjoyable battles of his career. He knew there would be plenty more if smug, insufferable Willie actually had the gall to go ahead with his obvious plans and attempt to grab the brass ring at the White House.

Renny had enlisted long ago in the campaign, beginning almost on the first day Willie entered the House and now growing rapidly as his ultimate ambition became more and more apparent, to stop him in his tracks if it could possibly be done.

3

"Always the Judges, Never the Judged."

1

First came the medium.

Then came the message.

And then came the messengers, at first relatively modest and unknown, now in the latter half of the twentieth century so wise, so mighty, so superior, so smug—and so inviolate.

In the early days they were diligent, hardworking wage-slaves on weekly newspapers or on larger but often still struggling dailies, men and women who were in it partly for the hell of it, partly out of a really genuine sense of serving the public and helping to make society better, and partly out of sheer love for the business, which was then—and to this day—probably the most enjoyable, excitement-filled and generally satisfying profession there is. . . .

And then came radio and television, briefly alongside but soon far out ahead, and with them the birth of the great god Communication, with all its eager acolytes making major salaries and competing fiercely for national and international exposure and influence, and all its huge corporate entities making billions and competing fiercely for advantage and profits in the national and international markets, and all of them taking over America, and through it, the world.

And as a result of all this exposure and ambition and scrambling for fame and fortune, the messengers had become so all-powerful and so impregnable that they were able, virtually without successful challenge, to create, control, dominate and manipulate the opinions, attitudes, social standards, basic beliefs and everyday thinking of the majority of the inhabitants of a chaotic planet careening increasingly out of control, partly as a result of the messengers' own self-confident and often mistaken leadership. They never admitted it could be mistaken. Their self-confidence, like the power of the mediums in which they worked, grew ever greater.

Their conviction did not create a "conspiracy"; it was not even their "fault." It was just the way the business, and world society, developed in the enormous rush to technological change that overwhelmed the final decades of the century. It gave them a unique status in the world; one which many seemed to exercise without the slightest thought of their own responsibility to use their influence with fairness and balance, or the slightest sign of humility or understanding that they were especially favored. Their arrogance was beyond belief, and their united self-defensiveness awesome to behold.

"Always the judges, never the judged"—so Willie had described the media early in his career when some of their many leading lights were subjecting him to a particularly snide and vicious attack; and it was true enough, Tim agreed, even though in those early days he still had a lingering feeling that he should protect the herd even when it came thundering down in its implacable majesty upon himself, who so often flew in the face of its ruthless, set-in-stone conventional wisdom.

It was not always so, he reflected as he put aside Johnny Herbert's newsletter and Renny's insufferably pompous response, and turned to a contemplation of the day's news and how he would make use of it in his daily column for Anna Hastings's *Washington Inquirer.*

It was not always so.

When he first came into the business making sixteen dollars a week on a small weekly newspaper on the eve of World War II, there was still among his colleagues the old attitude of trying to be fair, trying to be balanced, trying to contribute something substantive to society, either in the way of supporting decent goals or exposing those whose shady, unethical, often criminal activities were subverting them.

This had lasted pretty well, as he saw it, up to about the early seventies, when Watergate enshrined adversarial investigative reporting and when the great ballooning of newspaper circulation and profits, together with the great door-opening of television and radio, made every place and everyone on earth vulnerable to the incessant drumbeat of instant news and instant opinion, tumbled out indiscriminately upon the world around the clock.

Television, radio, the press, the great god Communication—they had destroyed time. With it went humanity's ability to comprehend, adjust, absorb, reason—*think*. There was no time left for it. Everything was instantaneous. Now it was instant impact, instant reaction, instant result. The world was overwhelmed by immediate information. It was too much for mortals to handle in any thoughtful, rational way that might produce thoughtful, reasoned results.

And it was only going to get worse.

There was no turning back.

In such a climate, he often reassured himself (he often felt, wryly, that he had to), he continued to do his damnedest to find a balanced approach that would help his readers find some sort of reasonably steady basis from which to cope with the increasingly crazy world. This was not easy. His own nature made him skeptical of overblown claims to certainty about anything; yet he had often found himself pushed over the edge into responses as one-sided and intolerant as those that were flung against him. His critics had early begun to attack him as "conservative," that great pejorative dear to "liberals" who found—in the intolerant climate they themselves had done so much to create—that it was much easier, and much more effective, to smear than to reason.

He had always tried to avoid using the label "liberal." He reflected now with a certain irony that he had plenty of other buzzwords to use: "herd orthodoxy . . . Group-Think . . . Right-Think . . . herd-think . . . the Great Gullibles of the West . . . Everybody Who Is Anybody . . . Those Who Really Matter . . . Those Who Really Understand"—and so on. His was not an infertile mind: words usually seemed to be there when he wanted them. They gave his writings a certain distinctive cast when he commented on politics. "Liberal" was too easy; it became as automatic and meaningless a pejorative as "conservative" was for them. He liked to give things gloss of his own.

He realized—because they often told the world so—that those who clutched the description "liberal" to their bosoms fancied themselves as everything lush and loving and unutterably *good,* enlisted forever in the causes of the threatened this and the threatened that, the endangered this and the endangered that, the starving this and the starving that, the embattled this and the embattled that, the bereft, the belea-guered, the disadvantaged, the well-publicized woebegone.

Conversely, those who were attacked as "conservative" were sup-posed to be everything harsh, reactionary and evil, devoted incessantly to the destruction of the endangered this and the endangered that and all their beleaguered companions, in a hostile "conservative" universe.

All of this was absurd, on both sides, but it was the accepted norm for America, where people automatically went overboard on every controversial issue that came along. If it wasn't a controversial issue when it began, they would turn it into one as fast as possible. Though supported by an amazingly easygoing and tolerant population, the upper reaches of American intellectualism were inhabited by some of the most absolute and grimly intolerant individuals on the planet.

"Gosh!" he once exclaimed to Willie in mock dismay. "Where would we *be* without the 'liberals' to defend us and the 'conservatives' to give them something to defend us against? And vice versa?"

He put both terms in quotation marks whenever he couldn't avoid using them, and devoted himself as much as he could to trying to find a middle ground. This made no one really happy with him, on either side; but, as with Willie, it gave him a satisfying feeling of being a free spirit, and his own man.

"When it comes right down to it," he said thoughtfully, "I guess my basic attitude is: fuck 'em all."

Willie smiled.

"I'm with you. It doesn't make us very popular sometimes. But it's a lot more fun."

So, like a couple of political Peck's Bad Boys, they went side by side down life's highway (as Tim described it to himself with characteristic humor), impartially dealing out applause and strychnine to both sides as the occasion, in their judgment, demanded.

What their lives would have been without this amiable alliance, he could imagine: equally successful but not half so much fun. From the days when he was editor of the *Daily* and Willie the rising star headed for student-body president, they had worked together and generally agreed on most major things. When their interests and careers took them to Washington, the alliance only became stronger and more supportive. The Wilsons became his family, as he had told Donna on her deathbed, and he and Willie, first as fraternity brothers and then as think-alikes on the great stage, were as united as the best blood brothers could be. The conviction of absolute *rightness* that united their critics in a solid phalanx of disapproval of them in turn united them in a defiant and usually humorous bond against their critics.

"If we had a motto," Willie suggested, "I suppose it would be: the emperors have no clothes. Because none of the damned emperors has any, on either side of the spectrum."

This automatically brought them within the ideological rifle sights of Those Who Defend the Citadel against those who withhold from it that awed respect and worshipful obeisance so necessary to the egos of those who live and work inside it. The result was an automatic clumping together of Senator and columnist in critical columns, editorials, commentaries, news analyses. In actual fact, their seeing eye to eye was never really guaranteed at any time. Quite often Tim's writings expressed some reservations, not always gentle, about Willie's more emphatic political positions; and Willie in turn never hesitated to express his reservations about some of Tim's more free-swinging attacks on their mutual enemies.

The general assumption that they were inevitable allies, that Tim could always be counted upon to support everything Willie proposed or did, and vice versa, was simply an arbitrary and convenient shorthand for those who wished to attack them. It did not, Tim felt, give him credit for the independence he had always felt he possessed, lived by and expressed. Nor did it give him credit for the abilities he had, nor did it sufficiently separate his success from Willie's. It gave Willie a certain claim on his success (which Willie himself never claimed, or even thought), which in Tim's mind really belonged primarily to himself and secondly to Anna Hastings and her stubbornly independent newspaper. It was the only one in the capital, he knew, where he could possibly have found a home over so many controversial years. He was much too independent to fit into the rigidly defined ideological rightthink of Washington's Daily Conscience, or of its more plodding and generally less exciting competitors.

That he had been at one time in love with the proprietor of the

Enquirer, which only Anna and Willie knew, gave his present position with the paper an extra dimension for him. It in no way affected his position, the success of his column or his steady rise to national prominence. Anna would have liked to think she was responsible for all this, but she wasn't and she knew it. It was to her credit, as well as his, that after initially giving him the job which guaranteed his inevitable rise, she had refrained from doing anything but furnish him with a pulpit for his thoughts on the world. It was up to him to make it as "bully" as he could (to use the catchword inherited from Theodore Roosevelt, which later became so popular with the media that play and replay ad nauseam the latest fashionable buzz).

Anna did give him the space to make his columns and articles exciting; and after they had moved on beyond what Tim always referred to in his own mind as "all that," they had settled into a comfortable and absolutely reliable friendship that became, along with Willie's friendship, one of the two safe havens of his life.

2

He sometimes reflected, with a wry (and increasingly rather fatherly) smile, on the career of the brash young editor of the University *Daily* who had laid down the law with such imperious certainty from his editor's chair in the then-tumbledown old *Daily* building; who got his start at sixteen dollars a week on a tiny country weekly; who, disqualified for military service in World War II by bad eyesight, then went to Washington because politics had always fascinated him; who briefly became a minor member of the *New York Daily News* bureau, then a Senate reporter for ever-penurious-ever-struggling-always-about-to-collapse-but-miraculously-hanging-on United Press; and finally to Washington's newest and liveliest newspaper, Anna's *Washington Inquirer.* For three years he was one of its foreign correspondents. He came home to find its astute young publisher willing to give him a place as columnist and special features writer, a post he held to this day and would, he knew, have as long as he wanted it: which, as far as he was concerned, would be as long as he could think of a word or pound a typewriter.

Anna, as everyone who knew her sooner or later remarked, was something else. Something else than *what* they could not always say, except that it seemed to mean a combination of brains, beauty, ceaseless ambition and an imperious refusal to accept any obstacles that stood in her way, either as a human being or as an editor and publisher in the capital's highly competitive media world.

When she first came to town she had been "just little Anna Kowalczek from Punxsutawney, Pa.," as old Senator Seab Cooney had once described her to Tim, when he was interviewing Seab for some UP story. Seab was very fond of Anna; she was, in fact, the pet of many men in the Senate, some of whose close interest was a bit more than paternal. But only a young Gordon Hastings, junior Senator from Texas, was permitted anything more than a long-range, wistfully lustful, eyes-only, no-touch friendship. Unbeknownst to "poor Gordon," as she always referred to him to this day, her ambitions coincided nicely with his oil millions, and in no time at all she was Mrs. Gordon Hastings and busy establishing her independent-minded newspaper and achieving her dream of becoming a powerful Washington editor and publisher.

Eventually, after the arrival of a son and daughter whom she produced rather absentmindedly along with all her other duties, there came the sad day when Gordon, increasingly relegated to the sidelines of her life and increasingly unhappy, committed suicide. It was a wound Anna never discussed with anyone, after the initial period when she shared days of wild sorrow and frantic protest with her most intimate circle of editorial advisers. It took her ten years to even mention his name, let alone refer to him lightly (and rather patronizingly) as "poor Gordon," as she did now.

From that point on, alienated from the kids, who had taken their father's side in the increasingly tense final days of the marriage, she devoted herself almost exclusively to becoming "one of America's most powerful women," always contesting in her own mind with the handful of others who competed, informally but fiercely, for that media-generated title. As she added more newspapers, and in time television and radio stations, to her growing empire, she became, at least as far as the public knew, what she sometimes referred to wryly as "the recluse of power." The degree of one's power always determined where one stood on Washington's ever-changing ladder of who's in, who's out; and Anna, once on the ladder, never faltered or failed in her steady determination to reach the uppermost rung.

She still attracted many men, not only because of her power but also because, well into middle age, she remained a very beautiful, very appealing and of course very brilliant woman. But with few exceptions, she never let herself become emotionally involved with any of them.

One of those most powerfully attracted, as he confessed rather desperately to Willie after his brief affair with Anna had gone on for a cou-

ple of months, was her increasingly successful and influential columnist. He often reflected later, with a still-wistful regret that slackened
with the years but never entirely left him, that he was ready-made for
her attentions: he liked her, he admired her, he was even a bit in awe of
her ruthless determination to acquire and exercise power. And he was
alone—more alone than he liked to admit, even to himself.

So when Anna decided, as she had decided with Gordon, that Tim
was what she wanted, she got him. The thing he did not realize until
later was that he was essentially what he described to Willie, "an anti-
dote for Gordon."

"I didn't know she cared that much for Gordon," Willie remarked.

Tim assured him that his impression, which was held by most of
political and media Washington, was wrong.

"She's still grieving a decade after," he said. "Gordy must have had
something we outsiders didn't know."

"Who ever knows about a marriage?" Willie inquired, rather mood-
ily: he and Donna were having "a bit of a rough patch" at the moment,
he said, and it made him a little morose. But he was sympathetic, of
course. Tim could always rely on Willie to respond with sympathy and
whatever encouragement and strengthening he could give whenever
Tim hit professional or personal rough patches of his own. For a short
time Anna was quite the roughest, until Tim pulled himself up
abruptly and decided he was never going to be allowed more than a
brief entry into the closely guarded inner keep of her emotions.

But for a little while it was most enjoyable and he really thought he
was going to be a profound part of her life. He even entertained
visions of marriage. Having known Anna since they were beginning
young reporters trudging the Senate corridors for news together in
Franklin Roosevelt's final year, he thought he could tell when her
emotions were genuine. But maybe he couldn't, he confessed rather
forlornly to Willie later.

"I *thought* I knew her," he said, "After all, we were kids together in
the Senate. And I've been with her for the bulk of my working life
since. I *thought* I knew her."

"Nobody knows Anna," Willie said with profundity, for like many,
he thought he did. "I guess you were just taken along for the ride."

"I guess so," Tim agreed. His expression, quite sad at the moment, brightened. "It was fun while it lasted, though."

Which had been roughly eight months, until the day he decided that he was indeed just "along for the ride," and had better get out of it gracefully before termination could be too embarrassing for him. As he ruefully expected, it was no problem for Anna.

"That's good," she said, looking at him thoughtfully as they sat side by side on her terrace in the Watergate, overlooking the broad Potomac and the traffic going by on the Virginia side (the historic house in Georgetown long since sold). "I've felt you were taking me too seriously. You know you shouldn't." She uttered a wry little laugh. "I'm *such* a femme fatale!"

"You could be," he said, finally deciding to be blunt after eight months of sometimes rather abject adulation, "if you'd just relax and put your heart into it."

"I can't afford that," she said. "I've got too many demands on my heart and my emotions, what with the papers, and the media and the TV stations, and the magazines, and the kids and all. Anyway, maybe I don't even have a heart by now. Lots of people think I don't."

"That's not fair to you," he said. "Of course you do."

"I wonder," she said. Her eyes widened, her tone became remote and almost as though he weren't even there. "I wonder . . ."

"Sure you do," he said firmly. She stood up suddenly, gave him her hands, helped pull him out of his chair, gave him a long, hard hug that he sensed had suddenly become maternal instead of provocative. It was obviously over.

"Thank you for everything, dear Timmy," she said. "I don't deserve you and I thank you for your kindness and patience with me."

"Am I to see you at the office tomorrow?" he inquired, thinking she might fire him, his presence too painful to have around. He might have known.

Her expression changed to one of quite genuine surprise.

"Why ever not?" she demanded. "We have a paper to put out!"

And next day, and all the days thereafter, it was as though nothing had happened between them. Their close friendship continued, if anything closer now, and after about ten minutes, thanks to Anna's completely matter-of-fact behavior, he dismissed any lingering embarrassment he might feel. You took Anna on her own terms, and you emerged thinking none the less of her, and in many cases, including his own, even more of her.

She was, as Seab Cooney had told him in those early Senate days, "*Sui generis.* A force of nature. A real force of nature. Yes, sir, that little lady is a *force* of *nature!*"

Taken on that basis, one could love her for life. Tim expected he always would. The emotion had suddenly become painless, deep fondness. And so it would remain forever after.

He resumed his place in the world of Washington, which had slipped a little in the involvement of their affair. His columns and writings had lost a little of their bite, which he was unaware of, but so much so that some of his journalistic rivals began to ask one another with some pleased anticipation, "What's happened to Tim?"

Just in time he was back at it, leveling his sights on the major issues of the day, subjecting them to his sometimes scathing but, he felt, basically honest and rational consideration.

He accepted that quite probably he was never going to meet anyone who could match Anna, that he was quite probably going to remain unmarried. But that was all right. He could manage, in one way or another; and there were compensations in hard work, particularly when one was running ahead of most of the Washington herd and carving a distinctive place for oneself among the nation's opinion-makers.

3   That place, as his detractors noted, was to a certain degree devoted to furthering the public career of Willie Wilson. But it had many more far-reaching aspects, and it was not long before it drew down upon him all the organized malevolence of that segment of the nation's intelligentsia whom he took to describing scornfully, in response, as "right-thinkers . . . group-thinkers . . . phony liberals," and the like.

And that, of course, brought him directly into target range of his fraternity brother back at the University, also embarked on his own successful national career.

The issues were often major as the decades unfolded. He could be absolutely certain that he would find Renny on the other side, and be called upon to either ignore, or respond acridly to, Renny's frequent sarcastic attacks. Renny had been a sour opponent of Tim's reasoning when Tim, as editor of the *Daily*, was, as Renny saw it, "always doing his damnedest to drag us into war against the will of the American people" (a position that changed when Hitler attacked Russia). That had been Tim's first big crusade and it had symbolized in microcosm the basic pattern of his later professional life: a strong position, a strong statement of it, a strong rebuttal to all who offered argument. This required at that time a lot of youthful arrogance. Fortunately for the kind of commentator he became, sufficient quantities of that carried over so that he could face the opposition he aroused without flinching or changing course in response to what he was able to dismiss as "ill-founded comment by uninformed people." This public response of course did not increase their love for him.

At the University, Renny's opposition took the form of an acrid tongue in many heated fraternity bull sessions on the imminent war. He had not yet acquired the outlets to match what Tim already had in the editorship, which added an extra note of jealousy to what he had to say. Later, when he too became a public man and a national figure with his own written and vocal channels of communication, his opposition became more formidable. But it never stopped Timmy, as Timmy often remarked with satisfaction. Renny only embodied and defined what he had to contend with.

"He's such a good weather vane," Tim said. "I can always tell which way the wind is going to blow in that sector when I hear from old Renny. He never fails me."

It was only much later that Tim, looking back, thought he had found the reason for much of Renny's opposition. It paralleled closely the general attitude and reactions of America's great adversary of the century, then midway in its seventy-year domination of the unhappy land of Russia.

Not that Tim ever joined the ranks of those frustrated and angry citizens who thought Renny was "a damned Red," or "a damned Communist stooge," or "a damned Commie," period. There was never any proof of it, and Tim regarded it as too easy an argument. Renny simply represented the sort of fashionable thing that right-thinkers did in those hectic decades. To allege otherwise was unfair to a mind whose opinions, for all its owner's adversarial ways, were usually quite genuine. The convictions expressed, while often deliberately perverse just for the sake of being perverse—and arousing controversy—were often sincere.

"Renny, Renny, quite contrary, how does your garden grow?" Tim once mused sarcastically to Willie, who snorted.

"With dead snails and puppy dogs' tails and a bucket full of crap," he responded. "That's how that garden grows."

Fortunately for the general argument, there were other critics whose reactions to Tim's writing, while quite similar and often equally automatic, possessed more validity in his mind. With them, and with his own conscience, he struggled valiantly over the years as he attempted to adhere to the standards he had early set himself—to be strong in the expression of opinion but to be sure that it was genuine opinion, that it was basically fair to his opponents and that he accorded their arguments space and weight as equal as possible to his. And then go for it.

That was how he summarized it to Anna at the end of his first year as columnist, when she called him into her office for a review of "where you stand and where you're going."

This was when she was beginning to take a more personal interest, but no matter what that might be—and he suspected then that it could be considerable—it was typical Anna that she should approach his professional record with that same cool ("cold," her critics said) analysis with which she approached all other aspects of her growing media empire.

"I think you know where I stand," he said. "That's clear enough every day. I like to think I stand for the puncturing of pretense and the upholding of truth, wherever it occurs, on whatever side of the issues, and whoever expresses it. And I like to think my own ideas are expressed with reasonable fairness and balance, and with a certain fundamental generosity of heart that permits me to accord their arguments full scope even as I demolish them." He grinned suddenly. "At least, I *hope* I demolish them. It's my principal aim."

"Yes, Timmy," she said with a wry little smile. "You certainly do try to demolish them, all right. And I will say, you often succeed. At least from where I sit."

"That's good," he said, more relieved than he wanted her to know.

"I know you're relieved," she said, always Anna, "because I know you've been worried about my reaction. It's all been fine with me. I think you're doing just great. Most of the time I agree with you, and when I don't, enough people disagree along with me, and squawk so loudly, that it all adds up to controversy, publicity and increased readership. And that's the name of the game. Or part of it, anyway."

"Well, thank you, Anna," he said, amused, and letting himself sound as relieved as he did feel. "I have wondered, and since you've never said anything—"

"Oh, I would have," she said. "You can rest assured that if I really disapproved, if I thought you weren't justifying the freedom I've given you—you'd know it. Of course"—she smiled—"you're getting so big that I can't afford to sound that patronizing anymore. Maybe I gave you the freedom initially, but you're rapidly making your own freedom now. You could be out of here like a shot and land somewhere else with the same freedom, if you felt you had to."

"Where?" he inquired. "I'm not all that popular with most people who share your power as a publisher. They're mostly on the other side of the fence. You don't think I could go to—" He named a famous D.C. street address from which all things Right and Good flowed each morning with an unctuous, superior certainty. "Not likely!"

She joined him in laughter, not terribly amused by the gap between pretense and performance which that particular address too often represented.

"Not likely," she agreed. "Not—very—likely. But there are other outlets . . . magazines . . . think-tanks . . ." Her voice trailed off. "But that's nonsense. You aren't going anywhere. You're staying right here where you belong, to adorn the *Inquirer* with your piercing analysis and rapierlike typewriter. Right?"

"Oh, right," he conceded with a smile. "I wouldn't have it any other way."

"Or I," she said. "And don't you forget it. Here you belong and here you stay. Let 'em have it!" And being Anna, she could not resist one last reminder: "It's why I hired you. Don't let me down."

"I wouldn't dream of it," he said, solemnity broken only by a gleam of amusement at the difference in their relative positions. "Let me at 'em!"

4 The years moved on, and with them the steady deterioration of the standards and principles of the profession, the steady increase in Tim's own stature and influence.

There were a few, tagged "conservatives," whom the "liberals" gave a certain grudging carte blanche to—just to be able to say that they were there, that they were tolerated, that the "liberals" were not really as reactionary as *their* critics charged, that they were broad-minded enough to extend their charity to a few misguided souls ("pet conservatives," Tim called them), who thought that they, too, were entitled to a few First Amendment rights.

There weren't many of these, he often thought with a wry smile; and certainly he was not among them.

"I exist in spite of, not because of," he told Willie with a smile. Willie nodded.

"You and me both, pal," he said. "A few whom they call 'conservatives' are *allowed*—if they're well behaved and don't get too obstreperous. You and I are not *allowed*. We bite too deeply and the teeth marks last a long time. If the people on that side of things don't have anything else, they do have long memories. They never forget and never forgive."

"Do you mind?" Tim inquired.

Willie gave him a look.

"Are you kidding?" Then, more seriously: "Oh, it's bothersome, sometimes. They can be so vicious and so intolerant and so unfair. But one gets used to it. If you want to have any kind of independent mind, by God, you'd better!"

Well, Tim thought: he did have an independent mind, and he wouldn't have any other kind; but it wasn't always easy.

When Anna was just beginning to circulate his column through the

Inquirer's "Writers' Syndicate," they were both startled to find that rival syndicates were actually soliciting newspaper clients throughout the country with veiled attacks upon him and his column. In some cases they were not so veiled. Somebody, as he remarked with some wonderment, "actually dug up old Renny and got him to say something derogatory about me. Not unusual, for Renny, but a little startling to find him operative in this area."

"He's everywhere," Willie said, "sparkling like the dew on a pile of horse dung."

"May I quote you?" Tim asked. Willie grinned.

"Please do. He's beginning to pop up in critical articles about me, too. We must stop this cancer before it spreads!"

"Impossible," Tim said. "The only good thing is, we know it won't be fatal."

But it was the first real indication that he would, for a while, have an uphill battle to become established as the national voice he hoped to be. Renny, himself moving toward prominence, was already becoming a good bellwether.

For the first couple of years, Tim's column did not move very fast. Twenty-three clients the first year, an additional twelve the second.

"Wait till the third year, "Anna said. "If you're like the things I grow in my garden, the third year will be the charm."

And, infallible as always, Anna proved to be right. The third year brought an additional forty, the fifth year fifty more; by the time he had been at it eight years he had leveled off at the respectable 273 he would continue to hold for most of his subsequent professional career. Most were small- to mid-sized papers, mostly in small communities, though he did have major outlets in the eight or ten metropolitan areas he had hoped to reach.

Two or three of these actually agreed with him on most issues; the remainder represented that painfully "broad-minded, tolerant and well-balanced" attitude their editors and publishers liked to have associated with their names in the popular mind. And, most had to admit, he did write well if at times a bit flamboyantly, and he did make some good points, which they had to acknowledge were good antidotes to the steady diet of right-think they customarily gave their readers.

So, in time, he too became "allowed"—and, he was ironically amused to find, on his own terms. Along with the rise of his column there came, in due course, recognition from the great mastodons that began to dominate the business as the century wore on. They, too, did not approve of many of his ideas, but they, too, basked in the glow of righteousness that surrounded their ostentatious, well-publicized tolerance.

"If I'm going to open our pages to that reactionary son of a bitch," said the editor of the Mother of All Newspapers, "we're going to get some credit for it. This'll show the smarmy bastards who say we're so arrogant and intolerant! If this isn't true tolerance, I don't know what is!"

And so, while they could never quite bring themselves to buy his column on a regular basis, Mother's editorial board began a carefully calculated campaign of inviting him to write for them three or four times a year, usually in their Sunday magazine. Dutifully across the country that group of earnest imitators that followed where Mother led did likewise; and so his fame and influence gradually grew until, by the time he was fifty, he had become recognized by All the People Who Really Matter as "one of America's leading conservative thinkers . . . a writer whose trenchant pen represents a point of view that, while it does not appeal to many, has an indubitable place in our national cogitations."

That was Mother, justifying her otherwise inexplicable and outrageous cohabiting with one who, to many "liberals," was anathema, as Renny faithfully reflected. For a while he fell into the habit of writing Tim exasperated and increasingly personal letters objecting to his articles.

"Dear Tim," he would write, "I was, as usual, shocked and offended by your article on 'The Kennedy Legacy: Guide for America or Public Relations Myth?' It has been typical of you, ever since you were editor of the *Daily,* to pose the most ridiculous questions and then provide the most offensive answers. You have challenged the memory of one of the greatest Presidents we have ever had. Who are you, may I ask?"

Or, "Dear Tim: Your analysis of the situation in China vis-à-vis the United States is, as always, flawed in conception and skewed in execution. You know we have to deal with them. You know we have to get along with them. You know any other course would be sheer disaster not only for Asia but for the West, and particularly for us. Why do you write and publish such nonsensical stuff? You might as well unfurl the flag and form Tim's Rough Riders to attack the Great Wall. It would make as much sense as your articles do."

Or, as years passed and his tone became harsher, "Tim: Why don't you just knock it off? You've always verged on the hysterical. I remember your *Daily* days when you were the laughingstock of the campus with your pro-war rhetoric. Your rhetoric is as exaggerated as ever and your desire for war even more obvious. Who are you going to fight? Surely not the Soviets, whose desire for peace is obvious and unassailable!"

And finally, when Tim wrote an article that tried quite successfully to present the arguments for and against the possible existence of subversives in the government (concluding that there were probably some but certainly no massive "conspiracy"), there came an almost illegible scrawl: "You and McCarthy! What a pair!"

For a while, Tim tried to answer as reasonably as he could without letting personal animus get the upper hand; but eventually he ran out of patience and replied to some particularly angry blurt:

"Dear Renny: For Christ's sake, shut up. You've never made any sense and you don't now. Please don't write me again."

For a wonder, Renny obeyed and there were no further personal letters. But he then went public with his complaints, since he too now possessed national and international outlets, including Mother and all her would-be children in America and abroad. Her editorial board gave him op-ed space in fullest measure, and Renny used it perhaps twenty times over the years to challenge, criticize and, he was satisfied, completely refute Tim's miserable logic and horribly reactionary views.

Nonetheless, Tim continued to plug along, Anna well satisfied and Willie always there as comforting sounding board and supporter when he needed one. And the reputation grew, always attacked by vociferous critics from the other side but growing in spite of that, as a certain stubborn honesty and unshakable integrity gradually wore down the opposition.

Anna submitted his name and work several times to the Pulitzer committee. Each time her friends on the inside told her that this occasioned some of the bloodier internecine feuds that often racked the closed-door sessions of that august body. Mother's behind-the-scenes influence, always heavy with the committee, often proved decisive for candidates her editorial board liked, devastating for candidates it didn't. Tim was never allowed to make it, but he thanked Anna most gratefully for trying.

"I'll keep trying," she promised. "You deserve it and I'm going to see that you get it, damn it!"

But Anna's own reputation also weighed against him, which he never mentioned but which she knew. There was always the lingering feeling in the profession that she was somehow an upstart in Washington who had no right to be successful in a city that was supposed to be owned by the Daily Conscience and its ditzy bediamonded Doyenne.

His books, which came out at the rate of one every three or four years, were automatically attacked, not only by Mother and the Conscience but by all the reviewers around the country who took their lead from those two far from objective sources. His most popular, a calmly analytical and coolly devastating analysis of the failed administration of the hero of the desert sands, agreed with their own views but of course came from a tainted source, in their minds. So it too got savaged in the initial reviews, such as they were, and then was completely suppressed thereafter, never mentioned again, never referred to, never given the automatic puffery given the books authored by those on The Right Side of Things.

He wasn't, and that was that; the media's great nonperson curtain came down and his book was heard of no more. Renny reviewed it for Mother, a scathing and unrestrained attack that appeared on page twenty-three of the book review (even though Renny, also, harshly criticized the hero of the desert sands—but in his own way, and when he wanted to: Tim obviously had no right to be heard on the subject). But that was all. The book sold well to the general public but nowhere near what it would have sold if the usual suspects had given it the heavy promotion they always gave one of their own.

"I'll bet no one outside the political world realizes the shafting they always give you," Willie said. "Either they censor and suppress you and bury you entirely, or they dump on you with that kind of crap. Either way, they do you as much damage as they can."

Tim shook his head with a rueful but undaunted smile.

"The general public," he agreed, "never stops to realize that reviews don't just happen—news stories and news pictures don't just happen. These things don't just fly on and off the page or the screen of their own volition. *Somebody* decides what's to be done, *somebody* selects the reviewer or the news story or the picture that will do it, *somebody* twists, *somebody* slants, *somebody* manages the news to manipulate the readership or the viewership. Minds are at work here, biases and prejudices control. No slant of a newspaper story, no position of a photograph on the page, no size or prominence of a headline, no radio commentary or television show, springs full-blown from the brow of Jove. *Somebody,* corporate or individual, makes the decision."

"You realize what a fight lies ahead if I decide to go for it," Willie said, associating the two of them finally in what he referred to with utmost privacy as "my ultimate project."

Tim grinned.

"I'm game if you are. Say when."

"Not yet," Willie said. "But I'll let you know."

From that point on, quietly and discreetly but always with the objective in mind, their lives and actions became dominated to considerable degree by Willie's ultimate project.

And not so quietly or discreetly but with equal dedication, the forces Renny symbolized and spoke for began to put themselves in place to thwart it, even though Willie was most careful to keep his intentions to himself.

"I just *know* that's what he intends to do," Renny told his friends and ideological allies; soon found himself obsessed with his attempts to defeat it; and never missed a chance to criticize, demean, belittle, attack, never knowing when events might place in his hands some weapon of scandal or detriment that would be the decisive factor, but always keeping himself alert for it, knowing that he would use it to the full if it ever came to him.

4

"An awesomely broad-gauged intellect,
truly one of the masterminds of the twentieth century . . . a glowing flame in the great
eternal struggle between good and evil
in our land. With such a one to give us counsel,
good's triumph may sometimes be delayed.
It can never be denied."

1 For his attacks on Willie's project, and on all the other necessary targets he felt he must assail in his long, contentious life, Renny congratulated himself that he was ideally equipped for battle. As he reached the full flowering of his quite formidable talents in the seventies and eighties, he found with happy satisfaction that he was in the right place at the right time, with powerful supporters to welcome him aboard with open-armed enthusiasm. They all believed, none more fervently than he, that they had exclusive rights to defend American civilization and the freedoms of the world, as they saw them. To that herculean task he was confident he brought herculean abilities. This was recognized early and late by what Tim referred to scathingly as "the forward-looking, right-thinking leaders of media, academe, Broadway, Hollywood and the law."

Tim, in fact, in one of his more lighthearted, what-the-hell moments, sent Willie a paragraph from "a column I am *not* going to write." It commented on Renny's support at midpoint:

"Now we see him hailed, that indefatigable spirit and devotee of all things Right and Good, by some of the leading institutions of the New American Enlightenment . . . *The New York Review of (Each Other's) Books* . . . The National (Right-Thinking) Book Critics Circle . . . The National Book Award (for Those Who Mind Their P's and Q's) . . . membership in the American Academy of Arts and Letters (for Those Who Toe the Line) . . . Mother's Book Review (of Good Little Boys and Girls) . . . the Daily Conscience's Book Review (of Those Who Know Which Side Their Sales Are Buttered On) . . . and so on. It is a noble roll call, nobly deserved by Dr. Suratt, harbinger of the brave new world."

In a more serious vein, Tim analyzed him in an article for Mother's

Sunday Magazine, whose editors, as always, printed his thoughts with some misgivings but, to their credit, stuck by their uneasy arrangement with him. The encomiums of some of Renny's high-level supporters, Tim wrote, "would humble a lesser man, which Dr. Suratt is not. The quotes are golden:

"'One of the major social and political theorists of our time . . . a voice of sanity and reason in a troubled age . . . a prophet of coming events whose dynamic and exciting views must be studied and absorbed by all who wish to understand the profound transformations of the twentieth century . . . one of those paradigmatic figures who illuminate the world for all of us . . . a guru for the enlightened, a leader for our times . . . an awesomely broad-gauged intellect, truly one of the masterminds of the twentieth century . . . a glowing flame in the great eternal struggle between good and evil in our land. With such a one to give us counsel, good's triumph may sometimes be delayed. It can never be denied.'

"From his privileged and securely tenured position on the University faculty, he is now a major institution on the national scene. He has become an entity almost separate from himself, whose writings, lectures, books, statements and actions in mobilizing dissident thought are accorded instant and automatic approval by that 'establishment' his critics are so fond of attacking.

"In fact, Dr. Suratt now *is* the establishment, as much as any one individual could possibly be.

"Devoted disciples know him as one of those seminal figures whose challenging and disrespectful views of the *other* establishment blend with his magnetic platform presence to make him a formidable, slavishly admired icon. It does not seem exaggeration to say that he is worshiped from Martha's Vineyard to Beverly Hills and the Golden Gate.

"He has become an inseparable and necessary part of that great interlocking directorate of mutual puffery, publicity and back-patting that controls the American intellectual community. They review his books—he reviews their books. They praise his speeches—he praises their speeches. They quote him—he quotes them. He tells the world how wonderful they are—they tell the world how wonderful he is. The drumbeat is incessant, implacable and irresistible."

(The following two paragraphs were cut by the editors of the *Sunday Magazine,* but the article otherwise was allowed to stand intact.)

"From the winding back roads of Martha's Vineyard to the windswept dunes of old Nantucket to the lush green lawns of Georgetown and the sands of Malibu, they pass the word. On campus after campus, at political fund-raisers and at increasingly violent protest rallies, wherever the four winds blow, Dr. Suratt remembers his friends. And they remember him.

"It is all very jolly and completely typical of what passes for independent American intellectual thought in the second half of the twentieth century."

More privately, in areas Tim did not touch upon even though Duke Offenberg, Johnny Herbert and Moose Musavich had fully informed him of the campus gossip when he was doing research for the article, Renny also followed a style of living most predictable for the times and for the national community of think-alikes and act-alikes into which he fitted so securely.

From about age thirty-five, when he achieved the status of full professor, to about sixty-five, when he finally decided it had become rather pointless and even ridiculous, perhaps not really suitable for his final metamorphosis into elder statesman, his classroom persona was classic: hair long and unkempt, fingernails ragged and dirty, jeans, shirts and tennis shoes carefully tattered and sloppy (though secretly well laundered and clean, because he couldn't abide the thought of anything soiled against his skin). His sexual life kept pace in the extreme—and often quite pathetic—pattern of many in the sixties who thought that by escaping into the eternal juvenility of mindless, automatic sex they could somehow cheat Mother Nature into relieving them of the simple but terrible burden of just growing up to be mature human beings.

Outwardly, and as far as his special world knew (or preferred to admit), his life followed a clear and quite predictable pattern—at least professionally.

Soon after the end of the war, when he returned to the campus from his family home in the wealthy enclave of Hillsborough, he persuaded then-President Chalmers to give him an instructor's job in the English department. Dr. Chalmers did so with some misgivings, belonging as he did to an earlier generation that found Renny's aggressive politics and free-swinging lifestyle both bizarre and daunting. He did not foresee then how extreme both would become, but having presided over a major university for some years by that time, he had an uneasy inkling. But he could not deny that Renny was, as Dr. Chalmers reluctantly admitted when challenged by such trustees as Walter Emerson, "a very bright young man and a spellbinding teacher. The kids like him."

"The kids like anybody who challenges authority," Walter returned with a snort. "That goes with the territory. It doesn't mean the son of a bitch makes sense. You mark my words, that boy means trouble."

Dr. Chalmers, startled by Walter's vehemence and not entirely sure but what he was right, murmured something vague about, "Well, we'll have to wait and see."

Which, Walter confided to several close friends on the board, "is typical of Chalmers. He's a nice man but he's weak. He sure isn't equipped to handle the type of teachers and kids who are going to be flooding into this campus in the next few years."

And in this, of course, Walter was entirely right. A new age was dawning and Renny was one of its major spokesmen and "gurus," as his followers described him. He was ideally positioned to raise hell; and he was confronted by a school administration that was not necessarily "weak" but was so conditioned by the experience and background of a gentler, more honorable, more gentlemanly time that it was simply unable to control him. He so speedily acquired a reputation and standing with the major intellectual elements of the country that it was impossible to do what Walter constantly urged, "get rid of him."

Renny very cleverly made sure that this could never happen. There were several other young members of the faculty who thought and acted much as he did, but they didn't have his genius for publicity or his instinctive ability, as he described it, "to know where the buttons are and how to push them."

It took him little more than a year on campus to begin to acquire the fawning attentions of the media and the academic and literary worlds, through which he knew he could have a major impact on his times.

―――――

Just as it took him about the same period of time to begin to acquire the sort of secret personal reputation that both repelled and intrigued the younger minds and bodies he sought, with quite frequent success, to take advantage of. Many were as fascinated by his attentions as they might have been by the act of playing with a mamba. He was about equally dangerous to their morals (not very strong at that age), their principles (quite vague at that age) and their health and good looks (both superb at that age).

But what the hell, you were only young once; and "Old Renny," as they began to refer to him on campus, would show you things you had only dreamed about when you were dawdling in the shower or masturbating in front of Rita Hayworth's picture on the wall of your dormitory or fraternity room. Old Renny made it all come true and also introduced you, at first it seemed quite painlessly, to drugs.

It was amazing how he got away with it, his young friends remarked to one another after some particularly energetic night in his converted gatehouse at the mansion in Hillsborough. He was a perfect guru indeed as the fifties moved into the sixties and seventies and he knowingly and deliberately helped the weaker members of a generation fall apart, even as he challenged the politics and beliefs of their parents across the land.

How did it all begin? How did he become such a sanctified untouchable in the world of Those Who Really Mattered, such a voracious playmate in the world of the randy young?

"It's like everything," he confided to his fellow celebrants with a rather grim little smile. "Sheer determination. The disarray of my enemies. And the protection of my friends."

2   And how *did* it all begin, the parallel rise of "one of the major social and political theorists of our times . . . a voice of sanity and reason in a troubled age" . . . and the naked master of ceremonies enjoying and dispensing his drugs and his favors to youths of both sexes and all genders who flocked to his gatehouse, helplessly intrigued by his excitingly sinister reputation?

Back in the fraternity house, on the eve of World War II, Renny's prickly personality warranted the reputation he had there: "a sour, unpleasant son of a bitch who doesn't seem to like anybody."

This was the almost universal judgment. Only gentle Bill Lattimer, shortly before his tragic death in the accident on Palm Drive when he took his fatal last ride with Randy Carrero, made any real attempt to find out if the reputation was justified.

As he admitted with some chagrin to Willie later, "I felt there must be some good there that we haven't tapped into. I thought it might be our fault."

"And did you decide it was?" Willie inquired dryly. Lattimer gave him a frustrated and rather shamefaced smile.

"Nope," he admitted, not liking to acknowledge that his own genuine goodwill toward the world was in no way shared by their difficult fraternity brother. "I decided it was innate and endemic."

"I could have told you that," Willie said, not knowing then how often down the years he would have occasion to reaffirm that bleak judgment.

Thanks to Renny's shrewd marketing of his opinions and talents (particularly the former), the judgment was not shared by the leaders of the snug little, smug little world to which he soon belonged. Their influence depended almost entirely upon the great god Communication and the fact that they all had much the same education and had been subjected to the same academic and literary attacks upon principle and common sense. This created the same mind-set, which they happily inflicted upon their countrymen in an age of great uncertainty. It was a time when, as Renny put it, "the whole tree can be shaken by a few determined people pounding on the trunk." It was an exciting time for those whom Tim, scornfully reciprocating, dubbed "The Mind-Benders," a time not only exciting but highly rewarding, if you were on the Right Side. Tim certainly was not and, as Renny often jeered, "could only splutter, offstage right, in frustration and futility."

Renny and his establishment friends, influencing through "the interlocking directorate" all the major means of communication in America and generally throughout what was known somewhat euphemistically as "the free world," were able to shake the tree on nearly all the major issues of the day. One of their most effective means was the written word. Books of the correct persuasion were often the surest guarantee of entry into the inner circle. Once you received the gracious anointing of favorable reviews in Mother, the Daily Conscience and all their slavish journalistic copiers across the country, your influence rapidly became enormous. Your national and international reputations soared, and with them your material fortunes.

Renny had grasped this early when, lazing by the family pool in Hillsborough in his sun-filled, safe-haven, conscientious-objector days in World War II, he had contemplated what he wished to make of his future.

His first book, *America: The Myth That Couldn't*, was a scathing analysis of what he called "the Little Train 'I-Think-I-Can'" mentality of unimaginative middle-class America. The volume was received with hosannahs ("a brilliant new social thinker has been found") by Mother and the Conscience and their group of happy campers, and he was on his way. The front-page reviews he received in the book sections of every right-thinking publication on that occasion proved to be a sure harbinger of things to come. His patrons were determined to secure for him national attention and major influence. Their efforts were successful from the start.

The list up to now was impressive.

The Balding Eagle: America's Uncertain Role in World Affairs came next, in which he argued "with the incisive insight and devastating logic that we have come already to associate with Dr. Suratt's name" that the country's post-war policies were leading straight to what he described as "appalling disaster—a situation in which the twin dreams of 'world peace' and 'a stable world society' supersede and cancel out effective concepts of simple right and justice on this unhappy globe."

Then came *Janus: America's Two-Faced Foreign Policy* (by then he had taken the necessary catch-up courses and switched from the English department to political science, where he was much more at home and where prominence came easy). *Janus*, the reviews said, displayed "his usual infallible choice of the right word, the right phrase, the right thesis with which to demolish all those old-fashioned ideas that hinder the clear perception of the inevitable curtailment of the arrogant dreams and foolish imperialist ambitions that besmirch America's present world record."

That was followed by the timely *American Abyss: Disaster in Vietnam?* "warning, with his usual characteristic searing pen and irrefutable logic, of the tragic catastrophe that will soon engulf America if the administration does not speedily reverse its course in that unhappy sector of the world."

Number five was *Crossroads: America Waits for Social Justice*, which, by coincidence unhappy for Bayard Johnson but great for the book, was published a month after By's death in the University riot organized by Renny and his followers—"a tragic coincidence, but one which nonetheless serves to emphasize Dr. Suratt's customary sensing of the moment and his impeccable logic as he warns against just the sort of extreme divisions that apparently resulted in the recent death of Bayard Johnson. It need not have happened. The sad event came too late for inclusion in Dr. Suratt's book, but it demonstrates most grimly the essential soundness of his argument." ("Now we know why that riot happened," Tim wrote bitterly in his own review of Renny's book. "It sold books." Renny did not dignify that with a rejoinder, but his supporters made up for it with a number of scathing denunciations of Tim.)

Book number six, just recently published, was *Kaleidoscope: America's Racial Divisions, No Longer Black and White,* "a book of extreme prescience and profound reasoning, a chilling forecast of the clashes between Asians and blacks, Hispanics and blacks, that may soon begin to rend the nation as the hardworking successes of fast-rising newcomers to America supersede and submerge the traditional patterns of black-white relationships. A call for enlightened leadership in all races; an ominous warning of what could happen to our democracy if such leadership does not arise."

For once, Tim approved and said so, in his column and in an op-ed piece for Mother. Willie did the same in a brief statement for the *Congressional Record* that called attention to the book and endorsed its reasoning. Asked by Mother's editors to comment, Renny responded with a grim smile and said, "I'm touched by the approval of my two old fraternity brothers, Senator Wilson and Mr. Bates. It comes late, but welcome." And said no more; nor did they. It was the last time the two of them showed the slightest public civility toward Renny, or he toward them.

Renny often told himself with an ironic humor that there was one other book he really should write: *How It's Done, A Guide to Achieving Fame and Fortune in Late Twentieth Century America.*

He knew he wouldn't write it, of course, but his own career offered a perfect example. It could be summed up in one sentence: Toe the line—don't be too independent—agree with establishment thinking on all major issues—if you have the talent (and he did), carry it one step further and become a vigorous advocate—and watch the glory roll in.

It was so simple that he marveled sometimes that Tim and Willie (whom he consistently referred to in the classroom as "Tantrum Tim" and "Senator Squeak-In") had never recognized the classic practicality of it and conducted themselves accordingly. Willie could have been the darling of the establishment and Tim would have won his Pulitzer years ago. (As Renny had been assured he himself would, sometime in the next two or three years "after we've taken care of ———" naming two or three other pets of the in-group. So Renny knew it would soon happen for him, and was content. And maybe even a Nobel? It did happen, sometimes, for those who were reliable apples that never fell far from the tree. The tree had powerful roots in Europe, too.)

He knew that his career sometimes provoked the disrespectful comment, from those who were always jealous of success, that he had no real principles or beliefs, just a desire for fame backed by a formidable pen and hypnotic platform presence; but he knew the jape was not correct. He knew how to work the angles, true enough, none better; but there was something deeper, just as there was something deeper in his private life than just the cheap thrills provided by young bodies and easily seduced experimenters. He genuinely wanted to help "his kids," as he thought of them, to achieve the fullest expression of their natures and the freest possible development of their personalities.

As he wanted to help the country overcome and finally defeat the stupid, ill-informed, incorrigibly reactionary beliefs of so many of their parents.

It was no wonder the parents, exemplified by Walter Emerson and his blindly conservative contemporaries, regarded Renny as "dangerous."

He *was* dangerous, he told himself with some relish, dangerous to all their silly, half-baked, half-assed, "patriotic" assumptions, their complacent lives, their sick, confused country, their greedy, money-grubbing, off-balance, unequal, unfair society—dangerous to the very foundations upon which they lived—dangerous, as they saw it, to their children, whom they wished to have inherit their own dangerous assumptions and their crazy, mixed-up world.

Not because he believed in Communism or any other stupid foreign-born ideology; he was too smart and independent for that—not because he had any particular alternatives to offer except "Do it differently"— but just because, as Duke Offenberg remarked when Renny's attacks on him were at their height, "He likes to destroy."

Renny knew that "destroy" was too harsh a word. He liked to challenge, he liked to turn things upside down, he took perverse pleasure in being different, the longhair, the drugs advocate, the sexual "liberator," the radical. He had always been, and was becoming more so, the spoiler—but spoiler, he was satisfied, in the interest of good causes.

And so be it, he thought grimly. They deserved it and he was going to let them have it as long as he could draw breath and wield pen.

Not, of course, that it had all been smooth sailing. There had been a couple of times when he seemed to be under almost insuperable attack, his own assumptions challenged, his life's work put at desperate jeopardy.

His supporters had rushed to his defense. The noisy invocation of his many triumphs, the prompt media and academic glorification of "what he stands for" were sufficient to overcome his adversities. He had emerged more impregnable than ever. But for a time, in both cases, the outcome did not seem all that inevitable.

3   "I don't care if you sleep with my boys, but God damn it, lay off them with the drugs!" Moose snapped. "Or you and I are going to have big trouble!"

His face was flushed with anger; the long, jagged scar from the war in the Pacific that disfigured his face from eye to chin was swollen and protuberant, as it became when he was truly enraged. He had walked the quarter mile between the athletic offices and the political science department growing angrier by the minute.

It was the first time since fraternity days almost thirty years ago, aside from a terse hello at faculty senate meetings or when happening to cross paths on campus, that they had actually confronted each other. Renny knew at once that Moose's mood would play to his own advantage, as it always had in their brief and usually hostile exchanges in the house. They hadn't liked each other then and liked each other even less now. Renny, confident from past experience that he could always dance around old Mooser like a wasp he tried to slap but couldn't quite reach, was not overly perturbed by their growing argument this morning.

"Sit down, Moose," he said, with what he prided himself was an outwardly perfect calm, though he couldn't deny that he did feel some trace of apprehension. Moose was so *physical*. He had never quite "bashed your head in," though he had threatened to several times in undergraduate days. Renny could not quite dismiss the possibility.

It would be so like Moose, the stupid Polack football player. And not even a very good one, at that.

"Maybe I will sit down and maybe I won't," Moose growled, but did, after a moment, facing Renny squarely across his cluttered desk, resting his two hamlike paws side by side in front of him.

"Good," Renny said crisply. "Surely you don't intend to give me carte blanche to sleep with the football team, Moose. Why would I want to do that?"

"You do everything else, from what I hear," Moose said darkly. "And even that, too, if you get the chance. Of course I'm not giving you carte blanche. I'm just mad."

"About the drugs," Renny said with a chuckle. Moose looked like a thundercloud.

"God damn it, how can you be so lighthearted?" he demanded. "Don't you have any conscience about it at all? You're ruining a lot of kids on this campus, and a lot of other campuses too, where they hear your crazy ideas." His scowl deepened, his tone became flat and accusatory. "You ruin everything you touch and always have. I ought to be used to it by this time. But I can't keep still when my boys are involved, and I won't, by God, I'll go to Chalmers if I have to. And we'll see what happens to smug old Renny then."

"I'm not smug," Renny said, reminding himself that he must keep his temper or this big ox would figuratively if not literally knock him off balance.

"You've always been smug," Moose retorted. "Nobody in the house could stand you then and nobody can stand you now. Certainly I can't."

"You didn't have to come over," Renny pointed out with determined mildness. "Give me a call. Write me a letter. Talk to Chalmers. We didn't have to have a big dramatic confrontation."

"It's all you understand," Moose said scornfully. "Drama. Melodrama." He uttered a derisory sound. "Big deal! God, I despise what you've become." He thought for a moment, decided to use the weapon he knew would hurt Renny most—if he could be hurt, which Moose doubted. *How I pity you.*

And that, Moose saw with grim satisfaction and Renny with angry dismay as his carefully maintained control slipped away, really got to old Renny.

"Don't you dare pity me, you ignorant football player!" he cried. "You hunk of—of nothing! All you've ever done in your life is chase the skin of a pig around the field and pretend you're a big shot. You were never very good at it, with your 'fucking asshole touchdowns,' as Franky Miller used to say. What a pathetic life *you've* led! Head coach to a bunch of morons who don't know any better! You ought to be ashamed!"

"Better than a bunch of kids who don't know any better than to let a pervert debauch their bodies and destroy their characters!" Moose retorted, breathing heavily. With an obvious effort, he spoke in a quieter but still adamant tone. "I am proud to be head football coach at a great university, and I am proud of the boys who come out for the team and work their asses off for me. And I don't want them hurt by you, understand? I know kids can't be stopped from experimenting with sex. We've got a couple of pairings on the team right now; they think I don't know but I do. But it won't last, they'll get over it—or maybe they won't, I don't know, but it's their business as long as they're discreet about it and it isn't cold-blooded God damned *organizing,* the way you're doing. It's spontaneous and, I suspect, even happy, or they wouldn't be doing it. At least that's *human.* You're a God damned machine experimenting with other machines."

"How do you know about that?" Renny demanded with a fine show of surprised indignation. "What makes you think—"

"I hear things," Moose said grimly. "They tell me a lot, our young friends. It's all over campus, anyway. You think it isn't, but that's where the great sophisticated Professor Suratt is a naive jerk. Plenty of people know. Just because you're famous in your circles—"

"In my circles," Renny echoed with a sort of jeering complacency, "I am untouchable."

"Yes," Moose said. "Well. Your circles don't control the whole world, you know."

"Just about," Renny said in a tone he knew would infuriate his hopelessly stolid and tradition-bound fraternity brother.

"We may have a chance to find out about that," Moose said, "unless you lay off. Particularly the drugs. And particularly Bill Gregorio."

For a moment Renny looked genuinely startled; decided to bluster it out; and switched to determinedly indignant.

"Who's Bill Gregorio?" he demanded. "I don't know any Bill Gregorio—"

"The hell you don't," Moose overrode him angrily. "Stop the crap, Renny. Bill Gregorio is in the news every weekend. He's one of my best players and a hell of a nice kid. Or was. Until you got hold of him."

"But I don't know—" Renny began. Moose scowled him down.

"Stop it," he ordered. "Just stop it, O.K.?"

Renny did stop, and for a long moment they stared at each other across the desk, Renny maintaining his air of self-righteous innocence, Moose his unrelenting insistence. Then Renny sniffed.

"Well!" he said. "Assuming for the sake of argument—"

"Sake of argument, nothing, you poseur—" Moose began. Renny interrupted.

"Oh!" he exclaimed archly. "I didn't know you knew such a word!"

"I know lots of words," Moose said "and I'm going to use them all on you in public if you don't keep your dirty hands off Gregorio and anyone else on the team you may have your eyes on."

"Don't be so melodramatic yourself!" Renny snapped. "I don't 'have my eyes on' anybody. They come to me. I don't pursue them."

"Sometimes yes, sometimes no," Moose said. "I hear about it. Anyway, *leave them alone,* that's my point. Just leave them the God damned hell *alone,* all right?"

"I can't help it," Renny said, "if young friends in search of enlightenment about themselves and their bodies and their inner truths come to me and—"

"What crap!" Moose snorted. "What holy crap! You make me sick. Bill Gregorio called me last night at home and wanted to come over. I told him to come ahead. Diana took the kids to a movie and left us alone. Bill spent two hours in my house, crying. That's what you've done to a fine kid, Renny. Look yourself in the face for once. *That's what you've done.*"

"I haven't done anything to anybody that he or she didn't want," Renny said sharply. "I always make sure they know what they're doing and that they're entirely agreeable—"

"Hell," Moose said. "You know kids that age as well as I do. Catch them right and they'll agree to almost anything. I repeat, leave Bill alone and leave the team alone, or there's going to be one hell of a scandal and by God, I'm going to break you if I can. Chalmers wants you out, the trustees want you out, and a lot of parents do too. We'll get you, if that's what you want."

"You'll never touch me," Renny said with a calm defiance he did not entirely feel: who knew what trouble this oaf could stir up if he really went public and started raising hell with parents and alumni? Most of the faculty and most of the student body would be on Renny's side, but what about the reactionaries who always came out of the woodwork when anybody with Renny's views started to stumble? That could be another matter.

He repeated with a calm assurance, "You'll never touch me."

Moose laughed grimly and stood up, not offering to shake hands, which Renny wouldn't have done anyway.

"Watch yourself, Renny," he said. "Mark my words and behave yourself. Or you won't like what happens."

"Fuck you," Renny said viciously, "you ignorant clod."

Moose paused briefly at the door.

"Rave on," he suggested. "But behave yourself."

And turned on his heel and was gone, surprisingly fast for a big man.

Four days later the University *Daily,* the Bay Area papers, the wire services and even such journals as Mother and the Daily Conscience far away in the happy East brought sobering news, which received bigger headlines in the West but still commanded attention everywhere.

STAR GRID PLAYER A SUICIDE.
BILL GREGORIO, COLLEGE HERO,
SHOOTS SELF AT UNIVERSITY.
Coach Says, "He Was One Of
Our Finest. A Great Tragedy."

The month following was the most devastating—and decisive—of Renny's life. Before it, he might have been tripped up by his enemies; after its successful conclusion, never.

The outcome fully justified his confidence in himself. He never doubted he would come through it all right, though for a brief while he wasn't sure just how. Which was not the way he liked to lead his life, and shook him badly; but only for a brief time, and not in any way that could really interfere with what the Conscience, in a strong editorial of support, called "his most worthy career."

First came Moose, as good as his word:

COACH HINTS POSSIBLE DRUG TIE TO GREGORIO DEATH—"I THINK THERE'S A SUPPLIER ON THE FACULTY"—BUT REFUSES TO NAME HIM "FOR NOW."

Then came the interview with Dr. Chalmers, which was not easy but Renny overcame it.

And then came the full baying of media, academe and all right-thinkers in his defense.

And the crisis passed.

"Sit down, Professor Suratt," Dr. Chalmers said, always polite, always gracious, always the gentleman—always the well-bred weakling, Renny thought with a sarcastic superiority that almost—almost—canceled out the very real trepidation with which he had answered the president's request that he come to his office.

"Thank you," he said, working to keep the hostility out of his tone because Chalmers, for all his mild, old-fashioned courtesy, could still pack a wallop when aroused. "Why did you wish to see me?"

For several seconds the president did not reply, simply stared at him thoughtfully as he sat where so many recalcitrants, students and faculty alike, had sat over the years, awaiting what Renny referred to among friends as "the sermon on the mount."

"Why do you think I want to see you?" Dr. Chalmers inquired finally. "Examining the broad field of subjects on which I might want to interrogate you, which would be your guess?"

"I don't know," Renny said blandly, thinking: *two can play that game, you old fraud. You tell me.*

"No inkling," the president said gently.

"No inkling," Renny responded in the same bland way.

"A great tragedy, young Gregorio," Dr. Chalmers remarked.

Renny nodded and looked grave.

"Always one or two, every quarter," he said. "Always a tragedy. And always, in the last analysis, unexplained—and perhaps unexplainable."

"Do you think this was?" the president inquired. "I get intimations that it might not have been so unexplainable."

"Oh?" Renny said with interest. "What could it have been?"

"Your fraternity brother has his ideas," the president noted.

Renny permitted himself a skeptical chuckle.

"Moose? Moose always had ideas, even as an undergrad."

"I've always thought his main idea—aside from fielding a team that would always win, that is—" The president smiled the fatherly, there-goes-lovable-Moose-again smile that so many people conferred on Moose; but Renny refused to respond, only looked attentive and interested. "Aside from fielding a winning team all the time," Dr. Chalmers repeated, "I've thought his main idea has always been to help raise as many fine, decent, morally worthy young men as he could manage with the material he has on the team, insofar as a coach can influence them in that direction."

"Yes," Renny agreed, and could not keep the sarcasm entirely out of his voice. "Old Mooser has always fancied himself to be A Molder of Men."

"A worthy objective," Dr. Chalmers remarked gently, "and one to which I am sure all decent faculty members try to adhere. Molder of men—and women. Don't you agree, Professor Suratt?"

Look, Renny almost let himself shout, *why don't you stop the pussy-footing and come to the point, you old phony?* But of course that would never do. He rearranged his face to its respectful mode and again looked interested and attentive.

"Why would I not, Dr. Chalmers?" he inquired. "Why would I not? It is, as you say, the objective of every decent man and woman on the faculty to exercise such uplifting influence on the young minds and just-forming characters of the youths who pass through our hands—"

"An interesting phrase," the president murmured.

"Er—yes," Renny agreed, momentarily—but only momentarily, he congratulated himself, thrown off balance—and resumed with appropriate earnestness—"As I say, we all have that objective, to be good influences, to help them develop in the way they should go, to help them, if I may use the cliché, to find themselves. It is one of the greatest and most serious duties—and one of the greatest pleasures [*take that, you old smart-ass*] a teacher can have. There is no higher satisfaction."

"Providing, of course," Dr. Chalmers remarked thoughtfully, "that it goes in the right direction and not in some—other."

"I don't know of a single faculty member," Renny said solemnly, "who would so betray his—or her—trust. It would be unthinkable."

"Unthinkable?" Dr. Chalmers echoed thoughtfully.

"Unthinkable," Renny said firmly.

"Coach Musavich seems to feel that there was a drug connection to young Gregorio's death," the president said, and his tone suddenly became quite impersonal and all business. "Would you know anything about that, Professor Suratt?"

"No, sir," Renny said calmly.

"Are you sure?" the president asked. "Coach Musavich—Moose— seems to think you do."

"I shall sue Coach Musavich—Moose—for slander if he—or you— or anyone ever says such a thing outside this office," Renny said in an even tone as flintlike as the president's. "It is a lie and I defy him—or you—or anyone to produce any proof that would indicate otherwise."

"Moose says Bill Gregorio told him all about it in a private conversation at Moose's home a few days ago."

"Did Moose write it down?" Renny demanded, and felt an iron hand grip his interior as the president hesitated for a moment.

"I believe he did, yes," he said finally. He searched among his papers, held up one, started to slip it back in the pile.

"Don't put it away," Renny said sharply. "I'm being challenged, I'm being slandered. I have a right to see it, I *think*."

Again Dr. Chalmers hesitated for a moment, retrieved the paper and passed it over, face impassive. Renny scanned it hastily, aware suddenly of fresh young voices calling to one another in the Quad outside, the metallic rattle of passing bicycles, the hum of a soft spring day. Then he tossed it back scornfully.

"Does Moose have a witness to this so-called revelatory conversation with an obviously distraught young man?" he demanded.

"I don't believe he does," Dr. Chalmers said calmly. "But that doesn't mean I don't believe him."

"And what do you intend to do about it?"

"What do you think I should do?" Dr. Chalmers inquired, still calmly.

"Without proof, what can you do?" Renny asked, equally calm, for now he was convinced he was home free.

"I can suggest that you seek employment elsewhere," the president said.

Renny actually turned pale, not from fright but from fury and disgust.

"You can suggest," he spat out, "but I'll fight it."

"I can always terminate your appointment outright," the president noted. "I'm sure a majority of the board will support me."

"But on what grounds?" Renny demanded. "I repeat, on what grounds? There are none. I meet all my classes, I fulfill all my obligations as a faculty member, I write books that are acclaimed not only nationally but internationally, my lectures are extremely popular, *I* am extremely popular. What on earth can you say against me that won't make you simply a laughingstock?"

"I don't have to defend my decision to anyone but the board—" Dr. Chalmers began. Renny uttered a scornful laugh.

"You'll have to defend it to a lot more people than that," he said. "Most of the faculty—most of the student body—the academic community throughout the country—all my supporters in the media—"

"Yes, I know," Dr. Chalmers agreed, annoyingly unperturbed. "You've made sure you have a lot of friends in powerful places. But they don't control what happens here."

"Oh, yes, they do," Renny retorted. "Wait and see."

"I had rather this did not become public," Dr. Chalmers remarked. Renny gave a sarcastic hoot.

"I'll bet you'd rather it didn't!" he exclaimed. "You know damned well—very well—what the reaction would be, your word against mine—"

"And Coach Musavich's—and poor Bill Gregorio's—and I dare say there will be others who will come forward," Dr. Chalmers said. "Once this can of worms is opened, there will be others who will speak up. There have been rumors about you for years."

"Because my views are too progressive for this reactionary place!" Renny exclaimed. "Because I have some vision for America that is worthy of respect and doesn't fit with the old-fashioned, reactionary thinking that has always dominated the University! Because I believe in going forward with a new vision for America—"

"That is nonsense," Dr. Chalmers said quietly.

"Yes," Renny said, breathing heavily. "It may be nonsense but it will be believed. That's the important thing from where I sit. *It will be believed.* And you'll get slaughtered in the media because you're attacking one of the most original and forward-looking social progressives in America!"

And he stood up abruptly and, with scant courtesy or none, stormed out, leaving Dr. Chalmers with a thoughtful, but not unduly perturbed, expression on his face.

Two days later at the regular trustees' meeting, Dr. Chalmers, backed vigorously by Walter Emerson and a clear majority of the board, announced that he thought Dr. Suratt was "a bad influence on the student body and a detriment to the University," and asked them to support his decision to ask for Dr. Suratt's resignation. He was vigorously opposed by Anne Greeley, who spoke for several of the younger board members.

"I am not concerned with unfounded rumors," she said, as their long, angry wrangle drew to a close. "There is no real proof of any of these allegations, Dr. Chalmers. It seems to me that you make yourself very vulnerable when you challenge a popular teacher on such flimsy grounds, when it is widely recognized in the media and throughout the country that his progressive political and social views are really at the heart of this. You and a majority of the board obviously regard him as a radical revolutionary, a subversive influence. His many supporters on campus and in national intellectual circles regard him as an enlightened, challenging and most stimulating commentator on the American scene. He is highly popular with the student body, faithfully conducts his courses and his other duties as a faculty member and contributes to the fame and standing of the University with his brilliant, highly thought of books.

"Any attempt to get rid of him would, as soon as it became public, become the focus of a major firestorm surrounding the University that I fear you could not win.

"I think the board should take this into consideration most seriously before we authorize the president to embark on any such highly controversial course."

Dr. Chalmers and Walter, however, had the votes. Two-thirds of the board voted favorably. The president was authorized to request the resignation of Dr. René Suratt on the ground of "questionable circumstances that tend to discredit and demean the University."

The decision was announced immediately in a formal statement to the media. Since the "questionable circumstances" were not specified or explained (at Walter's suggestion—"We don't have all the facts, and it's the sort of thing we ought to 'keep in the family,' so to speak") the door was left wide open for attack; and attack came, hot and heavy. The firestorm Anne had predicted very soon consumed not only the campus but the major media and intellectual forces of the country as well.

His two leading defenders on the other side of the continent knew very well what lay behind the board's decision, because reporters from both immediately called the editor of the *Daily* to ask.

The editor, light-years away from the days when Tim Bates sat in her chair and beat the drums for entry into World War II, told them candidly what the campus gossip was about Renny.

"We hope you aren't going to mention *that*!" they both exclaimed with some alarm.

"Are you crazy?" she demanded. "This is our guy out here. *We like him*. We aren't going to play into the enemy's hands by printing stuff like *that*."

"We aren't either," they assured her cheerfully. "He's our guy, too."

And made note that if she ever turned up on their doorsteps looking for a job, she would certainly be welcomed with open arms. It was heartening to see another generation coming along in journalism that knew what the score was and didn't have to be educated.

Three hours after the announcement was made, a "Save Suratt" rally was organized and held in the University's main plaza. Renny made a fighting speech, skillfully deprecating his own achievements while calling attention to them; attacking "the reactionary forces that control the University and are always seeking to drive us into a faceless conformity"; modestly picturing himself as "one of those who, in contrast, seek always to open up the minds of students to the possibilities inherent in this wonderful country of ours, wonderful, if we always fight to keep it wonderful and free to the probings of independent minds and courageous spirits."

He concluded by whipping his audience into a frenzy of support as he cried:

"René Suratt is only a symbol! A symbol of freedom! A symbol of curiosity and discovery! A spirit of independent research and independent thought into *all* aspects of human living! A symbol of that freedom which this university was founded to ensure, and which this university must never abandon or betray!

"I will never give in to reactionary pressures! I will never resign! Let them fire me if they will—*if they dare*! [Shouts and banners, YEA, RENNY! YO, RENNY! GO, GO, GO RENNY!] I will never let them kill my mind *or your minds either,* my dear young friends! Let us show them what they have taken on, when they attempt to suppress freedom and independent thought in America!"

And on a dying fall, the plaza hushed, the whole world, it seemed, hushed:

"I thank you from the bottom of my heart, my wonderful young friends, all. You reaffirm my faith in you. May I always justify your faith in me."

There were a couple of students, returning by car to the University, who told the *Daily* they could hear the resulting roar of approval at the upper end of Palm Drive, a mile away.

In the East, immediately shifting the basis of the debate as Renny had predicted his supporters would, Mother editorialized:

"And now we have an attempt by the anti-thought brigade to drive from public life ["Only from the University," Dr. Chalmers murmured with bleak amusement when he read this. "Only from the University."] one of the leading young intellectuals of our times, Dr. René Suratt, whose dismissal from the University's faculty is now the aim of a reactionary board of trustees and a reactionary president.

"We cannot tell from the official statement—the board and Dr. Chalmers do not say—what the 'questionable circumstances' are that have prompted this extraordinary vendetta against one of America's most brilliant advocates of social reform. We do know that Dr. Suratt's credentials are impeccable with everyone who gives an instant's thought to what is best for America, and for the University to whose name he brings such luster with his powerfully written, profoundly well-reasoned books. We also know that in recent years he has become a symbol not only to enlightened minds here and abroad but particularly to students on his own campus and many others. His is a light that shines with a rare exuberance and clarity. It must not be snuffed out by reactionary forces."

And in the same vein, the Conscience:

"The battle for freedom of thought never ends. Now it is being taken up again, this time in the cause of Dr. René Suratt, one of America's leading thinkers and one of its most brilliant and profound commentators. He is under attack from the board of trustees and the president of the great university which he distinguished by his presence on its faculty. Everyone who values powerful writing, clear thinking and far-seeing analysis must come to his assistance. The attack on him is no less than shameful.

"What dire things lie behind the board's ominous charge of 'questionable circumstances' to justify the attempt to force Dr. Suratt's resignation? Its members do not tell us. We can only conclude that a shabby pretext is being used to try to support a shabby act. Obviously the reasons for seeking Dr. Suratt's ouster are personal. He speaks too bravely. He thinks too deeply. He is too independent by far.

"He frightens them.

"For shame, we say to the board and the president. You are not worthy of your university's founders and its long tradition of free thought and free speech.

"And we say to everyone who values that tradition wherever it is expressed in America: rally behind Dr. Suratt. He deserves your generous and unstinting support."

And rally they did. What Willie referred to sarcastically as "the Free Renny campaign" was in high gear within two days. Editorials in most of the nation's major papers, TV and radio news programs and commentaries, fellow faculty members and academic leaders at many other higher institutions, all came to his support.

Within four days the tone of letters and phone calls received by Dr. Chalmers began to change. The first alumni to contact him were unanimously in favor of the board's action; soon, there was a subtle shift. Doubts began to be expressed; hesitations surfaced; "Are you very sure—?" began to hang in the air. Even Walter Emerson was shaken by the well-coordinated campaign. A week after the original announcement he called Dr. Chalmers from his home in Piedmont in the East Bay.

"I wonder—" he began without other preliminary. The president responded with a rather grim little chuckle.

"Yes, Walter," he said. "I'm not wondering about the wisdom of what we did, but I am wondering if we can make it stick. What do you and your fellow board members think?"

"I've polled them," Walter admitted. "And God damn it, they're beginning to crumble. I never thought I'd see the day when this university or this board caved in to organized pressure from the crackpots of the world, but I'm beginning to think this may be the time."

"What do you want to do?" the president asked. Walter uttered a frustrated sound.

"What do you want us to do?" he countered.

"Cut our losses and move on," Dr. Chalmers said. "There are more important things for this university than one little twisted soul on the faculty."

"He's certainly made himself important," Walter said glumly.

"I'll draft a statement and call you back in an hour," Dr. Chalmers said. "If we're going to surrender, I think it had better be fast."

"Absolutely," Walter agreed.

Two hours later the board's second statement reached the media:

"The board of trustees, acting in concurrence with the president of

---

the University, has decided to rescind its action calling for the resignation of Dr. Suratt from the faculty."

"Very terse," Walter observed, giving it his approval.

"I don't think we should argue with him in public," Dr. Chalmers said. "I'll write him a letter so he'll be formally put on notice in case he's tempted to get out of line again."

"He won't pay any attention to it," Walter predicted.

"He'd better," Dr. Chalmers said; but knew as he said it that they were dealing now with a sanctified recalcitrant. Now Renny was fortified by his supporters all over the country, even more than before a national figure, free to give his popular lectures and conduct himself on his own terms.

Nonetheless the president's letter was firm and to the point, ending with a blunt warning:

"If such an episode [Gregorio's suicide] ever happens again, or if I hear further rumors about sexual transgressions betraying your implicit trust as teacher vis-à-vis students, I shall promptly issue specific and detailed charges, together with any and all pieces of evidence that the University may be able to gather. Never forget, Dr. Suratt, that somebody will talk. Somebody always talks. You have escaped this time by the skin of your teeth, but you will not escape again should you be so stupidly unwise."

But you never laid a hand on me, Renny gloated as he read it. *I never made any concessions or any promises, did I? My friends and I were just too big for you, weren't we? We've beaten you, little reactionary, pathetic, two-bit people. So sorry.*

That evening Moose, watching television at home after a pleasant dinner, received a phone call. There was heavy breathing and then, clear, distinct and triumphant, "Ha, *ha!*"

"Get off my line, you fucking pervert," he replied. "If you ever hurt anybody on this campus again I'll cut your nuts off and stuff them down your throat."

"Ho, ho, *ho!*" the voice said. "Sleep easy, Moose. You're a sterling soul, but a little too big for your britches."

"Oh, shut up!" Moose said, and slammed down the receiver.

Secure in his gatehouse in Hillsborough, preparing to host a jolly little naked party celebrating his triumph, Renny laughed. He was about to receive five eager young guests and, he thought with happy anticipation, they would use drugs and do things and have a hell of a fine old time.

So much for those who would try to humble one of the masterminds of the twentieth century . . . a guru for our times.

The second time he was seriously at risk—a decade later—was a little more uncomfortable for him, but aided by his hands-down victory on the first go-around, he survived that one, too. It only served to confirm him in his contempt for, and opposition to, another major figure in his lifelong list of hates.

And it brought that pious fraud Willie Wilson back into the center of his concerns—although Willie actually was never far from them, so successfully did he represent all those forces of conservatism, reaction and old-fashioned morality that Renny so despised and so diligently flouted in both his professional and personal lives.

Willie was a real enemy—along with his lapdog, the famous columnist. Renny became even more determined to thwart their high and mighty ambitions, if he could.

4   *"Darling,"* the breathy little voice said in the final days of Renny's second "occasion." *"Darling,* I *must* see you."

Oh, Christ, Renny thought; and for the first time in six months of what she obviously regarded as their great romance and what he characterized in his own mind as "her insufferable sticking like glue," serious apprehension began to enter his mind. This was not what he had planned at all when she had first thrust herself forward after one of his classes; not even when she eagerly accepted a murmured invitation to, and eagerly participated in, one of his gatehouse romps.

Usually these things ended as they began, a brief fling seldom repeated except by a few very determined participants. She swiftly made it clear that she was, as he put it, more determined than anybody. And it wasn't as though she was all that attractive, he reflected bitterly as the insistent stream of phone calls, notes slipped under his office door, coy worshipful looks and accidental-on-purpose body-bumpings began to make him feel increasingly hemmed in.

Did he go out on the Quad for a quiet smoke? There she was, waiting for him on one of the benches under the palm trees. Did he walk, all unsuspecting, down the hall? Fancy who would be waiting for him around the corner! When he was talking to a group of fellow faculty members or a group of adoring students, guess who he bumped into, standing squarely behind him, when he inadvertently stepped back? She was, God damn it, always underfoot. It had begun by being fairly amusing. In a month it became absurd. Very rapidly it escalated into something unbearable. And by now it was beginning to become downright frightening.

And all from such a plain, unattractive source. She was tall, thin, unkempt and rather dirty; eyes big and usually lackluster from drugs when they weren't alight in pursuit of him; broad brow unfurrowed by uncertainty, serene in the comfort of absolute political conviction; an aura ablaze with youthful idealism, somewhat askew but violently self-righteous, burning bright. Borrowing from Bertolt Brecht and "Mack the Knife," he took to thinking of her as "Suki Tawdry." The name was really Helen, but she certainly was tawdry enough. And somehow "Suki" suited too.

He had finally looked her up in the registrar's office, pretending he wanted information on someone else. She was nineteen, a junior, majoring in political science—and men, he thought bitterly. Why she had fixated on him, he couldn't understand; for once his ego, sensing potential disaster, refused to let him believe that it was his fatal charm. He worried that it might turn out to *be* fatal. The thought, far out and fantastic as it might be, soon took hold of him. Old Renny had some sweaty moments as he contemplated the possible results of what had begun as just another happy fling. He was determined it would not happen. Somehow she must be discouraged, told to fuck off in a way she wouldn't forget. He himself temporarily forgot, in his worried calculations, the ultimate female weapon. Her latest phone call, summarily dismissed, was followed by a direct confrontation outside one of his classes next day. She told him, under threat of a loud public confrontation, which he recognized might be quite disastrous, that he must listen.

"Now you've done it," she said, eyes for once looking really alive, glittering with a mixture of anger, amusement and smug satisfaction. "You've done it now, *darling*. And what are you going to do about it?"

"What?" he demanded, although instinctively he knew.

"Knocked me up," she said. "I'm pregnant. What now, brown cow?"

"I'm not your 'brown cow,' " he snapped. "Act your age, Suk— Helen. How do you know it's me?"

"Oh, I don't," she said cheerfully. "But who's to prove I'm wrong?"

"There are tests," he said, struggling to keep things rational.

"Not until the baby's born," she said. "And by then you and I are going to be the University's newest and happiest couple."

"You're crazy," he said.

"Could be," she agreed with a complacent smile that did strike him as seriously off-balance. "So what? Nobody will notice when I'm wife to Professor Suratt, great thinker of America."

"Now, listen," he said, and despite his desperate efforts to sound calm, a certain strain was evident. "Surely we can work this out like two adults. There are ways of getting rid of—"

"Oh, no!" she said, so loudly that it seemed for a moment that a public confrontation would take place—several students, passing, looked around, surprised and interested. "Oh, no, we won't do that! *I* won't do that. After all"— and an unpleasant, sarcastic smile twisted her mouth—"I'm carrying the seed of genius, aren't I? Everybody says that. Professor Suratt, he's our genius. Professor Suratt, he's a great man. Well, Professor Suratt can jolly well be a great man and stand by little Baby Genius here, can't he? He'd better, is all I can say. He'd better!"

"Now, look—" he tried again, but again she cut him off.

"*You* look," she said with a sudden vicious emphasis. "If you don't do the right thing"— the irony of appealing to what Renny often described with heavy sarcasm as "simple, honest, middle-class morality" obviously escaped her; and him, too, at this particular moment—"if you don't do the right thing, my parents will raise hell with the whole damned University. And there goes your career, famous man. This time you aren't going to escape."

This echo of something now a decade in the past momentarily shook him. A surge of anger came to his rescue.

"Listen to me," he said, voice low but suddenly as vicious as hers, "*tramp*. If you *dare* to try to make trouble for me, you'll be crucified, my girl. My academic friends and my friends in the media will *destroy* you. Just for starters, President Offenberg is my fraternity brother and he'll see to it you're kicked out of school immediately. I'll deny everything. What will become of you then?"

She had flinched at the whiplash of his emphasis on the word "tramp," but came back strong.

"I wouldn't be so sure," she said. "I'll call the *Daily* and announce our wedding plans and then where will *you* be?"

"Announce and be damned!" he said grandly.

The hoot of her laughter followed him halfway across the Quad as he turned and strode away through more passing students who, startled and intrigued, looked at him with new speculation in their eyes.

Ten minutes later he received a call from the current editor of the *Daily*, an earnest young man who would go far in his chosen profession. He was obviously upset.

"Professor Suratt," he said hesitantly, "I've received a very strange call from a student named Helen Carlson."

"Yes?" he said calmly: he was not going to make this comfortable for him; the boy's tone indicated he might be easily intimidated.

"She says—well, you know what she says," the editor said. Renny thought: not so simple, after all. And became instantly cautious.

"No, I don't," he responded without missing a beat. "What did she say—Bob, isn't it?"

"Yes, sir," Bob said, sounding flattered that his name would be remembered by one so distinguished and so burdened with the world's affairs. "She said you two are going to be married in Memorial Church next month. Is this true?"

"It is not," he said with firm indignation. "It is absolutely untrue. The young lady is obviously off-balance a bit; there's a screw loose somewhere. Don't quote me on that, but you can use 'unbalanced,' if you like. She's obviously under some delusion, some twisted fantasy. It sometimes happens to people like me when one is—shall we say, famous? Or at least well known. It is something that sometimes goes with the territory. I don't even know the girl."

"She says she has been to your house, sir," the editor persisted, politely but doggedly. "She hinted she may be—"

"Yes?" he inquired, tone a demand.

"Pregnant, sir," Bob said.

"Do you believe her, Bob?" Renny asked in an amused, between-us-men-of-the-world mode.

"Should I, sir?" Bob asked, still sounding like a meek little soul, but obviously not.

Renny snorted.

"You believe what you like!" he said flatly. "I'm telling you it's a dreadful lie and I'm predicting that young lady will be on her way off this campus just as soon as I can reach President Offenberg, which I am going to do as soon as you've had enough and hang up."

"I'm sorry, sir," Bob said hastily. "I think I do have enough for now. I think maybe the best thing at the moment is to simply put the whole thing on the back burner and not print anything at all until something specific happens."

"I think you would be wise," Renny said.

"Yes, sir," Bob said, and rang off with a nervous laugh.

Renny picked up the phone again immediately and called the president's office. Within ten minutes Duke called back.

"Renny," he said, his tone impersonal, neither showing his permanent dislike for the difficult fraternity brother who had become his most difficult and uncontrollable faculty member, nor straining for any artificial cordiality.

"Good afternoon, Duke," Renny responded with similar enthusiasm. The dislike was mutual, originating in the house, increased over the years by Renny's opposition to what he saw as Duke's unwarranted rise to the presidency and his quiet, implicit, irritatingly adamant hostility to Renny's ideas and way of living.

"What can I do for you?" Duke inquired politely.

Renny told him with succinct brevity, concluding, "You must get rid of her. I don't know who else she may blame for her condition, but the basic fact is that it is her responsibility. I regard this as a deliberate attempt to entrap me. That girl is a menace."

"She wouldn't be if he could ever keep his cock in his pants," Moose would say later when Duke told him about it in confidence, seeking reinforcements for what he intended to do. Duke was never so blunt or so direct, but it was good to have Moose's unblinking candor on his side.

He also had Willie's. A call to Washington produced equally emphatic approval of his decision, which was to expel the girl—and simultaneously use the episode as a means of getting rid of Renny.

The suggestion provoked, as he had known it would, violent reaction from Professor Suratt. It also threatened to provoke another "firestorm," as Anne Greeley had described the original episode, which had long since passed into campus legend. Renny was confident the outcome of that guaranteed the outcome of this.

"Go ahead and try it, Duke," he suggested angrily. "Chalmers couldn't do it and you can't do it. Particularly since you're not the fighter he was."

Duke, who had successfully ridden out the seventies and the long, lingering aftermath of Vietnam, didn't dignify that one by arguing. He just said, "We shall see," in a very firm tone that gave Renny pause for several minutes after their brief conversation ended. Then he thought, just as he had with Chalmers: he wouldn't dare.

He did dare, but like his predecessor, found what Willie referred to as "The Organized Friends of Renny Suratt" too well entrenched, throughout the country and the world, to be overcome.

Not that it came to an open battle this time. Both Duke and Renny were much more mature now. The conflict was short, intense and fought out in private. It was a matter of Renny "alerting his God damned network" (Moose) and Duke "standing firm on principle, which I've found doesn't always help much" (Willie).

And Willie of course was right. Standing on principle was a dying art as the century staggered into its closing decades—dying and, frequently, foredoomed. It was still considered by many an admirable thing to *have* principles, but if you were so naive as to think you could succeed by acting upon them, well, good luck to you, brother. Not in the politicized world in which Willie, Duke and Renny all lived and operated.

The *Daily* editor's decision to keep quiet about "the latest Renny episode" (Duke) was endorsed with much more unhesitating decisiveness by all his seniors in the media and in the academic, literary, political and theatrical circles that clustered so tightly together when one of their own was challenged or threatened by what they all considered to be "right-wing reactionaries." (The description "right-wing" was increasingly linked to "reactionaries" in all their writings, programs and speeches. By the end of the century it would be an automatic mantra; impossible for them to say the one without the other. The concept of "left-wing reactionaries" was beyond their abilities to comprehend.)

It was decided, in one of those behind-the-scenes, off-the-record, instinctive gatherings of the clans, that no word of Renny's latest imbroglio and the University administration's latest attempt to get rid of him should appear anywhere, aside from those right-wing reactionary publications that could always be counted upon, in their spiteful fashion, to spread the news about anything embarrassing to the other side. And who listened to them, anyway? The iron curtain of freedom (On Our Terms) descended on the matter and remained unbroken.

(At one point Renny triumphantly showed Duke a cable from Australia—"Aus*tralia,* for God's sake!" Moose exclaimed when he heard about it—pledging the "support, cooperation and silence" of the most powerful journalistic figure in the Antipodes.)

The matter was complicated a week later when lawyers for Suki's parents informed Duke that they were suing the University for $2 million for their daughter's "embarrassment and humiliation, the destruction of her reputation and the endangerment of her health." The suit associated "one Professor René Suratt" as co-defendant.

The board was finally aroused, though it was now headed by Rudolph Krohl, another fraternity brother enemy of Duke's. ("You really have very few enemies at all," Shahna remarked with a helpless little laugh, "but it does sound so *awful!*") Rudy, whom Franky Miller once described in pre–World War II days as "our anti-Semitic, junior American Nazi," fortunately despised Renny even more than he did Duke. He called the board immediately into emergency session. Its members, encouraged by a very strong letter from Willie, who was unable to attend, decided to fight the suit. They also directed Duke to fire Renny "forthwith."

Renny demanded to be heard; appeared, buoyed up by seemingly unbounded righteous indignation that enabled him to withstand Rudy's merciless bullying; and threatened to explode the whole thing into the national media and everywhere else he could think of.

"I have friends!" he kept warning. "I have friends! They'll ruin this University!"

Three hours after he stormed out, defiant and threatening to the end, the board was still in anguished session. Finally, at Duke's request and on Rudy's own disgusted motion, it was decided by a substantial majority to seek an out-of-court settlement. Within a week the transaction was completed for $200,000, a most drastic reduction achieved by Renny himself when he wrote Helen's father a scathing letter pointing out that he was not alone in enjoying her company—"I could name a baker's dozen" who had enjoyed the same privilege. The reference in the board's minutes was reduced to an innocuous, uninformative, "A vote was held on the Suratt matter," and that was that.

Renny again emerged triumphant, his position at the University now completely unassailable. A month later the father telephoned him, shattered and bitter: he had arranged an abortion for her but . . . "something went wrong . . . she didn't make it."

"Oh, well, at least you have the money," Renny told him with a cheerful chortle, for now he really was home free. "That should be some consolation."

And hung up on the father's anguished howl of rage, sorrow and disgust.

And Duke, having weathered the crisis not very adequately but at least having kept the University out of the headlines (which he regarded as one of his principal responsibilities), returned to the job he had wanted ever since undergraduate days. He was unable to foresee the nature of the next crisis but he was sure there would be one. There always was.

He was not surprised when it soon began to develop; or that Renny should be involved in this one, too; or that Willie should also be involved, and Rudy Krohl; and, finally, the whole big world of government, politics and people, which now in the Age of Communication permitted no smallest corner to go unilluminated, no tiniest rock to go unturned.

5   Past events, present consequences, the inexorable unfolding of life's threats and promises made long ago. They often amused—and bemused—the president of the University. Work down layer through layer, he told Shahna, and you often came finally to a fraternity house with all its crosscurrents of youthful tensions, lasting friendships, never quite forgotten animosities.

Today it was a situation created by himself, Rudy Krohl, Renny and Willie. The latest recasting of the story of their lifelong relationships would be played out against the growing probability that Willie would finally make his formal run for the White House. It was clear now, as the seventies merged into the eighties and material indulgence replaced Vietnam as the principal obsession of the citizenry, that if he wished to have any chance at all his candidacy could not be much longer delayed. Stable men were needed to challenge the hand of rigid leftist conformity that was clamping down ever more heavily on the independence of American thought. Farsighted men were needed to try to bring the national focus back to the foreign relations that were deciding every day the question of whether America could long remain a major player in the world.

Many Americans believed Willie had the answers. Rudy Krohl possibly shared this belief, though Duke suspected that it was not from any love of Willie that Rudy had intervened to help shape the forum that was about to bring them all together. It was more likely prompted by his sheer hostile desire to see them all become entangled, in public, in their conflicting views of what was best for the country and the world.

It was fitting, in any case, as Duke remarked to Shahna (he was always remarking to Shahna; he told her everything just as he always had since their first meeting on the Quad almost forty-five years ago), that the event should occur on the campus from which they had launched the private lives that in many cases had become the public lives of public men.

About his own life, he could not complain even if he had been of a temperament to do so. Dr. Alan Frederick Offenberg, a true son of the University, had fallen in love with it the moment he set foot on campus. He was quite content with the way things had worked out for him from that moment on.

He had, first, joined the house, one of the major influences on his life.

He was the child of a modestly well-to-do family in Cleveland, where his father was principal of one of the city's high schools. Restricted by the family budget, he had taken a Greyhound bus to San Francisco, transferred to another to take him down the Peninsula, emerged exhausted and uncertain in the then rather sleepy little town that adjoined the University. He had been standing in front of the bus depot with his tennis racket and a hand-me-down suitcase of his father's, uncertain for the moment how he would get out to the campus, when a chariot of the gods in the form of the Packard roadster Gil Gulbransen's father had given him on his nineteenth birthday roared up and came to an abrupt halt. In it were Gil, Willie and Hack Haggerty, on their way back to the house after a foray to Sticky Wilson's ice cream and soda parlor downtown.

Gil stopped the car with a flourish. Willie made the first impression, as he did with so many—a lasting one, as Duke often remembered with a fond smile.

"There's a live one!" Willie cried happily, jumping out and seizing Duke's bag before he knew what was happening to him. "Jump in, sire! Your slaves will transport you to the campus! Which I'm sure is where you're going?"

"Y-yes," Duke managed, overwhelmed by the sudden presence of what he knew must be upperclassmen, and by the way he was being summarily included in something—he wasn't sure just what, but he liked it enormously and found it terribly reassuring in that bewildered, uncertain moment. He held out his hand tentatively.

"M-my name's D-Duke Off-offenberg."

"Do you always stammer?" Gil inquired as they all shook his hand vigorously and took off again for Palm Drive and the campus. Duke, feeling as though he had suddenly been swaddled in a warm blanket of instant cordiality, spoke more strongly.

"No, I don't. But you guys are sort of—sort of overwhelming, you know."

"Better over than under," Gil said cheerfully, and Willie said, "That's *right*, Doctor!" And they all laughed heartily at some reference Duke thought he got, but wasn't quite sure. Did college guys talk like that? Not many in his high school had, and he certainly wasn't one of them.

"Stay with us, kid," Willie advised, "and you'll learn things!"

"Not necessarily always good ones," Hack observed with the kindly smile Duke soon found was unfailingly characteristic of him. "But I won't let them warp your youthful innocence too much."

"Thanks," Duke said, sounding suddenly so fervently young and earnest that they all, even Hack, couldn't help laughing.

"You'll do," Willie said. "Where are you from and what do you plan to study here?"

And they were off on a conversation that lasted until they reached the freshman dorm and he was deposited with all the other earnest, anxious, trying-not-to-appear-frightened new arrivals.

"Why did you guys stop and pick me up that first day?" he inquired years later.

"You looked handsome, confused and lonely as hell," Willie said.

"And nice as hell, too," Hack said.

"So there you were," Gil said. "And there we were. And here we all are now. Any regrets?"

"Not a one," Duke said fervently. "Not a one."

Forty-five years ago, he reflected now, and he still remembered their meeting as vividly as yesterday, and with the same warm glow.

After that, things moved along. They took him out to dinner a couple of times, and when pledge time arrived they invited him up to the house twice more. Two other houses made bids but when Willie called with their formal invitation he accepted immediately.

"And we all lived happily ever after," he often remarked.

Except that they didn't, entirely. A year later Rudy came along and things for a while got quite tense. And to this day still were.

Rudy came to the house from Ridgewood, New Jersey (the names of his original sponsors becoming quite hazy as members tried to distance themselves from his increasingly abrasive attitudes as World War II approached). His father, an immigrant fifteen years out of Germany, had already built up a reasonably prosperous trucking and haulage business when the war began. With the great boost the conflict gave to many industries necessary to defense, Krohl and Son emerged in 1945 as one of the world's leading trucking firms. When his father died fifteen years later Rudy took over and brought it to its present near-dominance of the industry. Not even great commercial success changed "the hard-nosed bastard, the Rudy we know and love," as Guy Unruh characterized him.

And for his fraternity brothers, nothing could change the bad memories that would always cling to his name in their minds; not even the millions he subsequently lavished on the University in what they regarded as "a belated attempt to get right with God and everybody."

It was a relationship whose sharp edges time could not dull, let alone erase; symbolized and forever summed up by a tiny incident inflamed into major antagonism by youthful tensions and by the virulent anti-Semitism Rudy got from his father and other German-born in the New York–New Jersey area, which was such a wartime hotbed of sympathy for the old country.

It occurred on a beautiful spring day when a lot of members of the house were out sunning on the upstairs balconies, studying in a half-hearted, drowsy way. Duke came out and walked past a recumbent Rudy. Rudy immediately flared up and charged Duke with deliberately kicking his foot. When Rudy, spouting profanities, tried to stand up, Duke, finally fed up with his many snide comments and personal innuendos, pushed him back down so strongly that he sprawled at Duke's feet.

Rudy came up roaring that Duke was "a damned Jew." Duke struck him so solidly that he not only knocked him down but, for a moment, knocked him out. An emergency house meeting was held; the resentments Rudy had been building up against himself for his loudly voiced pro-Nazi sentiments boiled over, and he was expelled from the house. The episode, so minor in fact, so illustrative of greater tensions, seemed to many of them to sum up the terrible emotions that were rending the country on the eve of war.

Rudy never forgave Duke, and to this day, though he was president of the board and Duke president of the University, their relations, while reasonably polite and sometimes necessarily congruous, were still frigid and essentially hostile.

Along the way Rudy, as a means of leaving his parents' names and his own indelibly on the University, established the annual Herman and Gretchen Krohl Memorial Lecture, to be given by a distinguished alumnus or alumna. Unfortunately from his standpoint, he gave the University the right to choose the annual speaker. President Chalmers chose By Johnson; and it was at that inaugural lecture that the riot inspired by Renny resulted in By's death.

Rudy, who had always despised Renny at the best of times and now harbored a permanent grudge because he had ruined the inaugural, successfully asserted his right to have an equal voice in the selection of speakers. It made for an uneasy partnership but both he and the University rocked along with it on a reasonably practical basis.

And all of this, Duke sometimes thought with wry disbelief, originating out of one little fraternity house, decades ago.

When Rudy had called six months ago, his tone was as usual blunt and autocratic. (Some things noticeably didn't change. What Shahna referred to as "the Rudy manner—very rude-y"— was an example.)

"This is Rudy," he said, wasting no time on pleasantries and, as always, not addressing Duke by name if he could possibly avoid it. "What's this I hear about you planning to invite Willie to give the Krohl Lecture this year?"

"Where did you hear that?" Duke inquired. Rudy snorted.

"None of your games," he said flatly. "Have you already invited him?"

"I have," Duke said calmly. "And he's accepted, and I think that's great and I'm sure it will be a great evening."

Rudy didn't quite say, "Not if I can help it," but the resolve was clear in his tone.

"Shouldn't you have consulted me?" he demanded. "A lot of people don't like Willie."

"I've never regarded the Krohl Lecture as a popularity contest," Duke remarked. "We try to invite people who are worthy of the honor, and reasonably interesting."

"Obviously Willie is both," Rudy said with heavy sarcasm.

"Yes," Duke replied crisply. "I think so."

"Well, I don't," Rudy said harshly. "I want him out of there."

"No," Duke said firmly, and braced himself for the explosion. It came.

"God *damn* it," Rudy said. "You bastards at the University think you can run everything. That's my lecture. I'm financing it and I can have who I want speak there."

"Not quite," Duke said. "It's not that simple. After By's death we said we'd keep essential control but agreed to give you substantial input."

"You mean, after Chalmers and the rest of you fucked it up and *then* By died, you agreed to give me 'equal control,' and that's not 'substantial input,' it's 'equal control' and we wrote it into the grant and we all signed it. And that's that, and I want Willie out of there."

"No," Duke said, still managing to speak calmly, though with difficulty.

"Listen!" Rudy said, obviously also striving for some control. "I am not going to have the Krohl Lecture turned into a political platform for that fading has-been. Next thing I know he'll be using it to announce he's running for President. We don't need that kind of crap from him after all these years."

"I think Willie understands well enough the nonpolitical nature of your lecture," Duke said, adding with sarcasm he thought Rudy probably wouldn't get, "but I'll remind him of it, just to satisfy you."

"Put it in writing and send me a copy," Rudy said.

"Are you kidding?" Duke demanded, finally exasperated. "If I tell you I'll remind him, I'll remind him."

"Put it in writing—" Rudy began, but this time Duke cut him off.

"You're impossible," he said. "I will *not* put it in writing. Now, if that's all you have to say, I'm going to hang up. All right?"

"I knew you'd be like this," Rudy said. His tone shifted, subtly but unmistakably. "You people never change, do you?"

"Not unless we're killed," Duke said evenly.

There was silence for a moment. Then Rudy uttered a tired sound.

"Oh, Christ!" he said. "*That* old chestnut! I'm not interested in that old stuff. O.K., so you won't put it in writing. You won't withdraw the invitation. You won't do anything I want—you think. But oh, yes, you will. If you won't withdraw Willie I'll exercise my right and demand that he have company. We'll turn it into a debate this time, and see what happens. How would that be?"

"Who would you suggest?" Duke inquired, thinking, Oh, no, that would be too much of an irony, Rudy would never think of anything like that.

But of course he had.

"You have somebody right there on campus who can do it," he said, a happy triumph in his voice. "An expert on politics, a great leader of American thought, a mastermind of the twentieth century and all the other bullshit his media pals shower on him. Frankly, I think he's as full of shit as Willie is. It would give me great pleasure to see them destroy each other in open meeting."

"Surely you're not thinking of *him*," Duke said, hoping his skeptical tone would intimidate Rudy but knowing it wouldn't.

"Of course I am," Rudy said with smug satisfaction. "And don't you try to get around it. I'm going to tell the *Daily* and the papers up in the City about it, and then it will go all over the country."

"And suddenly we'll have a real media circus at the lecture," Duke said, "and no doubt a real political brawl to boot. Maybe that would be a good thing, after all."

"You betcha," Rudy said complacently.

"Are you insisting on this?"

"Of course," Rudy said. "Either way, you lose. If you agree, you run the risk that the evening may get out of hand and turn into something really dangerous, like it did with By. If you don't agree, the national media will be on your ass like a ton of bricks because you're trying to squelch their pet professor. You can't win."

"I thought you despised Renny."

"He has his uses," Rudy observed. "And so do you. You can be the moderator. Then three of my favorite people will go down in flames together. How great!"

"You want to watch out, Rudy," Duke suggested. "You're going to wind up as the darling of the liberals yet."

"Fuck 'em," Rudy said. "They're worthless people, in my mind." His tone turned businesslike. "Do you want to put out a joint statement from there saying the University and I have agreed to invite Willie and Renny for a political debate, as this year's Krohl Lecture, or do you want me to do it from here?"

Duke uttered an exasperated sigh.

"I'll do it."

"Good for you," Rudy said with a cruel little relish. "I've always said you knew how to trim your sails to meet the wind."

"Yes, Rudy," Duke said, sounding tired because he *was* tired of this arrogant, intolerant jerk of an ex–fraternity brother who had turned out to be a recurrent element in his life long after Duke had thought of him as disposed of by graduation and distance. "Why don't you go back and play with your trucks. I have a university to run."

"If you ran it half as well as I run my trucks," Rudy snapped, "you'd be worthy of the job."

"Ho, ho, ho, *ho,*" Duke said. "Run along, buster."

And hung up, cutting off some still further unpleasant rejoinder. He supposed Rudy would be even more hostile at the next board meeting, but he didn't give a damn. They had to get along officially, but otherwise their decades-long mutual dislike would never change. Rudy had won this round, of that there was no doubt.

"I think," Shahna said firmly when Duke returned to President's Knoll that evening and she saw his troubled face, "that you had better have a good stiff drink and tell me all about it."

When he had complied and discharged some of his angry feelings, she said something so unlike gentle Shahna that it brought from him startled laughter and a further easing of tensions.

"That bastard," she said. "That *bastard!*"

"Why, Mrs. Offenberg!" he said, much amused. "What a thing for you to say!"

"Well, he is," she said stubbornly. "He really is."

"Wish me luck," he said, "when I call the other one and let him know he's going to have some more of the limelight he loves so much."

But first he had to call Willie and give him the news. It was 10 P.M. in Washington and Willie was probably "out on the circuit," as he often described it; but Duke made the call anyway, to his private number at home. Rather to his surprise, Willie answered.

"Well, well," he said, tone warming as it always did for the few people in his world whom he considered really genuine friends. "What's up, pal? An earthquake? A fifty-million-buck donation? Or Rudy raising hell again?"

"You hit it on the third try," Duke said. "How did you know?"

"It's usually a fair guess most of the time. What's the problem now?"

"You are."

"Oh, God," Willie said with a mock groan. "Not *again.*"

"Sunday, Monday and always," Duke said. "You remember I've invited you to give the Krohl Lecture."

"Oh, no," Willie said. "You did? I quite forgot."

"Not game time," Duke said soberly. "Quite serious, in fact. Rudy wants to turn it into a debate. You and guess who."

"Oh, *God,*" Willie repeated, genuinely annoyed this time. "Surely he doesn't want—"

"Of course he does," Duke said. "Nothing could be more delightfully controversial. And self-destructive for all of us, Rudy thinks. His motivation is, as always, mischievous. So is Renny's."

"I hope you told Rudy no."

Duke sighed.

"He does have a certain whip-hand, when all is said and done. It is his money, after all. I told him no, but of course that made no impression, as I'm sure you can guess."

"Suppose I just withdraw my name," Willie suggested. "You haven't really publicized it yet. Why don't I just get out? 'Press of official business' is one of the standard excuses we use around here."

"That wouldn't suit *your* plans, would it? I'm sure you accepted for a specific purpose. Rudy, incidentally, assumes you accepted for the same specific purpose. You don't want to disappoint both of us, do you?"

"You're both too suspicious," Willie began patiently, but Duke wouldn't permit it.

"Now, Willie," he said, "we know you, from way, way back, so stop being disingenuous. Obviously if you're going to run at all it's got to be this time around or never. Grizzled old turkey buzzards are beginning to be passé. The country is getting ready for bright young things now."

" 'Grizzled old turkey buzzards!' " Willie exclaimed. "Well, thank *you*, Dr. Offenberg! 'Grizzled old turkey buzzards!' You really know how to hurt a guy!"

"You know I'm right," Duke said, joining in Willie's growing laughter. "And Rudy's right, too. He suspects you might use the occasion to announce, but he doesn't want his lecture to be used by 'a tired old has-been' for that purpose. Is that better than 'grizzled old turkey buzzard'? "

"Why, that smarmy two-bit Nazi bastard!" Willie said, suddenly sounding not amused at all. "He's got a hell of a nerve!"

"Good," Duke said with a chuckle. "I knew that would do it. And don't try to tell me that's not what you intended, Brother Wilson. I've known you too long."

"You're not saying I'm devious, are you?" Willie asked, instantly recovered from his indignation and sounding amicable and in charge again. "Furthermore, why did you invite me in the first place, knowing what a tricky soul I am, if you didn't want me to seize the opportunity?"

"I thought it was time for you to get off the dime if you're ever going to," Duke said. "I hoped this might precipitate it."

"Just between you and me—"

"How else?" Duke inquired.

"Just between you and me, I have decided to do the foul deed next year. Too many incompetents, too much decline, too many second-rate bozos trying to move into 1600 Pennsylvania. The country deserves better."

"And Richard Emmett Wilson is it."

"Name a better," Willie suggested, and Duke responded with a chuckle.

"You know I wouldn't dare. Even if I could think of one, which I really can't."

"That's the spirit," Willie said, the amusement that so often lurked in his voice surfacing as it was apt to do on serious occasions. "I knew I could count on you."

"You really can," Duke said, completely serious for a moment. "You know that."

"How about Secretary of Education?"

"Oh, come on," Duke said. "I don't want secretary of anything. You don't have to bribe me to have my support . . . So, good. That will really make Renny's day."

"Don't tell him," Willie said. "This is just between you and me and Shahna. Let him be surprised along with everyone else."

"He won't be. I'm not even sure I could muster the verbal contortions necessary to keep him from guessing."

"You can do it," Willie said encouragingly.

But when Duke called Renny a few minutes later at home in Hillsborough he found that Rudy had already called and planted his suspicions firmly in fertile ground.

"I think it is most disgusting the way Willie always tries to manipulate things for his own political advantage," Renny observed in his most righteously disapproving tone. Duke could not refrain from a sardonic chuckle.

"Something you would never dream of doing."

"I am not interested in cheap political shots," Renny said sternly. "My motivations are a lot better than that. And, I think," he added sourly, "a lot more noble than our distinguished Senator's. However, it's no skin off my nose. I'll be ready for him. I think his purpose here is so blatantly self-serving that it should be very easy to reduce him to size."

"You've tried for forty years," Duke observed, "and you haven't succeeded yet. What makes you think it's going to come easy now?"

"Most of the principal factors are on my side," Renny noted with some smugness. "I don't know who's supporting Willie, really. Most of the major media are against him, the academic community certainly is, he doesn't have very much political support anywhere in the country except here in California, and that's not very strong. He's always been something of a fluke at the best of times. Why he wants to run now is beyond me, but maybe he'll clue us all in when we debate."

"I'm sure you can draw him out on the subject."

"I shall certainly do my best," Renny promised, with such absolute lack of humor that Duke couldn't suppress some amusement.

"What's the matter?" Renny demanded sharply. "Am I saying something funny?"

"I'm not sure," Duke said. "We'll have to wait for the debate to find out."

"I'm ready for him," Renny repeated, sounding for a moment so defensive that it was all Duke could do not to laugh aloud.

"I don't have any doubt of it," he said. "And all your cohorts too, I presume."

"My 'cohorts,' as you put it," Renny said tartly, "are most of my colleagues on the faculty and a great many students who see things as I do. You know how effective they can be."

"Yes," Duke agreed dryly. "And I know how effective you can be as their leader, with all your brilliant intellect and savage pen, so famous and so praised in all the circles that really matter in American life. For instance—let me find it"—he paused and pretended to search, though it was one of the quotes he treasured and kept under the glass top of his big executive desk—"yes, here it is. I quote: 'A reactionary fluke, unworthy of the University—a threat, because of his unjustified prominence at a great institution, to the future of higher education in America.' That was one of your real goodies. Do you remember that one?"

"Yes, I remember that one!" Renny snapped. "It was true then and it's true now. You haven't changed one iota."

"That's right," Duke agreed with satisfaction. "I was president then and I'm president now. And you and your cohorts are still out there yapping at my heels. Futilely. Right?"

"We didn't get you then, but—" Renny began.

"You certainly did not," Duke interrupted. "And you never will."

"We almost did," Renny observed.

"Yes," Duke agreed. "How well I remember the rallies, the demonstrations on the Quad, the newspaper and television interviews from coast to coast, the stirring headlines when you and your friends tried to get rid of me. 'UNIVERSITY IN UPROAR AS SURATT LEADS OFFENBERG OUSTER CAMPAIGN. PRESIDENT'S PRO-WAR STANCE ENRAGES FACULTY-STUDENT COALITION. ATTEMPT TO OCCUPY HIS OFFICE THWARTED BY CAMPUS POLICE. SURATT AND STUDENT LEADERS JAILED FOR ONE NIGHT. TRUSTEES UNANIMOUSLY SUPPORT OFFENBERG, GRANT NEW LONG-TERM CONTRACT.' Exciting times, Renny. Exciting times!"

"Yes," Renny said sourly. "And don't fool yourself that it can't happen again."

"I think not," Duke said calmly. "The great days are over, Renny, the fire is gone. Even the most determined are growing up and settling down. Except for you, of course. You'll never give up your gallant battle."

"That's right!" Renny, said, genuinely angry now. "Because it is never over. It never stops, the battle between the reactionaries of this world like yourself and Willie and that worthless son of a bitch Krohl, and people like myself who have some vision of what this country and this world could be if your constant opposition was removed. There are plenty like me. We will never stop fighting you. You think 'the fire is gone,' but it isn't gone, it's just banked for a while. Wait till the sixties generation really grows up, Duke. They're quiet right now because they're busy maturing and gradually closing in on the levers of power. But give them time; give them time. Ten, fifteen, twenty years from now, they'll be back and in place to run things, and you people won't be able to stop them then. They'll be in our schools teaching the next generation what to think, they'll be in our legislatures and courts making the laws, they'll be in the media controlling public opinion. You think they're gone: it's a futile hope. They're not gone, they're just dormant. They're coming back. Wait and see."

"And you, I suppose, will still be here, leading the parade from your wheelchair!" Duke said angrily, provoked finally to a personalized sarcasm he rarely used, because he knew that Renny, essentially, was right.

Time would secure for that generation what they had tried to seize, too young, ahead of their season.

Time, as Renny predicted, would rescue them.

Their true season would come, and they would return and triumph.

"I'll be here when they carry you out," Renny said grimly as he slammed down the receiver. "And I'll have plenty to say in the meantime!"

And so he did, most notably when, six months later, the Krohl Debate, as it came to be known for easy political reference, took place between the senior Senator from California and "the undisputed leader of enlightened American thought," as the Mother of All Newspapers described him in its highly favorable (to him) editorial post-mortem.

5

"A futile gesture, as befits a futile politician,
foredoomed to failure, as he has
always been foredoomed to failure,
by his faulty perception of events."

1   It was like the slow gathering of a great wave, Willie reflected as he sat in his private hideaway on the Senate side of the Capitol and looked down across the hazy summer landscape of the District, the Potomac and the heavily wooded hills of Virginia beyond, somnolent in the humid heat.

It was as though he could see in mind's eye a tumult of thousands and thousands of tiny streams and currents, tumbling, growing, swelling, converging gradually into one overpowering tide that was sweeping toward him inexorably in one overwhelming surge, set in motion by his own ambitions, fed by the faith and conviction of millions of his supporters throughout America. He could not escape even if he wanted to, which now he did not. He could only direct it, if he was lucky, into channels conducive to his own victory and, if all went well and he and America were greatly lucky, to the ultimate good of the country.

As with all would-be candidates for President, personal ambition and idealistic dreams were so inextricably mixed in his mind and heart that he could not have said honestly which predominated at any given moment. They jockeyed for importance, now one and then the other rising to control his thoughts and actions, the personal yielding to the national, the national to the personal as events unfolded.

Right now ambition was in charge, concerned with how he might frame what he intended to say when he spoke in the Krohl Lecture— "the Krohl Dogfight," as he referred to it privately, knowing that was what Rudy and Renny would like to turn it into if he would take the bait. He rejected the idea with impatience even as he thought how enjoyable it might be. He would love to take the measure of those two insufferable lifelong gadflies left over from undergraduate days "to periodically annoy their betters," as Guy Unruh once described it . . .

"the two unlikeliest candidates for best-loved fraternity brothers," as Franky Miller used to refer to them.

Renny could always be counted upon for his incessant personal put-downs, Rudy for his opposition to Willie's views in trustees' meetings and his outright political opposition to Willie's campaigns for office. A lot of Rudy's money had gone quite publicly into the campaigns of Willie's opponents. "I despise those two sons of bitches," Willie told Tim, and he knew they responded in kind.

He pulled himself away from the contemplation of their unattractive and annoying personalities and concentrated for a few minutes on what he would say when he appeared at the lecture in October. It was basically very simple:

"I will be a candidate for President next year. You all know my record; you will know it even better when I get through explaining it and my opponents get through trying to tear it down. I think my long years in public service, my extensive experience in government, my record as your Senator serving this great nation-state of ours during its phenomenal growth in population and prosperity, speak for themselves. As the campaign goes forward I shall set forth in detail my positions on domestic policy, foreign affairs, how to best protect and preserve America and what its overall aims and purposes should be in the closing decades of a turbulent century.

"I ask the support of those who approve of me and I welcome the opposition of the small-bore minds who will oppose me. I hope the issues can be decided on a higher tone than that, but I serve notice now that I am quite prepared to meet my opponents on whatever ground they choose, be it as high as I would like or as low as they will get."

When he read these words to Tim, Tim uttered a startled little laugh and exclaimed, "You can't say that!"

"And why not?" he demanded. "They've never given me any quarter."

"You haven't given them any, either," Tim observed.

Willie laughed rather grimly.

"So what's the problem?"

"You sound too arrogant," Tim said.

Willie snorted.

"I *am* arrogant, didn't you know? Everybody's always said so, from the time I first got into politics back at school. It hasn't seemed to matter much. In fact, the fear that I might give as good as I got has had a very salutary effect on a lot of would-be opponents, in my estimation. Anyway, 'that's Willie.' "

"In his less attractive guise," Tim said. "Soften it, friend. That's my advice."

"And try to be a please-all pantywaist like—" and he named one of his likely opponents, a small-state Southern governor so consumed with ambition that, as one of his hometown critics remarked, "He eats ballots for breakfast and shits ballots at night. It's nonstop political alimentation."

"I didn't say please everybody," Tim said mildly. "I just meant curb your high-flying tongue and be reasonably diplomatic. I know it's hard, but try. You might be surprised at the results."

"It's too late to be good," Willie said lightly. "I'm bad, bad Willie Wilson, the baddest man in the whole damn town. I'd upset everybody's plans if I attempted some other configuration. They have my slot all worked out, after all these years. It wouldn't be fair of me to move into some other."

"Oh, nonsense," Tim said. "You're a perfectly reasonable soul—most of the time. I know you rather enjoy having the reputation of a Terrible-Tempered Mr. Bang, but those of us who know you intimately know that's not the essential Willie."

"I'm a kindly soul at heart?"

"Yes. So redo that statement, please, and take out the knives and daggers. They know you'll snap back if they snap at you. A lot of 'em will walk very wide. You don't have to put signs on the grass."

"Nonetheless—"

"Think about it. Who are you going to get to handle media relations for your campaign?"

"I thought maybe I'd get you to do it."

Tim snorted.

"At my age? All that stress and strain? No, thank you."

"At my age, run for President?" Willie mocked. "All that stress and strain? Anyway, you'd only be the titular head. We'd get some hard-working ambitious young soul to handle the details and take the day-to-day crap from your distinguished colleagues. You'd just coast along and enjoy the ride."

"Oh, thanks," Tim said. "That *would* be a picnic. Anyway, Anna wouldn't give me leave from the column. And anyway, I don't want to tie myself too closely to any one candidate. Even you."

"The media tied you to me a long time ago," Willie said. "Prior to that youth, college, propinquity, congeniality of personalities and views, et cetera, et cetera, et cetera, also tied us together. You'll be considered an unofficial spokesman anyway. Might as well make it formal."

"No, thanks," Tim said firmly. "I appreciate your trust and generosity, but no, thanks. Why don't you get Latt?"

"As a matter of fact, I have been thinking of Latt, in one capacity or other. I'm not sure what he would take, though. I'm not even sure he'd want to be associated with my campaign. He has his own row to hoe, in the House. He'll probably feel he can't do both."

"Don't underestimate Latt," Tim suggested. "He's not his father's son for nothing."

"How do you know?" Willie demanded. "Have you talked to him?"

"I have, as a matter of fact. We had lunch just last week."

"Good for you," Willie said. "I haven't seen him for a month. I guess I'll have to get an appointment."

"It might help," Tim said, amused. "He's a busy boy these days."

"He's doing very well in the House," Willie agreed with satisfaction. "He may run against me for the Senate if I don't watch out."

"No," Tim said, more seriously. "That's one thing I'm sure he never will do. But if you ever decide to retire—or *are* retired, let's say—"

"Let's don't say that," Willie suggested with a chuckle. "I'd rather like it to be voluntary, when the time comes."

"Anyway, talk to him," Tim said. "He sounded as though he's missed hearing from you. Give him a call. He won't hang up."

"No, he won't," Willie agreed. "Maybe I will call him, about the campaign if nothing else. I really have been thinking about using him somewhere, if he's agreeable."

"Donna would be pleased."

"Yes," Willie said, tone suddenly sad, as her loss could still do to him almost a decade later.

———

"And I'm sure Anne would be, too. And Fran, of course. Fran thinks Latt is *her* son, almost. They've become quite a team in the House."

"They're both very shrewd operators," Willie agreed, tone lighter and showing his pride in both of them. He sighed, mocking himself a little.

"Me and my women," he said. "Where are Anne and Fran going to fit into the campaign picture?"

"That will no doubt be thoroughly discussed by the media," Tim said cheerfully, "so be prepared. You could marry either one of them in a shot, so why don't you? Why haven't you? You have two of the longest-running affairs in the history of the republic. Does the Guinness Book of Records know about this?"

"Everybody knows about it," Willie said dryly. "Anyway, it isn't two affairs. Fran and I don't have an affair, we have an 'understanding.' The basic elements are mutual admiration—no strings—no conflicts—just two political minds well met." He chuckled. "Don't you understand my motivation? It's the only way I can keep *her* from running against me for the Senate."

"Sure, sure," Tim said. "She really admires you, Willie. She thinks you're too necessary to challenge. And too well established. And too popular."

"I'm not all that well established," Willie said. "I never have been, I'm too independent. In California, that quality does guarantee a certain basic popularity, however. It's seen me through a good many close calls."

"And as for Anne—" Tim suggested.

"As for Anne," Willie said, more seriously, "the years go by and things don't seem to reach a conclusion one way or the other. I've asked her twice to marry me and each time she's begged off. She's afraid of her ex-husband."

"Hasn't he remarried?"

"I don't think it matters. There's some sort of fixation there, some sort of tie, still. He seems to have a fairly violent nature, I gather. She's afraid of that and of something more disturbing—he's unpredictable. He's threatened her and the girls a couple of times; never done anything overt, as far as I know, and I think she'd tell me, but enough to keep her perpetually uneasy."

"That's a shame," Tim said. "You'd be good for each other."

"We are good for each other," Willie said, "otherwise it wouldn't have lasted this long."

"It'll all come out, you know, when you run. Once you announce, it'll be open season."

"Oh, of course. But as you know, it's hardly a secret. We've been attending parties and official functions together for years. And it was all thrashed over in my last campaign, and I know it will be again. I'll do what I always do, be polite, stonewall it and go on."

"Maybe you'd better ask her again," Tim suggested, half humorously. "Explain to her how if you're going into the really big time, it ought to be settled once and for all. She's got a good political mind, too. She'll understand."

"Maybe you could put in a good word for me," Willie said, not entirely in jest. "She admires and respects you, you know."

"Not my column or my ideas. But I'll give it a try, if it comes right."

"So will I," Willie said, somewhat ruefully, "but I'm not too hopeful."

So many things to think of in a campaign, he reflected as he said good-bye to Timmy and put in a call to Latt. Particularly any little bit of anything that could be misinterpreted, turned into a scandal, exposed in some unexpected and embarrassing way. Tim's colleagues were always watching, always searching. Whatever they produced would never be charitable; any candidate could count on that. Nine times out of ten it would be derogatory, derisive, destructive. That was how the game went, as the century hurried on.

"Congressman Wilson of California," his receptionist announced in prim and tortured tones. "Cain Ay helll—*pew?*"

"Perhaps," Willie said, thinking: I wonder if he's ever called his own office? Not a good image at all. Better replace this little lady filled with her own importance, sucking on a pickle, with someone more welcoming. "This is the Congressman's father. Is he in?"

"Oh, yais, sir," she said, a little more obliging. "Ay mean, naoh, he's nott. But his appointments secretary is. Please hole-don."

"Yes, Senator," said another female voice, much warmer. "What can we do for you?"

"I want to corral His Majesty for lunch," Willie said. "Any chance?"

"Yes," she said promptly. "Farm Bureau people in town today as I'm sure you know, but tomorrow's free. All right with you?"

"Fine," Willie said. "My place or his?"

She chuckled.

"Defense appropriations bill on the floor here tomorrow afternoon, quite serious from about two P.M. on."

"Speeches, insertions in the *Congressional Record* and various assorted ego trips over here," he said. "I'll meet him at the House restaurant."

"Twelve-fifteen?"

"Fine," he said. Twenty-four hours later he was responding with obvious pride as a tall, handsome gentleman with a cane, beginning to get a bit gray and thus becoming even more handsome, came toward him, opened his arms, gave him a hug and pressed his cheek against Willie's.

"Hey, Dad," he said, clearly pleased, while assorted tourists, waiting for their Congress members to come and take them to lunch, beamed approval. "I'm glad you called me. I've been wanting to do this for a month, but you know how things go over here—"

"Senator—Congressman"—the maître d' said, adhering strictly to protocol as the older members of the service staffs still do on the Hill—"I have a nice table for you in the corner, where you can talk."

She was a stately, dignified black woman with a pleasant smile and an efficient manner who had been on the job for years and knew practically everyone on both sides of the Capitol.

"Thank you, Odell," Willie said. "You remembered."

"Never forget a face as handsome as yours, Senator," she said heartily. "Never forget one as handsome as your son's, either. You two are something, when you get together. Enjoy your meal."

"Stop grinning," Latt said in a stage whisper as she turned away to help someone else. "You know she flatters everybody."

"I know," Willie said, "but I'm putty in her hands. It just turns me to jelly."

"From putty to jelly," Latt remarked with a grin. "There's a smooth political transition for you. How've you been?"

"I've been fine," Willie said. "How about you?"

Latt rubbed his eyes and for a moment looked genuinely tired.

"Busy. Busy. And you?"

"Likewise."

"Gearing up to run, finally," his son observed after they had scanned the familiar menu, decided on soup and a half sandwich each and two glasses of wine. "Napa Valley, of course," Latt said with mock solemnity. "Of course," Willie agreed as they settled back to look at each other appraisingly.

"Am I too late?" Willie inquired. Latt shrugged.

"Nope. Not yet. Not quite. But advisable now and no later, I think. Otherwise forget it."

"Are you with me?"

"As I've remarked before," Latt said, looking a little severe, "I *am* your son. And while I cannot agree with all your ideas, being one who tries to be consistent and not all over the place—"

"Ouch," Willie said. "Do I really deserve that?"

"—I certainly would not expect to find myself backing anybody else if you were a candidate."

"That will greatly disappoint the media," Willie said. "They're slavering to drag us into a father-son confrontation if they possibly can."

"We've had those," Latt remarked. "They had their place and their time. But there *is* a season, as the Bible says, and the season for that has passed. I can't imagine you advocating anything that would seriously turn me off. Unless there's another Vietnam, which does not appear to be on the horizon."

"I hope not," Willie said fervently. "And if there were, I would expect us to be pretty much on the same side anyway."

"Good," Latt said with a sudden smile. "I've never been entirely sure, even now. So: when do you announce?"

"Well, you know who Rudy Krohl is, and the Krohl Lectures—"

"I've listened to a few in my time," Latt said. "What's our multi-million-dollar relic of the Third Reich up to now?"

"He's pitting me and your old pal Renny Suratt in a debate in October."

"And you'll announce then."

"I'm thinking about it."

"Well, why not?" Latt asked. His eyes narrowed, a political brain as good as his father's obviously clicking in. "Want me to come out there and introduce you?"

Willie looked pleasantly surprised; it was something he had hoped for but wasn't about to suggest.

"That would be very nice," he said. "In fact, that would be wonderful."

Latt smiled.

"I'll collect next time I want a companion bill introduced in the Senate simultaneously with one of mine in the House."

"The Double Wilson," Willie said. "Rather like the double whammy. We've never done that before."

"I've been thinking we ought to get in the habit," Latt said. "It would make a nice little publicity package." The smile broadened. "If there's that much we could agree on."

"Once or twice a year would be enough," Willie suggested wryly.

"Probably difficult to manage even that," Latt said. "But let's try."

"It's a deal," Willie said. "In the meantime—"

"Who's going to manage your campaign?" his son inquired as their soup arrived and the sound of politics being talked, deals being made and awkward tourist-legislator conversations being doggedly pushed ahead surrounded them.

"I haven't decided yet," Willie said. "Who would you suggest?"

"*Moi,*" Latt said with a grin. "Who better than little old *moi?*"

"You're kidding," Willie said, trying not to look too openly pleased. "Where would you find the time?"

"I'll manage," Latt said. "You won't even have to pay me minimum wage. You couldn't afford to pay me very much anyway, the press would make such a stink. I'll explain that I'm doing it largely for love, which few will believe and fewer appreciate. But away from the professional arena, a lot of ordinary citizens with ordinary families will understand and approve."

"Are we ordinary?" Willie inquired.

"Oh, pretty much," Latt said. "I've got a black wife and three black kids, Amos is a brilliant young actor living with his boyfriend in New York, Clayne is married to a millionaire twice her age in Portland, Oregon, who manufactures cardboard packaging. And you're the longest-running Casanova on the Hill. We qualify."

"I'm the one who has to qualify," Willie said. "As long as you three are all happy in your various ways, I'm content on that score. As for me, you raise an interesting point. Tim thinks I should hurry up and marry Anne without further ado. I've tried to tell him I've asked and she won't have me. There's also the question of the ex. He could still make trouble, which I think is why she's still hesitating after all these years."

"He is a case," Latt agreed soberly, "but I think you should go ahead anyway. I've never met the guy but he's a very successful lobbyist downtown for a lot of financial interests. I've heard he's more bluster than bite."

"I'm not so sure," Willie said. "I have met him, and Anne and I have talked about him. Not very stable, I think; definitely odd, in fact."

"Well, I don't know," Latt said thoughtfully. "It's something you two have to decide. Have you told her you're finally going to run?"

"Let's just say I'm going to run and leave out the 'finally,' " Willie suggested, not entirely in jest. "It makes me sound so ancient. I've just been waiting for the proper time. How's your family?"

"Everybody fine at latest accounting," Latt said. "The kids are doing brilliantly in school, Ti-Anna's still deeply involved with the N.A.A.C.P., which keeps her busy; my brother-in-law Melrick works for me on minority matters here in the office, and dear old Maryetta is always off somewhere on some crusade for blacks or women or some damned thing."

"She never stops, does she?" Willie remarked.

"But at least her heart's in the right place," Latt said and Willie nodded.

"Yes. It's taken me forty years to come to terms with Maryetta, but I guess I finally have. She does mean well—and God help the world if it doesn't agree with her. I can only imagine the joy with which she's going to greet my candidacy. All the venom glands will be churning. Trying to defeat me will add a good ten years to her life."

Latt chuckled.

"You sound positively anticipatory. You'll announce my chairmanship when we appear together at the University, right?"

"Perfect timing," Willie said, amused. "I can hear Renny now. Taking after me, that is. You're still a permanent pet."

"Oh, old Renny's all right," Latt said. "He served a purpose for me—once. His kind of absolute certainties appeal to kids who are trying to find their way toward some coherent view of the world. I'll admit he was quite the Pied Piper at one point. And probably still is, for another generation of wide-eyed brats who fall for his anti-establishment line."

"And his sexual invitations," Willie remarked. He gave Latt an appraising glance—he had never ventured to inquire about this before. "Did you ever accept any of them?"

"I did not," Latt said flatly. Willie looked relieved. "However," his son went on, "I won't deny I was very tempted on several occasions. But I was never exactly deprived in that area. There were plenty of young ladies—and some others, if I'd wanted them—who were very willing. I was lucky."

"Not lucky at all," Willie said. "Just a gift of nature. You were a very handsome young animal, very attractive—very appealing—very—"

" 'Sexy' is the word, I believe," Latt said with a grin. "You ought to know. You were too. Still are, as a matter of fact."

"And you," his father said.

"Well, let's don't overdo it," Latt said with mock sternness. "I try to behave myself now, and you do the same, please. If I'm going to be your chairman I'm going to insist on absolute purity all down the line. No unexpected scandals for this campaign, I *hope*."

"Nary a one," Willie said, "except my unexpected marriage to Anne Greeley. Or expected, as the case may be. If she'll have me. Which she probably still won't."

"Give it a try," Latt said. "All she can do is say no. Again."

"That's what inhibits me," Willie admitted with a rueful grin. "I don't like to feel rejected."

"Poor ba-by!" Latt exclaimed. "My poor old beleaguered daddy, a great big old U.S. Senator acting like a schoolboy!"

"Ridiculous, I know," Willie agreed as they finished their coffees and stood up. "But there it is. Give my love to Ti-Anna and the kids."

"I will," Latt said. "Why don't you come over Sunday for dinner?"

"I have to leave for Chicago to see some people and then speak there Monday night. But how about Tuesday or Wednesday?"

"I'll be on a committee trip to Houston first part of the week," Latt said, "and we have a debate on the crime bill here later in the week, as I believe you do too. And so it goes."

"Anyway," Willie said, as they stepped into the hall, hugged again and again aroused maternal and paternal murmurs of approval from the tourists still waiting to get in, "I am very grateful to have you with me in the campaign. Maybe we can find time for a cup of coffee in New Hampshire."

"It's a date," Latt said with a grin. "Give my love to Anne."

And turned away to proceed with dignity on his cane, his artificial right leg giving him his slight, distinctive limp, through adoring visitors who greeted Willie with equal enthusiasm as he followed.

There goes my son, he thought with a strange, disbelieving wonderment, thinking back on all the argumentative years of Latt's youth: my son, my love, my life. How unpredictably life turned out, sometimes; but how naturally, too, when one reviewed its endless convolutions in sequence. They were back together now: apparently Latt had decided to be with him on this final great adventure. Willie felt as though his endorsement made the battle half-won; although one of its basic problems was far from resolved, as Anne made clear when he stopped by her charming little Federal-era house near the Capitol for dinner.

She was busy in the kitchen; he was watching the news; her two cats were in attendance, the younger pestering her for food, the other sitting in his lap. Couldn't be more domestic, he thought half-wryly, half-gratefully; only her adamant determination had always kept it from being complete. He decided to challenge her on it after they finished eating. He would take Latt's advice, and try again.

"Duke Offenberg called me today," he said when dinner was over and they were seated together on their favorite sofa facing the illuminated Capitol, perfectly framed in the living room bay window.

"Oh, how is he?"

"Fine," he said. "I know you've never really approved of him as president of the University—"

"He's handled himself very well," she conceded, "under great provocation from many of the students and most of the faculty. I hope he was in good spirits."

"Yes," he said as she settled comfortably against his chest and leaned back into the curve of his arm, the two cats settling into their laps in further proof of domesticity. "He had good news for me. You know he's invited me to give the Krohl Lecture this year. Now your pal Rudy Krohl—"

"Not my pal," she said firmly, tone reflecting her many bitter arguments with Rudy during their years together on the board of trustees. "He's insufferable. What does he want to do now, put up a statue of Hitler in front of Memorial Church?"

Willie chuckled.

"Not quite. Though that may yet come. No, he just wants to turn the lecture into a debate."

"You and who?" she inquired, adding with dismissive scorn, "Renny Suratt?"

"Yes, as a matter of fact," he said. "Now, there *is* a pal of yours, right? I'm sure you're pleased."

"I am *not*," she said, so vehemently that the cats stirred in protest. "He's another of the Great Insufferables, even if we have agreed on a good many things relative to the general nature of national decline."

"Which he has helped to speed on its merry way," Willie remarked. "I never have been able to understand how you could agree with him even part of the time, he's such a destructive influence and never constructive. However," he added as her expression began to turn stubborn, "no point in rehashing that old argument. Although I do like it when you get hot and bothered. It's cute."

She laughed and settled back, mood swiftly changing.

"I am not cute," she said. "That is one thing I am not, cute. So what are you two old fraternity buddies going to talk about?"

"I'm going to announce for President," he said. "Early. In fact, practically the moment I'm introduced by my son."

She looked pleased.

"That will be nice," she said. "I'm glad he's going to do that. It will help you, and I know how much it will mean to you."

"Yes," he said, "it will indeed . . . but what about the announcement? Don't you have any comment to make on that?"

She smiled.

"Of course I'm pleased about that. But if you think I'm going to pretend that I'm surprised, Senator, you have another think coming. You have to, this time, or not at all. It would have been a shame if you hadn't at least taken a good shot at it."

"Do you think I have a chance?"

She hesitated for a moment, mentally reviewing the field.

"The alternatives aren't exactly sensational," she said. "Certainly you have a chance. A good chance."

"But not a *really* good chance," he said, surprised to find how important it was, suddenly, for her to give him a ringing and completely unqualified endorsement. But that wouldn't be Anne, one of the most honest people he had ever known.

"Certainly a good chance to win," she said with some impatience.

He couldn't resist pushing it.

"But not a certainty to win."

She smiled but shook her head.

"If you want me to say it's all over for you but the shouting, I won't, because it isn't. But as I see it, you do have as good a chance as anybody and perhaps better than all the rest. Somebody has to come out on top. Why not you?"

"I am overwhelmed," he said with mock gravity, "by your enthusiastic, irresistible, completely confident support for me. It is really an endorsement, what I mean, a *real* endorsement! It sends me into battle girded to smite mine enemies hip, thigh and brisket. It strengthens me to meet the greatest challenge, confront the most savage enemy, climb the highest mountain—"

"Oh, you," she said, reaching up to kiss his cheek with an affection so accustomed as to be really domestic. "You know the real reason you might not win the presidency?"

"No," he said. "What?"

"You have a sense of humor. You're too irreverent and too unexpected. Men who are elected President are predictable and they certainly have no sense of humor. Go over the list and there isn't one, except possibly Jack Kennedy and that was probably because his health made it all so uncertain anyway, who had a real sense of humor about himself. They don't have time for it, and mostly it isn't in them anyway. It's your only weakness."

"Hah!" he said. "I'd say the unpredictability, even more than the sense of humor. And of course there's one more thing."

"What?" she asked, idly but interested.

"You."

"Me?" she demanded, sitting bolt upright so abruptly that the cats protested, jumped down and sought refuge in a chair across the room. She turned to fix him with the intent look that was one of the major weapons in her arsenal as one of the capital's most brilliant and successful lawyers.

"Why me? Surely there isn't anything anybody can say about me at this late date. We've been a public item for a decade. What can anybody make of that?" She broke into laughter, quite genuine and spontaneous. "If I'm the biggest scandal they can dig up about you, you're home free." She swung around to face him squarely. "I *am* the biggest, aren't I?"

"You're the biggest."

"Well, all right, then. Relax."

"Which is why," he said, suddenly serious, having forced the issue and thinking that this might, with luck, be the time to settle it once and for all, "I cannot understand and do not understand and will never understand why you won't marry me. It would be the perfect start to my campaign."

"That's why!" she said, returning to laughter, voice lightly mocking. "You're always so political. Always thinking of yourself. Always worried about your career. Why, at this very moment—tender, intimate, romantic—discussing as we are the most solemn question that can be raised between man and woman—you still—you *still*—relate every-thing to your campaign. It's disgusting, Willie Wilson! It's absolutely *disgusting*!"

And she mussed his hair, thumped him on the stomach, poked him in the ribs and generally acted quite unlike the dignified lawyer her clients knew.

After that moment of hilarity, which was not so unknown to them in their more playful moods, he tried to reestablish a serious tone.

"Nonetheless," he said doggedly, "I don't understand it, and I don't like it, and I don't know why I continue to put up with it year in and year out, when—when—"

"When we live perfectly happily in sin?" she said, laughter gradu-ally diminishing. "Well"—finally sober and serious again—"I'll tell you once more, Willie, though I've told you a thousand times already—because I find it quite comfortable and complete just the way it is. No ties, no strings, no muss, no fuss—"

He interrupted.

"Except for David."

"Except for David," she agreed, abruptly, completely serious. "Except for David."

"You've been divorced forever," he said. "Twelve years. Why is he such a burden for you now?"

"You don't understand," she said, moving away from him slightly.

"No, I do not. Tell me."

"He bothers the girls, for one thing. He's still trying to dominate their lives, demanding they visit him, threatening to make public scenes if they won't, threatening to do something that might embarrass me personally or professionally—"

"Such as what?"

"I don't know, some item in the *Post* or something, some public scandal—something, I don't know. He's just always there—and always threatening—and always making me uneasy and uncomfort-able just to know he's around."

"But he's married again. It isn't normal for him to act this way."

"That's the point," she said unhappily. "He isn't normal. He's obsessed. He's off-balance, somehow—way off-balance. And he keeps me off-balance, too." Her expression became wry. "Surely you've noticed!"

"Yes, I've noticed," he said grimly, "and that's why I want to put a stop to it once and for all. Once again, marry me and get out of all that. He wouldn't bother you then."

Suddenly she looked sad, and quite terrifyingly alone.

"I'm not sure of that. I think he would. And that's where I think of your career. I couldn't bear it if he hurt you in some way because of me. That would kill me. It really would."

"Look," he said, desperately earnest, one last try—"marry me. Don't worry, don't hesitate, don't let anything, particularly a twisted psychopath, which I think he is, cripple your life and mine any longer. Just don't worry. *Just do it.* O.K.?"

For several long moments, they were silent, while he sat very still and scarcely dared breathe. She stared straight ahead, face torn and tense, hands clenching and unclenching, more agitated than he had ever seen her in all their long relationship.

Finally, she shuddered and uttered a long sigh that seemed to come from the depths of her heart.

"All right," she said, voice very low. "As you will."

There were muttered endearments for a while. He held her very tightly, then neither of them said anything. The cats returned and, mollified by their silence, hopped back up on their laps and settled down again; time lengthened . . . but she did not, as he dreaded she might, suddenly announce a change of heart. She simply held him very tightly in return; and finally he knew he could proceed now as he wanted to do, his own heart, at last, assured of some inner serenity it had lacked ever since Donna's death and through all the incomplete years since.

His office issued a formal announcement the next day. They were married two weeks later in little St. John's Church just off Lafayette Square, before an overflow audience that included many of Willie's fellow Senators; most of the California delegation in the House including Fran Haggerty, looking very pleased; Tim, best man, equally pleased; a large working group from the media recording the event on film, tape and notepad; Anne's two girls and his three children, all looking happy and relaxed, Latt with Ti-Anna and the grandchildren, Clayne with her millionaire, Amos handsome and alone. ("Bring him along," Willie urged. "I'm not ashamed of him." Amos said he appreciated that, he wasn't either, "but I think this is best." Latt agreed.)

They went to Bermuda on their honeymoon, kept it successfully incognito and very short, four days spent mostly on the beach in front of the vacation home of one of Anne's clients; then they returned and got back to work.

The wave formed, overtook them and swept them away.

2   The debate at first seemed to promise something for everyone.
He had the opportunity to launch his candidacy from a major platform. Rudy and Renny had the chance to do him damage if they
could. His supporters had the opportunity to applaud him vocifer-
ously. His opponents, including many students and a sizable number
of faculty, had the pleasure of shouting slogans, screaming, waving
banners and jumping up and down in a well-planned demonstration
in front of Memorial Hall. The media, many of whom had flown out
from the East as rumors spread of Willie's intention, had the opportunity to enjoy "a mass orgy," as Tim put it, of picture-taking, interviewing and editorializing, which would bring national and international
publicity and hopefully guarantee that his entry into the race would,
for a few brief days at least, dominate the news everywhere.

The first things that greeted him, when he and Anne and Latt and
Tim arrived from a private dinner at the Offenbergs', were shouted
slogans and hand-drawn placards denouncing him. Typical was, "Wee
Willie Winkie We Think You Stinkie!"

Latt hooted.

"If that's the best they can do," he said, "you're safe."

There was a good deal of laughter in the crowd, even some good-
natured applause when their party arrived. For the moment, at least,
the mood was relatively amicable and nonthreatening. Anne's comment was, "They seem to be having fun."

"Let's hope they stay that way," he said grimly, remembering the
savage bitterness that had greeted By Johnson's fatal address in this
same place.

Despite his apprehension, the crowd remained relatively calm,
exhausting most of its energies on loudly cheering Renny's sallies,

groaning and occasionally booing his own emphatic responses. There was no physical violence, which perhaps indicated that the country, as represented in microcosm here, was finally coming out of its long Vietnam indulgence.

Promptly at eight o'clock, Duke rose from his seat in the row of chairs behind the speakers' lecterns and went to the middle of the three that had been set up. A silence, restless but mostly attentive, greeted his opening, and his introduction of Rudy and Rudy's customary words welcoming them to "this lecture presented every year in honor of my dear parents, an event which has grown steadily in importance and national prestige." There were some scattered cries of dislike, the word "Nazi!" still hissed out here and there, decades after war's end; but Rudy ignored it and bulled his way ahead with characteristic arrogant impatience to introduce "the moderator of the evening—a young man selected with enthusiasm by both our participants—one of our leading Congressmen from California, the Honorable Latt Wilson."

At this there was an upsurge of really genuine applause from all across the hall. Latt's record as a Vietnam veteran who had become one of the earliest leaders of Vietnam protest, his war wound and the cane and limp that certified it, plus his commanding physical presence and his general popularity across a wide spectrum of the generations, always guaranteed him this same warm welcome wherever he appeared. "You're the one who ought to be running for President," Willie had told him a little while ago at dinner. "Give me time," Latt replied with a smile. "Give me time." No one who knew him or of him had the slightest doubt it would someday happen.

"Mr. Krohl—" he said formally, "Dr. Suratt—Senator"—he suddenly abandoned formality and let his face relax into the easy smile whose charm he had tested innumerable times since entering public life—"Dad"—again there was laughter and general applause—"ladies and gentlemen:

"I thank you for coming out tonight to attend the latest in a series of always interesting, always enlightening and always significant lectures honoring Herman and Gretchen Krohl. It is a great gift from their son Mr. Rudolph Krohl to the University and to all of us. It has become one of the University's major contributions to the culture and thought of this country. What has been said here has many times reverberated across America and, indeed, across the world. So I hope"—again the flash of quick, charming smile—"it will do tonight."

Good-natured laughter, though a bit more reserved this time.

"Professor Suratt," Latt went on, "you all know. He is one of America's most prominent and most active social critics, a constant prod to our consciences, a persistent gadfly to our complacencies. I am one of his many former pupils who will always remember the impact of René Suratt on our young lives. In many cases it has been unique; in some it has been quite surprising. For us all it is, has been, and always will be, unforgettable."

Again heavy applause, though Renny looked, for just a second before he caught himself, a little uncertain and upset. Latt's tone did not seem to match his words, somehow—Renny could almost believe it had been deliberately designed to make people remember many things. He forced himself to look graciously dignified, politely attentive, carefully unreactive.

"My father," Latt said, "the senior United States Senator from California, you also know. Not as well as I do"—again the easy smile—"but certainly as well as constant publicity and prominence can make a public man known to his constituents. Some of you here tonight are his constituents willingly. Some are captives of geography who wouldn't be caught dead as his constituents unless, as it has turned out, you happen to live in California and can't help yourselves." There was rueful laughter from some, applause from others. "I don't think many can deny, however, that Richard Emmett Wilson is one of the Senate's most famous and, I and many others think, one of its most able and effective members.

"He and Dr. Suratt, as you know, disagree on many things. You may agree or disagree with one or the other, but you know they are going to give us a lively exchange.

"Professor Suratt, by the luck of the draw, will open.

"Gentlemen, have at it!"

Applause rose, somewhat mixed but generally in Renny's favor, as he came forward with a fatherly smile, shook Latt's hand vigorously, clapped him affectionately on the shoulder and stepped to the lectern to Latt's left. The audience quieted quickly and Renny began.

"Mr. Moderator," he said—"Congressman, my old and dear pupil and friend, Latt—Mr. Krohl—Senator—President Offenberg—ladies and gentlemen:

"The Congressman is, as always, gracious, effective and appealing—even when one must disagree with what he says. He does indeed, as he says, know my opponent of the evening better than any of the rest of us. Familiarity, in his case undergirded by familial and filial ties, has obviously not bred contempt. I wonder if we would all be able to say the same, were we as close to the Senator as he is.

"For myself, the relationship is not so deep or so lifelong, but fairly close nonetheless. Most of you are aware that the Senator and I were fraternity brothers on this campus for three years; I have had the opportunity, then and for all these decades following, to study him; not, perhaps, as closely as his son but not as blindly either. And my impressions are somewhat different.

"Senator Wilson is a man who has been favored more by circumstance than by real achievement. He has always been a favored individual, one of those who rise lightly to the top with little effort, requiring little accomplishment."

There were murmurs—"Renny's out for blood. Go get him, Renny!" Students and faculty members geared up for a satisfying evening with their resident brain. Anne and Tim looked openly annoyed. Wilsons, father and son, remained impassive. Rudy Krohl, disliking both speakers, did not know exactly how to look at this particular moment.

"I must say to you," Renny resumed, tone growing harsh and accusatory, "that Willie Wilson has always had it easy. Things have always come to him virtually without trying. For the most part he has been more highly rewarded by fortune than his character and actions have deserved. The role of golden boy, superbly played, has always concealed a straw man hiding behind it, an empty shell without real convictions or principles. Such is what we have representing us in the United States Senate."

"Professor Suratt," Latt said, mildly but firmly, resting against his lectern and chatting in a comfortable, down-home way, "did you come here to dissect what you see as my father's character—or lack of it—or did you come to debate major issues facing the country? Perhaps we are straying a bit from the purposes of the Krohl Lecture? What do you think?"

"My understanding," Renny said, a characteristic tartness creeping into his tone, "is that the Krohl Lecture has no real parameters. It is designed to challenge thought, disturb certainties, generate controversy and perhaps, if speakers are lucky, provide enlightenment. I believe the character and record of our Senator is pertinent to all of these. Unless the moderator wishes me to take my seat?"

There were cries of "No! No! Give 'em hell, Renny!"

Latt remained unflustered.

"Certainly not, Professor," he said. "In some years of acquaintance I have never yet known you to be silenced by anyone, although"—a rueful smile—"there have been times as a student when I have wished I could. But certainly not now. Just try to keep it civil, that's all. I do believe that's a parameter worth preserving."

"Oh, yes," Renny agreed with a shrug. "Oh, certainly. I know how tender the Senator's feelings are, I can remember way back on that: and your feelings as his son, of course. It is only when I see incompetence enshrined and pretension given the status of reality that I balk. It is then that I think his character and actions become very important to this debate, and to any subsequent debates in which he may appear in the months ahead."

Head him off, Willie silently urged his son; he's going to blow my little surprise, such as it is. But of this Latt of course was quite aware.

"Well, Professor," he said, still comfortably but also firmly, "you have now blackguarded my father virtually unchallenged for the better part of ten minutes. I think that if that is the way you intend to debate, he should in all fairness be permitted to respond before you exceed the bounds of civil discourse any further. I would hope he would not respond in kind but that, of course, is up to him. Senator?"

"Thank you," Willie said, coming forward to the lectern on Latt's right. "I appreciate your attempt to restore some fairness to this encounter, which seems so far to have brought out little but the venom in Dr. Suratt's soul. I'm sure there are gentler elements there, and thoughts more worthy of his high and far-famed reputation in all those circles of enlightenment that really matter in America."

He uttered an audible stage sigh and shook his head as if saddened by his own irresponsibility.

"I am afraid the professor will not like what I am about to say. But while it does not attempt to demean the professor's character, or portray him as he often seems to many of us, as the very embodiment and symbol of all those elements of decay and decline that threaten America"— angry boos from Renny's partisans, hearty applause from his—"still I think I should say it now. And nowhere more fittingly, I think, than at this great university, on this campus from which so many of us have gone forth to make our individual records and leave our imprints on our times.

"A presidential election is coming.

"I shall be a candidate in that election."

There was a gasp, a minor tumult, some applause, some booing, all recorded avidly by the television cameras stationed around the hall. When all this died down, tension and excitement having been raised to an enjoyable degree, Willie went calmly on.

"You all know my record," he said, just as he had planned some months ago with Tim, who felt his own tensions rising, not knowing whether his advice in favor of moderation was to be taken or not.

"You will know it even better when I get through explaining it and my opponents get through trying to tear it down.

"I think my long years in public service, my extensive experience in both houses of Congress, my record as your Senator serving this great nation-state of ours during its phenomenal growth in population and prosperity, speak for themselves.

"As the campaign goes forward, I will set forth in detail my positions on domestic policy, foreign policy, how best to protect and preserve the United States, and what its aims and purposes should be in the closing decades of this turbulent century.

"I ask the support of those who approve of me and I welcome the opposition of the small-bore minds that will oppose me."

Again there was a gasp; Tim cringed; but the audience quickly subsided and Willie proceeded calmly on.

"I hope the issue can be decided on a higher level than that—and on a higher level than Dr. Suratt is attempting to impose upon us all tonight. But I am serving notice that I am quite prepared to meet my opponents on whatever ground they choose, be it as high as I would like it to be, or as low as Dr. Suratt and his kind would have us descend.

"I am very pleased and proud to announce that my son Latt, Congressman from California, will head my campaign as chairman.

"And now, Mr. Moderator, could I have just a word or two more at this point? I have not directly answered Professor Suratt's kind malignancies about my character. I would like to do so."

"I think perhaps," Latt responded with a smile, "that the announcement you have just made should be quite enough to give Dr. Suratt and your other critics pause, creating as it does a sudden rearrangement of national politics. I think perhaps we should return—or try to return—to a more direct discussion of the issues in this debate. And incidentally"—the smile broadened—"I think that you have really disqualified me as moderator, having created a conflict of interest that I can't resolve right now. Dr. Offenberg, would you take the chair, please?"

He withdrew to take a seat between Anne and Tim. Duke came forward to the middle lectern. For a moment an awkward little silence fell. Willie broke it to say quietly, "Mr. Moderator, I was about to respond directly to Dr. Suratt's personal attack—"

"Oh, yes," Duke said. "I'm sorry. Certainly. You have the floor."

"Mr. Moderator," Renny said angrily, "I object. I object to this obviously carefully staged game of musical chairs which centers control of this debate in the hands of my opponent and his friends. And I object most vigorously to the obvious favoring of the Senator as a result of the change in moderator. The Senator was given full license by his son to divert this debate and turn it into a launching pad for his candidacy, which I sincerely hope will crash on takeoff. It is a futile gesture, as befits a futile politician, foredoomed to failure, as he has always been foredoomed to failure, by his faulty perception of events." Again, raucous audience response, laughter and applause from Renny's supporters competing with boos and hisses from Willie's. "I object to his being permitted to hold the floor unchecked for his partisan announcement. And now he wants time to make a personal attack on me. I resent this, Mr. Moderator. I resent it!"

"*I* attack *him?*" Willie demanded, real irritation and disgust in his voice. "What in the—what has *he* been doing to *me?* As always, he turns the facts on their heads, which has always been typical of the way he thinks and operates. He began the personal attacks, now he must take the consequences. This is something known as simple fairness, which is something Dr. Suratt has never understood."

There was a gasp from the audience and Renny started to retort. Duke overrode him with a calm, "The Senator will proceed." Renny subsided for the moment. Willie studied him briefly and then resumed, tone and face registering open distaste as though he were seeing something unpleasant in the road.

"Who is this person," he demanded, "who, as my son says, attempts to blackguard me here on the campus of our alma mater? I know he is considered to be a great man in some of the more precious circles of American academic, intellectual and political thought, but what a fraud, Mr. Moderator, what a fraud. As he has noted, we have known each other a long time, starting with day-to-day familiarity in our mutual fraternity house. I have studied him as he has studied me; his dislike for me is minor compared to what I feel for him. He is a poor excuse for a teacher, a poor excuse for a thinker, a poor excuse for a man. I too prefer to match pretensions with reality. The professor does not fare well in such a comparison. His pretensions are so grand as to be outright laughable, were it not for all the minds he has damaged and misled. The reality is so devastating that it cannot be evaded when placed beside his pompous pronouncements and his curious personal life."

There was a sudden ugly note in the response of Renny's friends, a hissing and an angry susurrus.

"The natives are restless on that one," Latt murmured to Anne, who nodded unhappily.

"I wish he wouldn't get down to Renny's level," she said, "but what can he do? Renny really did start it."

"Mr. Moderator," Willie said, voice deliberately level, almost disinterested, "I hope we can proceed without further personal exchanges and attacks such as the professor has launched upon me. My announcement is partisan, yes, but only for myself; I am not attacking anyone else, it is not partisan per se. I respect the divergent views of those—most of those—who oppose me. If they treat me fairly, I shall reciprocate; if they do not, I shall respond. I hope the professor and I may now proceed like gentlemen to have a debate on those issues which really concern the country far more than his personal vendetta against me."

And he turned to his opponent with the relaxed and easy smile that had always struck Renny, from their first meeting in the house forty years ago, as one of his most repulsive features.

"Well, Mr. Moderator," Renny snapped, "I know I am supposed to bow to the famous fatal charm of the Senator and be mollified into forgetting the weakness of his character and the viciousness of the personal attack he has just made upon me. I too hope we can proceed like gentlemen. It takes two," he observed with heavy sarcastic emphasis, "to make that bargain."

"Mr. Moderator," Willie said, remaining calm and steadfastly imperturbable, which he knew would infuriate Renny most, "I refuse to engage in this exchange of personal pleasantries any longer. I was aware, from our first days in the house, that Renny Suratt was very jealous of me; people like me seem to invite it from people like him. I have had many occasions over the years, as he has attacked me and my record so ruthlessly and so relentlessly, to see that jealousy manifest itself. But I did not realize until today, Mr. Moderator, how deep and how vicious—and how infinitely sad, for him—that sick obsession is. I pity him for it but I am afraid there is nothing I can do to appease or lessen it. It is a personal problem, like others he has, which I am afraid no one can assuage."

For a full minute, Renny did not respond. Anger, envy, hatred, frustration, seemed almost physically to consume him. His sharp features looked even sharper against his dark-complected face framed by its carefully careless swatch of graying hair. His spare body, beginning to thicken and stoop a little as time began to move in on him, as it has a way of doing to even the most profound of great thinkers, seemed bent and contorted with some savage inner turmoil.

Then he straightened abruptly, grasped the lectern firmly and spoke, with a control that obviously cost him much, in a flat and impersonal voice.

"Duke," he said quietly, "can we proceed?"

"To what?" Tim murmured wryly to Latt. "Everything else will be anti-climactic."

And from the media's standpoint, and in the minds of the opposing factions in Memorial Hall, it was. The argument went on for another forty-five minutes, more quietly and much less personally. Both speakers felt later that they had made many effective points in scanning the nation's problems, but it was of course the "personal vendetta" and the "futile gesture" that caught journalistic fancy and received the major publicity. Willie's announcement was almost overshadowed by the explosion of personal animosity that had overtaken him and his lifelong gadfly. In most major accounts it was seen as a battle between "liberal" and "conservative."

That was how the media interpreted it and that was how it was presented to the world.

It would be years before Willie would admit publicly that he had been mistaken to make his announcement at that particular time in that particular place with that particular opponent, so beloved of America's opinion-makers despite his "colorful personal life," which they always protected from the public gaze even as they blithely savaged transgressors of a different political stripe. But he knew it immediately that night, even before he read and heard and saw the anvil chorus.

Back on President's Knoll, having run the gauntlet of scornful protesters whose good-bye, now that Renny had set the tone, was even less cordial than their hello had been, he admitted his error with a humorous chagrin that did not quite conceal the pain of it.

"I was too good-natured," he told Duke as they sat on the terrace of President's House having a nightcap, looking down on the scattered lights of the University below. "When you called me about Renny I should either have put my foot down right then and refused to appear with him, or I should have skipped the lecture if Rudy wouldn't agree." He laughed without much amusement. "I'm afraid I was Mr. Nice Guy just once too often this time."

"Oh, I don't think so," Anne protested. "I don't think it's hurt you as much as you think."

"With all respects, Annie," Latt said, "I think you're being Mrs.

Nice Girl. Dad's right. It was a mistake. He shouldn't have done it. It just made him an even more attractive target for the goo-heads."

"The damage isn't irreparable, though," Shahna remarked, and added in such an uncertain tone that they all laughed, "Is it?"

"It could be," Tim said. "I'd put the chances at about a thousand to one. If I know my colleagues in the media, Renny's attacks will get far more prominence than any reprisal or defense of Willie's."

"It would be great if anybody even notices the announcement," Latt said wryly. "No, that's too gloomy. It'll be noticed, all right, but it will receive the spin: the spin will be put upon it. It won't get the respect it deserves. They'll twist it. It will range from 'He's got a nerve' to 'Who cares?' "

" 'A futile gesture . . . foredoomed to failure,' " Duke remarked, "as Renny so kindly put it."

"And the record will be tagged 'conservative,' " Latt said, "even though it's far from that easy smear."

"It is far from that," Willie said. "It's always been middle of the road, which is something people have a hard time grasping, particularly ideologues who don't want to grasp it and deliberately close their minds to it."

"Hunt with the foxes, run with the hares," Tim said. "I've always warned you about that, old pal, but you've always persisted."

"He can't help himself," Latt said with an affectionate smile. "It's known as fairness—balance—integrity. Nothing so unusual about that. Except that it's very unusual in this world we live in."

"Hey, Diogenes!" Willie exclaimed. "Bring your lamp over here! Here I am, your honest man—all by my little lonesome."

"A hell of a basis for a presidential campaign," Latt remarked, "but we'll give it a whirl, and do our damnedest, and see what happens."

When they got back to Washington next day, they were greeted by exactly what they had predicted. The pack was in full cry: LIBERAL LEADER ATTACKS WILSON CONSERVATIVE RECORD, the Mother of All Newspapers reported in New York. SURATT CALLS WILSON CANDIDACY "FUTILE GESTURE," the Daily Conscience of the Universe reported in Washington. WILSON CONSERVATISM EASY TARGET FOR LIBERAL ATTACK, echoed many another me-too publication across the nation. And from editorials, columns, TV programs and commentaries the agreed-upon official wisdom poured forth.

"We must confess," Mother's editorial said, in a tone more rueful than condemnatory—and therefore more hurtful—"that we find Senator Wilson's citing of his conservative record as a reason to support his long-delayed run for the White House to be a rather forlorn and unworthy response to the well-grounded attacks made upon him by such brilliant liberal leaders as Dr. René Suratt.

"Coming as it did on the heels of his announcement of candidacy, the Senator's cry of foul—his plaintive accusation that Dr. Suratt was engaged in a 'personal vendetta' when he called the Senator's candidacy a 'futile gesture . . . foredoomed to failure'—did not strengthen the Senator's hand. On the contrary it weakened it, and invited more such attacks from those who cannot agree with a record which has wavered over the years between a moderate objectivity and an unabashed conservatism.

"Senator Wilson is in the race. It remains to be seen how long he can remain in it, given a history so vulnerable to attack from such recognized and highly respected leaders of American thought as Dr. Suratt."

"Senator Wilson— 'Wee Willie Winkie,' as demonstrators referred to him at his debate with Dr. René Suratt—did not, we think, make a very convincing defense of his legislative record," the Daily Conscience agreed. "To use it to buttress his formal entry into the presidential campaign is, we think, to open himself to justifiable attack from all, like Dr. Suratt, who hold to a higher and more consistent vision of what America is all about.

"Dr. Suratt's lifelong liberalism stands in stark contrast to Senator Wilson's incorrigible conservatism and his ruthless disregard for the best interests of the nation in his avid pursuit of his conservative goals.

"The Senator has finally ended whatever suspense there may have been about his presidential intentions. We think Dr. Suratt may have been a bit harsh when he referred to the Wilson candidacy as 'a futile gesture . . . foredoomed to failure,' but we agree with his basic judgment.

"Never has the Senator's record stood in more glaring contrast with the enlightened forces represented by Dr. Suratt. His candidacy is not futile, in the sense that it opens up further national dialogue on the future shape of government, which is always helpful. But we are forced to concur that his attempt may well be 'foredoomed.'

"It will be interesting to see how far he gets with it."

"So saith the 'liberal media,' " Latt remarked dryly, "in all their well-regimented might."

"I'm afraid you have your work cut out for you, Willie," Tim said.

"We'll give it our damnedest, Uncle Tim," Latt said with an amicable echo of childhood days.

"That we will," Willie promised grimly. "At least they'll know we've been in the battle."

And so they did.

3　　From the debate and Willie's announcement, the wave spread back out across the country as smoothly as might have been expected, which meant as smoothly as campaigns ever take form, shape and effectiveness. From headquarters on Pennsylvania Avenue, in offices leased four months before through a fictitious corporation to escape advance publicity before they were ready for it, Latt moved skillfully to put together the necessary machinery.

Like everything in American politics, some aspects of what he and his coworkers did were skilled and brilliant, others sloppy and filled with human error despite their most earnest efforts. All presidential campaigns strive to give the impression of clockwork efficiency, which hopefully will encourage the popular impression that this is how the candidate will act if elected to office. In reality, campaigns are as helter-skelter, uncertain and subject to human weakness and error as national administrations, in fact, are. Somehow candidates get elected, somehow they administer the country. It is far more a matter of luck and happenstance in both instances than it is of any really astute and infallible planning. Astuteness and infallibility live uneasily with democracy, most unastute and fallible of systems, although, as Willie and the great majority of his countrymen believed, the best.

To the pursuit of this elusive miracle, Latt brought his considerable political talents. His first move was to round up a few old friends. Reaching back over forty years and half a dozen of his father's campaigns for House and Senate, he called Aram Katanian at his law offices in Fresno.

"You made my dad president of the student body in 1938," he began without other preliminary. "Will you help make him President of the United States now?"

"Latt!" Aram exclaimed, pleased. "I'll be delighted. But where is the old bastard? Is he too important to talk to me now?"

"On the Hill in committee, I believe," Latt said. "Call his office, I know he'll get back to you just as soon as he can. He'll be very pleased to have you aboard."

"We did it before and we can do it again!" Aram sang in a croaky reprise of a World War II ditty. "Although," he added thoughtfully, "it may not be so easy now. After all, I made him president of the student body by being his opposition and he licked me cold. Now we're up against bigger guns than I ever was, and it ain't going to be no picnic, buster."

"I know that," Latt said. "He knows that. But you've been such a help with his subsequent campaigns that he's convinced if anybody can mount a winning effort this time, you can."

"Perhaps," Aram Katanian said. "I thought you were going to do it, though. Wasn't that the big sensation that came out of the big debate with Renny Suratt, King of the Wild Frontier, the Unfettered Mind and the Hyperactive Body?"

Latt chuckled.

"There were bigger sensations than me, in that debate. Anyway, I'm just chairman, lots of pomp and not much circumstance. I need hands-on, day-by-day, nuts-and-bolts people to really move things. My time is limited. I have my own office to run, unfortunately."

"And I don't?" Aram inquired with a challenge not entirely humorous. "That's the trouble with you giant egos in politics. You're all alike. You expect your families and friends to drop everything and tote the bale for you whenever you feel like snapping your fingers."

"You won't do it, then?" Latt inquired with mock concern.

Aram sighed, again not entirely in jest.

"Why do I always fall for this? I'll try. Four partners, five associates and a dozen bright and shiny juniors ought to be able to handle almost anything. And I'll always be at the other end of the phone when they need me. When am I supposed to be in charge?"

"Good man," Latt said. "How about next Monday?"

"I'll be there," Aram said, voice beginning to fill with the zest of coming political battle. "I'll probably need at least three secretaries."

"We'll share some," Latt promised "We're going to have all sorts of people. You won't lack for assistance, never fear."

"I saw Bill Nagatani at Rotary a couple of days ago," Aram noted. "We were wondering if either of us would hear from you."

"Wonder no more," Latt said. "He's next on the list. Dad and I believe in keeping good teams together. Tim won't take a formal position, but he'll be hovering in the background, full of advice—you know Timmy. Do you need help with finding a place to stay?"

"I always stay at the University Club when I'm in town," Aram said. "Two long blocks and a hop, skip and a jump through Lafayette Park to the White House. So near and yet so far!"

"You and Bill must close the distance," Latt said, and left Aram chuckling and anxious to get on with the job.

Bill Nagatani, now head of ten-thousand-acre Nagatani Farms nearby Selma and a long way from World War II internment with his parents and siblings in Manzanar—and a long way from his once-cherished dream of establishing a Japanese-American newspaper in California—proved equally obliging and anxious to get into the thick of it.

"Hi, Bill," Latt began. "This is Latt Wilson—"

"Of course I will," Bill Nagatani interrupted with a chuckle. "What do I do and when do I start?"

"How about the same job you had in the last Senate campaign, chairman of minorities?"

"We are beginning to get a lot of those," Nagatani remarked. "You sure you want an Asian-American in charge of the whole shebang? Won't all the others object?"

"You aren't an 'Asian-American,' " Latt said with some impatience, "you're an American. And why not? If anybody complains, we'll get precious and give you some individual ethnic subchairman to make everybody happy—if we all decide that's the right way to go, when you get back here."

"I don't know," Bill said thoughtfully. "I know that's the big trend right now, but whether it's good for the country to divide us along ethnic lines instead of unite us as Americans, I don't know. It used to be united we stand, divided we fall; now all the smart thinking seems to be devoted to dividing us just as much as possible along ethnic lines in the hope, in my judgment, that ultimately this will make us fall. Does Willie really want to be part of that?"

"Look at it as a temporary recognition of apparent reality," Latt said dryly. "It isn't reality, and it isn't wise, and it is a danger in a world already too divided, but it's the fashionable thing at the moment. Dad won't ever do or say anything to disrupt national unity, you know that, but you know how it is in a campaign. A lot of it is apparent reality, designed for instant perception, not actual reality based on long-range fact. Everybody else will have minorities represented in the most blatant possible way. Wilson for President will at least have to make the matching gesture."

"Oh, I understand all that," Nagatani said. "It's a matter of protecting against vulnerabilities. It makes me uneasy, that's all—having once suffered the consequences of assumed ethnic superiorities run rampant."

"There were lots of factors involved in those days," Latt said. "But," he added firmly, to head off Nagatani's tendency to grow argumentative on this subject, which understandably still rankled after almost forty-five years, "now we're confronted with campaign necessities—"

"And vulnerabilities," Bill repeated dryly. "Anyway, I'm glad you're including me in your gallant effort. I've worked my tail off for Willie in previous campaigns, and I'll work it off in this one. Ibu and I will arrive at the Willard, where we always like to stay, next Monday. Where do I report in to you?"

"Thanks, Bill," Latt said; gave him the address, the official phone number and his own private number; and made a confirming note on the organizational chart that was beginning to take shape on the headquarters wall.

There only remained fifty state chairmen to be selected; twenty or thirty liaison people to handle women, labor, industry, sexual groupings and other special interests; innumerable county and local workers, mostly the faithful who had labored long and hard in the party vineyard and now demanded their just, quadrennial recognition; a small press staff to pander to the endless demands of the pander-demanding media; and several dozen "nuts-and-bolts" people to handle routine administrative duties. But day by day the structure grew and the organization took shape.

Willie found himself well satisfied with the way things were proceeding as the holiday season approached. It would be followed rapidly by the season of primaries and debates—the "campaign before the campaign" that would define, delimit and in some ways sharply restrict the free democratic flow of the conventions. Their ability to make decisions, which had so often out of partisan turmoil in the past produced startlingly effective results, was increasingly bound by rules, quotas, arbitrary restrictions and the crippling fact that the primaries more and more controlled the final decisions in both parties. By convention time in both, it was virtually all over. The conventions, once so fluid and exciting, were rapidly becoming so rigid and preordained that, veteran hands wistfully complained, not only all the fun but all the real democracy as well were being inexorably drained away.

But, as Latt remarked, "You do the best you can with what you've got," and against that measure the Wilson campaign's efforts to provide the public with "temporary recognition of apparent reality" moved ahead with encouraging speed. So too, as Bill Nagatani pointed out, did their efforts to provide "permanent recognition of genuine reality" where Willie was concerned. He was already on the killing schedule that all would-be Presidents now seem forced to follow, the speeches, the television programs and radio talk shows, the physical forays into various parts of the country that are considered worth the personal effort of the candidate.

Out of all this there was beginning to emerge, despite highly vociferous opponents and relentlessly active critics, something of the picture of himself that he wanted the country to see: intelligent, honest, stubborn, devoted to a moderate vision of America, grounded in a basic good nature and common sense that added up to stability and trustworthiness in an increasing number of minds. Week by week he rose in the polls, confiding to Anne and Timmy that, "I don't believe in the damned things but the media makes such a fuss about them you have to pay at least minimal attention." And, he added with a grin, "I wouldn't like it if they showed me trailing badly, of course. That simply would—not—do."

Nagatani, whose shrewd mind saw many things, said that he too was satisfied with both "temporary recognition" and "permanent recognition," but cautioned: "Now all we have to worry about is the matter of protecting against vulnerabilities."

"Don't have any," Willie responded cheerfully. Both Bill and Latt squelched that smugness promptly.

"Are you sure?" Bill inquired. "Don't be so positive, Willie. There's always something that can be made to look like scandal, whether it really is or not."

"Better think and think hard," Latt advised. "If there's the slightest scrap of anything, anytime, anywhere, they'll dig it up, inflate it and turn it into sensation. Better be prepared."

"I honestly don't have anything like that in my record," Willie said. "Honestly, I don't."

"I'd suggest we keep our powder dry," Nagatani said. " 'Be prepared' is a good motto."

"The best," Latt agreed.

It never occurred to any of them, though they realized later that it had probably been obvious, that the really hurtful attacks, when they came, would not be directly upon Willie but upon those closest to him, whom he was most helpless to defend.

For the time being the targets were obvious. The first of course was themselves—"the inner circle," as it was referred to in the media. Every potential candidate had an inner circle, old friends and supporters, people long known and most trusted, intimates and advisers most of whom had been around a long time. This was only human nature, but, particularly with candidates who were disapproved of, it often became a thing of much tut-tutting.

Regularly since Bill and Aram had come to Washington, Willie's inner circle—those two, Latt, Tim and Anne—had met regularly twice a week for private brainstorming sessions on political realities, campaign necessities and overall strategy.

Very soon Mother and the Conscience and their attack-alikes across the country were deploring this in regretful tones.

"We must confess," Mother editorialized, "that we are saddened by the air of unctuous cronyism that already seems to surround the Wilson campaign. It shuts out original thought, suffocates the campaign like few other aspects of American political life. It is sad to see the Senator so unsure that he seems to be falling victim to this old routine.

"We hope the Congressman knows what he is doing when he makes a reasonably worthwhile career ["Just 'reasonably,' you'll note," Willie said with a chuckle] hostage to the Senator's quite possibly terminal one. It could mean throwing good legislative substance after bad. . . ."

"Surely," the Conscience chided, "Congressman Wilson must know how recklessly he is jeopardizing his own fairly respectable career in support of the presidential ambitions of Senator Wilson. A father-son team can sometimes be of real effectiveness in politics; but when it it based on so glaring a divergence of views, and is so clearly dictated by crude ambition on the father's part and impulsive and unthinking loyalty on the son's, then it becomes not a strength but a weakness for the elder's campaign. To say nothing of what it will do to the career of the younger. . . ."

"Get out while you can!" Willie cried in mock exhortation. "The dam has broken! Go east, go east!"

"They really strain for it, don't they?" Latt remarked, shaking his head. "I wonder. These are grown men?"

"If that's their damnedest," Willie said, "I think we can survive it."

"I hope so," said Bill Nagatani, ever cautious. "We have a way to go, yet."

4   But for several months all proceeded well in what was rapidly becoming the locked-in, undeviating, stately ritual of presidential politics.

There were the primaries, tumbling one after another, in which Willie did brilliantly in several, trailed in several more, broke more or less even in still others. There were the endless pontificatings of Mother, the Conscience and all their busy brood, along with those of television commentaries, talk-show participants, columnists, editorialists, writers and talking heads of all kinds and persuasions. Not a political sparrow fell but its demise was faithfully recorded in the media; not a word slipped up that was not determinedly magnified out of all proportion into major error by sources eager to denigrate and cut down. Not a physical slip occurred, a stumble, a momentarily uncertain look, an inadvertent grasp for the support of a friendly arm when going up or down stairs, a second's hesitation in speech, but what it was instantly blown up, exaggerated, emphasized, made the subject of endless speculation and conjecture. On and on and on it went, the American media, and more particularly its Washington, or Know-It-All, division pumping out literally millions of words upon endless, mindless, immaterial trivia.

As happened every four years, the citizenry in general very soon became thoroughly exhausted and disgusted with this; but the media would not let them rest. They were going to be told, by God, whether they wanted to be or not. Space had to be filled, time slots had to be occupied; and if that had something to do with the disinclination of many to exercise the voting franchise they never really understood or properly valued in a world where freedom was always on the defensive, then that was just too bad. The behemoth of unstoppable publicity and frequently completely frivolous information (or in some cases, deliberate misinformation) rolled on.

Caught squarely in its ravenous glare along with his fellow candidates, Willie had no choice but to perform according to the dictates of the imperial media. Most of their major practitioners were openly against him. He was not only independent, he was irreverent, and that was the ultimate sin. His sense of the ridiculous, his impatience with cant and hypocrisy, and his tendency to let fly with a razor tongue when under pressure did not endear him to Mother, the Conscience and others of their august ilk who took themselves dreadfully, dreadfully seriously and demanded that they be worshiped very, very respectfully. He could not resist showing a flash of contempt for them now and then, and that did it.

Powerful media figures didn't like what they consistently described as his "conservative agenda"; his "attitude" inflamed them even more. They disliked him with a consuming passion because he made it obvious that he considered them dubious people, as slanted, unfair, bigoted and unworthy of their privileges and responsibilities as the most rabid of what they termed "right-wing extremists."

It was his observation that no right-winger was ever more slanted and unfair than Mother and the Conscience on a good day. He described both extremes, in a letter to Guy Unruh (which somehow found its way into the *Honolulu Star-Bulletin*), as "all skunks in the same barrel, fighting one another blindly in a universal stink." Such sentiments did not endear him to either side, though a great many of his fellow citizens agreed.

There were many times, reflecting on all this, when he paused to wonder whether anything was worth the punishment of being at the center of such a maelstrom of vindictiveness and backbiting, which could be so vicious and so destructive of the good purposes for which he and his opponents had set out on the long, rough road to the White House. He found himself examining many times the assumptions that had finally brought him into the race.

"I still think," he stubbornly told the "inner circle," none of whom had challenged him on it but whom he felt, in some self-conscious way, he must continually convince, "that there is still a place in America for an honest, decent moderate who is possessed of goodwill toward his fellow citizens and who advocates some reasonably middle-of-the-road view of what is best for America."

"Millions agree with you," Latt reassured him, but his tone at times was so uncertain that Willie couldn't resist a grin and a challenge.

"Except that they probably won't vote for me," he suggested. "Is that how it's beginning to shape up?"

"It could," Aram Katanian said, and Bill Nagatani nodded soberly.

"It's possible," he said. "I'm sure you're prepared for that."

"You guys from the San Joaquin Valley," Willie said, "are too damned conservative for me. Think big! We have another month of primaries to go. I'm in pretty good shape right now. If I can take three or four of the big ones remaining—"

"And nothing comes along to blindside you," Nagatani remarked.

Willie laughed.

"You're a damned pessimist, aren't you, Bill? You're determined to keep my feet on the ground. You may be right, but I don't want to contemplate it just yet. I certainly don't see anything at the moment that would be insurmountable."

"You never know," Anne said, and shivered almost imperceptibly at the thought of her ex-husband, which Willie of course understood. But all had been quiet from that sector since their marriage. And there were no other possibilities that he could see right now.

But, as Latt and Bill had agreed months ago, "Be prepared" is a good motto.

He thought of it quite a lot; but even so, he was not prepared when the blow came, though he knew instinctively what it was the moment he picked up the phone and heard the voice of his second son.

"Dad?" Amos said; and there was that in his trembling voice which prompted instant recognition, based on subconscious misgivings, that the time had come.

How long it had been, he reflected now, since he and Donna had first begun to fear that the world might be unusually rough for Amos the gentle and vulnerable, so kind, good-hearted and trusting that he almost seemed to be inviting something crushing from life. It must have been twenty years ago, for he was thirty-five now and he must have been about fifteen when they began to share the conviction that he was going to find his path strewn with difficulties that might well break his heart and destroy his spirit.

For a time they had the usual worries about the cliché of a boy too retiring and too studious, fitting too neatly all the anti-clichés of bounding American masculinity. He wasn't rough, he wasn't aggressive, his tastes tended to be "literary" and "artistic" rather than rough-and-ready, he had rather read than play football or baseball with the gang. Later on he seemed to find more satisfaction in associating with a few close friends of his own sex than in embarking upon the endless routine of advance-and-retreat with nubile femininity that in many cases dominated the lives of men "from nine to ninety," as one of his friends put it sarcastically years later. More, perhaps, than society then realized did not want to participate in this because they were by inclination, taste, desire and inherent nature, unable. Their way was never easy even under the most favoring of conditions; and being the son of a rising national politician could not qualify as "favoring" by any judgment.

So, at some time in his eighteenth year, at a time when his parents were beginning to wonder with worried unhappiness how they might approach the subject and, as Donna put it, "do something about it" ("What would you suggest?" Willie inquired. She didn't know). Amos had startled, and at first dismayed, them, with an action so completely honest that they were initially unable to recognize it as the quite logical result of having two completely honest parents. He simply told them.

He first approached his father. Willie would never forget the summer's day when this happened, back home on the family ranch near Terra Bella in the middle of the San Joaquin Valley. It came at the end of a long, hot working day together in the orange groves, as Willie liked to do "to keep my hand in" whenever official duties permitted him a little leisure time at home. This was not often, and when it did happen he liked to have his sons join him if they could, so that they too could "keep their hands in." They all enjoyed this; it was one area where Amos never hesitated to participate to the full. Their ties to the land were strong, after all the years their grandfather and their father and Uncle Billy had devoted to the ranch. It was in them instinctively, a part of them; just as, for Amos, was something else.

As Willie learned later on, Latt had known this for several years before he did. Amos had always followed the lead of his more aggressive and dazzling older brother. It was quite obvious from age one that he worshiped Latt; imitated him, followed him in the groves and fields, tumbling in the dirt and gurgling with pleasure as soon as he could toddle along after. As he grew he imitated Latt's actions, adopted his ways of speech, tried to follow in Latt's footsteps as much as he could. Apparently when he was about thirteen, Latt seventeen, it had become obvious to Latt that something was lacking: Amos wasn't quite a perfect imitation. One day when Amos found himself physically incapable of keeping up in some heavy chore around the ranch, Latt had lashed out at him impatiently with their father's cutting tongue. He had not intended to use the words he did, had not really known that he knew what he knew, or thought what he thought: it all just came out.

They were alone in the groves. Willie had already gone back to the house to answer some call from Washington. Amos had collapsed helplessly in tears, so heavy for a little while, and so paralyzing of all speech and movement, that Latt was genuinely scared; and since he genuinely loved his little brother and had always been very protective of him, the moment of revelation was equally devastating for them both.

Out of it had come a heightened awareness, a deeper sympathy, a stricken apology from Latt, a sob-muffled confidence and desperate plea from Amos.

"It's the always being afraid," he said. "Always protecting myself . . . always trying to be what I'm not . . . always pretending . . ."

He looked up, eyes still brimming with tears, at his golden brother, so tall and protective standing beside him, so secure and invulnerable, and said in a voice so utterly desolate and alone that Latt never forgot it, "It is so hard . . . so *hard*."

For once struck silent, by a glimpse into a hell he would happily never have to contend with, Latt put a hand on his brother's shoulder and squeezed it, hard.

"You won't—won't—tell anybody, will you?" Amos asked. "You'll help me, won't you? You'll take care of me?"

And, suddenly much older in an instant, suddenly aware that he had it in his hands to literally destroy another were he to be so irresponsible, Latt gave the only answer a human being as decent as he could give.

"Why, sure, kid," he said huskily. "Of course I will. I always have. You know that."

"Don't tell the folks," Amos said, suddenly anxious.

"Never," Latt said quietly. "But sometime, I think you'd better. Not now," he added hastily as Amos looked stricken again, "but later on, when you feel like it. They won't let you down. Mom might be awfully upset for a little while, but she'll come around. I'm sure Dad will be kind. He always is. He may be upset for a while, too, but he'll get over it."

"I don't really want to tell them," Amos said, voice forlorn again. Again Latt squeezed his shoulder, hard.

"No," he said. "But I really think you'd better. When you feel like it."

Five years later, at a low point when he was feeling especially helpless about it, Amos decided the time had come. The results had been about what Latt had foreseen.

Donna, who had never had any close contact with what she persisted in calling "that sort of thing," went around the house weeping from time to time until Willie brought her up short by saying, "This is your son, Donn. Relax, O.K.? Just relax."

Her first reaction had been horrified dismay, personal guilt, "What have we done to deserve this?" and similar standard reactions. Again Willie brought her up short by inquiring soberly, "What has *he* done to deserve this? And what exactly *is* 'this'? I don't think we know one half there is to be known about it. I doubt if anybody ever does. Or probably ever will."

And had finally told her what he had never told her before, the sad little episode of Tony Andrade being caught in the act in a men's room on the Quad one night, and of how he and Hack Haggerty had saved Tony's neck and probably his life; and of how he and Billy later that spring had virtually forced North McAllister, in spite of his agonized forebodings and his quite genuine love for Billy, to go through with his scheduled marriage to Betty June Letterman, "which I'm still not sure was the right thing to do. I never will be sure.

"But anyway," he had concluded, "those things give me a history. I handled them as best I could in the context of those times, and it probably, in North's case, wasn't the perfect way to do it. But at least I was tolerant, I didn't shout and holler and damn them up and down; I tried to help, however imperfectly. I tried to be decent and kind. I can't do less for my own son."

"How did he seem when he told you?" Donna asked presently. "Humbled? Crushed? Belligerent? Defiant?"

"Amos?" he said. "You know how he seemed. 'Humbled' and 'crushed' are pretty accurate descriptions."

"And did you tell him it was all right with us?"

"Should I have?"

She uttered a long, heavy sigh and suddenly blew her nose with an air of emphatic decisiveness.

"Yes," she said. "You should, and I hope you did."

"Yes," he said quietly. "Can he come and talk to you now?"

"It won't be easy for me," she said. "But of course I want to talk to him."

"Just remember it isn't easy for him, either. It's hard as hell. I'll call him now."

"Yes," she said.

Willie never knew exactly what transpired. But she told him the gist of it, which was that Amos could count on her too, she loved him and would stand by him. More realistically than Willie, she described her misgivings about the future and warned her son to avoid the public eye as much as possible.

"Is that for Dad's career?" he asked, for the first time something of his brother's tart challenges in his voice.

She looked at him and said quite simply, "No, it's for your own happiness, which happens to concern all of us a great deal. I hope you'll concede us that."

"Oh, I do," he said hastily. "Have you told Clayne?"

"No," she said, "but I expect she knows. You might do her the courtesy, though."

And when he did, the next time Clayne came home from the University, his sister proved as sympathetic and supportive as his parents and brother.

"I am very blessed," he told his mother. "I've met some guys whose families have put them through absolute hell about this."

Donna, who cringed inwardly at the vista opened up by "I've met

263

some guys," as her imagination leaped to where and when and how and under what circumstances such a confidence might have been forthcoming, managed to smile gravely and say, "Good. We'll never let you down. And we hope you'll never let us down. But most importantly of all, my dear son Amos, I hope you won't let yourself down. Be kind, and be careful."

"Two good rules," he said, for the first time in weeks managing a wan little smile. "I can't go wrong with those."

"Don't flaunt it," his mother said, sounding suddenly practical. "That's all we ask—don't flaunt it."

"I'm not a flaunter," he said, smile a little more confident. "I wouldn't do that for your sake, and particularly for Dad's."

"And for yours too," she suggested.

Amos nodded, completely serious again.

"For mine too."

From that point on, the subject had never been mentioned in the family. Amos, like his uncle Billy, showed considerable theatrical talent and took an increasingly active interest in the theater, particularly musical theater. He had an excellent tenor, a fine melodic ear, a genuine creativity and a real talent for composition. Ideas bubbled up, he developed them and committed them to paper, got an agent and began peddling them around. Like his brother, he was a handsome young man, tall and commanding, with an excellent stage presence and, as Latt noted, "no obvious stigmata to arouse the hostile." After graduation from the University he sought roles in small companies in San Francisco and Los Angeles, moved on soon to Washington and from there to New York, where he scored increasing success in supporting roles, culminating as the male lead in a musical romance that received encouraging reviews and lasted a total of eleven performances off-Broadway. But it was a start. His agent was negotiating for what appeared to be a sure thing, the lead in Hack Haggerty's latest comic operetta, *Lorraine,* when Willie announced his candidacy.

By that time the pattern of Amos's private life was well established. After a series of "fly-by-nights," as Latt described them privately to Clayne, Amos met Joel, a young stockbroker, also successful in his field, which was a long way from Amos's so that there were no career conflicts. Very quietly and very discreetly they had taken an apartment together on Central Park West, and appeared to be settling in for the long haul. And then the harsh world impinged.

"Dad?" Amos said.

"Yes?" Willie said, his tone more challenging than he had intended, but instinctively he knew that this meant trouble. He struggled to make his voice more welcoming and matter-of-fact.

"What is it, buddy?" he asked. "Is it official about Hack's show? Have you got the part?"

"I think so," Amos said. His voice turned suddenly bitter, confirming Willie's worst fears. "If it matters to anybody now."

"What do you mean?" Willie demanded with a determined heartiness. "Of course it matters, to a lot of people, including your family. And what do you mean, 'now'? Why wouldn't it matter 'now'?"

"Because they're after you, Dad," Amos said bleakly. "And they've decided to go after you through me. And I don't know"—his voice threatened to break for a moment but he steadied it and forced it on— "I don't know wh-whether I can take it, if you get hurt because of me."

"And I don't know whether I can take it if you get hurt because of me," Willie responded gravely. "Tell me about it."

"You'll see it soon enough," Amos said in the same bitter tone. "It's going to be front-page in all the supermarket sleaze rags and all the majors will pick it up from there. CANDIDATE'S SON IN GAY LOVE-NEST . . . WILLIE'S LITTLE BOY LIVES WITH MALE LOVER . . . CHURCH LEADERS DENOUNCE "CORRUPT LIFESTYLE" OF WILLIE'S SON . . . WILLIE'S PRINCIPLES BETRAYED BY GAY SON. Oh, you'll see it."

"Do they have any proof?" Willie inquired.

"Do they have to?" Amos asked.

"They'd better if we sue them," his father said grimly. Amos uttered a tired little laugh.

"We aren't going to sue."

"At least we can deny," Willie said, and again his son uttered a tired little snort.

"What good would that do? It's the truth and all they have to do is raise the question in the public mind. They don't have to prove anything at all. Particularly when it's the truth."

"We can deny it," Willie said stubbornly. Again Amos voiced weary dissent.

"Dad," he said, "you aren't going to deny anything. I don't want you to perjure yourself on my account. You can't do it. They've got a copy of the apartment lease with both our names on it, and although that alone doesn't necessarily mean anything, they're going to base all kinds of hints and charges on it, and the public is going to believe them. *Because it's the truth.* I think it comes down to two choices."

"Yes," Willie said, grimly abandoning what he knew was a futile line of defense. "Either I stand by you or I repudiate you. Which shall it be?"

"I hope you don't want me to reply to that," Amos said. "I hope I don't have to make up your mind for you. I don't want to influence your judgment. That's your problem."

"It isn't even a problem," Willie said. "Do you think you could stand the pressures of a joint press conference in which I defend you? Because of course that's what I'm going to do."

"Thank you, Daddy," Amos said, sounding suddenly about four years old. "But," he added, sounding suddenly a hundred years older than that, "I don't think I *could* stand the pressure. I'd be grateful to you to the day I die, but it would be too much of an ordeal for both of us. Why don't you just issue a statement from your office and let that be the end of any comment from the Wilson family. And Joel and I will get out of town for a while."

"I agree we all should be in on this," Willie said.

"I'd appreciate that," Amos said, near to tears but managing to speak with a shaky gratitude.

"Did they give you any indication how soon this will become public?"

"I didn't talk to them directly, but my source is on the staff of *Eye.* He says in next week's issue. He thinks several of the others probably have it already. So—any minute now."

"And the majors, in their pious way," Willie said, "will pick it up, consciences clear and shining, and give it a royal run, and there will be the latest sensation from the Wilson camp. Well, we might as well get ready. I'll set up a conference call with you and Latt and Clayne as soon as possible, probably tonight, and we'll be prepared for them."

"If we ever can be," Amos said bitterly, sounding so close to losing control that Willie knew he must be as firm and determined as he could be, if his son was to come out of this with his future stability relatively protected.

"I think you're right about you and Joel lying low for a bit," he said matter-of-factly. "Do you have any idea where you'll go?"

"We haven't really discussed it yet, but we might go up to Montreal. There's a great little hotel where we spent a week last winter, in the city but very private and out of the way. They have no idea who I am, which"—he sounded wry and for a moment more like himself—"is not surprising for a third-rate minor actor—and I've always made sure that nobody connected me with you. So I think we'd be safely out of the way there."

"Always be vigilant, though," Willie advised. "Never underestimate the media's ability to do damage, particularly where I'm concerned."

"I'm afraid Hack will dump me from his new musical," Amos said, forlorn but honest.

"I think you'll find Hack a better friend than that," Willie said. "He and I went through something together at the University that ought to make him supportive. I don't think I'll have to remind him of it."

"Dad!" Amos said, mock horror, disbelief and (thank goodness, Willie thought) a little reviving humor in his voice. "You don't mean that you and Hack—"

"No, no," Willie said, beginning to laugh in response. "But somebody did, and Hack and I had to come to his rescue."

"I hope you saved him."

"We did," Willie said. "And we'll save you too."

But in the four days following the family conference in which Latt and Clayne had unhesitatingly come to their brother's support, he was not so sure. Particularly when the break came and everybody from the lowest to the highest in the righteous world leaped happily into the act.

Amos had given him a sad and sarcastic prediction of what the headlines would be in the gutter press and he proved to be entirely correct. And exactly on cue, as Willie had predicted, the nation's major publications and commentators, relieved of any responsibility because of course they had not floated the original story but were only reporting the resultant furor solemnly in their smug outlets, joined eagerly in.

"We deplore the tactics of the gutter press in attempting to smear Senator Wilson's son for his unorthodox lifestyle," Mother said gravely, "but we do find a rather surprising gap between the Senator's profound moral pronouncements on the cares of our age, and the casual way in which he appears to have accepted the morally questionable personal predilections of his younger son, Amos. A remarkable political family which includes the Senator and his older son, Representative Latt Wilson, also apparently includes a member whose presence is gravely damaging to his father and brother. We expect the country has not heard the last of this deplorable episode. . . ."

"Just as the primary campaigns roar to a conclusion," the Conscience commented, "with Senator Wilson appearing to be holding his own in a contest that seems destined to go right down to the wire in his own party, it is revealed that his second son, Amos, a minor but heretofore respectable theatrical figure, is pursuing a lifestyle that can only bring the condemnation of many church groups and other Main Street elements that support his father's candidacy. The Senator's expected defense of his son will be understandable in human terms, but in political terms this may be one of those disclosures that can seriously damage a candidate one of whose claimed strengths is his appeal to 'the moral fiber of the nation.'

"In the case of Senator Wilson and his unhappy second son, the fiber seems a little frayed, to us. . . ."

And in his most recent public appearance, an address to the annual meeting of the American Society of Newspaper Editors, that paragon of social enlightenment and moral sturdiness, Professor René Suratt, let fly with equal vigor and a noticeable satisfaction:

"Those who live by the moral sword sometimes seem destined to die by it. Such appears to be the case with the candidate of 'the moral forces of America' and his unhappy son, who apparently is not as strictly 'moral' in conventional terms as Senator Wilson's fervent supporters would like to believe all things Wilsonian to be.

"I was privileged to teach at the University both the brilliant young Representative Latt Wilson, now one of the finest and most able members of the United States House of Representatives, and his younger brother, Amos, now an able young actor just beginning to make a real impression in American theatrical circles. Even in those embryonic days it was obvious that Amos Wilson had his problems. He was one of that small coterie, found on every campus, whose moral pretenses live sadly askew alongside the reality of a questionable moral lifestyle. Now that dichotomy has suddenly entered the public domain just at the time when his father's presidential candidacy appeared to be nearing a possibly successful climax.

"That possible success is now sadly and perhaps fatally damaged by his own son. It is a tragedy in human terms, though it may turn out to be a blessing for the United States. Americans expect their presidential candidates to be men of moral stature. Senator Wilson apparently falls short of that high standard. In fairness to himself, his son and the country, he should promptly withdraw."

Over the next week Wilson campaign headquarters received close to one hundred thousand letters and telegrams. Of these, 20 percent expressed unqualified support for "whatever course you, as father and candidate, decide to pursue." Twenty percent were upset, condemnatory and in many cases outright savage and hurtful. All the rest wavered somewhere in the middle, as he told Amos when he called in from Montreal to ask how things were going.

"Do many of them think you should withdraw?" his son inquired. Willie snorted.

"There are always gullibles who will pick up on any line handed them by major media and such hypocrites as Renny Suratt."

"Some do want you out, then," Amos said. "What do you want me to do?"

"Sit tight," Willie said firmly. "Stay where you are. Avoid the media like the plague and say nothing. It will blow over. How is Joel taking it?"

"Not very well," Amos said, sounding bleak. "He isn't used to it, like you are."

"I'm sorry," Willie said unhappily. "I'd give anything to save you two from all this—"

"It's probably always been inevitable that it would hurt you some day," Amos said. A little sob, quite unexpected, apparently quite spontaneous, welled up. "I'm sorry."

"Let's get it straight who's hurting whom," Willie said with some severity. "I don't want you apologizing for anything anymore. Your mother and I made the decision to stand by you years ago, and that's that."

"I'm glad—" Amos began, and his voice cracked suddenly with emotion. "I'm glad she isn't here to have to go through all this with us."

"So am I," Willie said, "but she would have come through with flying colors. That was your mother, if you recall. Anyway, tell Joel not to take it too hard. We're all pulling together. It will all work out all right."

"I hope so," Amos said. He sighed deeply. "It's very tough for him. He's really taking it awfully hard."

"Tell him he mustn't. Nobody's blaming him."

"Easy to say," Amos said bleakly, "but it isn't that easy in person."

"I can't come up there and talk to him personally, or I would."

"No, no, of course not. We wouldn't expect you to. And we can't come down there."

"Sadly, no. Again, I'm sorry. But that's just the way it is right now. My love to you, and to him. Good luck to you both."

"Thanks, Dad," Amos said, voice threatening to break. "We'll be all right."

"You will," Willie said firmly, adding fervently to himself, *God, I hope so.*

Two calls came in later that day, the first from Napa Valley, the other from Salt Lake City. From his beautiful home overlooking the valley at Collina Bella Winery, Tony Andrade sounded grave but determined.

"Willie!" he said. "You're in trouble. Can I help?"

"I don't quite see how," Willie said, "but I do appreciate the offer very much, Tony. It's wonderful of you."

"Well, you helped me when I needed it," Tony said. "I want to do what I can."

"Just think good thoughts," Willie said. "That's a great help."

"Is there anything I could do," Tony asked with an uncharacteristic hesitation, "to—to try to explain it to Amos and his friend that might be helpful to them?" He uttered a sudden sarcastic laugh at his own expense. "Hell, I don't know that anybody *can* explain it. But I'll try, if you think it would help."

"You're noble, Andrade," Willie said with an affectionate wryness to hide the surge of gratitude he felt, "but I agree, I don't think anybody can. It's just *there,* right?"

"It's just there," Tony agreed. "And some of us get a handle on it and manage to live with it, and many others don't. How's Amos doing?"

"He's a gentle soul," Willie remarked, "all right when left alone to proceed at his own pace but not always able to stand up to the world when it gets too rough. Which is now."

"And his friend?"

"He's the same type," Willie said. "Amos needs a strong man at his side right now"—he chuckled, without much humor—"somebody like you, Tony—but unfortunately he's got a kindred soul instead of a counterbalancing force. I get the impression they're both being tossed on heavy seas."

"Well, tell them to hang in there," Tony said. "Tell them about me, if you think it would help. I rode out a pretty heavy sea myself, didn't I?"

"You did indeed," Willie said soberly, "and I've always admired you for it. I thank you for your permission to tell them. I may do just that, if I decide it would help them. I don't know, at this point."

"And as for you," Tony said, "I don't have to tell you to be tough, you *are* tough. I see the pressure is really on to make you quit, though. What do they think you are, anyway?"

"The vulnerable father of an extremely vulnerable son," Willie said. "I may be able to ride it out politically, but whether he can ride it out personally, I don't know. He's worried now about what Hack is going to do. He was confident Hack was going to announce his selection as one of the leads in Hack's new musical, but now he doesn't know."

"I'll talk to Hack," Tony said firmly. "I can't imagine he'd be swayed by this any more than you would, but who knows. I'll give him a pep talk if I find he needs one. Where is he now, do you know?"

"At the Carlyle in New York, about to start work on the production," Willie said. "Got in late last night from Rome, Amos tells me. I know he'll be glad to hear from you."

"Right," Tony said. "Hang in there, pal. None of this is your fault."

"Except for running for President," Willie said. "That's my most egregious fault, according to major media and distinguished figures like Professor Suratt."

"Fuck Professor Suratt," Tony said. "Perverted bastard." He laughed abruptly at his choice of words. "Now, there's a *really* perverted bastard. Louise and the kids all send their love. Keep laughing, Willie. This will all work out."

"So I tell Amos," Willie said unhappily. "But I'm not sure he believes me."

Within the hour he heard also from Salt Lake City. North McAllister, never as jaunty as Tony in the face of their similar challenge, was grave and concerned.

"I just thought I'd call," he said, "to tell you how heartily I support you, and to ask you to convey to Amos my strongest support and best wishes. Have you ever told him about me?"

(At this immediate indication that he, like Tony, would unhesitatingly share his most intimate fact with Amos if Willie thought it would help, Willie was momentarily almost overcome by a gratitude so deep he could not articulate it.)

"I haven't told him about you by name," he said, "just that there was someone at school who was involved but who got married and overcame it."

"Which is comforting," North said dryly, "but not exactly the entire truth-so-help-me-God. I take it Amos doesn't show any signs of getting married, does he? Not one of your heroic, do-the-right-thing cases beloved of Dr. Willie?"

"I suppose I deserve that," Willie said, "but Billy and I did what seemed best at the time. You couldn't marry Billy."

"I love him to this day," North said evenly. "When he died something died in me. But there it is."

"Did you ever regret marrying B.J.?"

"No," North said. "But it would have made a lot of things a lot easier if I hadn't."

"You wouldn't have had your successful medical practice, I'll wager, And your two fine kids. And years of settled life with B.J., before the cancer got her. So—"

"So it's a balance," North said. "Life's always a balance. Just a little more difficult for people like me and Tony and Amos, that's all. But I don't go around being afraid. And neither does Tony. And neither must Amos . . . How did we get to this point, anyway? I called to give you some support, though knowing Willie, you probably don't need it—"

"I do," Willie said gravely. "I do."

"—and I also want you to pass on to Amos my sincerest good wishes and my hope—and my confidence—that he will weather this O.K."

"I think he will," Willie said, still gravely. "I'm not so sure about his partner. But I'll see that they get your message. They'll appreciate it. And so do I, old friend."

"I hope you don't have any foolish ideas about withdrawing," North said. "Much though your opponents would like you to."

Willie made a disparaging sound.

"Like Renny."

"That monumental, insufferable twit," North said. "I should hope *not*."

But Renny did not stop his attacks, nor did the major media. Nor, of course, did all those elements opposed to Willie's candidacy that the major media were able to stir up against him.

CHURCH LEADERS AGAIN DEMAND WITHDRAWAL . . . PARTY HEADS CONFER ON WILSON CANDIDACY . . . REPORT AMOS WILSON AND FRIEND IN CANADA . . . PRESSURE GROWS FOR WILSON DISAVOWAL OF SON'S LIFESTYLE . . . FAILURE TO DENOUNCE SON'S LIFESTYLE BRINGS SAG IN WILSON POLLS . . .

It was time, Willie decided, to release the family statement he had

---

been holding in reserve. Latt had been urging it for a week, Clayne was becoming impatient, Amos reluctantly agreed, fearing it would only make matters worse but grateful for the support.

Willie decided not to hold a press conference; it would only dignify the situation more than he wanted to, and would swiftly slip out of his control under the hostile questioning of the media's best and brightest. To say nothing of what it might do to his beleaguered son and his friend.

The statement dominated the news for two days until it was overtaken by the event he had sometimes imagined but had never really believed would occur.

"My son Latt, my daughter Clayne, and I," the statement said, "wish to state our unshaken love for, and complete support of, our son and brother, Amos Wilson.

"We do so without either condemning or endorsing the private life which, we must emphasize, is *his* private life.

"We do not have the colossal arrogance which some have shown in commenting upon his private life. Nor could we possibly match the viciously intolerant opportunism with which many in the media and elsewhere have seized upon this episode as an excuse to demand my withdrawal from the presidential campaign.

"This is an attempt to smear me with a totally spurious 'guilt by association.' I am only guilty of a profound love for my son, and of a father's pride in his growing record of professional accomplishment.

"I will not be deflected from my determination to restore decency, stability and balance to American government and to American life. I will not withdraw nor will I in any way repudiate my dear son Amos. If his critics and mine possessed one-tenth his integrity, they would respect his determination to lead a quiet and productive life, and leave him alone. I say to them: you cannot use the miserable excuse of a spurious moral righteousness to drive me from the campaign, nor can you use a hypocritical claim of sexual superiority to attack one who asks only to be allowed to exercise his right to be left alone to pursue a constructive and worthwhile life."

"Them," said Aram Katanian, "is fightin' words, pardner. But I admire you for them, Willie."

"The roof may fall in," Bill Nagatani remarked, "but you've done what you had to do—for his sake, if perhaps not for yours."

"His sake is what I have to think about right now," Willie said grimly. "I can survive, whatever. I'm not so sure he can."

For the next two days the story continued to hold the noisy attention of front pages, editorials, columns, headline-writers and major news programs.

Mother, as usual, set the pace:

"The angry defiance with which Senator Wilson has defended the son whose lifestyle has so sadly shadowed his presidential campaign perhaps does him credit as a father but it does little to salvage his suddenly threatened run for the White House.

"Many of his major supporters are demanding that he withdraw from the race. ["Not many," Tim remarked in angry frustration. "*Some.* But how do you get habitual liars to tell the truth?"] That demand is now becoming a roar. His statement declared that he would not yield to the pressure. But how long can he defy it?"

During the brief interlude between the sensation's launching and its end, Willie traversed the country twice, made four major campaign speeches in states as far apart as California and North Carolina, and issued through campaign headquarters four major position papers on major foreign policy issues. He was met with a few hostile placards, an occasional shouted hostile question; but basically his crowds did not diminish, his support appeared to hold, the enthusiastic response continued strong. He smiled, waved, performed effectively as always. His heart and mind were dominated by worries known only to his children and the inner circle—where was Amos, what was he thinking, what was he doing, how was all this affecting him?

Amos did not choose to communicate and they did not know where to reach him.

Just as his father reached a point of frustration at which he was about to call the director of the FBI and ask for his assistance, Clayne received a telephone call at her home in Oregon and promptly called Willie as he was about to leave his hotel in Atlanta to make a major speech.

"Daddy," she said, her voice filled with a desperate concern that instantly chilled Willie's heart, "Amos just called me. He sounded awful."

"Where is he?" Willie demanded. "Did he tell you?"

"Still in Canada," she said, "but planning to come home—I think. He wanted to know if he and Joel could stay here. I said of course."

"When?"

"He didn't say. He seemed very"—her voice trembled on the edge of breaking—"very distracted. He said he wanted to 'get this thing taken care of, as soon as possible.' I don't know quite what he meant, but I'm scared, Daddy. He sounded so—so forlorn, somehow, and all alone. He said to tell you to stop worrying, 'we'll handle it.' He said to tell you how sorry they both are to be such a—such a 'burden' to you. He said he wanted to apologize to all of us for having—having"—she started to cry and barely got the words out—"messed up our lives so terribly."

"Oh, my poor son," he said with a crushing sorrow. "If he calls you again, tell him to please call me. I'm his friend too."

"I told him that already. He said you'd be hearing from him 'before long.'"

"Let me know the minute he calls or shows up. I'm afraid the two of them, being gentle souls, will work on each other and"—his voice broke—"and who knows?"

"I know," Clayne said in a desolate little voice. "I'm terrified."

Twenty minutes later one of the leading figures of American politics strode onto the stage in Atlanta to the wild applause and enthusiastic cries of his supporters. Lights flashed, cameras rolled, tapes began to turn. The inner circle, its members as troubled as he, agreed that it was one of his most effective performances. Never had he seemed more calm and more sure of himself. It seemed to them that he had successfully faced and overcome the major crisis of his campaign; though, being realists, they could not maintain this conviction for long.

Next day, inexorable, implacable, doing their jobs as the well-paid functionaries of a highly competent profession, the members of the media relayed their findings to an interested public:

———

AMOS WILSON AND FRIEND FOUND IN VANCOUVER. FLEE MEDIA.

And a photograph of them doing just that, running down a rain-swept street with newspapers over their heads, the picture taken from a balcony above so that they were foreshortened, giving a searing impression of two frightened little animals running from the pack, which is what they were.

"I wish he'd call me," Willie said, deeply worried. "He can handle the media all right. It isn't that difficult."

"He doesn't believe that, obviously," Latt said. "He's obviously scared to death of them."

"They can be frightening when the feeding frenzy is on," Tim said. "It's a game to them now. They won't give up until they've got him in front of the cameras and forced him to say something."

"If they can catch him," Latt agreed with wry amusement. "I think he figures anything he might say would damage Dad."

"It couldn't be any more damaging than this attempt to outrun them," Willie said with an annoyance he would regret bitterly later. "He's just making himself look ridiculous."

But it was obvious the situation was not going to change, at least for the moment:

WILSON SON AND FRIEND AGAIN DODGE MEDIA AS DEMAND FOR SENATOR'S WITHDRAWAL GROWS.

Followed next day by:

WILSON SON AND FRIEND REPORTED BACK IN STATES. MEDIA TRACKS THEM TO IDAHO HOTEL. WITHDRAWAL CLAMOR GROWS.

And the next day, tersely:

NO WORD FROM AMOS.

Followed eight hours later, with startling, sledgehammer impact, by word from Amos:

AMOS WILSON AND FRIEND FOUND DEAD IN APPAR-ENT SUICIDE PACT IN IDAHO MOTEL. AMOS NOTE CLAIMS MEDIA "HOUNDED US TO DEATH IN ATTEMPT TO DESTROY MY FATHER'S CANDIDACY." SENATOR IN SECLU-SION, SUSPENDS CAMPAIGN.

And a stunned silence and a hasty rethinking, too late, by many in the media, followed by the usual defensive regrouping and the suave, responsibility-shifting excuses:

"It's tragic," admitted the famous editor who spoke piously for them all on *60 Minutes* a week later, "but what could we do? We didn't have a choice, once the story became public. Our obligation, after all, is to the First Amendment ["which is in the Constitution," Tim conceded] and the people's right to know." ["Which, created by the media to justify their most egregious excesses, is not."]

Two days later at the ranch, where they were gathered to bury Amos, Willie looked up through what seemed infinite layers of blackness to see Latt standing before him with an opened letter in his hand. He was crying. Willie thought dully that he hadn't seen Latt cry in thirty years.

"What is it?" he asked wearily, and held out his hand.

"It just came," Latt said, giving it to him. "It must have been the last thing—" and could not go on.

"Dear Daddy," Amos wrote, reverting like Clayne to childhood locution in times of trouble, "by the time you get this, the major obstacle to your candidacy will no longer exist. Joel and I have talked it over and we believe we have no choice. I hope you will forgive us all the pain we have caused you and the family, and for whatever added pain our decision will bring you. Yet we feel we have no choice.

"I had thought, foolishly I now know, that I could lead my life quietly and honorably out of the public eye insofar as my personal problems were concerned. With Joel it had begun to seem possible that this might be so. But now the media have made it impossible, and have added the increased burden of attempting to use our basic hope, which was just to be left alone to be at peace with each other and with the world, as a means to attack you and, if possible, bring you down.

"It seems increasingly that this may occur. Neither of us ever wanted it to happen. We feel that the only solution that seems to make sense is to remove ourselves once and for all from your life so that you may achieve the final great service to the country that we, and many millions more, feel confident you can do.

"I want to thank you, Daddy, for being a wonderful father to me all the days of my life. You always loved me, understood me, never criticized or condemned, always supported and defended me. I'm afraid I have given you a very poor return for that love and support. Perhaps this final small sacrifice will repay you for all you have done, and free you from the burden I have unwittingly imposed upon you. We both hope you can forgive us, one last time.

"I love you, Daddy. May God give you the final triumph you deserve.

"Your loving son,

"Amos."

5 Far off a dog barked, closer at hand he heard the rhythmic murmur of a pump bringing water to the groves: sounds of his youth, endlessly repeated in this home place.

It had been a hot day, the heat gathering force in the cool hush of dawn, rising to its usual afternoon peak of near one hundred or a little over, then falling gently away into the cooling twilight and deep velvet silence of the Valley night. The old house was still, its occupants gone early and emotionally exhausted to bed. He supposed he was not the only one awake in these lonely after-midnight hours, but there was no indication. No human sound intruded.

Under six feet of good Valley earth his second son slept; endlessly around and around went his own mind, reliving, as it would many times in years to come, the quiet ceremony in which Amos had been laid to rest in the small family cemetery halfway up the slope of the bare brown foothill behind the house, created by Amos's great-grandfather when he buried his first wife soon after they had come as pioneers from New England to the Valley and founded what became, in time, Wilson Ranch.

It had been a simple ceremony, held in the fresh hour of morning, attended by immediate family and a handful of Washington and Valley friends. There had been no eulogy: neither he nor Latt was steady enough to give one, and they did not think the impersonal remarks of a local minister who had never really known Amos could contribute anything. He had offered Joel's parents the opportunity to have their son buried next to Amos if they so desired; they had been genuinely grateful but had their own family arrangements in faraway Pennsylvania. Amos, now as always, was essentially alone. More alone, Willie now knew, than he had ever realized as he watched, over the years, the stubborn courage of a gallant life.

The dog barked again, the pump murmured on, another repetition occurred. This was a conversation, silent, endless, pointless, nobody to listen, nobody to respond . . . but for now, he seemed powerless to turn it off:

Oh, my dear son, you shouldn't have, *you shouldn't have*. It just wasn't as bad as you, in your overly sensitive mind, obviously thought it was. Your situation wasn't the shock to people that it might have been in an earlier time, you didn't threaten my campaign except in minds that will never change on that particular subject. The fuss would have died down, I could have toughed it out, Latt could have toughed it out, you could have toughed—only you couldn't, could you? You weren't us. You were just gentle Amos, who only wanted to be left alone to quietly lead your private life, express publicly whatever was in you artistically, make a home with somebody you could trust, and not bother anybody . . . always so quiet, so decent, so friendly and so kind to the world . . . which, because of your father, was not willing to be kind to you.

It was my fault. You didn't do it, I did, just by being who I am. They *are* trying to destroy my candidacy and maybe, in killing you, they have succeeded. I don't know, yet. It's too soon. I don't know right now what I'll do, except grieve for you; and that I do, more bitterly than you could ever imagine. Because it was all so unnecessary. You panicked, and that was fatal, literally fatal. You could have faced them down, you didn't have to give them the satisfaction of dying, or even of running away. The minute you started to run, they knew they had you; but not even they, I think, thought that you would be so sensitive that it would end like this. They knew I was tough and they knew your brother was tough and they thought they could indulge their feeding frenzy and play their damnable games and you'd be tough too. But you weren't, were you? You weren't really suited for this horrible world we live in now, and so maybe you're better off being out of it. But I can't accept that, as I stand humbled in the face of the infinite bravery and generosity of your sacrifice.

I'll never cease to mourn you, my solemn, loving little boy. It was so unnecessary, such a terrible waste. . . . My dear son . . . you shouldn't have . . . *you shouldn't have* . . .

In the week-long hiatus from his campaign the conversation

echoed through his head in all his waking hours, whenever he had a quiet moment.

He said good-bye to Billy's family, left the ranch and returned to Washington with Anne and Tim, ignoring the clamoring media; proceeded grim-faced and tight-lipped to his offices on the Hill, refused all press calls and interviews, adamantly and successfully evaded reporters. Presently habit and political instinct began to reassert themselves. Simultaneously with his sad unanswerable colloquies with his son he began an unhappy inner battle with himself as he considered his political and personal options and tried to decide what to do.

From the expected sources he received the expected advice. Mother and the Conscience and all their think-alike-do-alikes of newsprint and television were virtually unanimous. Having gone so far and achieved so unexpected and devastating a result, they were trapped in their own irresponsibility and could neither admit fault nor reverse course now.

"Senator Wilson's predicament in the wake of his son Amos's death is tragically difficult," Mother averred. "For his own sake, and the country's, there seems logically only one fitting and viable solution, considering the enormous emotional burden he now carries, which can only adversely affect his judgment and his actions in the final stages of the campaign.

"He should withdraw.

"He can do so honorably and with the full support and sympathetic understanding of his countrymen. No one possessed of an ounce of human feeling and sympathy would begrudge him this, or expect him to do otherwise. . . ."

"We, like all decent and understanding Americans, can only sympathize deeply and sincerely with Senator Wilson in this dark night of the soul brought about by the tragic death of his son Amos," the Conscience agreed.

"Under emotional pressures such as few public men have experienced, and faced with the likelihood that these will make it extraordinarily difficult for him to handle the remainder of his campaign for the White House—or to adequately administer the government, were he to be elected—we can only do what a prudent regard for his own health and the welfare of the country dictate:

―――――

"We urge him to withdraw.

"He has fought a good campaign, ably and effectively stated his moderate, middle-of-the-road positions. They have not, perhaps, put him within closing distance of his White House goal, but they have been honorable and worthy of his long career. It is a campaign he need not be ashamed of, and one which he can point to with pride, should it now be coming to an end.

"We think in all conscience that this would be best for him and best for America. We hope he will not long delay in reaching the decision which in our estimation this tragic episode makes inevitable. . . ."

"They have it all decided for you, don't they?" Latt inquired dryly as he and Willie sat in their headquarters office with these and similar unctuous advisories from around the country spread out before them. "Miserable, pious, hypocritical bastards," he added bitterly. "Now you're 'moderate'—'middle-of-the-road'—and 'honorable'—and here's your hat, what's your hurry? Are you going to give them the satisfaction?"

Willie sighed deeply, staring out the window down the long parade of Pennsylvania Avenue, over the hurrying traffic to the distant White House, hidden in its trees.

"I don't know yet," he said finally. "Let me think."

"Certainly," Latt said. "But they aren't going to give you much time."

Nor did they. In the next five days it turned into a national drumbeat. Voices urging him to remain seemed few and far between; many of them, like Anna Hastings in the *Washington Inquirer,* were forceful and eloquent, but they were virtually drowned out in the well-organized clamor from the other side. Unity of view, loudly if not always truthfully proclaimed, began to have its effect. The citizenry, "always suckers for pressure," as Tim remarked with annoyance, began to respond. Polls, at first 62 percent in his favor, 34 percent against, reversed rapidly to 56 percent against, 40 percent in his favor.

He had said he wanted to think.

His opponents were giving him plenty to think about.

But, being Willie, it took something more than popular clamor to make him reconsider a goal he had worked so long and patiently to achieve.

6 Five days after Amos's death he called together the inner circle to ask their advice; not that it would be controlling, but he wanted their judgments to fortify his own in whatever his decision might be.

He knew he could not delay it much longer. So far, he had left his name in the primaries but had already canceled three major speeches and two trips, one to California and the other to Denver and the upper Northwest. Anguished appeals from his partisans all over the country were mounting in worry, desperation and number. It was imperative that he make a decision immediately and either get out or return to the campaign with renewed vigor and the enthusiasm he must show, whatever his private feelings. He owed it to himself and above all to the many thousands of campaign workers and millions of voters who had invested efforts, hopes and in many instances prayers in his cause.

With the exception of Anne, who had a case to try that morning before the Supreme Court—"but you know what I think, anyway"— they were all there: Latt, Tim, Bill Nagatani, Aram Katanian. He had managed very little sleep in the past six nights: his appetite was off— he looked tired and drawn—he felt as though he was walking around half-dead all the time—a heavy weight, almost physical, seemed to be wearing him down. All were excellent reasons to continue avoiding the media as long as he could, but not encouraging for his friends.

He really felt that this was the low point of his life. Their dismayed expressions as they entered his office, quickly concealed after the first moment of shock, made it clear they agreed with him. "Willie the Magnificent," as Tim had referred to him, ironically but with an affectionate admiration in a campus editorial long ago, obviously needed all the help they could give.

They took their seats soberly in a half-circle facing him across his cluttered desk piled high with letters, telegrams, newspapers. (NATION AWAITS WILSON DECISION. SUPPORTERS FEAR "DEFEAT BY DEFAULT" AS OTHERS CONTINUE DEMAND FOR WITH-DRAWAL.)

There was an uneasy silence for a moment, uncertain, heavy with sympathy. Latt broke it in his usual direct, no-nonsense manner.

"Dad wants us to help him decide what to do," he said. "You know the options. Bill?"

Nagatani drew in his breath sharply, a habit he had inherited from his parents and never quite been able to shake. It gave him an odd lit-tle aura of ancestral throwback for a second.

"I'd rather wait until we've discussed it a little," he said slowly. "Aram?"

"So had I," Katanian said.

"With all respects to your feelings, Willie," Tim said, "which you know I share, I think you should stay in and complete the run."

"So do I," Latt agreed, "and nobody knows better what you're going through because I'm going through it too. But I'd think a lot before I let the bastards win in this situation."

"I am thinking," Willie said with a sigh, and rubbed his face slowly in his cupped hands, a gesture that revealed how tired he was. "But it isn't only the bastards I have to worry about. There are millions of good people out there who are also involved. Withdrawing might let the bastards win, but it would free all those people to get behind someone more worthy of all the liking and support they've been pour-ing out on me."

"There's nobody more worthy," Nagatani said. "Let's don't have false modesty at this late date, Willie."

"Or self-dramatization, either," Aram said, a little apprehensive at his own temerity but encouraged when Willie flared up and sounded more like himself for a moment.

"I'm not 'self-dramatizing,' " he said sharply, "and don't say I am, Aram Katanian. I'm sincerely worried about these people. Where will they go?"

"There are several," Aram said, standing his ground and naming two other contenders, one from each party. "They'll find a home—and with all respect to you, Willie. I'm convinced you're the best and I'd feel that way even if I hadn't"—he smiled, softening his tone—"even if I hadn't been part of the tail of the Wilson kite for the past forty years. You're still the best. Maybe you've already proved that in your campaign to date, and maybe that's enough, under the circumstances."

"But there are so many things I want to do!" Willie exclaimed. "So many things. And the 'circumstances'—well, people expect their President to keep going under almost any circumstances. A son who couldn't"—he tried again—"a son who couldn't—a son who couldn't"—but had to stop, voice choked.

"I know, I know," Aram said, voice gentle. "It's a hell of a thing."

"It is," Latt said, also close to tears at the sight of his father so powerfully affected and so, uncharacteristically, giving way to his own emotions. "But maybe there's salvation in overcoming it and just going on. It won't be easy, but they expect it of you and they'll admire you for it. You'll have an enormous sympathy vote, to begin with—"

"I'm not going to use Amos that way!" Willie interrupted harshly. "And don't you *ever* treat your brother with such contempt!"

"It isn't contempt!" Latt protested. "It isn't contempt! I loved my brother, you know that! I loved my brother!"

And the tears did come, and for a moment father and son were in their world of grief apart, in a place where the others could not follow. Tim stared determinedly out the window, Aram at the desk, Bill at the cheerful signed photographs of Willie with various Presidents that adorned the wall.

Presently the moment passed. Willie spoke in a more normal voice.

"I'm sorry," he said to Latt. "I was wrong to say that. I know how you feel. And you know how I feel. And you're right, we have to judge this as calmly and objectively as we can. Amos is at the ranch and we're here, and this is our responsibility now. Timmy, why do you think I should stay with this?"

"Because you do owe them a great deal," Tim said soberly. "Many of your supporters have been with you since you first came to the House. They stayed with you when you went to the Senate. They've always wanted you to run for President because they genuinely admire and respect you and think you'd be a great one. And many of them have already put a great deal of time, effort and money into this, many for no particular material reward but just because they believe in you. That means something."

"Public belief?" Willie repeated gravely. "Yes, it does. You'll never any of you know how much—or Latt does, probably, because he seems to be acquiring a good bit of it himself—"

"It's the name," Latt said more lightly, giving his father an affectionate look. "Without that I'd be nothing, zilch, nada. *You* know that, Daddy."

"I don't either," Willie said firmly. "Why do you think you're beginning to get respect from the *Washington Post* and the *New York Times?*"

"*Ha!*" Latt said, and said no more of his sentiments on that subject: his tone sufficed. "So," he said, "two more countries to be heard from. Bill?"

"It's hard for me to separate Willie now from Willie then," Nagatani confessed. "Back in the days when Tim was editor of the *Daily*—and when I succeeded him as editor of the *Daily*—and when we had to comment, it seemed like every day, on this glamorous star from the Valley who dominated our campus world and bedazzled our campus ladies—"

"Only Donna," Willie said. "Only Donna."

"That was enough," Bill said with a smile. "Quite a star there, too. Anyway, in those days Willie Wilson was a real hero to us all. And then he went on—and on—and on. Congressman, Senator, major legislator, leader in domestic and foreign issues, major figure—and husband, father, paterfamilias—what a character! But always, in my mind, the same genuine human being I knew on campus a long, long time ago. And that human figure I would not want to submit to the further punishment of this campaign, after all he has been through in the past week. I know it would mean the sacrifice of a great ambition—high hopes—big dreams—but I think he's earned the right to take it easy now. I say you have the excuse, Willie—not 'excuse,'" he added quickly as Willie shifted uneasily in his chair, "but perfectly justifiable and understandable necessity—to withdraw and let the other contenders tear each other to pieces. You're still in the Senate, you'll have that platform probably as long as you want it, and nobody will think less of you for bowing to an extraordinarily bad piece of luck and coming back here to resume duties you have so admirably performed in the past."

He looked around and smiled. "Which is enough speech for little Bill Nagatani from Fresno, California. Aram?"

Aram Katanian thought for a moment, leaned forward earnestly.

"Little Aram Katanian from Fresno, California," he said, "will not be so verbose as my colleague, here. Is this the descendant of the Inscrutable East? Certainly scrutable this time, I'd say; and, I must say, I couldn't agree with him more. You have a fine record up to this point, Willie, and you'll have a fine record for years to come. You've run a good campaign, a fine campaign, and we who have helped you will always be able to take pride in it and feel that we labored in a good cause. But, as Bill says, there's a limit to what you should be expected to take as a human being; and nobody I can remember has taken a blow equal to this in the midst of a campaign.

"I know your ultimate aim has always been the White House, and I know your basic motivation has always been based on the highest concepts of civic duty and national good. God knows, a lot will be lost if you don't get there. But there is a limit on the price you should have to pay; and also, Willie"—his tone, always reasonable, became grave, and ready for whatever reaction his words might provoke—"there are others—there are always others—and some of them would do a good job, too. Some of them are quite capable of carrying the burden—and one of them will. I know you're not so naive or so egotistical as to believe in the myth of the indispensable man. One of the great strengths of the system is that it produces so many who are capable; and as long as it allows one of them to win, the republic will be in reasonably good shape. One of them will emerge the victor and nine times out of ten he will do an often passable, sometimes excellent, once in a while superb, job. If the tenth one we get is a jerk, well, the country will survive him and go on.

"I have no doubt where Willie Wilson would fit in—the good-to-brilliant, in my estimation. But my vote now is for withdrawal. You aren't that ancient, you can try again next time if you want to. But for now, you're under such a burden that it's bound to affect you, sometimes in ways you probably won't even be conscious of. No one will think less of you if you quit—better for you, maybe better for the country, if you do . . . At least," he concluded, somewhat self-consciously, "that's what *I* think. . . ."

They were silent for a while after he finished. Outside in the hall they could hear the morning sounds of a Senate office building hitting workday stride, messengers rattling up and down with their little carts filled with reference books and official reports, Senators cheerfully greeting one another, staff members chatting amicably as they passed; and an extra little bustle which, to their experienced ears, signified that the media had tracked them down and were waiting, with all exits covered, to clamor for information and comments when they emerged.

"I still vote to continue," Tim said finally. "You owe it to the country. And the country needs you. I say, stay in."

"I agree," Latt said. "It sounds corny and pretentious, but it's true. You have too much to offer to be driven out by—by—" He searched for the words, finally decided on "a private sorrow." His voice became quiet as he invoked his brother and repeated from Aram the word he knew would weigh most heavily with his father. "Amos would want you to, Daddy. He wouldn't want you to quit."

Again they were silent, as the morning sounds continued pleasantly outside in the corridor, and in the room Willie turned his chair, back to them, to stare out the window.

Finally, after what seemed to them many minutes but were probably only two or three, he swung back with a sudden decisiveness they were delighted to see, though two of them knew inevitably he would disappoint them.

"Two for, two against," he observed. "And Willie in the middle. Now," he asked with a playful note that pleased them because he sounded like himself, "*what* do you think I'm going to do? Well, I'll tell you." He leaned back and surveyed them thoughtfully one by one as they leaned forward, intent.

"I don't want to be didactic or bombastic or overly eloquent, so I'll try to keep it simple. I am not a quitter, and, as Latt so eloquently puts it, I don't want to give the bastards the satisfaction of driving me out." Latt and Tim looked pleased; he went on, and their expressions turned to doubt again. "At the same time, the family and I have received a terrible blow and I wouldn't be human if it didn't affect me profoundly. I walk around outwardly the same—minus," he noted wryly, "a good many hours of sleep and a few pounds of weight—but inside, as you can imagine, it isn't the same." He sighed and repeated, "It isn't the same. . . . I won't burden you with my grief over my son, and I thank God the other one is still at my side and strong and active in my cause—but it hurts. It hurts like hell and I know it always will, somewhere inside, though I know I'll manage quite well regardless, as I think people do manage with a deep sadness. Usually they manage to keep going and I will too, there's no doubt in my mind about that. So it comes down to: how long will it take me to regain my flying speed, and how much should I subordinate my life at the moment to a grief that will, in time, grow gentler and more endurable? And how quick should I be to take advantage of an excuse—a good one, but perhaps still just an excuse, remembering how many people in this world have blows of sorrow and pick themselves up and keep going. . . .

"It will be hard"—his voice grew stronger—"but I think I shall stay in. I thank you for your advice, Bill and Aram, which is heartfelt and I know sincerely concerned for me; but I don't think I can let my friends all over the country down. I really think I do have millions of them, in spite of my opponents' attempts to convince the world otherwise; and we're at a point right now where I still think I have a reasonable chance, and where, if I can manage the extra effort and stay with it, I just may get the nomination, and after that—? Well, who knows? But at least I will have given it my best shot and stayed the course. And that's the record I'd like to leave, and maybe the Lord will reward me for it and maybe He won't, but at least people will know that Willie Wilson didn't quit. He never has and I hope never will."

He stood. They stood. Solemnly they shook his hand, returning his pressure with concern and affection.

"No word to the boys and girls outside, of course," he said, "and no hint of my decision. I know I don't have to tell you that. Latt, tell them I'll hold a press conference in the Caucus Room at three P.M."

"Washington, May 3," the wire services wrote. "Odds grew today that Senator Richard Emmett Wilson will remain in the race for President despite the tragic death of his son Amos, who committed suicide five days ago after his gay lifestyle was exposed.

"An obviously relieved Rep. Latt Wilson, the Senator's older son and his campaign chairman, told reporters that the Senator will hold a news conference at 3 P.M. today at which 'he will tell you all about his plans.'

"Rep. Wilson refused to answer questions about his father's intentions, but it was clear that he approved of his father's decision. It has been known that the Congressman was among those in the Senator's inner circle of campaign advisers who have been urging him to continue in the race. . . ."

Five minutes after the "inner circle" had moved off down the corridor, followed by an eager and highly vocal press corps demanding answers to questions that were ignored, Anne slipped into his office. One glance and his welcoming smile turned instantly to concern. He went to the door, told his staff to hold all calls, turned back, gave her a kiss, held her at arm's length and studied her face with an astute and loving eye.

He realized that she was actually pale with agitation. He felt apprehension as heavy as that of a week ago. He thought, Dear God, what now?

"Sit down," he directed. "What's the matter?"

"They brought me this a few minutes ago at the Court," she said. She held out a letter, much as Latt had five days ago. The action, so reminiscent, increased his tension. "Fortunately I had a couple of colleagues with me who could take over. I begged the Court's indulgence and started out. On the way, the bailiff handed me this." She opened her purse, took out a standard phone-message form. "Read this with the letter. They obviously go together."

"You received a call from: *Eye*," the message said. "At: *10:21* A.M. Please call at: *your early convenience*."

The letter was handwritten in a calligraphy he had come to know well over the years of complaints, accusations, alternating supplications and threats. The "David" scrawled unevenly at the bottom confirmed it. Going on for fifteen years now, and the sick obsession was not diminished.

"Dear Anne: Your famous husband obviously thinks he can do any damned thing and get away with it. What they did to his boy they can do to you. I know you won't kill yourself, you're too much of a bitch to do that, but what you've done to me can sure as hell destroy his campaign if I tell the media about it. Nothing would give me more pleasure. They've got me all fired up to do it, and I think I will.

"After that I'll tend to you. I've been patient for years. Reckoning is long overdue. Don't laugh your superior laugh. This time I mean it. You won't hear from me again. By letter, that is.

"Love, dear Annie, from your dear little David."

He finished reading, tossed it on his desk atop all the other communications he had received in recent hours. This one was as special as its writer had intended, but how significant was it, really?

"Standard psychopath's bluff?" he mused (of the sort he had received routinely, as most of them did, throughout his public life). "Or something we should pay attention to?"

She shivered.

"He's never been this crude or openly threatening before," she said. "Let's call *Eye* and find out. They've obviously got him highly agitated."

"They're fools," he said. "They don't know what they're dealing with."

He picked up the phone, asked his secretary to get the editor but not say who was calling. He took Annie's hand and held it while they waited. It was trembling, and very cold.

"You believe him, don't you?" he asked gently. "He really has you frightened this time."

"Petrified," she admitted. "I think this may finally be it."

"I wish I could understand why," he remarked, frustrated. Her expression for a moment was grimly amused.

"Who knows? I've tried to understand it for years, without success. One can't understand everything rationally in this world. It's just something in his mind, and that's all we're ever going to know. I suppose it all began with love. Lots of weird things do."

The phone rang, he picked it up. The editor's secretary was starchy: she would have to know who was calling, or—

"The caller is Anne Greeley," he said coldly. There was a flurry of voices; the editor came on.

"Yes?" he said cautiously. Anne replied, Willie on the extension but silent. "Ah, Miss Greeley," the editor said. "Mrs. Wilson. How are you?"

"I'm fine," Anne said in her best lawyer's voice, polite, even, unwelcoming, empty. "What can I do for you?"

"You can answer some questions we have, arising out of a conversation we've just had with your husband," the editor said, and corrected himself elaborately. "Your *ex*-husband. Mr. David Greeley."

" 'Ex' a long time ago," she observed in the same cold, uncommunicative tone. "What have you been hearing from Mr. Greeley?"

"He is unhappy with you."

"Oh?"

"Quite, I gather," the editor said. His tone indicated some wonder at the depth of Mr. Greeley's feelings. "Quite angry, quite embittered, in fact."

"Yes," she said. "I have heard from him. He indicates that you looked him up and deliberately inflamed an already unbalanced mind."

"Mrs. Wilson!" the editor exclaimed, shocked and aggrieved. "We would never be so unethical and so irresponsible as to—"

"If there are unpleasant consequences of this," Anne said flatly, "we will hold you responsible."

"I am sure you will," the editor said smoothly. "But about Mr. Greeley. He says he is prepared to tell us, and I quote, 'everything.' Whatever that means."

"I'm sure I have no idea."

"I gathered from his remarks that it perhaps involved your present husband, the Senator."

"He is my husband, yes," Anne said, and could not resist: "At least you have that factually correct."

"Mrs. Wilson," the editor said sharply. "I did not call to engage in verbal fencing with you—"

"Then why did you call?" she asked with equal sharpness. "I am supposed to be in the Supreme Court at this very moment, arguing a case for a client. Yet here I am, wasting time on you. Why?"

"I think it would behoove you to speak with a little more respect," the editor said. "You will remember that it was *Eye* that broke the sordid story of the Senator's son, thereby almost terminating the Senator's campaign, though I understand now that he has decided to go on with it—"

"I sincerely hope so," she said. "It would be a great loss if such a qualified candidate were hounded from office by the likes of *Eye.*"

"We were not alone," the editor said smugly.

"And more shame to *all of you,*" Anne said.

"None of us would be sorry to see the Senator depart the presidential scene," the editor said. "We may all yet succeed in encouraging him to do so. We shall have to see what happens if your lack of cooperation forces us to reveal the equally sordid story of your affair with the Senator, prior to your marriage and while his first wife was dying. Coming on top of the scandal about his son, it will certainly give the public a whole new picture of one who used to pretend to be a paragon of moral virtue."

"A distinction to which you have never had to aspire," Anne observed. "Luckily for you."

"Do you deny you had an affair?"

"I did not date the Senator until after my divorce," Anne said. "Other than that, I have no comment to make on any of your false and ridiculous allegations about anything. Now, if you will excuse me, I must get back to the Court—"

"Mrs. Wilson!" the editor said sharply. "Your ex-husband, Mr. David Greeley, has furnished us with many details of your behavior both before and after your divorce. Mr. David Greeley has the same interest we have in bringing to the public full information about the behavior of a man who might possibly become President of the United States. He is as dedicated as we are to the public's right to know. Neither he nor we will be deterred in the performance of that noble duty."

"You 'noble'?" Anne said. "*Eye* 'noble'? There's twisted language for a twisted time, I'm afraid. A scummy, sleazebag magazine, as I see it, run by scummy, sleazebag people. Yet I suppose you will go home to wife and kiddies tonight genuinely convinced that you're a good and decent human being. By such grand self-delusions is society often held together. Now if you will excuse me—"

"Mrs. *Wilson!*"

"If you will excuse me!"

"Well," Willie said, amused, the crash of her banged-down receiver still ringing in his ears. "I didn't know my little girl had it in her."

"I'm not sure I do," she said soberly, as the flush of righteous battle faded from her cheeks and the exhilaration of it left her, to be replaced by more characteristic caution. "I think we had better consider again, very carefully, what you should do. These people aren't through with you yet, obviously, or with me either. They can do great damage to both of us. I don't worry about me, but my kids—and your kids—and your campaign—" She stopped suddenly and looked as though about to cry. "Oh, Willie, what a miserable world. What a miserable world!"

"I know," he said soothingly, rising and taking her in his arms. "I know. But somebody has to keep trying to make it better. We can't all just give up."

"What did you tell them when your meeting broke up?"

"I didn't tell them anything. I had Latt tell them that I'd hold a press conference at three—"

"To withdraw?"

"I don't want to withdraw!" he said sharply.

"I know," she said, loosening his arms gently, repairing her makeup, getting ready to go back to the Court and the public stage. "I don't want you to. But maybe we should talk about it again very seriously, when we have a little more time."

"There isn't time," he said stubbornly.

"Make some," she said.

WILSON SPECULATION SUDDENLY REVIVED.

"Washington, May 4 Senator Richard Emmett Wilson today abruptly canceled a press conference at which he was expected to announce his intention to stay in the presidential race. He rescheduled it for 10 A.M. tomorrow.

"Speculation immediately arose that the abrupt change of plans might indicate a change of heart.

"No explanation was given by his son, Rep. Latt Wilson, chairman of his campaign. But it was obvious to reporters that Congressman

Wilson was puzzled and upset by his father's surprising change of plan. He refused to speculate whether this meant a change in the Senator's presumed decision to remain a candidate. . . ."

He arrived home shortly after 7 P.M., having spent most of his working day answering his mail. He had asked his staff to keep a running count: it gave him roughly 60–40 in favor of continued candidacy. He was feeling pleased with this as he swung into the driveway of the rambling old house in Bethesda where he had brought Donna, helped raise their kids, seen Donna die and, presently, brought Anne.

He opened the door and called out, "Hi! I'm home!"

She came forward out of the dimly lighted living room and he knew instantly that something was terribly wrong. She looked devastated, was crying and, as he sensed immediately, so palpably frightened that it formed almost a physical miasma around her.

"Annie!" he exclaimed. *"What is it?"*

"It's T-Rex," she said. "He's—he's—"

"Did he die?" he asked, voice filled with concern for the amiable, loving Labrador who had galloped through their recent years knocking things over and smothering humans with his slobbering affections. "Is he all right?"

"He's dead," she said in a desolate voice.

"Well, he *was* ten," he said reasonably. "That's not bad for a Lab—"

"He was murdered," she said bleakly. "He was waiting for us on the porch. David cut his throat."

"No," he said, horrified.

"Oh, yes," she said. "I almost brought my work home this afternoon, in which case I too—" Her eyes widened; she uttered again her anguished cry in his office: "Oh, Willie! What a miserable world we live in. What a miserable world! . . ."

"How do you know it was David?" he asked, still desperately trying to find a rationale where he knew there was none. "Did he leave a note?"

"In your chair."

"I can't believe this," he said a couple of minutes later. "I can't believe this."

"You thought I was kidding," David had written in an obviously agitated hand. "This is the first installment. I've had it."

For perhaps five minutes Willie sat in his chair while the television, unnoticed, babbled on about his shifted press conference, renewed speculation about what he might do, what he might not do, on and on and on in the news anchor's most profound and knowing tones.

Finally he spoke.

"I've had it too," he said, voice infinitely tired and defeated. "This is it. No more. No more melodrama, no more pain. Nothing more to disturb, and perhaps kill, members of my family. I'm out of it. They've won. Nothing more. I'm through."

"But you can't just—" she began.

"Oh, yes, I can," he said; and said again, quietly, "No more. Nothing again. No more."

7

His press conference next morning played to an overflow audience in the old Senate Caucus Room, site of so many historic events in the nation's history. Every seat was occupied, standees lined the walls, a long queue waited in the corridor outside in the vain hope that some of the overflow might yet get in. The press tables were filled hip to hip and elbow to elbow, microphones were live, television cameras ready. Still photographers pushed and shoved one another raucously for advantage. An excited babble rose. His supporters were there to encourage, his opponents, they hoped, to gloat. Capitol police moved nervously among the crowd, fearful they might be called upon to quell disturbance.

When he entered from his office down the long corridor to the left, pandemonium briefly occurred. His supporters applauded and shouted wildly, his derogators booed and hissed. The police shouted warnings, warnings were ignored. A small cordon escorted him and his family. They moved forward in a glare of floodlights, strobe lights, the angry fuss of photographers exchanging courtesies. In three minutes, though to them it seemed like eight or ten, they reached the chairs and lectern set up on the dais at the end of the room. They seated themselves and looked out upon the crowd, in which they were able to spot Nagatani and Katanian, and Tim, waving encouragingly from a press table.

Willie was in the center, Anne to his right, Latt at his left. They waited impassively while the crowd settled down and the reporters examined him intently.

When all that remained was a buzzing of whispers and private comments, Latt stepped to the podium.

"Ladies and gentlemen," he said without embellishment, "Senator Wilson."

Willie gave Anne's hand a squeeze, smiled at his son, stepped forward. Applause and boos again surged up. He smiled and held up his hands requesting quiet, which provoked even more vigorous response from both sides. He began to speak in an untroubled, steady voice. His advisers and his wife felt that he had come to terms with it. He appeared to become more relaxed as he spoke, and so did they.

"Ladies and gentlemen," he said, "thank you for coming. Many of you were here when I began this campaign. It is good to have you here when I"—he paused for a second, the room became instantly quiet, a little gleam of humor came into his eyes—"when I tell you now what I am going to do."

There was a groan from his supporters, who had thought they were going to be told immediately, a wave of subdued but sarcastic laughter from his enemies.

"God damn it," somebody murmured under his or her voice at the press tables, "stop playing cutesy and get on with it." But he had his own agenda and did not intend to be hurried.

"I began this campaign," he said, "convinced that I had a reasonable chance to secure the nomination of my party and, perhaps, go on to win the approval of a majority of my countrymen and so become their President.

"I still," he said, pleasantly but firmly, "have that conviction. Nothing that has occurred in the campaign has convinced me that I should abandon that belief. My record in the primaries is good, I am favored to win several of those remaining, the goal still seems achievable . . . if I remain in the race."

Again the groans, the laughter, the impatience from the media, who only wanted their news flash, and then up and out of there to inform whoever in the world had not already seen it on television.

"There have been, as you know"—his voice became grave and, in deference to his tragedy and with a reasonable respect even from his opponents, silence ensued—"certain personal aspects of my campaign which I shall not go into here."

" 'Aspects'?" somebody whispered at the press tables. "I thought there was only one, his gay kid."

"Probably just a slip," somebody else rejoined.

"Willie doesn't make slips," a third contributed.

"Shhhh," whispered somebody else.

"Suffice it to say," he went on, "that I have had to take all this into account. Yet I do not think that anything has changed the essential message I have hoped to bring to the American people."

"Oh, oh!" somebody whispered. "Here we go. Speech! Speech!"

"Campaign Speech 101-A," somebody else agreed.

"Either preparatory or farewell," another offered.

"You guess," still another suggested.

"*Shhhhh!*" admonished yet another.

"I have suggested to the American people," he continued, aware of the private interplay at the press tables that usually accompanies the public moments of public men, but ignoring it as public men learn to do, "that there is a place in this land for honesty, for integrity, for an approach to governing that is neither right nor left but somewhere in the middle.

"A rational, caring, compassionate middle; an imaginative, far-seeing, productive middle; a middle where all decent citizens can find a common ground and solve their differences with one another creatively and responsibly, as the heirs of our great Founding Fathers should be able to do if they are true to that awesome example. This I have advocated, this I do advocate and this I will continue to advocate—"

"Oh, oh!" somebody whispered. "He's in."

"—in whatever capacity I may find myself in the days and years ahead."

"Oh, oh, yourself," a colleague commented with a chuckle. "He's out."

He paused for a moment, looked out over the crowd, caught Aram's eye, Bill's, Tim's. He smiled briefly at them and at the crowd that now hung silent on his words.

"I have asked myself in these recent days how I might best push forward to achieve this goal. I am aware that many millions have already expressed their faith in me. Many, I hope, will continue to do so. This is a tremendous honor and a heavy burden. Many millions more"—his smile broadened for a moment—"have made it clear that they would much prefer me to lay down the honor and reject the burden. To the former I say: I will never abandon the basic belief on which I have based this campaign, the belief that has always inspired me throughout my public life. To the latter I say: I will *never* abandon that belief, which is central to my approach to American government."

There was a burst of approval from his supporters, an abrupt renewal of hostile feeling from his opponents.

"But," he said, and the room grew absolutely still again as something in his tone signaled that he was nearing his conclusion, "there are factors which I, as father and husband, must take into account." His voice became very grave. "They weigh very heavily with me. To them I must submit the final decision. The conclusion to be drawn from them is inescapable.

"I shall withdraw from this campaign and cease to seek the presidency."

There was a genuine, long-drawn-out groan from his supporters, a burst of wild applause from his opponents.

"I shall return to the Senate immediately and resume my duties there as strongly and actively as I know how. I will continue to do so as long as my fellow Californians keep me here.

"My principles"—he concluded as the television cameras swung from his earnest face to the rapidly dissolving crowd and back again, and members of the print media dashed out in what was soon to become an antiquated, outdated routine to file their stories. "My principles remain unchanged. My vigorous advocacy of them remains unchanged.

"Willie Wilson is back at the old stand, doing business.

"I have not been silenced, nor will I be.

"God bless you all, and God bless America."

"We must confess," Mother confessed, "that Senator Wilson's abandonment of his presidential campaign was done with dispatch, decisiveness and dignity. There may be some who will criticize him for permitting personal tragedy (tragedies? He did not make clear) to influence him unduly, some who regard this as weakness. We prefer to think it not weakness, but strength. We prefer to think that this was only one of many factors that prompted a decision that can only redound to his credit and to the best interests of America.

"Now the presidential picture is much clearer. The battle between right and left, conservatism and liberalism, can be decided free from the sometimes confusing, always disturbing, always difficult appeals of moderation and middle-of-the-road.

"The country needs clear-cut decisions on clear-cut propositions.

"These the withdrawal of Senator Wilson now makes possible. . . ."

"Senator Wilson from the first has been a divisive element in the presidential race," the Conscience declared. "Old-fashioned principles of moderation, balance, middle-of-the-road 'fairness' and 'common sense' have less place in present-day American politics, we suspect, than clear-cut stands on clear-cut issues. Fuzzy ideas offered as solutions for major problems do more to confuse than enlighten, more to thwart progressive objectives than achieve them.

"There will be some who will charge him with personal weakness for allowing personal problems to terminate his campaign for a prize he has always wanted. Such an argument could be made. But the overriding fact is: he is out, and for that citizens who believe in a truly progressive approach to our national agenda must be genuinely thankful.

"His candidacy raised the specter of an American President too moderate, too middle-of-the-road, perhaps too tolerant of too many divergent views—too 'balanced,' to use one of the Senator's favorite words, to accomplish anything.

"A President who wants to be 'fair' to everybody runs the risk of becoming mush. Tolerance of opposing views can often lead to paralysis. This is not what our hectic times demand. This is not what we believe to be best for America. . . ."

Out in California, an enterprising staffer on San Francisco's painful excuse for a big-city newspaper had the bright idea of calling Professor Suratt at the University.

Renny sniffed.

"I told him when we had our debate that his presidential campaign would be a futile effort foredoomed to failure. And so it was. But he had to find out. He had to do it his way. That's our Willie. He was always like that, even in our fraternity house. I didn't expect him to change."

*　　　　*　　　　*

Nor would he, he thought grimly next day when he saw Renny quoted prominently in Mother and the Conscience, and heard his words repeated ad nauseam in television commentaries, talk shows, news programs. Not for you, Renny, and not for the big guns of the media, and not for the arrogant proprietors of Mother or the arrogant Ditzy Doyenne of the Conscience, or the holy trinity of the networks or the jabberwocks of the radio talk shows.

Much remained to be done before he could resume the familiar tenor of his Senate ways.

He went back to the floor that afternoon, was greeted with many cordial handshakes and slaps on the back. He had managed to check in during every break he got throughout the campaign, but everybody seemed to want to make a big thing of it when he returned full-time; many because they were genuinely glad to see him back and supported his decision, others because they were delighted to have him out of the race—and supported his decision.

"The Senator from California is recognized," said Randolph Merrill of Virginia, in the chair; and everything was as before.

There ensued a month of hard work, dismantling the campaign machinery and struggling in his own mind, still not easily, with all the aspects, temporary and lasting, of his decision to withdraw.

On one level, the level of Amos and the very real threat to Anne, he had no doubts. He turned David's two handwritten notes over to the police and the FBI. In due course this brought his arrest and internment, which the judge indicated might well be permanent. In the ponderous way of American justice, however, David had been allowed to roam free for the better part of two months before he was taken into custody, during which time Willie knew he could have done major, possibly fatal damage to Anne; so that he did not regret having given up his campaign for her, or the guard that was put on the house, or the protective surveillance to which they were both subjected when they left it. It had been an extraordinarily tense and frightening time, and he could easily envisage what it would have been were he still out campaigning with both himself and Anne exposed to sudden insane attack that not even the most rigorous protections could prevent.

When the frightening time was over, and David safely consigned to

St. Elizabeth's mental hospital in the District, he and the family could relax. Anne in particular did, at ease and happier than he had ever seen her.

Amos, of course, would not go away, a poignant familiar who was with his father at some point in every hour of every day. Slowly the pain began to ease, little by little life returned to balance; but it would be a long time, if ever, before he could contemplate what had happened without a sudden desolate sense of the world dropping away beneath his feet.

He knew from experience that the cliché was right: when you lost a loved one, it took just about a year to get over it; and some deaths you never really got over, just pushed them back into a special inner place of mourning so that life could go on. Amos and the manner of his going would never leave him, he knew that; but he knew that in time he would come to terms with it. He thanked God that he had been able to realize the devastating blow it was to him, and to recognize that it might indeed adversely affect his campaign and his future public life. Thank God he had recognized instantly that if it were compounded by something happening to Anne almost within the week, the two together would cripple him permanently, ruin his campaign and throw the remainder of his life completely off-balance.

They managed to keep the conclusion of what Anne called "the David business" concealed from the media, even though *Eye* and several of its big brothers kept worrying the subject and trying to find out from time to time. Consequently there were a good many snide comments in various quarters about his withdrawal: his reason wasn't really valid, his decision simply showed a weakness of courage and character that would have been bad for the country anyway. Or, his reason perhaps was valid but it gave him an ideal excuse to abandon a campaign that was faltering and would have ended in humiliating defeat anyway.

He made no attempt to answer these. He couldn't catch up with them, he would only make himself look defensive and foolish, and what was the point? It was obvious from the outpouring of sympathy he received that ordinary citizens free from inside-the-Beltway disease gave him credence for his grief and for his courage in handling it the way he did. Many expressed the earnest hope that he would run again in four years' time.

He composed a statement, which his office sent out to all who wrote or called. Even then he remained the astute politician: he closed no doors, though he was convinced in his own mind that he had made his run and would never make another:

"I want to thank you most sincerely for your kind expression of sympathy and support. I appreciate and highly value your understanding now and your encouragement for the future. I have returned to my Senate duties and I shall dedicate all my energies to serving my state and America in whatever capacity Providence decrees. In this, your friendship, good wishes and support will be an inestimable source of strength."

And bit by bit, as rapidly as it could be done, the campaign machinery came down. Advertising plans, scheduled speeches, scheduled trips, were canceled. Warm letters of thanks went out over his signature to all his many hosts and many workers across the country. Headquarters were closed, the lease canceled. Final records of bills and expenditures were consolidated and handed to his finance chairman for settlement. (Overall cost of the campaign, that hardworking gentleman estimated, had been approximately $6,723,000, which, in the way of campaign costs, would be settled sometime, somewhere, somehow by somebody, hopefully before the erstwhile candidate passed entirely from the mortal scene. Some such burdens stayed on the books for decades, though he like all campaigners hoped that wouldn't be the case with him. To work out an eventual cents-on-the-dollar liquidation was what finance committees were for, after the drums and bugles fell silent.)

Staff were dismissed with personal letters of thanks and commendation from the candidate, accompanied by two weeks' pay and the promise of whatever help could be given in finding new employment.

Bill Nagatani and Aram Katanian went home to Fresno, Latt went home to Ti-Anna and the Hill. Tim, who had managed to continue his column throughout, went back to Anna and the *Inquirer,* determined to take on his colleagues and their wayward ways with a renewed zeal. And life resumed its customary rounds and went on.

He was still, he told himself—a bit defiantly now but it was true—a relatively young man. With luck, he had perhaps two decades. He was still a public man and intended to remain one. There was still much to do; still a lot of life to be lived.

Things didn't stop. The wave rolled on, returning to old channels, bringing new challenges.

Much was still expected of Willie Wilson.

By his family.

By his friends.

And above all, by himself.

6

The Very Occasional Newsletter, Vol. 3

1

Ten years later, again prompted by Willie, "who seems to feel we ought to keep at least minimal contact with our misspent youths and the youths we misspent them with," Johnny Herbert has gathered the information and prepared the final *Very Occasional Newsletter.* This is the third of the very sporadic reports he and Willie began shortly after the end of World War II, when everyone wanted to find out what had happened to them all in the great conflict.

Reporting at that time, Johnny had noted that five, including himself, had been excused from service for physical or psychological reasons. The rest had gone to war. Four had not returned—amiable, easygoing Buff Richardson, supremely ambitious Bob Godwin, steady, hardworking Ray Baker, quiet little unobtrusive Hank Moore.

All, distinct individuals.

All, worthwhile citizens.

All, full of promise for themselves and their individual worlds.

And all wasted.

Even now, more than five decades later, it is still possible at times to feel a sudden flash of anger and resentment at the terrible waste of their lives and of so many millions of others in the global cataclysm so ruthlessly precipitated by the mad genius in Berlin. He is gone, too, leaving a world permanently dislodged from all its old, relative stabilities. The many bitter harvests of his vast dislocations of nations and peoples continue to have their reverberations and repercussions down the unhappy century whose sadly twisted course he more than any other man determined.

But resentment and regret, while permanent, are now buried deep beneath the hurrying realities of the workaday world. Many other concerns weigh upon those members of the house who, as Johnny writes, "are moving now into our seventies but still alive and kicking." Alive and kicking, he wryly adds, "even though Mother Nature is not always as kind as she used to be with once-minor aches and pains that now too easily become major, irritating handicaps."

He is pleased to report, however, that the "alive and kicking" are also "still actively contributing." He says he thinks this "is a pretty good record for the old house, and we all ought to be proud of it."

"The major one, of course," he begins the roster, "and was there ever a time in our mutual history when he wasn't the major one?—is our ever-lovin', ineffable Willie, who still, in his seventies, occupies the Senate seat from which many have tried to dislodge him, but which he still hangs on to with all the tenacity, hard work and skill we remember from his days on campus."

(Johnny is too kind to mention—and this isn't the proper place to do it, anyway—that Willie now faces the strongest challenge he has ever faced, and from a source he had always expected might someday confront him. Congresswoman Francine Magruder Haggerty, as much a fixture in her House seat from the Bay Area as Willie has been in his Senate seat, has finally decided to take him on. His deep personal friendship with Hack Haggerty's long-since-divorced first wife continues unabated, but politically she considers him to be, finally, a possible target. The seismic political consequences of his failed bid for the White House still proliferate; and although he was subsequently reelected to another term in the Senate, it was by a very slim margin and many ambitious souls now believe him vulnerable. Fran has preempted the field by announcing early and campaigning hard. The outcome next time has become very iffy, as he has confessed to Latt, who is solidly ensconced in his own House seat and, although urged publicly by Renny Suratt and others, will under no circumstances challenge his father.

"You can always retire," Latt says reasonably. "You don't have to let Fran humiliate you." He grins suddenly and says humorously what is seriously on his mind. "Why don't you retire and let me have a crack at it? I love Fran but I can beat her."

"I know you can," Willie says, "but I think I can too."

"Maybe," Latt says, "and of course I won't lift a finger for myself as long as you want it. But if you should decide—"

"I'll think about it," Willie says. His son knows this is as close to a concession and an endorsement as he is going to get, until such time as Willie faces up to the years that now seem opponents, where once they were comrades. He confesses to Latt that they are becoming a tide that is running faster and faster. So far he has stayed afloat, but as his son perceives with a loving eye sharpened by his own ambition, it is becoming harder. But Latt also realizes the great pride involved, and accepts it gracefully. He knows he will have Willie's full and active support when the time comes, and rests content—if now and then inwardly a little impatient and anxious to get moving on his own—"to keep the seat for the imperial Wilson family," as Renny can't resist jibing.

None of this appears in *The Very Occasional Newsletter,* Vol. 3, although its general outlines are of course known to Johnny and to everyone else who follows politics with reasonable perception.

"Willie," he writes, "remains one of the dominant figures on the national scene, a major player still in the Senate in both domestic and foreign policy. This despite the personal unhappiness with which you are all familiar from the news accounts, the loss of his second wife, the former Anne Greeley, to breast cancer at the age of sixty. Anne, like Willie, was a longtime member of the University board of trustees; a brilliant lawyer and charming woman, as all who met her will remember; and a great companion for Willie in his various political battles. Willie's son Latt, who as you know is Congressman from their home district in the central San Joaquin, tells me that his father is 'well adjusted, reasonably content and working hard at the legislative tasks he loves so well.' We who watch his career in print and on the tube are aware of this, benefit from it as citizens and appreciate it. As always, we wish Willie well and look forward with interest to what he will accomplish next. He remains a leader and an encouragement as we round the turn and begin the home stretch.

"Tim Bates is another who continues to fill his special niche in Washington. His column on national affairs continues to be one of the most perceptive and popular out of our nation's capital, in an age where all such endeavors operate in a fiercely competitive climate. Tim has his critics who attack him fiercely; knowing our Timmy, and remembering some of his writings when he was editor of the *Daily,* we are not surprised that he gives as good as he gets. Those of us who see his column frequently are aware that his generally middle-of-the-road views are sometimes expressed with a vigor that stings his critics, but we also know that he is quite capable of taking care of himself. His column appears, as it has for many years, in the *Washington Inquirer,* whose editor and publisher, Anna Hastings, has always been one of his most loyal supporters.

"You are also aware that he won the Pulitzer Prize for column writing two years ago, a fitting recognition long and, many of us think, unjustly, delayed. We are glad that his years of maintaining his column at a consistently high level of thought and expression finally paid off. Congratulations, Timmy! We're proud of you.

"Hack Haggerty is another who continues to produce and perform at his usual consistent high level. He still lives in Rome in that beautiful old house on the Janiculum where many of us have visited over the years with him and his late, lovely wife, Flavia Lampadini.

"Their son, Paolo, and daughter, Sophia, both married, have given Hack six grandchildren between them, and they seem to keep him occupied, he says, 'when I have nothing better to do.' For one who has now published his Fourth Symphony, numerous shorter pieces, and in recent years has composed the scores for three highly successful Broadway productions, two of them musical comedies, the third the more serious *Octagon,* we doubt that Hack has 'nothing better to do.' But those of us who have grandchildren undoubtedly know what he means.

"(Which does not include our four bachelors, yours truly, now retired from the history department here at the University; Randy Carrero, now a cardinal in the Vatican; Galen Bryce, still holding the hands and mopping the brows of the psychologically discombobulated of Hollywood; and Renny Suratt, social gadfly and leader of political forces about as far from Willie as one could get.)

"North McAllister, retired after a highly successful medical career in Salt Lake City, is now active in a number of civic betterment causes. He has won many medical and civic awards; never remarried after the tragic death from lymphoma (that damned cancer again) of his delightful little wife Betty June Letterman. B.J., whom we all remember fondly, shared with our dear Bill Lattimer the honor of having the two highest grade averages in the entire student body. North is one of our grandfathers, his daughter, Eileen, having provided him with three. He says that he is feeling 'a few aches and pains that a cane seems to help a little, although I'm afraid I won't be running any foot races any time soon. And there's some high blood pressure, kept at bay by the usual medications. And a few arthritic creaks and squeaks, here and there. But other than those standard complaints of antique decrepitude, I'm getting along just fine!' You touch a few familiar chords, North, and ring a few increasingly insistent bells. Most of us can sympathize with you, or if we can't right now, we're getting there! But, so it goes. That's life in a pickle factory, as my dear mother used to say.

"And so we move on to Moose the Mooser, our man on the football field, the distinguished Theodore Krasnik Musavich, retired as head coach at the University after many sterling (and sometimes startling) triumphs. Many a team has stumbled into the stadium a jumble of awkward adolescents, only to be transformed into a football juggernaut by the training of Our Moose, Molder of Men. He's still contributing as a special adviser, he tells me, and certainly no sensible coaching staff would ever refuse his highly knowledgeable and experienced input. He is also, one can say without fear of contradiction, one of the most popular and well-loved men who ever coached a varsity team. For the better part of forty years, Moose and the University have been almost synonymous. This is no mean accomplishment, to come down through all these turbulent decades still riding high and still so highly popular with everyone on campus. Congratulations, Mooser, on a job well done.

"Guy Unruh is still basking, as well he should be, in his sharing of the recent Nobel Prize in medicine, given for his pioneer work studying native remedies for cancer around the world. Guy is one of the leaders of the growing school of medicine that thinks there may be much of value, for many diseases, in less sophisticated, more traditional methods of treatment; his lifelong experience as one of the world's leading oncologists led him naturally into this more specialized study. His many awards and his outstanding reputation have brought him back to campus on several occasions to give special lectures in the School of Medicine. And he, too, like Hack in Rome and Tony Andrade in Napa Valley, has been the lucky possessor of a spectacular home, on the slopes of the Pali in Hawaii, which has made him highly popular with shameless fraternity brothers like myself who have several times taken advantage of his generous hospitality. He and Maggie (Marguerite Johnson), who is busily involved in island charities and historical groups, are always most welcoming. He will be back on campus next semester lecturing in med school. Guy is one alumnus who likes to stay close to the alma mater, and we're always glad to see him here.

"Tony Andrade continues to manage famous Collina Bella Winery in Rutherford, up in the Napa Valley. He and his shrewd and lovely Louise (Gianfalco) have made the winery (originally established by Louise's father) into one of the leading labels in the American market. Tony continues to hold his solid place as one of the principal growers and vintners in the Valley, recipient of many awards for C.B. wines and a spokesman in both Sacramento and Washington for the wine industry. He and Louise have eight grandchildren among their two sons and two daughters, and we all remember that wonderful house above the Valley where we had the picnic during the reunion many years ago. Again, the hospitality is warm and endless, and again, many of us have been blessed to enjoy it over the years.

"Loren Davis, Tony's best buddy in school and best buddy ever after, continues to run the family company, Davis Oil, now an international operation that seems to acquire new fields and new businesses every time one turns around. Lor and his charming wife, Louise's cousin Angie (Angela D'Allessandro), manage to keep in close touch with the Andrades, Lor tells me, their most recent adventure being a University tour of Egypt, Syria and Israel. Lor has nothing but good to say about these tours, and those of us who have taken one or more of them can only agree that they're delightful experiences. As always, one can only envy Lor and Tony their close and lasting friendship, which does not always last beyond school days in such good shape, once family and business obligations come along. More power to 'em, we say. It's good to see some things last.

"Galen Bryce is still, as I already noted, holding the trembling hands and soothing the jittery egos of Hollywood's brightest—in the luminary, not the intellectual, sense. He's so good at it that he now reigns undisputed as the king of Hollywood shrinks. If anyone missed his prominent featuring in the *Time* magazine cover story 'Hollywood Goes to the Docs,' about a year ago, you ought to look it up. Those of you who remember Gale and his profound analyses of our juvenile ids, which always took place when he managed to corner us around midnight when the house was silent and most sensible people were sound asleep, will be able to imagine what he contributes to the movie capital's mental balance. If they have any problems, Gale can solve them—or at least rearrange them so that they'll *think* he's solved them. Of that we can be sure.

"Dr. Alan Frederick Offenberg retired a decade ago and from time to time still acts as a very successful consultant in education to the University and other major colleges. Duke weathered his fifteen years as president in good shape. He and Shahna (Epstein) handled most of the hectic times of Vietnam protest and resulting challenges to the stability and soundness of the University with firmness and dignity, and emerged in good shape in the final years of his term, admired by many and even (if grudgingly) accorded decency and goodwill by all but the most radical. He and Shahna have moved to a comfortable house, still overlooking the campus, near President's Knoll. He has a book on his experiences coming out soon, which will no doubt be reviewed in some hoity-toity journal in the East by his loudest campus critic and opponent, Dr. René Suratt.

And what should one say about Renny, except that he's just the same and hasn't seemed to change a bit in all these years? He's still one of the best-known teachers, commentators and speakers on a certain political side of things, and as such always receives the highest plaudits for his own books and speeches from all the major publications and news analysts that seem to dominate a lot of academic and political thinking these days. Renny can do no wrong as far as these folks are concerned. Although he now has many critics of his own at the University as well as elsewhere, he seems to withstand them all and go his merry, backbiting way, to the detriment of many of our national ideals and aspirations, many think. But Renny remains undaunted—and very vocal. Boy, is he vocal! (And don't make me the subject of another mass mailing, Renny, you know you love the notoriety!)

"Jefferson Davis Barnett remains, like Lor and Tony and Marc Taylor (and Smitty Carriger, who has never been heard from to this day and remains officially 'lost, somewhere in Southeast Asia'), a prime example of a highly capable son taking over and steadily enlarging the corporate inheritance he received from his father. Jeff also remains a very active and very visible national figure in the ongoing campaign for racial equality. He and Willie's son the Congressman for a time worked very closely together in the more moderate (but actively progressive) wing of that endeavor, along with Maryetta Johnson, widow of our late almost-member By Johnson, and her daughter Ti-Anna, Latt's wife. Lately Jeff has reduced some of his more conspicuous national activities and is, like many of us, pulling in his horns a bit as the calendar marches on, but his dedication and loyalty to the cause, together with many major financial contributions, make him still one of the major moving forces. His most recent service has been on a special task force set up by the President to report on achievements to date since the passage of Lyndon Johnson's Civil Rights Act.

"Randolph Cardinal Carrero, to give him his formal title, which Randy still urges old friends to ignore, is concluding just as we knew he would, as a dominant figure in Vatican foreign policy. He said once in an interview with the alumni magazine that he hoped to contribute 'something imaginative but solid' to whatever assignment he received in the Church, and this he seems to be doing, in a field which has always fascinated him. One can only applaud this, as God knows foreign policy all around our harried globe seems to be royally screwed up, and maybe Randy can help. If anybody can, we're convinced he can. He says he and Hack see each other often in Rome—"I'm practically a second father to his kids and a second grandfather to their kids. This suits me fine and gives me a home base I really enjoy." And as for Rome—'You who have been here know. One never tires. Like London, it's inexhaustible. If the present is ever dull (which it rarely is), just go back a few hundred years and pop yourself into history. Things will liven up again in an instant. It's for me. I couldn't be happier here.' Which is very nice to know, for such a nice guy.

"Dr. Roger Leighton, sadly, has recently lost his charming Juliette (Cambron) to recurring heart disease. Rodge continues his very active life as an adviser to the International Atomic Energy Agency and a crusader for rigid international controls of that frightening force. He remains undaunted that the task seems even more formidable now than it was when he first became inspired by it, flying over Hiroshima two days after the first bomb fell in 1945 at the end of World War II. He has long been one of the most savvy and dogged negotiators with the current (and growing) group of atomic powers, and one of the most effective teachers, writers and advocates of atomic controls. He speaks here quite regularly and some of you may have heard him elsewhere, for he 'makes the rounds,' as he puts it, about every two years. He shows no signs of slacking off. 'We have to keep fighting,' he writes. 'We can't stop trying to pin the beast down. If we don't succeed, one of these years it will kill us all for sure.' More power to Rodge, a fine world citizen who labors on despite the odds of resistance and indifference which make the job so formidable and, one suspects, so heartbreaking when all is said and done.

"Marcus Andrew Taylor has emerged over the years as a most effective head of his inherited Taylorite Corporation. The Marc we knew in the house, the quiet Marc, the shy and self-effacing Marc, is, we are sure, still there somewhere. But behind that retiring, self-effacing aspect there seems to have developed (or broken out) a firm and decisive character who apparently has been able to bring to the family business a shrewd and effective leadership that continues to make Taylorite one of the most successful major corporations in America. He has also been a major benefactor of the University; the new Marcus Andrew Taylor Annex to the School of Business will be dedicated in February. Marc informs me that there will be various festivities in connection with that, and he and his wife, Helen, whom he met during our first reunion, 'expect as many of you as possible to be there and be our guests.' A long way from 'shy little Marc' of undergraduate days, and more power to him!

"Just one other, final, note. You all remember—who could ever forget?—our ousted former member, Rudolph John Krohl, the only man ever expelled from the fraternity. Rudy went on, as you know, to achieve great success with his Krohl Inc. (also father-founded), which now is one of the world's most successful trucking and haulage firms (and many other things, as it has become an international conglomerate in recent years). He too has been a great benefactor of the University, having founded the Krohl Memorial Lectures in honor of his parents (the forum at which Willie and Renny had their famous debate when Willie announced his unhappily aborted campaign for President). Rudy also financed the Krohl Business Library. You probably saw the news last November when he and his wife Helga (Berger) were killed in the crash of their corporate jet when they were flying from Chicago to New York and got caught in a sudden blizzard. It is sad that Rudy, who obviously had many talents in the business field, should have missed so badly on the human level with those of us who knew him in adolescence.

"So that's it, for now. Maybe Willie will round us all up for another reunion someday. Let's hope so. It would be good if we could meet together one more time and exchange details of our lives and reminisce about the happy days we had together on this beautiful campus, now so greatly grown but still so beautiful, and wonderful for the hopeful young.

"Fond best to you all—

"Johnny Herbert"

"*Addendum:*

"It is my sad task to inform you that Dr. John Thomas Herbert, chairman emeritus of the history department, passed away a week ago of a respiratory seizure at his desk in his departmental office. From his days as a freshman, when he was exposed to a storm for several hours during an innocent undergraduate prank, he suffered from weak lungs and continued respiratory problems. It was an incident that changed his entire life, yet as we all know, he suffered its consequences without complaining and with a spirit of undaunted cheerfulness and goodwill that was a never to be forgotten example to all who knew him. He was always a brave, gallant and gentle soul who contributed greatly to the University, to his chosen discipline and to the friends, students and colleagues whose lives touched his over the years. He was a fine scholar, teacher, writer and, above all, man. Everyone will sorely miss him, none more so than we, his fraternity brothers, who first knew, and became so fond of him, so many long years ago.

"He had prepared this newsletter and it was on his desk awaiting mailing by his secretary when he died. I have taken the liberty of sending it on to you.

"Fraternal, and warmest greetings,

"Duke"

7

**The last reunion:
home, in a different season**

1 Recalling that sad little postscript a decade later, Willie reflected that even then the tone of Johnny's *Very Occasional Newsletter* had been a little heavier, not quite so lighthearted, not quite so carefree and undaunted, as its predecessor had been ten short years before. And naturally so, he supposed: the years themselves were shorter, he and his friends were older and on them all the not so gentle hand of advancing age was beginning to impose its not so subtle intimations.

His own life had changed substantially. Fran Haggerty, far from running against him for the Senate, had married him instead, a development that had prompted startled but wholehearted approval from his two remaining children, affectionate support from his closest friends, generally good-natured and less acrid than usual comments from his critics. The jibe around the Hill was "If you can't lick 'em, marry 'em," directed more at Fran, whom everyone liked, than at him, whom many liked but whose views were deplored by quite a few. In general, comments were not so sharp—except for Renny, but, then, nobody expected Renny to change. Guy Unruh had analyzed it years ago in the fraternity: "It's an extra gene, left out of most people but implanted in Renny by a passing werewolf. It comes out in the dark of the moon."

The marriage, when it finally happened, seemed a perfectly natural and inevitable culmination of their lifelong friendship, her general support of his political career despite occasional divergences, her sympathetic support during Donna's illness and, later, Anne's.

"You've had your share of bad luck, now," she said, enough in jest so that it didn't sound patronizing, enough in sincerity so that he could willingly once again accept her support. "I think it's time you settled down with me and enjoyed your golden years."

"One more election," he said, "and then if I win that, I'll feel I can shut up shop with dignity and retire."

"If you win it," she remarked. "But if you don't?"

He gave her a quizzical glance.

"I don't think marrying you will be conditional on whether or not I win an election, Fran."

"Well, thank God!" she said with mock relief. "I thought for a minute, there, you were establishing a condition."

His response was a sudden sharp look.

"You don't think I'm going to win it, then."

"Speaking as one old pol to another," she said with an unabashed smile, "I think it's going to be damned close."

"Then why not stay in and beat me?" he inquired, rather grumpily. "You've always wanted to be in the Senate—"

"I've always wanted to be Mrs. Willie Wilson."

"I'll bet you say that to all the boys," he said, more humorously.

"Well," she said thoughtfully, "not all. Not all."

Next day she issued a strong endorsement of his reelection, and a week later, amused at themselves for, as she said, "spitting in the face of the media," they drove off quietly into Maryland, found an obscure little church and a modest little minister, and said their vows attended only by Tim and Latt.

Six months later he won his last reelection, but by so narrow a margin that Renny, out at the University, revived his "Senator Squeak-In" label and was pleased to see it picked up gleefully by Mother, the Conscience, and the media and political worlds in general.

"I think this one had better be it," Fran remarked as they went through a district-by-district post-mortem with Latt.

"I agree," Latt said.

"You know," Willie said—in a mocking tone, but words he had never thought he would say—"so do I."

Soon thereafter he issued a statement announcing his retirement at the end of the term "so that others who may wish to run will have plenty of time to prepare themselves."

Renny remarked acridly that "The only obvious one at the moment is Latt Wilson, so this is obviously just another Wilson family Tinkersto-Evers-to-Chance, or rather Daddy-to-Daddy's-Boy. It is time to stop this everlasting, egregious, insufferable exercise in barefaced nepotism."

"Renny doesn't love me the way he used to do," Latt remarked wryly. "I wonder if he's still giving those parties at the old family homestead in Hillsborough. Maybe I should go out and see if I can't get him back on my side."

His father snorted and Fran said, "Over my dead body."

And so in due course Willie retired, after forty years in public life. And presently Fran died, after seven happy years of marriage that spanned his final term and the first year of a very active retirement, when the cancer Guy Unruh thought he had conquered for her at age sixty-one came back to destroy her at age seventy-four. And suddenly, and to his complete surprise, Willie found himself again in the Senate, on appointment of the governor of California, who had a political problem on his hands and called on Willie in some desperation to help him solve it.

It was one of those classic situations in political life that sometimes surprise an unsophisticated electorate whose members rarely catch a glimpse of the inside workings that produce the desired result.

One day, Willie was a retired Senator, usefully and happily employed as a special consultant to three of the Beltway's largest and most prestigious think-tanks, his public hours occupied with helping to prepare political analyses and reports, his private time devoted to Latt, Ti-Anna, their charming daughters Donna and Maryetta and by now very big "Little By," grown into a six-foot-four, two-hundred-pound quarterback about to graduate magna cum laude from the University; and Clayne, now the very wealthy widow of her much older husband, active in many good causes in Oregon, where she had lived for years, and her three bright and lively kids, all doing very well in their studies and headed for what appeared to be worthwhile and productive lives.

Next day, Willie was back in his almost lifelong home, once again the junior Senator from California, "starting all over again at the bottom of the seniority ladder," as he remarked a bit woefully to Latt, who with the same suddenness had become his senior Senator. He had won his own election to the upper house when Willie's then-colleague dropped dead of cardiac arrest on the Senate floor.

Willie's unexpired term would run for three years. On the day he was sworn in he issued a statement establishing the final parameters:

"I am deeply grateful for the honor shown me by the governor. I shall do my best to give the people of California the same diligent service I gave them before.

"I shall permanently retire at the end of the term, and will under no circumstances seek, or accept, another public office. Common sense warns against it; age flatly says: No. But I do look forward with pleasure to helping the governor advance in Washington all the vital interests of the state, and I fully expect him to succeed me in due course when all his great contributions to California lead him inevitably to the Senate."

The governor, much pleased, thanked him privately for the endorsement and, even more, for helping to solve his own problem, which was to fill a suddenly vacant seat that had two equally insistent aspirants, one from San Francisco, the other from Los Angeles, equally powerful politically and equally vocal in their demands that they be selected. Willie, still highly visible and still receiving the sentimental loyalty of many millions in ever-growing California, was the obvious way out, although the governor's choice was never explained that way:

"His long service to California . . . his brilliant public record which we all remember so well . . . the obvious need for continuity and experience to serve the state . . . no finer man could be found to continue the high level of California's representation in the upper house . . ." and so on.

"Oh, *God,*" Renny exclaimed to the students in one of the seminars he still conducted as professor emeritus. "Did you ever hear such crap?"

The "continuing voice of reason on the national scene," as Mother and the Conscience always called him, was still unrelenting and always would be. But Renny, like his journalistic and academic cohorts, was no longer of particular interest to Willie. He was delighted to be back in the Senate "for one last strut on the public stage," as he agreed amicably when Latt so described it; and he was thoroughly enjoying it when he got the bright idea one day of calling the remaining members of the house together for one last reunion on the eve of his final retirement in the year 2000.

Along the way somewhere, other annoyances had also dropped by the wayside or been reduced by time to minor irritations.

Maryetta Johnson, obstreperous to the end, had died at seventy-three after a long, contentious life devoted mainly to civil rights causes and the careful deification of By Johnson's memory. She had become over time an icon to the professional leaders of black advancement, a name they trotted out on frequent occasions, an increasingly frail little woman crippled with age and osteoporosis whom they still brought to the platform at major events. She was inevitably "simmering down," as Willie described it to Tim. But she, like Renny, never let up on Willie.

Their last meeting, just before she died, had been at Latt's house on the Virginia side of the Potomac just outside the District, when he and Ti-Anna had gathered together her mother, his father, Clayne, Tim and assorted children for a Fourth of July barbecue. Everything had gone with reasonable, if occasionally prickly, amicability until almost the end when Maryetta finally let go with her pent-up frustration concerning Willie's appointment.

"Of all the arrogant, self-indulgent, self-aggrandizing, typical Willie Wilson moves," she snapped, "that takes the cake. Why didn't you have the self-respect and the dignity to refuse it, Willie? You're too old to be of any good now."

"You should talk," Willie retorted with a good-natured grin he knew would annoy. "Why don't you have the self-respect and dignity to calm down and enjoy your grandchildren and old friends? You're a pretty dilapidated spectacle yourself, I must say, trying to hang on to your youthful glories!"

"*I?*" Maryetta cried. "*I*, trying to hold on to youthful glories? You ought to be ashamed of yourself, Willie Wilson! At least I make sense. That's the difference. *I* make sense, not the same tired old stuff you've been giving us ever since college days! If you've had a new idea, or enlisted in a progressive cause, in almost sixty years, I don't remember it!"

"That's the problem," Willie said with mock gravity. "You *don't* remember. The old machinery's getting rusty, Maryetta. The old synapses are wearing away. The necessary thought-producing delays between emotion and reason are breaking down. You just don't remember my liberal ways."

"Ha!" Maryetta exclaimed, for once, he was pleased to note, almost speechless. *"Ha!"*

"I take that to mean consent," Willie said with a chuckle. "Will you pour your mother some more wine, please, Ti-Anna? I don't want her to have apoplexy."

"You'll give it to her if anybody can," Ti-Anna said with a laugh. "I'll pour you both some and you can both then drop the discussion, O.K.?"

"No problem," he said cheerfully.

"There's no point in arguing with you, anyway," Maryetta said. "You've always been too tricky to face an honest argument."

"And you too emotional to ever present one," he countered; and that was the end of their last contention.

But he was sorry to see her go, when the time came. She had always been an utterly predictable, utterly reliable weather vane, just as Renny had been—to Old Left, New Left, Middle Left, any kind of Left.

"You could always count on Maryetta," he remarked to Tim when they shared a cab back from her interment in Rock Creek Cemetery. "She was as predictable as Mount Rushmore."

"Where she probably deserved to be," Tim commented. "The Perfect Liberal, Second Half, Twentieth Century."

"Well, maybe she was right," Willie said. "About me, at least. I don't suppose I've changed much, either."

He was pleased that he would leave a respectable political legacy. He had sponsored some major pieces of legislation, successfully introduced moderating amendments to many more, had long ago lost count of how many. His general views had been stated for the permanent record in Senate debates, public speeches, magazine articles, op-ed pieces, interviews too numerous to mention or even recall. He had received many indications from around the country—and, pleasingly, from a number of younger members of Senate and House as the years drew on—that his ideas were well received and sometimes exercised an active influence, which he supposed was about as much as a good Senator could expect. And this despite the many bitter attacks on them, and on himself, by Mother, the Conscience, their worshipful followers in media and academe and such egregious paradigms as the Ditzy Doyenne with her diamond (dead at seventy-six, honored by a virtual state funeral in National Cathedral attended by Everybody Who Was Anybody in sycophantic Washington. He pointedly and conspicuously did not attend. He had always considered her overly emotional, vindictive and vicious, one of the few people in his life toward whom he had come close to feeling an active dislike).

It was time now to forget all that as much as possible and concentrate on the last reunion. The inevitable Renny was apparently going to attend, the oldest, most persistent and in many ways the most representative of all his critics, which, he supposed, was why he had always paid some attention to what Renny had to say: he spoke so definitively and completely for the pack. Hopefully there would be happier things to think about when they all came together. He knew he would not be alone in trying as much as possible to ignore Renny and concentrate instead on finding out what old friends of sixty years felt they had accomplished with their living, and what had really gone on with them, behind such barriers of privacy as they might have been able to maintain during their lives as public men.

2   Duke, as promised, had arranged accommodations for them in a single location on campus. Deciding to bow to Willie's mood and his own, he had chosen the most sentimental venue he could think of, the freshman dormitory from which they had started out on their long journey together so many years ago. It was early fall, the school year would not begin for another two weeks, the normally jumping, happily raucous old building was empty and silent. He had consulted Willie, Guy Unruh and Tony Andrade. Their verdict was pleased and unanimous, the others endorsing the choice in due course, except of course Renny, "who has to be different," Tony remarked in a tired tone. "That goes with the territory."

Choice of the dorm started things off in a generally amiable and nostalgic glow, although, as Guy remarked with a chuckle when Duke called him in Honolulu, "We really aren't freshmen, you know."

"Pretend," Duke suggested. "Think positively. You'll feel a lot better about your aches and pains if you do. Imagine you're seventeen again."

"God forbid," Unruh said. "Although," he added with a chuckle, "I can remember three or four little girls I'd like to get in the backseat of my dear old Chevy again if I *were* seventeen."

"And they were seventeen," Duke said.

"Aye," Guy said. "There's the rub, damn it. Where did the years go, Duke?"

"Gone forever," Duke said. "But nice to think about."

Awash in sentiment, which they indulged in varying degrees, they arrived on a Friday for the weekend. Marc Taylor was accompanied by his Helen, a pleasant little woman who hovered over him like a mother hen—"Just what he needed," North McAllister observed with an approval they all shared. The other four wives had agreed amicably to be absent but on call. Shahna Offenberg, Maggie Unruh and Diana Musavich were working together to prepare the Saturday night dinner at the Offenbergs' comfortable home on President's Knoll overlooking the campus. Louise Andrade was readying the picnic scheduled for Sunday at the Andrades' spectacular house overlooking Napa Valley. Helen elected to join Shahna, Maggie and Diana on the Knoll. The men—the widowers, the bachelors in fact and the bachelors for the weekend—were housed together on the third floor of the dorm, each with his individual room, a luxury they had not enjoyed in the original days when they were housed as freshmen, two by two. Only Moose was on the first floor, confined to a wheelchair because of what they discovered sadly to be advancing multiple sclerosis, but still mentally alert. ("Was he ever alert?" Renny remarked sourly to Marc, who was too polite to move away from him. "Was he ever known to do anything that could be classified even remotely as mental?")

They slept late on Saturday morning; lunched together, as Duke had arranged for them, at the Faculty Club; then separated by mutual consent and spent most of the afternoon wandering the campus, now enlarged threefold from the semi-rural original sandstone buildings, country lanes and open meadows that had welcomed them more than half a century ago.

Musings were complex, memories deep and not always happy. Sooner or later everyone drifted through Memorial Church, comforting as always to the soul, conducive to the long, long thoughts of age as it had always been to the long, long thoughts of youth. The sun slanted down through the stained-glass windows, the gentle hush of the beautiful room conferred its benisons upon the restless heart. Each for his own reasons realized how much that lovely place had meant to him over the racing years, seldom consciously recalled but always lying close to the surface in their memories of youth.

Sometime around four o'clock Tony wandered in, having just walked by a place on the Quad that still had the capacity to trouble him: even now, recalling the events of that unhappy night still hurt. He was alone in the dreaming Indian summer day and thankful that he was; only Willie and Hack would have understood his melancholy. He hesitated when he stepped inside the church and recognized the lone figure seated halfway down and over to one side, as if warning off intruders; head bowed in hands, aspect unhappy and alone. But after a start of recognition—for he had not realized at lunch how old his friend looked, how old, presumably, they all now looked—he thought: what the hell, walked down the aisle and eased into the pew beside him.

North McAllister glanced up with an expression of sadness he tried for a second to dissemble. Then he too seemed suddenly to relax, to cast away protections and pretenses, which were of no use or necessity with this fraternity brother, who shared with him the same burdens imposed by nature and by a society that still gave very little shrift to something it did not really understand or really accept, however staunchly defenders insisted that it did.

"Oh, hi," he said, voice quiet to suit the quiet they were in. "How are you?"

"I'm pretty good," Tony said, voice equally low; and, as was his instinctively kindly nature when confronted by anyone who seemed to need encouraging, added firmly, "Actually, pretty damned good. And you?"

North thought for a moment, considering. Then he smiled, some-what tentatively but responding to Tony's unfailing charm and his steadfast refusal to be overcome by life.

"Not bad," he said. "At times not good, but at other times not bad. Isn't that how it goes?"

"That's the way it's always been with me," Tony said. "Although, happily more good than bad, when I think about it."

"Does one ever stop thinking about it?" North inquired, again for a moment looking sad. Tony hesitated, then gave his arm a squeeze.

"Stop that," he ordered. "We're in our late seventies, man. Much too old for feelings like that. Cut it out."

"I'd like to cut it out," North said with a wry little smile, "but how can one—even in one's late seventies? I don't find that so easy, no matter how I try. But I suppose old Tony's come up with the magic formula."

"Oh, sure," Tony said with some sarcasm. "Abracadabra, it's done. No more worries, no more strain, no more false hopes, false starts, anguish, pain. Right?"

"I'll bet you've never had much," North said. "You're too practical.

I still agonize. I always have. That's been my problem, not the thing itself."

" 'The thing,' " Tony echoed thoughtfully. "I've never called it that, myself. It's always just been 'it.' But I suppose we all have our inner vocabularies. I never have agonized much, though, which I guess makes me a little bit different."

"A little bit lucky," North observed with some envy. "You've been saved a lot of unhappiness."

"Some people take it very heavily," Tony agreed. "I *am* very fortunate, in that respect. I've had good friends, but except when I was very young and first beginning to find out about things, nothing deep or shattering." His expression changed, became uncharacteristically dark and moody for a moment. "Until now, when poor Lor has left me and gone into the darkness."

"What is it?" North asked. "Alzheimer's?"

Tony nodded.

"Son of a bitching disease," he said. "He doesn't know me. He doesn't know anybody. The guy"—he hesitated again, went on honestly; he told himself nobody could say Tony Andrade wasn't honest— "the guy I have loved with my deepest heart all my life since I first got to know him in the house. We really have loved each other, North. It hasn't been any sometime thing."

"I know that," North said gently. "We all know that."

"Oh, I *hope* not!" Tony exclaimed with humorous exaggeration. Then he laughed.

"But, what the hell. Why not? I'm not ashamed of it, although I've never had the urge to go around boasting about it, or leading any parades, or anything. It's just been our lifelong private thing, that's all; and we've been really very happy with it. And it hasn't interfered with either of our other lives, either. I think I've made Louise happy, we have four great kids, it's been a happy house. And Lor has three, and I know Angie's happy too, and that's also been a happy house. So, who's to criticize? And who's to care?"

"But you wouldn't want to advertise," North said with a smile.

"Only to you, old friend," Tony said comfortably. "Only to you. And what about you?"

"To some extent the same," North said, "though unfortunately not quite so idyllic a story as yours. I have a friend about twenty years younger in Salt Lake who wasn't married when I met him but is now and has been for many years. Also three kids, a nice wife, reasonably happy, who has always been a bit suspicious, but we've managed. Nothing regular but, considering the odds against and the happiness we get out of it when we're together, well worth the effort to keep it going. And we have, for twenty-three years now. So I can't complain too much, either."

"And other than that?" Tony asked. Again North looked a little sad, but not entirely; life, Tony could see, had not been all that bad, however uptight his old fraternity friend might have been on occasion over the years.

"Casuals now and then, when I've been away to some medical meeting, or very occasionally with friends on camping trips back in the mountains. Nothing planned, usually quite surprising; you know how it is. Boom!—and there you are, sometimes with the most surprising people."

"I like that," Tony admitted. "Occasionally. I haven't gone out looking, that mostly ended when I met Lor, but now and then, even in Napa Valley, particularly since we got inundated with people from San Francisco. They bring their exaggerated wives for exaggerated weekends and occasionally they get a little itchy." He grinned suddenly. "They want to be scratched and I scratch 'em, now and then. But," he became more serious, "like you, very, very occasionally. Too much at stake to be promiscuous, under any circumstances. That ended with the war, and marriage to Louise. Among other reasons for being completely discreet is that I just happen to love her. As you, I take it, loved B.J."

"I did," North said gravely. "We got married right here in this room, you probably remember; I was remembering when you came in. I was very upset at the time, not at all sure, close to frantic. But Willie and Billy Wilson told me I should, and so I did."

"Especially hard," Tony observed, "because you were in love with Billy."

"How did you know that?" North asked, startled. Tony grinned.

"One senses these things when one is a member of the fraternity. And I don't mean Alpha Zeta . . . But you never regretted it, I hope."

"Never," North said, face clouding over as he remembered lively little B.J., all her bright, optimistic personality and high intelligence, all her happy days competing with Bill Lattimer when they were "the two brightest kids on campus," all her happy times when she and Donna Van Dyke (later Wilson) were the University's most active organizers, working together in happy tandem to plan parties, dances, charity events, picnics.

"I loved B.J. once I really made up my mind to it," North said soberly. "And I think she loved me."

"I'm sure she did," Tony said firmly. "I'm sure she did. And you have two kids, right?"

"Yes," North said. "Eileen is very happily married, lives in Denver with her oil-owning husband, has three kids. Jason is—on his own."

"Hasn't found anybody," Tony said. North nodded. "Well, I wish him well. . . . Wasn't that a hell of a thing about Willie's son? I called Willie at the time and told him to tell the boy about me if he thought it would be of any help."

"Did you?" North said, surprised. "So did I."

"Did you?" Tony echoed, equally surprised.

"Aren't *we* the ones! I admire you for that."

"And I you," North said. His expression became thoughtful and reflective; Tony could see the conversation had been easeful for them both. "I think we've done pretty well with our lives, all things considered. We've never shouted, we've never demonstrated, we've never done big, dramatic things. We've just lived quiet, steady, productive, responsible lives."

"Yes," Tony agreed soberly. "That's right. I think that's the point."

"What point is that?" Willie asked, and they both jumped, so quietly had he come down the aisle and slid into the pew behind them.

Tony chuckled.

"That we're quiet, decent guys and you've been God damned lucky all these years to have us for fraternity brothers. Don't you agree?"

"I do," Willie said with a smile. "I've never had the slightest doubt."

"Not even when—?" Tony couldn't resist.

"Or even when—?" North echoed.

"Even when and even when," Willie said, smile broadening. "And I mean it. Are you guys going back to the dorm before we head up the hill to Duke's for dinner?"

"I'd like to," Tony said. "I think I'll take a little nap. Personally," he added, lightly but meaning it, "I'm emotionally drained."

"Me, too," North agreed. "But I'm glad we talked."

"So am I, buddy," Tony said. "Maybe it was necessary."

"I think so," North said. "I didn't realize what a relief it would be."

"Well!" Willie said, secretly relieved too. "I guess that relieves *me* of being Father Confessor."

"You're relieved," North told him; and Tony poked him affectionately in the ribs.

"Get the hell out of here!" he ordered. "Let's walk!"

And so they did, back to the dorm through the sleepy golden afternoon, at peace with themselves, with each other and with the singing world.

Standing under the arches on the other side of the Quad, Hack Haggerty smiled to himself as he watched them go. He was glad he had not arrived earlier for his sentimental rendezvous with Memorial Church. He had practiced on the organ there so many times as an undergraduate, composed so many of his tentative early melodies in that benign atmosphere, that it had always been a special place for him. He would have been glad to play for the trio just departing had he arrived just a little sooner; but he was glad that he hadn't. He and Mem Chu, as he understood the kids called it now, had a special date he did not really want to share with anyone.

Not that he had ever been "anti-social," to use the jargon; he just usually liked to be alone, particularly when in a mood to practice or compose. Flavia had always understood this, freely giving him his privacy when he wanted it. Fran never quite had, sooner or later breaking in, politely but with a nagging little underlying impatience she tried dutifully to hide but could not, asking if he would be through soon so that they could go do something of more immediate concern to her career as a rising young lawyer. That, plus her increasingly sharp opposition to his frequent absences with Transit Obligations, the band he had organized for local engagements in the Bay Area and the occasional foray farther afield, ultimately doomed the marriage; plus increasing mutual boredom with habit and routine and a growing competition and jealousy of careers. "Incompatible career differences" became the official reason for divorce; it covered many things.

This was in their early San Francisco days soon after graduation, when their long and sometimes rocky undergraduate romance had flowered into marriage and maturity (!). He always thought of it, even now, as either "maturity (!)" or "maturity (?)" because it was a long way from maturity pure and simple. As with so many of their age, they were still children, though they would have denied it indignantly then. Maturity was something far different, as he came to realize after what he now regarded, with all respects to Fran, as the luckiest day of his life: the day when, wandering estranged, unhappy, confused and alone, he had met Flavia Lampadini near the House of Livia, on the Palatine Hill in Rome.

Flavia, always understanding, never demanding, recognizing very soon that she really had no rivals except a piano and some musical manuscript paper, had proved to be exactly what he needed and wanted. He was sensible enough to recognize this immediately; then came maturity, without exclamation or question. Then began his happy years, which, though he lost her to cardiac arrest after two peaceful and gratifyingly productive decades, left him with a blanket of love and support that enfolded him to this day; maintained, of course, by the younger generation and *their* younger generation— Paolo and Sophia, also living in Rome with Paolo's charming wife, and three, Sophia's handsome but reasonably faithful husband, and four. They had their domestic and emotional problems, but their loyalty and caring for him never wavered; and in the eyes of the seven grandchildren, he could do no wrong.

To a considerable extent, that applied to the world of music. He had some sharp and unrelenting critics but many who liked him, too; and "the creative juices flowed," as he had once written Willie, who had his own troubles with critics but also managed to survive them in reasonably good and combative spirits.

From the comfortable old eighteenth-century house on the Janiculum Hill, Hack watched with distant but constant interest as both Willie and Fran rose to become stars in the Washington galaxy. Neither success surprised him, though he had been a little taken aback when Willie pulled out of the presidential race and when Fran did not go on to seek a Senate seat but chose to marry Willie instead.

"We hope you will give us your blessing, old buddy," Willie had written in his usual jaunty style, which sometimes, as in this case, concealed more uncertainty than he would have cared to admit. "We're a couple of losers who just didn't make the final grade. That's what they say, and that's why we've finally decided to join forces and console each other. We hope you can forgive us for that, and forgive me for running off with one whom in some ways I will always consider 'your' lady. I put the 'your' in quotes because she's mine now, and you don't even have visitation rights. But we want you to come see us anyway, when you can. Because, seriously, you do have them, you know, always and any time."

At the bottom, in her neat, lawyer's hand: "He exaggerates, but that's our Willie. Do come see us if you get to Washington. Love, Fran."

He hadn't managed to very often, but he was glad when she died that he had been able to visit a total of four times over the years. After a little initial awkwardness, bad things rolled away and the old, familiar friendship from college days appeared to be happily restored. Not only appeared to be but was, as they became increasingly able to relax with one another. In some degree he and Fran were still in love and always would be, as they all realized; but by that much later time, maturity had indeed taken over, life had settled in different patterns, everybody respected everybody else, and all went well. They too strengthened him, as he hoped his friendship strengthened them.

Now as he opened the door of the church, some ten minutes after the others had left, he found Randy Carrero and Guy Unruh, an unlikely pair who brought a little smile to his lips, obviously enjoying a good visit. He hesitated for a moment, then went on in; they wouldn't disturb one another. He wondered what that other pair, Tony and North, had been discussing; and where Willie fitted in. He suspected he knew, though he had never been sure about North; but about Tony, his memories were all too vivid. His own levelheaded tolerance and personal steadiness had served him well on that unhappy night in the rain when Tony had been apprehended with a casual pickup in a men's room on the Quad. Hack's handling of it, along with Willie's had made of Tony a lasting friend, who had given him an unabashed and genuinely fond hug when they had met again this morning on the third floor of the freshman dorm.

"Hey, Hack!" Tony cried. "You old bastard, how's the great composer?"

"Fine, fine," Hack retorted, "old bastard yourself. How's the great little old winemaker?"

"I've brought along a case for dinner," Tony said, "and you'll get a chance to drink some and see. I'll catch you later. I'm going out and wander the Quad."

Their eyes met—no one else was around, the floor was deserted—they both succumbed to spontaneous laughter.

"Alone, I hope," Hack said. Tony let out a guffaw as he turned away and started down the stairs, not four at a time as he did six decades ago, but in admirably spry fashion for a septuagenarian.

"You damned betcha, boy," he tossed over his shoulder. "You *damned* betcha!"

Sometime during the week, Hank suspected, they might talk about that; then he decided it obviously wasn't necessary. All ghosts were banished between them. It had happened, Tony had survived it and had obviously lived his life within bounds that permitted him to achieve some peace of mind and retain his natural, charming lightness of spirit. What that had involved, Hack could imagine but didn't really want to have spelled out. It wasn't his area and he wasn't particularly interested in finding out more than he already knew from his contacts in the musical and theatrical worlds.

Which, he had to admit as he climbed the narrow stairs to the organ loft, had been very good to him, professionally and financially. After his first major symphonic works and many shorter pieces, he had turned to musicals; the results had been spectacularly successful. He had originally planned to share them with Billy Wilson, but Billy's decision to return to the ranch, and later his tragic death in the auto accident with Janie, had precluded that; lent an added poignancy, in Hack's mind, by the conviction that Billy had a genuine talent, along with a genuine desire to become involved in the theater. But he was a dutiful child and a loving brother, and had done what duty dictated when Willie left the ranch to go into politics.

Hack wondered now, as he had many times over the years, how Willie felt about it. Had he ever regretted the waste of Billy's talent, or had he believed Billy when he insisted, as he often did, that he was perfectly happy that things had worked out as they had? Knowing Willie as much as anyone ever knew Willie, Hack suspected that he had always felt uneasy about it, had always felt a somewhat guilty gratitude for what Billy had done to free him for his own career. Hack wondered if politics had really been enough for Willie, particularly when its basic cold-blooded ruthlessness finally resulted in his having to abandon the presidential goal he had always wanted.

Willie defeated was still not a concept the friends of his youth could quite become accustomed to; the glamorous figure of the handsome and handsomely successful Big Man On Campus still glimmered, faintly but ineradicably, from across the intervening years. Hack was sure the disappointment had hurt Willie more than he would ever acknowledge.

He felt a sudden surge of thankfulness that he had never had to absorb such a rebuff, even when some of his more hostile critics were at their most obnoxious, going on about the "uninspired themes" of his symphonies, the "standard melodies" of his shorter pieces, the "predictable popularity" of his Broadway and Hollywood scores. In his field, as in all others categorized as artistic, the standards of critical judgment were largely superficial, transitory and sneakingly personal. If by some shrewd adaptation or fluke you became one of their pets, you could do no wrong, however strained, tortured and basically for-the-shock-of-it your compositions might be. If you were not among the pets for some reason—personal integrity, publicly expressed skepticism of the current conventional wisdom, or failure to show properly humble respect for the more influential critics—you were often disparaged, castigated and put down.

But, he thought with satisfaction as he ran his fingers lovingly over the keys and experimented gently with the pedals, if you had integrity, remained true to yourself and were just plain ornery, as he was in his quiet way, you could still manage to do all right with your work and your life. You might not be ranked up there with Ludwig von or Wolfgang Amadeus, but you still made your mark and a lot of nice, amiable folk who didn't live by the backbiting customs of the inside group approved respectfully of what you did. And this, he suspected, was Willie's solace, too, even though he might have missed The Big One. And who knew? He might not have made it, anyway. No one could ever say for sure, which Hack supposed might be a satisfaction in itself.

He shook his head impatiently as if to clear it of distracting thoughts. He concentrated now, as he had with so many ideas over the years, on a simple little theme that had come to him as he walked beneath the arches. He thought he might entitle it "Return to the Quad": gentle, slow, soothing, restful; reminiscent, sentimental, nostalgic; winding in and out from mood to mood as his inspired fingers teased it from the organ in obedience to his kindly, decent heart.

Below in the otherwise deserted church, Randy Carrero and Guy Unruh, who had entered a short five minutes before Hack did, exchanged a fond smile for him, paused briefly to listen and then returned to the talk they had begun five minutes before when they had met unexpectedly in their sentimental wanderings along the Quad.

The gentle murmur of the organ in the background induced a relaxed attitude, and both become more unexpectedly candid than either had contemplated.

"I've never quite been able to imagine the life you lead," Guy remarked. "You've always had to be so pure and circumspect. Or have you? There seems to be a small army of former altar boys coming out the woodwork these days to charge that you—generic 'you,' that is, not you personally—haven't been all that pure."

"And they make big bucks with their charges, too," Randy said dryly. "I'm glad you specified generically, because that has never been my bag. Now, on the other side of the coin—" He chuckled. "But even there, Guy, I have to disappoint you. I've been pure and circumspect all over the place. It's disgusting, isn't it?"

"Well," Guy said with a grin, "not disgusting, exactly. But it does seem a little out of character, from what I remember of the young Randy Carrero here on campus."

"Young Randy Carrero," Randy said, "was not Randolph Cardinal Carrero, and therein lies the difference; a hell of a lot of difference, actually. I made a commitment, Guy, and I've stuck with it."

"I'll bet it hasn't been easy to keep," Guy suggested. Randy proved that he had lost none of his feisty combativeness, cardinal or no.

"Somewhat easier to keep, I imagine," he observed tartly, "than Guy's commitment to Maggie."

"Ouch," Guy conceded with the ready grin that had always eased him out of tight situations. "You—might—just—have something there."

"Now, you tell me," Randy said, "what you've been up to in that line. You always used to be such a busy skirt-chaser in school."

"And skirt-lifter," Guy said with satisfaction. He gave an exaggerated, humorous sigh. "Ah, yes, those were the days! Those were the days!"

"And not over yet, I'll bet," Randy suggested. Again Guy grinned.

"I don't know why I should tell you," he said, "except that you're a professional confessor, after all, so I suppose you've heard everything."

"There isn't much I haven't," Randy agreed with a wry smile. "So tell me all."

"And satisfy your prurient imagination?"

"It was surfeited about thirty years ago," Randy said. "O.K., we'll talk about the weather."

"There's a hell of a dull subject," Guy remarked. "No, I'll be honest with you. While you've been over there in Rome jacking off under your robes, I've been chasing after a little honest sex over here. Is there anything wrong with that?"

"I didn't say there was," Randy said, laughing in spite of himself. "And I'm not conceding anything about what I do under my robes, except to say that sex is a subject I don't pontificate on, at any time. It's much too complex for that."

"So *you* won't be honest with *me*," Guy said. "O.K. for you, buddy. I thought we used to be soul mates."

"I don't recall that, quite," Randy said, "but let's say we regarded each other's pastimes with tolerance and forbearance. Which I am still trying to do"—he grinned—"at this moment. So what does Maggie think about all this, at this late date in your full and busy life?"

"Maggie doesn't know a lot about it," Guy said, "and I make sure that she never will. Any more than the Pope—"

"Guy," Randy said, amused but firmly, "I am not going to satisfy *your* prurient imagination, so knock it off."

"O.K.," Guy said with a mock sigh. "If I must. You church guys are sure holy, I must say!"

"We get paid for it," Randy said lightly. "Also, as I said, it's a commitment. It isn't so hard once you get into it."

"And you do accomplish a great deal of good," Guy agreed. "I must say I do respect that, wholeheartedly."

"And so do you," Randy said, their elderly college-boy banter set aside for more serious contemplations of where they were now. "I really admire what you've done, Guy."

Guy gave him a sudden shrewd look.

"You, because of Latt. Right?"

Randy's expression turned somber, so rapidly and completely that Guy was afraid he had gone too far. He could tell that Randy was looking far back, to all the horror of his own special night, the terrible rainy night when, drunk and frustrated because of his futile romance with Fluff Stevens, he had driven up Palm Drive with Bill Lattimer as his passenger—slid off the road in the torrential downpour—gone head-on into a tree—totaled the car—and totaled Latt, the brightest student in school, always gentle, always kind, always decent, loyal and supportive—in many ways the finest human being they had ever known, or ever would. Willie had named his firstborn son after him, the rest still revered his memory. For sheer goodness, they had never known his like.

And he, Randy Carrero, had killed him.

It had happened more than sixty years ago but Guy realized that suddenly it was back with Randy in a blinding flash, as it must have been many times over the years, when he least expected it and was least prepared to handle it.

"I'm sorry," Guy said with genuine contrition. "I'm sorry. I know it must still hurt, even now. I had no right—"

Randy attempted a smile that didn't quite make it.

"Oh, that's O.K. You all have the right, if you want to. Latt in life

341

influenced me a lot. Latt in death sent me into the Church and drove me into good works, so I owe him a lot. If I've done any good for anybody, whoever I did it for owes him a lot. I've tried to make it up to him—" His voice sank very low, and he looked for a moment as though he might give way to tears; underwent what was obviously an intense internal struggle; worked his way out of it and spoke in a voice shaky but determined. "I've tried to make it up to him"—he looked toward the altar, flecked with light filtered down through the stained-glass windows—"I've tried to make it up to you, Latt. I know I never can, but—but I've tried."

"You've tried," Guy said huskily, "and by God, you've succeeded, friend. So try not to grieve too much now. You've lived a long, good life, you've more than made up for it. I know he's proud of you wherever—wherever he is."

"I hope so," Randy said in a near-whisper. "I sure hope so . . . Anyway, Guy," he said, forcing himself to return to a normal tone and normal discourse, "I do admire what *you've* done. It's been great."

Guy sighed, relieved to leave the subject of Latt but inevitably brought back to confronting his own private demon, his constant companion, what he often referred to as "the Great Enemy," cancer.

"Even though I'm no closer than anyone else to solving the riddle," he said. "The Great Enemy continues to kill its millions in spite of what many of us keep trying to do. I've contributed one little bit, and if it's helped even a handful of people, I feel it's been worth it. But the challenge is staggering . . . and endless. And so is yours, I imagine."

"Yes," Randy said gravely. "Mine is a Great Enemy, too: war." He also sighed and was momentarily far away as he contemplated the equally endless challenges it posed to humankind everywhere. "I suppose you and I are up against the two greatest enemies of all; and like you, whatever progress I can contribute to holding mine at bay is minuscule compared to its constant, grinding devastation of the globe."

For several moments they were silent, a long way from the lean, handsome, ever-jesting, ever-foraging Guy Unruh and the stocky, self-contained, pragmatic Randy Carrero of fraternity days; but there were still glimpses, beneath the now heavier, grayer but still handsome Guy, the heavier, grayer but still engaging Randy. A lifelong civic purpose, faithfully followed had transformed them both into formidably worthwhile citizens, however lightly they might minimize their contributions.

"How much progress are you making, actually?" Randy inquired. "We read a lot about you, of course, particularly when you got the Nobel, for which congratulations, incidentally—"

"Frosting on the cake," Guy said, and added with a wry smile, "not an exact metaphor, it's not exactly cake, what I do as an oncologist, but the prize, while it is nice—makes funding and backing easier to get— makes a nice addition in *Who's Who*—doesn't change the grunge work which goes on, as it has to, and will for many thousands of us until the enemy is licked at last . . . if that day ever comes."

"But year by year you're getting closer, I hope," Randy said earnestly. Guy made a dismissive grimace.

"Who knows? Who knows? Maybe yes, we are making some progress in some areas; but it really is an endless process. We haven't really unlocked the box within the box yet." He looked grim, and tired. "And never may . . . and never may. You must feel the same."

"Always," Randy said somberly. "Always. It never ends. Diplomacy aided by goodwill keeps trying, makes a few tentative advances; diplomacy aided by evil will makes sudden gains, cancels out the good, shifts the contest to new battlefields, new purposes, sometimes different but far more often very old, rooted in ancient hatreds and ambitions that often have no real solutions. Like you, many thousands of us try, many millions wait desperately on the outcome of our endeavors and are ultimately as defeated and disheartened as we are. But we can't stop, we have to keep trying, as you do . . . we have to keep trying."

"When I was much younger," Guy said, "when we were undergrads here together, I used to think there were conclusions in life, that things had reliable patterns, that you could set yourself a task, try something, and sooner or later there would be an ending, a 'closure' as the jargon goes nowadays, that would wrap it up neatly. In some ways that applies perhaps to some smaller things, but in the larger ones like yours and mine . . ."

"There are no endings," Randy agreed, "no pat conclusions, no final solutions. In some small things, maybe, but even there, many of them aren't small things for the people involved, everything is big to somebody. Many times they don't end, and certainly the big ones don't end. They just mutate and metastasize and appear somewhere else where you least expect them. They're like some eternally reviving monsters in a horror movie, except that there's no single Indiana Jones to cut them up and stamp them out. Just millions upon millions of very human little Indiana Joneses, doing their damnedest, always striving, always defeated. You can bid the monsters good-bye today but they'll be back tomorrow, so never relax, little man, little woman, little humanity. Never relax, never relax, never relax . . ."

Again they were silent. Then with the same sudden, decisive impulse, they both said, "Well—" held out their hands for a shake to end their now completely serious talk, stood up and made their way up the aisle. Overhead, Hack continued to create his gentle autumnal melodies that so suited the autumnal mood of their autumnal days.

At that moment, feeling quite autumnal himself, Tim Bates was seated at the editor's desk in what used to be known as "the *Daily Shack*," now the principal ornament of the latter-day "Department of Communication," a rather pompous title that sought to dignify and stultify what was still, for most of its students, excellent practical experience and a hell of a lot of fun.

Thanks to the generosity of a successful newspaper-owning alumnus who wanted his name enshrined on campus, the formerly tumbledown, ramshackle old building, filled with the exuberant chaos and crumpled copy paper of many generations of undergraduate would-be journalists, had been remodeled some years ago into a relatively modern, up-to-date newspaper facility. Right now it was uncharacteristically silent, clean and tidy. Tim knew that in a couple of weeks, when the incoming editorial and business staffs returned to school, it would soon again be engulfed by uproar and activity. He hoped the spirit of it, and the fun of it, had not been changed too much from the spirit and fun of his day.

He was alone with a thousand memories, many of them his. He was reminded, somewhat ironically, of a once-famous advertising slogan, which had not been applied to his profession or to his gender, but which he found amusingly pertinent still: You've come a long way, baby.

Thinking across-continent to Anna Hastings's *Washington Inquirer* and to all his famously contentious life as columnist and writer, he thought with satisfaction: You're damned right, baby. So I have.

Here in this place, still alive in his mind with all the days of ambition and triumph that had culminated in his editorship of the paper on the eve of World War II, he smiled an amused and affectionate smile for the very earnest young man who had pontificated on the coming crisis—when he was not laying out the school administration editorially for some crime of commission or omission.

These had been the two main targets of what had been even then a powerful pen, possessed of a freshness and vigor that still resonated across the decades when, as happened sometimes, he took down the bound volumes of the *Daily* from his library shelves and dipped casually into what he had written. It was good to remind himself occasionally of how often he had challenged authority, in the person of the University president, kindly Dr. Chalmers, now many years gone, as he sought to maintain balance on a campus increasingly shadowed by the oncoming conflict. And it was satisfying to recall how often he had been right, at that early age, on the basic principles of peace and freedom, whose validity had been proved innumerable times as the chaotic twentieth century unfolded.

Had there ever been such a time! He supposed so, in the minds of those who lived through the Hundred Years' War, for instance, or other battles of the Middle Ages, or the fall of the Roman Empire or some other perilous era in the endless turmoil of a humanity always struggling forward, only to fall back into the chaos endemic to the human condition. It had always been "the worst" to those living at the time of it, though he found it hard to imagine that anything could have been worse than his own constantly unraveling, constantly warring century.

And now it was over, the millennium turning, ever-hopeful humanity looking, against all the odds, for some magic to be wrought by the changing numbers on a calendar. How futile it was, and yet how human, to hope for the magic because the century was "new," the millennium was "new"—and the tale of human greed, ambition and cruelty just as unchanging and awful as ever.

Well, he had done his best, in all these hectic years, to try to make some sense of it; and, he told himself, with as much success and "infallibility" as anyone. He knew he wasn't infallible, but his profession imposed on its practitioners the necessity of thinking they were, otherwise it would be hard at times to generate the sort of imperious attempts to change and control public opinion that were so characteristic of the professional commentator's life.

With him, as with all his fellow pontificators of print, tube and movie screen, the pious label they applied to what they did was "educating the public." In actuality it was a non-stop battle to dominate, influence, direct and (to give it the blunt but honest word) manipulate the public opinion of the United States of America, and through it, the world. He did it, they all did it. Some, like himself, were convinced, and rightly, that their motives were more sincere and genuine than the rest, but the end-game was the same: to swing the country one way or the other, this way or that, and in some small or large way, depending upon circumstance, help direct the life and destinies of the confused and earnest republic in which they had been given such overwhelming influence.

In his case, he thought it was deserved—as, he thought wryly, so did they all. But he knew that many of his colleagues, many of his fellow citizens, and many in the political world and its closely associated allies in academe and Hollywood did not agree with his self-estimation. As he had told Willie, way back in their discussion of his long-ago but still famous article on "The Rise of the Scum," he treated his critics with an amused contempt rather than with the worshipful respect their fragile egos demanded; and that was fatal. It made them livid; and, he had to confess, gave him an extra delight in doing it.

Nonetheless, in spite of their decades-long opposition, he had finally received the accolade. Thanks to Anna's furious lobbying and her scathing public denunciations of the committee's "inbred, incestuous, insider politics," he had finally been awarded his Pulitzer—after Anna had shamed Mother and the Conscience into conceding, finally, that he really had been around a long time; after it had become more than a little obvious that their opposition was almost entirely personal and ideological; and after Mother's latest family proprietor snapped, "Let the bastard have it and let's get it over with. Otherwise we never will hear the last of it from Anna and all that crowd."

His first impulse was to send it back with a scathingly sarcastic letter, but Anna told him to stop being a damned fool, shut up and take it.

"I haven't busted my gut all these years for you to play high and mighty now," she said, "so calm down, Timmy. Be thankful for small favors, and just shut up."

And of course, though much too inexcusably long delayed, it was not a small favor but a well-earned honor he deserved. He had worked long and hard, not specifically for that particular honor, but to achieve the position of influence he still held to this day, now in his early eighties; and so he took her advice, thanked the committee, made the properly grateful remarks when asked to comment, and went on doing what he had been doing for more than sixty years, observing, analyzing, commenting upon and seeking to influence the course of his confused but, he felt, still essentially goodhearted and well-meaning country.

And being old friend, confidant, occasional adviser and political water boy for the Senator from California, now about to leave office again, irrevocably this time, on the completion of his surprise interim appointment by the governor. Tim had always found Willie to be an interesting personal and professional study as he fought with the same people Tim fought with and in the same public arena, where their opposition, if successful, could easily have sent Willie back to the ranch years ago.

Tim regarded it as something of a miracle that Willie was still here; but attributable, like his own survival, to a determined ambition, unwavering purpose and gifts of written word and spoken rhetoric that sometimes surpassed Tim's, and gave him very effective weapons in his lifelong battle to achieve and hold office for his own purposes of clarifying and moderating the major legislation of his time.

There had even been the moment when it appeared, for a little while, that Willie might actually achieve the ultimate prize of American politics and carry his stubborn ways and basically idealistic ideas all the way to the White House. The manner in which he had said good-bye to this opportunity was so typically Willie that Tim had always felt a strong admiration but an equally strong regret that Willie for once in his life had not stayed the course and followed it to the end. Being a realist, Tim knew that Willie probably could not have won the presidency. He knew from his knowledge of him then, and a conversation some years later, that Willie had made the same dispassionate analysis.

"I knew it would take a real miracle for me to win," he said, "but I just thought I'd give the bastards a run for their money and show them that they couldn't always have things their own way." His eyes had darkened with long-gone but never forgotten pain. "But, there was Amos . . . and Anne and her crazy ex . . . and my conclusion that it just wasn't worth it for my family, to be put through more of such stuff . . ." Then he grinned suddenly, a signal that Willie was still there, irrepressible and irreverent as ever. "But, oh, Timmy! Wouldn't it have been fun to sit behind that desk and give those bastards the finger from 1600 Pennsylvania! It would have been the biggest one since the Washington Monument!"

And he had laughed for the sheer fun of it, and whatever regrets there had been—and Tim knew they were many and lasting, whatever the outward show—he had successfully put them away and gone on about his own contentious life, and his own purposes for the country.

Now Tim was faced with a problem of his own: keep up the column on a part-time basis and write an occasional article, or simply devote himself to watching and enjoying the passing parade in Washington. Anna had given him the choice.

"As long as I control the paper," she said, "you'll always have a home here for anything you want to write."

He knew this wasn't entirely true, for Anna had always been a strong, and on occasion arbitrary, editor; but she had never been an unfair or unsupportive one, and he knew he really did have a home there as long as he wanted to keep it. On one level, nothing appealed to him more. It would be nice to follow without deadline responsibility the Washington routine: the major parties, the occasional White House state dinner invitation; politics winter, spring, summer and fall, which would include attendance at major Hill debates; interesting committee hearings; insider talks with friends in Senate and

House; holding what would amount to a permanent pass to the Senate and House press galleries through the kind auspices of the two
superintendents, both old friends, who assured him he would always
be welcome; privileged entree to everything official and most that was
not. Followed, in well-established ritual, by the standard trek to the
Vineyard, where he and Willie and Latt and Ti-Anna had frequently
leased a house together; or travel to Europe or Asia; or settling into
some favorite hideaway such as Sanibel to work on another book to
add to the twelve he had published already.

Keeping up the column and the writing on a casual basis appealed,
and he supposed he would continue to take Anna up on her offer from
time to time; but he could see the frequency diminishing. Because—
he did not like to admit it to himself—did anybody?—he was facing a
fundamental human problem. He was growing old.

A creak here and a squeak there, a groan here and an expletive
there, an ache here and a cringe there—somehow they were increasing, bit by bit, sly and sneaky. Where did they come from, how did
they grow? He found it hard to analyze sometimes, was amused by his
own discoveries of them. First you noticed something small and
insignificant, so minor that it barely caught your attention; and then
one day there it was, unmistakable and inexorable, quite as though it
had come upon you unexpected and full-blown, although of course it
had been creeping up on you all the time. "Another God damned
break in the machinery," as Guy Unruh put it cheerfully when the
subject came up, willy-nilly, at lunch. Nobody really wanted to discuss
it but inevitably everybody did, with varying degrees of good nature
and amusement, depending on how stable you were and how ready to
accept that when it came to the final battles between you and Mother
Nature, at this stage of your life old M.N. was always the one sure
winner.

He smiled at his thoughts and thanked God he had sufficient
strength and humor to weather it, whatever it might be. So far he had
been quite lucky: a couple of operations for cataracts, a hernia operation, a bad bout with pneumonia a couple of years ago, a broken leg in
a foolish tumble on the dunes, the other leg broken several years later
when, forgetting caution, he had tried to run for a cab in a blinding

D.C. snowstorm and taken another inexcusable fall. Everything had healed well—so far—but the basic machinery weakened a little more each time: M.N. getting ready to administer the final coup de grâce, whenever and however it might come.

He looked around the modernized *Daily* Shack with fond eyes that misted a bit as he visualized a tall, gawky, earnest kid with big horn-rimmed glasses, passing through on his way to adult glories. Hey, there, Timmy, there you go, kid! Bright and shiny and earnest and positive and knowing how the world should be run and telling it so every chance you got! How did it ever survive your conscientious attempts to improve it? How would it ever have managed to make it without your advice? And how will it manage when you are gone?

He shook his head, dashed a quick hand across his eyes, got up and walked slowly out of the silent building. In a couple of weeks they would come thundering in, the future Timmys and Annas and Willies and all the rest. They thought they had all the answers, and perhaps a few of them did have some. In any event, he wished them a happy time, not too many setbacks and tragedies, enough triumphs big and small to keep them hoping and keep them going. He hoped they would have as much contentious, cantankerous, slam-bang fun as he had enjoyed all his life with a gifted pen and a combative soul.

He wouldn't have changed it if he could.

And while he didn't want to hurry her any, he thought with an inner serenity that he would be quite ready to meet old M.N., when she came along for the final no-contest encounter.

Embarked on a slow pilgrimage around the main Quad and some of the outlying areas of buildings and walkways that had been added over the years, Roger Leighton and Moose Musavich also shared thoughts of mortality. Neither had ever had the gifts of expression that Tim and Willie had, but both were moved by similar recognitions of time passing; particularly since their present situation was reminiscent of so much in their long friendship, going back to the house, youth, World War II, maturity and all the rest.

Moose was now confined to a motorized wheelchair by multiple sclerosis. Rodge once again, as on other occasions they both remembered vividly, was helping his old friend through a difficult passage.

Their journey from dorm to Quad had been mostly silent as Moose rolled doggedly ahead and Rodge trudged along at his side, his pace slowed somewhat by age but his bright, interested personality as attentive and complementary to Moose's as always. Nobody in the house had ever quite figured out what the attraction was, Moose so big and burly, "such a typical football jock," as Gil Gulbransen used to say, Rodge "such an earnest, goodhearted grind." But a deep and permanent bond had rapidly grown between them. Later on, on Iwo Jima, the bond had become literally a matter of life and death for them both.

They had enlisted in the Marines together the morning after Pearl Harbor; by the inscrutable chances of war and headquarters, had arrived together a year later on Iwo. Two days later Moose, badly wounded, had been trapped with six fellow Marines in a shallow "cave" some sixty feet from the better-protected position of Rodge, now a captain (whom everybody called "Professor" to his face, but he didn't mind). Virtually certain death was waiting, but Rodge rescued them all, making his way across a hell of rifle fire, grenades and exploding bodies. First he brought Moose over, then went back, one by one, for the others—"Seven times!" Moose always exclaimed when he retold the story, as he often did. "Seven *times!*"

Moose came out of it with a jagged scar running from his right temple down to his jaw, a gimpy right leg and a gimpy right arm that would always thereafter be an inch or two shorter than his left. Rodge came out of it with the Congressional Medal of Honor, one of only two men from the University to receive the distinction. But it was more than courage that had done it, Moose realized later with awed and eternal gratitude. It was friendship as well, he knew, that had tipped the balance and brought Rodge to his rescue against all the odds.

"And now here you are," Moose remarked with a gruff humor as they entered the unchanging archways of their youth, "nursemaiding me again."

"Somebody's always had to do it," Rodge said with an amiable grin. "You've always had Diana. I'm just a temporary today."

"I had you before Diana came along," Moose said, and reached up, unabashedly and quite naturally, to give Rodge's hand a squeeze where it rested on his shoulder. "A long time before Diana came along. And thank God for that, otherwise I wouldn't be here."

"You'd be here, Moose," Rodge assured him affectionately. "You're a tough bastard—you always were a tough bastard. Too tough to die."

"Not on Iwo," Moose said, "thanks to you." He sighed suddenly, humor gone, eyes suddenly filled with the haunted loneliness of the irretrievably ill. He had lost a lot of weight, his heavy frame, shrunken by the years, wasted even more by his sickness. His expression grew sad, and grim. "But you can't help me now. Unfortunately."

"I'm sorry as hell, Moose," Rodge said gravely. "I wish I could. Oh, how I wish I could. But—"

"Don't I know," Moose said. "But don't grieve for me. I can take it."

"How can I not grieve for you, dear friend?" Rodge inquired gently. "Diana and I are in the same boat, I imagine. We both like a stubborn old football player who was guilty of "—he made his tone deliberately lighter—"what did Franky Miller always call them? Your F.A.T.s— Fucking Asshole Touchdowns. Those were the days. I can see and hear it now—the last couple of minutes of a game—the crowd going wild—Moose! Moose! Moose! And there's old Mooser, not exactly where he's supposed to be, nobody knows quite how he happened to get the ball, *but there he goes!* Touchdown! Touchdown! Touchdown! Musavich has done it again, by God! Don't ask how he did it, he just did! F.A.T. is right! Our hero!"

Persuaded temporarily out of his depression, Moose stopped his wheelchair and sat there laughing in the warm September sun.

"I really did it, didn't I?" he said. "Those were the days. Those *were* the days!" His expression darkened, not happy but at least, Rodge thought, not centered on himself for the moment, which was good. "I miss old Franky," Moose said soberly. "He was a hell of a good guy. He used to come down from Oregon to see me quite often when there was a good game. Why do you suppose he did a thing like that?"

"I don't know," Rodge said quietly. "It had been many years since I'd seen him or heard from him, so I don't know what finally tipped it over. Life as an auto dealer apparently just got to be too much for a free spirit, I guess. Who ever knows what really happens inside?"

"Mmm," Moose said, starting to roll again, taking them to the eastern side of the Quad where it faced out across the Oval and up Palm Drive toward the distant town, which now, like everywhere, was much larger, much more troubled, filled with problems of racial tension, crime and other unhappy things.

Suddenly Moose stopped again. He half-turned in the chair until his eyes could meet Rodge's. "What would you think if I said I've thought of that?"

For a moment Rodge felt ice-cold in the gentle afternoon. Then he took a deep breath and returned Moose's gaze steadily as he replied.

"I wouldn't be surprised," he said carefully. "And I wouldn't be shocked. And I wouldn't blame you."

Moose's look intensified, his voice dropped lower.

"Would you help me?"

Rodge was silent for several moments. A couple of students on bikes, summer quarter leftovers or advance troops for the imminent horde, swept by with cheerful hellos and a happy-go-lucky chime of bells. The Quad fell silent again. Moose repeated his question, muted but insistent. Rodge's eyes held his for a moment longer; then he spoke, quietly.

"I would, yes, if you needed me."

Moose didn't speak, just nodded. His expression looked so relieved, and so humbly grateful, that Rodge almost couldn't stand it.

"That's what Diana says, too," Moose said, very low. "I guess with you two guys on my side, I don't have to worry."

"No," Rodge said, with a rueful smile. "But now we do."

Moose managed a rather wan little laugh, so far from his once-powerful guffaw that Rodge winced. But Moose's tone was stronger.

"Well, don't worry," he said. "As I told Diana, you'll get plenty of notice if I ever decide. I won't catch you off-balance . . . but I don't expect I'll ever really do it. I'm not a quitter."

Rodge nodded.

"As I said, I wouldn't be shocked. And I wouldn't blame you. I could understand it, God knows. You don't face an easy time."

"Easier, now that I know I can count on you," Moose said. He touched a button, started his chair moving forward again. "As always."

"As always," Rodge agreed firmly.

Moose thought for a moment, offered an obvious change of subject. "How are things going over there in your shop in Vienna? Making any progress?"

"Virtually none," Rodge said, and added ironically, "I'm the one who often feels like committing suicide. The endless meetings of the International Atomic Energy Agency go on, the eternal empty promises are made and ignored, the big powers sit tight and the little wannabes cheat and connive and maneuver constantly, dishonestly and hypocritically to avoid any honest accounting of what they're up to. The Russians, tricky as always, continue to sell off anything atomic they can get away with, to anybody who has the money to pay—or whose purposes generally coincide with the Russians', who still believe in weakening us and whoever else they regard as a continuing threat. And our own government, in the usual damnable lightweight fashion of American politics, seems willing to put any kind of optimistic, giggling gloss on any kind of serious development as long as it can be presented in such a way that it won't alarm the American people—and cost the President, or the Congress, or somebody, popularity and votes. And so we soldier on," he concluded with a wry disgust. "And so we soldier on."

"Why don't you resign and get the hell out of it?" Moose inquired. "You're old enough."

"Yes, dear boy," Rodge agreed in the same wry tone. "I am indeed, creeping up on eighty before long. But I'm just stubborn enough to think I can contribute a little if I stay in there and fight."

"It won't do any good," Moose said gloomily. "Somebody will blow up the world. It's inevitable, as I see it." Again he looked up at Rodge, trudging along beside him as they turned the corner of the Quad and started along the north side. "Don't you agree?"

Rodge started to give the automatically optimistic answer he had given to a thousand audiences—"It won't be easy, but I think it can be done, with sufficient goodwill and determination on the part of people of goodwill everywhere." Then he asked himself, Why shadow-box with this old friend?

"Yes," he said gravely, "I do. I don't say that publicly, but that's what I really think, particularly now that biological and chemical weapons have been added to the mix. And it comes closer every day, slouching toward Bethlehem—or Washington—or Moscow—or Beijing—or Libya or Teheran or Baghdad or Pyongyang, you name it . . . waiting to be born and take us all with it."

"So maybe," Moose said, and there was a gleam of his old presickness humor for a moment, "it won't be necessary for me to do anything. I'll just sit and wait and the end will be taken care of for me without my having to arrange it. Is that what you recommend?"

"Ha, ha," Rodge said. "Very funny. But maybe that's the best way to look at it. Except that such passivity, applied worldwide, could only make things a little awkward for Diana and your three kids, and for my four, who are even more my constant concern now that Juliette's gone. I'd rather keep fighting, thank you. At least it keeps me out of mischief and gives me something to do."

"I wish I were so lucky," Moose said with a switch of mood so sudden and so bleak that it left Rodge without rejoinder.

"Well—" he began, and fell silent, for how could one respond to that?

They proceeded along the Quad in a silence basically amicable but a bit uneasy now, having reached something of a temporary dead-end; until Moose broke the mood by remarking, "Oh, oh! Who's that up ahead? Isn't that shy figure one of ours?"

"It is," Rodge agreed with a relieved chuckle. "I'll yell and you put on some speed."

And they did, and up ahead along the Quad, Marc Taylor turned "like a startled damned deer," as Moose murmured. Marc too was "coming up on eighty before long," but he had been overcome with shyness and virtually tongue-tied at lunch and nobody had managed to shake him loose from it. He seemed a little more receptive now, though still almost painfully uncertain with these old friends.

"Oh, hi, you guys," he said, obviously trying to be casual. "I was just—just walking around."

"So are we," Rodge said. "Let's find a bench and sit down and talk for a bit. Unless you've got an appointment somewhere."

"Oh, no," Marc said, looking startled but then smiling in a more relaxed fashion. "Only with my memories."

"I hope they're good ones," Moose remarked as they did find a bench and Rodge and Marc sat down, Moose parking his chair alongside.

Marc gave a shy little smile ("I'll be damned," Moose told Rodge later, "if that scared-rabbity smile has changed in sixty years") and said earnestly, "Oh, yes, very good, thank you."

"That's great," Moose said, and stopped, obviously at a loss.

"Where have you been?" Rodge inquired, filling the little silence that fell. "We've just been around the Quad and back."

"Oh," Marc said vaguely again, "I've just been—just around."

"Well," Moose said, making an effort, but amicably, "what have you seen? Anybody else out prowling?"

"I did run into Renny a few minutes ago," Marc said, tone noticeably cool.

Moose snorted.

"That was a great pleasure, I'll bet," he said. "What did the slimy perv— What did the great man have to say?"

"He told me I was an egotistical fool to want to go and see the building I gave the Business School," Marc said. He looked almost defiant and spoke up stoutly. "I didn't think I was."

"Jesus!" Moose said. "We don't think you were, either. Right, Rodge?"

"Of course not," Rodge said. "We want to see it ourselves. You have every right to be proud of it. Where is it?"

"Well, thank you," Marc said, sounding pleased and flattered. "Just keep heading in that direction"—he gestured vaguely north—"and you'll find it. You can't miss it." He smiled shyly. "It's pretty big. I didn't think it was going to be that big, when I gave the money." He laughed, also shyly. "But they fooled me!"

"Yes," Moose said. "Contractors and administrators on this campus have a way of doing that, when they get their hands on a building grant. I only hope they didn't come back at you for too much more money."

"Oh, no," Marc said, sounding for a second quite firmly in command of things. "I can afford it."

His fraternity brothers laughed, but fortunately in an affectionate way, or Marc, Rodge thought, would have taken off and flown away right over the Quad.

"I'll bet you can," Moose said admiringly. "You've really done the best of all of us, haven't you?"

"My dad started it," Marc said. "I just carried on."

"Pretty damned well, I'd say," Rodge remarked. "And I hear you've had a good personal life, too, which is wonderful for you."

"Yes," Marc said, suddenly smiling so expansively that he seemed temporarily transformed into quite another person, much more relaxed and happy. "My Helen has been wonderful for me, and we have wonderful children, and it's all been just—just wonderful. I never thought," he said, touchingly solemn for a moment, "I never thought I could ever be so happy, until she came along. You'll meet her tonight at Duke's."

"We look forward to it," Rodge said.

"Nobody deserved it more," Moose said; and spoke with the blunt candor that families don't often produce but sometimes old fraternity brothers do.

"You were a sad-sack son of a bitch when you were an undergrad."

Rodge made a restraining gesture, too late, but Marc was not at all nonplussed.

"I know," he said with a smile. "I deserve that, I know I was. And I suppose, really, I still am. At least Renny seemed to think so."

"Oh, Renny!" Moose said in a tone of great disgust. "What the hell was he doing prowling around, anyway? Trying to scare up some freshmen women out of the bushes?"

"I don't know," Marc said, relaxing into real laughter this time. "But I don't think he found any, if he was. He seemed pretty sour, to me."

"He's always sour," Moose said. "I've shared this campus with that bastard for fifty years, more or less, and he's never changed from the miserable asshole he was in the house."

"I don't think he's ever going to, either," Marc said.

"Too late now," Rodge agreed.

"Well," Marc said with awkward abruptness, standing up and obviously preparing to flee. "I think I'll wander on for a bit and let you guys have your visit—"

"We've had it," Rodge said. "We're on our way back to the dorm. Why don't you come with us?"

Marc gave a shamefaced grin.

"I appreciate it," he said, "but I think maybe—I think I'll go back and take another look at my building. They've put in some new land-scaping and it looks really good."

"And why shouldn't you?" Rodge inquired. "It's something to be proud of."

"No one has a better right," Moose agreed. "Mind if we come with you?"

"Why, no," Marc said, looking pleased. "Why no, not at all. I'd be flattered and pleased. Please do."

They went along to the small Business School quad, timing their pace to Moose's, who said he didn't want to be hurried and didn't want to be helped; and so came to the imposing Spanish-style building that housed administrative offices, graduate student seminar rooms, a small auditorium; and noted with approval the words MARCUS ANDREW TAYLOR ADMINISTRATION BUILDING on the pediment. They admired it with a now relaxed and openly proud Marc; said their good-byes and left him there in the gently receding afternoon after arranging to meet him at the dorm, where Diana would pick them up at seven in her car and take them up to the Offenbergs' for dinner.

"I'm glad to see him having some fun in life at last," Moose remarked as they moved slowly along across the center of the Quad.

"Yes," Rodge said, hesitated for a moment and then added thought-fully, "Now, there's one who thought he was going to give it all up in his sophomore year and take himself out of the big, bad world."

"We didn't let him, did we?" Moose said with satisfaction.

"No," Rodge said. "He decided to hang in there, and things eventu-ally worked out for him, and look at him now."

"Still a shy little rabbit," Moose said with amusement, "only, now, a shy little rabbit worth a hundred million bucks." His amusement ended, the haunted look came back into his eyes. "I know what you're trying to do, Rodge, but there isn't any reprieve for me, even if I had a hundred million bucks. So I appreciate it, but don't knock yourself out."

"Don't give up, damn it!" "Rodge said with the impatient anger of lifelong fondness. "They may yet find something—"

"Not for me," Moose said calmly. "It's too late. I'll be gone in a year, they tell me. So help me enjoy the reunion, and don't worry about it. I'm not."

"Like hell," Rodge began, but abandoned it. "The trouble with me," he said with shaky humor, "is that I hate to think that I made all that effort on Iwo, only to have it wasted—"

"What the hell do you mean?" Moose demanded, stopping his chair so suddenly he almost pitched himself out of it. "You gave me fifty years of happy life coaching at this place which I love, and all my years with Diana and the kids— Knock it off, Leighton. It's a good try but you're just digging yourself in deeper. So drop it. O.K.?"

For a long moment, again, their eyes held.

"Yes," Rodge said. "Yes, sir. I will."

"Well, all *right*!" Moose said. "That's better."

And he started his chair and they continued their slow progress through the golden afternoon, and did not speak again of what lay ahead for Moose, and how helpless it made his old friend feel, knowing that this time he really couldn't do anything for him, no matter how unstintingly he might offer friendship.

It was almost five o'clock. Only one member of the house still remained on the Quad—all alone, as he essentially always was and to this day defiantly told himself that he always wanted to be.

The "awesomely broad-gauged intellect . . . truly one of the master-minds of the twentieth century" was reviewing with satisfaction his harsh put-down of that insufferable little wimp Marc Taylor, he of the annoying shyness and irritating millions. Renny had always believed that the shyness was just a pretense, honed over the years to go along with the millions. He had always enjoyed upsetting Marc's seemingly fragile equilibrium and he had enjoyed it today.

"Why don't you organize a brass band and lead us all over here so we can properly worship your charitable achievement?" he had asked a few moments ago in a loud, sarcastic voice when he surprised Marc studying "his" building. "Surely it's worth more than your own silent adoration. Surely the presence of all of us must be demanded."

"I don't care whether you come see it or not," Marc replied with a rare defiance; among his other annoying characteristics was a deferential politeness that he showed automatically to everyone. It pleased Renny that he could still shake it a little. "Anyway," Marc added, "you work here, you must have seen it a thousand times when it was being built. Why should I care whether you see it now or not?"

"Well, you probably shouldn't," Renny conceded; looking, Marc thought with a sudden uncharacteristic harshness, like some stringy old tree, bent, gray-haired, gray-faced, a far cry from the lithe, long-limbed, rather saturnine figure, good-looking in a vaguely unpleasant way, who had been the Renny of their youth. He was aware that Renny was preparing some further cutting remark and decided to forestall it.

"Look, Renny," he said, "go away, all right? You and I never liked each other in the house, we've never had anything in common, you've always criticized me publicly along with what Rodge calls your 'other pet hates,' and I'm sick of it. I'm here for a nice reunion weekend with my friends and you're not one of them. So shove off, O.K.? It's my building, I paid for it, and if I want to enjoy it, that's my privilege. Now, *you* just go away and leave me alone."

"Are you asking me?" Renny inquired, unable to suppress a pleased smile at his successful breach of what he thought of as "Marc's shy-violet defenses."

"I'm telling you," Marc said firmly. "Now please go."

Renny studied him for a long moment, debating defiance, sarcasm, scorn, contempt, all effective weapons in his arsenal when enemy inspired or opposition warranted. He enjoyed stepping on the simple pleasures of the incorrigibly naive.

"Treasure it," he advised. "It's basically a very ugly building, I think. But the campus is getting full of them as all you old grads with more money than taste impose your egos on us."

"It isn't ego!" Marc protested, being too earnest and honest to do the most sensible thing, which was not to reply. "I wanted to do something for the school because I love it and I—I just wanted to do something in the way that's open to me."

"Sheer robber-baron boasting!" Renny exclaimed, with the satisfied thought that this would really get under Marc's skin. "Mere worthless capitalist self-aggrandizement!"

"Oh, go to hell!" Marc said. "You really are the damnedest jerk, Renny."

"At least I've made you react to something like a human being," Renny snapped, suddenly waspish. "That's something!"

"Why do you feel you have to 'make' me react to anything?" Marc inquired in a bemused tone. "Why can't you ever let people just live their lives as they want to? You don't know everything! What's the matter with you, Renny? You'd like to spoil my building for me; you're jealous and you'd like to. But you just can't."

"You're pathetic," Renny said. "Pathetic and childish. At least I've accomplished a damned sight more than a *building* in my life."

"That's right!" Marc agreed, tone unusually harsh. "Some ruined young bodies, even more ruined young minds, a pathetic, off-base sexuality, a twisted view of America and the world that you and your friends have succeeded in foisting on a couple of generations. That's what *you've* accomplished!"

"And I've made you positively eloquent," Renny said with a scornful laugh, and turned away, leaving Marc to the meeting a few minutes later with Rodge and Moose that fortunately did so much to restore his temper and equilibrium.

Renny always enjoyed such encounters with the benighted defenseless. They gave him the opportunity to exhibit his brilliance and his sheer intellectual dominance over the thoughts and emotions of lesser men.

Like Gertrude's rose, Renny was a Renny was a Renny. There really wasn't much more to be said about him at this stage of his life. Imprisoned forever in his liberal time-warp, he had performed for fifty years the functions his world expected of him, and it had repaid him greatly. Rewards, honors, international reputation and influence had come his way; he knew he had earned them and he accepted them as his rightful due. He had early established, and relentlessly maintained, his reputation as "the one necessary liberal gadfly of our age" (Mother), "the indispensable leader of enlightened thought in our hectic times" (the Conscience).

He thought he would say a few things to his complacent, stupid fraternity brothers this evening that they wouldn't forget. It was the last time he would probably see any of them, and he intended them to remember it. A grim little anticipatory smile settled on his face as he walked along. Many reactionaries had attempted to mock and thwart him in his long, bitter, greatly successful life, but in the minds of Those Who Really Mattered he had won out over them all.

He, too, had his Pulitzer—two, in fact, the first for *Janus: America's Two-Faced Foreign Policy,* the second for *Feckless Giant: How America Destroyed International Hope and Responsibility.* The second came the very next year after Tim finally received his, a sort of "So there!" gesture whose timing and intent were not lost upon amused insiders.

He and his think-alikes had achieved a dominance over American intellectual orthodoxy that Marc, Willie, Tim and all their stupid crew would always mistrust and despise but now, so deeply implanted was the hold of Renny and his kind, could never overcome.

3 Dinner was over. Well fed and relaxed, they were talking idly around the candlelit tables set up on the Offenbergs' ample terrace overlooking the campus. Major lighting emphasized the Quad and Memorial Church. More modest illuminations outlined the dimly lit streets and paths along which a few late-traveling cyclists, walkers and joggers were still passing at that peaceful hour. The campus, so soon to burst into noisy life, was still in presession somnolence—"the way we like it," Duke observed with a smile.

"Before the deluge," Shahna agreed. "When you can still hear yourself think."

"And the house," Willie said, walking to the edge of the terrace and gesturing down and to the right, "was somewhere—about—*there,* right?"

"That's right," Moose said. "Faculty housing now, but quite a place then." His tone softened, became surprisingly sentimental, for Moose. "Quite a place."

For a few moments they were silent, contemplating the ghosts of youth past, the inexorable tide of the years, the hold that particular small spot of ground, once so active with their own young lives, still exercised on most of them.

Guy Unruh broke the mood, half-jesting but serious enough.

"Anybody want to make a speech? Anybody want to tell us about your triumphs since you left this sinfully beautiful place devoted to the care and coddling of the well-endowed young?"

"Speak for yourself, Guy," Hack suggested. Everybody laughed.

"I didn't mean it that way," Guy said with a chuckle. "Although," he added with the ghost of a certain smugness he used to display in the shower in his undergraduate boastful days, "I will say that—"

"Don't," Maggie ordered, and they all laughed again.

"Yes, ma'am," he said with an obedient grin. "Hack, why don't you lead off?"

"Well," Hack agreed, "my story's briefly told. I married Fran Magruder, our careers diverged, we didn't have any kids, we divorced. I went to Rome, my favorite spot during the war, met Flavia Lampadini, we lived happily ever after with two kids and a reasonably successful musical career for me. I've achieved a fair success in my field and have no real complaints. Life has been good to me and I've tried to return the favor. Memories of the University and particularly the house, I am sure, underlie and inform some of my best work, often I'm sure without my conscious knowledge. Such are the gifts a great institution and a gang of scatter-brained adolescents can give one, often, I'm sure, not to their conscious knowledge, either. And how about yourself, Guy? You started the ball. Keep it rolling."

"Yes," Guy said thoughtfully. "Maggie and I are fortunate: we're both still here. It's been a long run, and I think a happy one. Although I don't press her too hard on that."

"Just as well," Maggie remarked, with the jovial chuckle they all remembered, which shook her pudgy little frame all over. "I'm one of those gals who has to be good-natured, just from the sheer weight of me. And it's a good thing I have been, sometimes. But he's not so bad. I've managed to put up with him."

"Thank God for that," Guy said, and again they all laughed. His tone turned serious.

"I've tried, within the small competence the good Lord saw fit to give me, to be a servant to mankind, in my own small way, in the direction my interests in medicine have led me. As you all know, it's a long, terrible, uphill slog, and we're still a long, long way from the top of the hill. But we keep trying, millions of us all over the world, doctors, nurses, scientists, technicians, ordinary folk using only the love and concern they feel for family members or friends. We haven't beaten it, we may never; but as long as we don't give up, there's hope that someday this scourge will be removed from the back of humanity. To be succeeded, as it is now accompanied by, humanity's seeming determination to destroy itself with nuclear war and monstrous weapons of biology and chemistry, if cancer and associated ailments don't. Right, Rodge?"

Rodge sighed.

"That's it," he said gravely, "'determination.' Maybe there is a determination, unconscious, subliminal, rising from an ancient instinct. The lemmings over the cliff—the moths into the flame—whatever. The urge to annihilate and, in the end, self-annihilate. Who knows? But it doesn't stop . . . and may not until it ends, and, ending, ends us all.

"The work goes on. Mooser tells me I'm too old, I ought to quit, but it's the old saw—somebody's got to do it. And why not me? I've been at it so long I'm the most famous guy on the block. 'There's that old crock Leighton again, send him out to make speeches, they love him on the lecture circuit. He peddles hope, or at least a modified pessimism we can manage to live with. He opens the door for us and tells us to be good girls and boys or we'll blow ourselves up.' But he doesn't tell us how to stop somebody *else* from blowing us up. That's the rub. The crazies rule the world as our sad old millennium ends and our wan and wistful new one wanly and wistfully begins. The world went mad on the night of December 31, 1999; we woke up to the same familiar grayness on January 1, 2000. So don't think, boys and girls. Don't think. I'm glad I've devoted my life to the cause I chose the day I was flown over Hiroshima. But I'm not fooling myself I've gotten very far with it—nor has anybody else. The threat has grown, exponentially, swollen by the new weapons. I'm not ashamed of my feeble efforts but I don't kid myself: feeble they are, and apparently ultimately pointless. But I can't complain. It's given me something to do, all these years."

Again they were silent, taken aback by his uncharacteristic bitterness. Always before when they thought of Rodge, it had been with a mental picture of his dogged optimism, his undaunted hope. Something had been lost. The chill of the age touched them and lingered. Moose cleared his throat and leaned forward in his chair.

"Well, buddy," he said, "that's not my Rodge speaking. I'm the guy who ought to be pessimistic, but I'm not. I've had a great run, thanks to you—you all know that story. And thanks of course to you, Diana, my wonderful wife . . . Things may look grim for me now. They aren't easy. But"—he looked around and smiled his wasted smile, with a gallantry that brought several close to tears—"I'm hangin' in there, and I shall continue to do so as long as the good Lord gives me strength.

Maybe with a little luck"—his voice thickened, he almost lost it, but he fought an obvious battle with himself, won and concluded shaky but determined—"maybe I'll make one more F.A.T. and beat this bastard yet. God bless you all."

In the ensuing silence as they sought to regain composure, Duke saw an opportunity and took it.

"Renny!" he said. "Surely you have some thoughts to give us?"—thinking, Yes, let's hear you break the mood now, you miserable bastard—which was heavy, for Duke. Renny saw the gambit, for just a second shot him a look of pure hatred, instantly masked; looked around the terrace with a slow, appraising blink, and spoke, as characteristically as they expected.

"Thank you," he said, tone edged with sarcasm. "Thank you all. I had thought we might speak a little more formally on this, probably the last occasion on which we will all see one another; but it seems to be catch-as-catch-can and I find it is now my turn. I shall oblige.

"First, let me say that my memories of the house are not as warm and cuddlesome as many of yours obviously are. Nobody ever liked me there—"

"And you never liked anyone," Tim remarked crisply.

"—and I never liked anyone," Renny agreed with equal crispness. "I tried to, when I first got there, but that was the age of the Big Jocks, you'll recall. It was people like Guy and Gil Gulbransen and Willie and the other skirt-chasing Big Men on Campus that I had to deal with." (There was a beginning of sympathy among the wives—Poor Little Renny—but it swiftly passed, casualty of years of husbandly dislike and Renny's inevitable withering attitude.)

"You guys didn't think much of brains in those days—"

"Perhaps because none of us doubted we had them," Guy remarked, and for a moment Renny's lifelong mask of superior judgment threatened to crack. But it had been tested in arenas far larger than this, and never failed him. He blinked and went on.

"The war came and went and I returned here to teach. I began to make a name for myself in all the intellectual circles that matter in America. My fraternity brothers didn't acknowledge me, the University only did so grudgingly; but the rest of the world was kinder, at least my world of those whose views of America and the world I respect. And I prospered and became a public man like most of us from that carefree, happy little group we still think of as 'the house.' Most of my efforts have been directed, one way or another, toward preventing the reactionary mindset you all so beautifully epitomized, from taking over the country. My efforts, I am happy to say, have in the main been successful, even though in Willie we have the prime example of what I'm talking about.

"Willie represents one view of America, I the opposite. We've clashed over the years, as you know, almost all the time. His futile attempt to win the presidency stands as a monument to the basic conflict between our two philosophies. I'm not going into all that here, except to say that I have the satisfaction of knowing that I helped keep him out of that office"—there was an audible gasp from someone, probably Helen Taylor—"and that the views I speak for have in general dominated and controlled the direction of the country far more than his have. B.M.O.C.s don't always have the successes that we, as kids, expect they will have. I'll match my record against his any day. Mine satisfies *me*, although I know you all hate it.

"I couldn't have lived with myself if I had to contemplate an America run by Willie's ideas, or Rodge's ideas, or even Marc's ideas—although [never being one to miss the chance to twist a knife gratuitously] I'm not sure Marc has ever had any ideas except to parlay his inherited millions into more millions, no matter how much he's had to ride roughshod over his employees to do it—"

At this Helen Taylor really did speak up, rising angrily to her feet: a neat, pleasant-faced, gray-haired little lady, normally as retiring and soft-spoken as her husband but now suddenly swept out of her reticence by indignation at this unexpected attack on him.

"You have a nerve to say something like that!" she cried, while Marc, with a nervously embarrassed smile, tried to get her to sit down. "My husband is good to his employees! He doesn't do bad things to people! He's a *good* man!"

Renny gave her an ironic little bow.

"Certainly a lucky one, madam, to have acquired such a staunch defender, particularly a defender who really has so little to defend."

"Now, see here, Renny—" Willie broke in. Renny was ready for him.

"Yes, 'see here, Renny'!" he snapped. "That's the story of my life, reactionaries like you, Willie Wilson, crying, 'Now, see here' at me because you haven't been able to answer my ideas and challenges on fair ground. You trot out all the old, tired rhetoric every chance you get. 'Now, see here, Renny'! Yes, Renny will see here, he's always 'seen here,' and what he has seen has always been more pertinent to these times and this country than anything you've ever dreamed up to con a gullible electorate, Willie Wilson! You see here yourself, you—you pompous senatorial fraud!"

Willie was on his feet, not quite sure what if anything he intended to do but sure that his height would give him some advantage in what had suddenly become their personal debate. Before he could speak Helen Taylor gasped out, "Well, I never met such an awful man!" Adding, to her husband, "How did you ever take him into your fraternity, Marc?" And, to Renny, "I think you ought to go home, you unpleasant person! We don't want you here!"

"Well, now—" Duke began, trying desperately to restore some semblance of decorum and be a good host; but Renny had his opportunity for a grand farewell, and took it. He surveyed them with a scathing glance.

"You're right, Mrs. Taylor," he said. "You're absolutely right. I'll say this: I didn't want to be here, either. I only came because I thought there might be some decency left among my dear—old—fraternity brothers at this late date that would give me a fair hearing and an equal chance to boast along with the rest of you about what a perfect life I've had. You guys claim it, I've had it. Not one of you has been more famous or had a more influential life than I have. Not one of you has had more impact on America and on our times. Not wonderful Willie or pontificating Tim or noble Guy or idealistic Rodge—or even football hero Moose—"

"Oh, come on!" Tony Andrade spoke up with great disgust. "Knock it off, creep!"

"Exactly!" Renny cried. "Exactly! Old Creep Renny, that's how you think of me, that's how you despise me, all of you, all of you! Pious little Tony the fat-cat wine-maker included! How did you get *your* good life? Married it! Half of you very distinguished guys either married it or inherited it. I inherited it, too, but I made something of it. I wouldn't have had to do anything if I hadn't wanted to, but I did. And that made me famous and respected by people *I* respect. I've contributed more to my country than all of you combined. More people respect me than ever respected you, Willie!"

"You protest too much, Renny," North McAllister remarked. "Why don't you do as Tony suggests and just knock it off?"

"It would be less painful for us," Randy Carrero agreed, with a thoughtful air he knew would infuriate. "And less painful for you, too, I imagine. It must be awful to put yourself through something like this—to have to struggle with envy the way you do."

"And don't *you* patronize me, either, holy man!" Renny snapped. "You and your pious ways and your evil, antiquated Church that's destroyed half the world with overpopulation and privilege! You're in no position to talk, half-man! What do you know about life, anyway?"

"More than you ever will," Randy said quietly. "Why don't you do as Helen suggests, and go home? Just go home."

"Oh, I'm going!" Renny said. "I knew I shouldn't have bothered to come. I don't know what misplaced sentiment brought me here. It couldn't have been respect, it couldn't have been affection. I think it was just plain dumb curiosity to see what you complacent bastards have become since we all lived *down there*"—he repeated Willie's gesture with a bitter mockery—"sixty years ago. Now I know. You haven't changed a bit. Crude, stupid, blindered individuals, the ruination of America!" His voice sank to a near-whisper, his eyes narrowed with contempt and hatred, his expression was harsh and unyielding. "How I despise you! How I despise you!"

And with a dramatic flourish—"Oh, Christ," Moose said—he flung away off the terrace and disappeared in the darkness down the drive. They heard his car start up; he gunned it; the sound dwindled swiftly away.

"Well!" Guy Unruh said into a silence that was half-stunned, half-amused. "Another drink, anybody?"

"Better make it doubles all around," Tim suggested.

Everybody shifted, moved, relaxed. Tensions eased. Humor returned. The informal roll call resumed.

———

Tim said with some sarcasm that he, too, thought he had contributed a good deal to America, was well satisfied with his life, added
humorously that he considered anybody who didn't faithfully read his
column "ignorant, hopeless and subversive of all good things." North
cited his medical accomplishments, his children, his civic contributions to Salt Lake City. Tony followed with an account of his lifelong
contributions to viticulture and the special world of Napa Valley.
Randy gave them a brief tour through higher Vatican politics and
declared himself well satisfied with his life even though, like Rodge, he
confessed to some despair over humanity's continuing determined
slide toward self-destruction.

The roll call ended, by tacit agreement, where in a sense it had
begun so many years ago. Nobody called on Willie to speak until the
others had finished; it just seemed to them fitting that he, their most
public of public men as long as they had known him, should conclude
this more formal part of their reunion. A cool little breeze had arisen,
the first faint touch of autumn's chill succeeding autumn's afternoon.
People pulled on sweaters, settled back. Willie looked at them with the
confident and happy grin they remembered from all their days "down
there," and began.

"Well," he said, "after that little lecture from Brother Suratt, I can't
think of anything to add. I think he covered it all. He told us how great
he is and how miserable we all are. What more can I say?

"However, there may be a little room for competing thoughts, even
so. I'd hate to have the evening's honors go to Renny by default; I'd
hate to have the winds waft to Hillsborough the news that he had
silenced me at last—"

"No, no!" Unruh cried with elaborate horror. "Never!" echoed
Tony sternly. Willie grinned and looked positively lighthearted.

"So I shall proceed. Suitably, I hope. And not too lengthily.

"We departed here as scared kids on the way to war. We have come
home in a different season. I'm glad Renny drew the distinction
between himself and us, because in a sense I think we have always represented the two poles in American political and social thought that
have battled for our generation and our children's generation. And I
think he is right to narrow it down, for purposes of argument"—he

smiled—"and invective—to the differences between himself and myself. For we have operated on the world stage and have to some extent symbolized in our two lives the line that splits the second half of the twentieth century.

"I like to think I have not been as extreme in my way as he has been in his, but the fundamental difference has always been clear. It is perhaps in his extremes and my somewhat milder approach that there lies a difference greater than any based on any particular view of things. His approach has always been slash-and-burn; mine, I hope, more reasoned and less savage—though equally devoted and equally determined. I will give him that. He has always believed in what he advocated, as have I. If I have accorded him his beliefs a little more generously than he has accorded me mine, that is, I suspect, a matter of personality." He grinned suddenly. "I like mine better . . .

"Unfortunately," he went on, voice graver now, "I now reach the end of my public career having to admit that he is probably right: he and his friends have won. Their ideas so dominate the most influential areas of American thinking, affect so heavily philosophical discourse and media presentation, are so overpoweringly influential in American education, that the more moderate point of view, which I like to think of as the more 'balanced' point of view, has hard going nowadays. And because it has hard going in the United States, it inevitably has hard going in most of the rest of the world. To use the cliché, trite but true, we really are one global village now, in a way we never were when you and I were debating the coming of World War II as undergrads in the house.

"Many of you have professed yourselves well satisfied with the way your lives have turned out, and I think we have a right to that satisfaction. We've all, I know, had our personal crises, our family problems, our emotional ups and downs, our bitter disappointments accompanying the happier days and happier triumphs. That's the human story, and none of us has been exempt. Because I've lived a life in the limelight, mine is well known to you all. I suppose"—he hesitated and then spoke quietly—"I suppose the death of my son Amos was probably the worst of it, though of course the deaths of my dear wives were devastating. Donna, Anne and Fran were wonderful to me, but their going in each case was expected, there was plenty of advance warning. The tragedy of Amos stands alone . . .

"Long ago, some of you may remember, Timmy wrote a famous article for the *Washington Inquirer* which he entitled 'The Rise of the Scum.' Unfortunately, nothing since has changed the somber picture he drew of the rapid decline of tolerance, kindness, good manners and common decency and the generosity of thought and action without which tolerance, kindness and decency cannot flourish. Everywhere our society continues to decline, to fray and erode, to find its grasp on safety and stability more and more tenuous.

"We live in a very fragile world now. Our hope is not so much that we can improve it generally, but that in our small, specific corner of it we can guarantee that we and those who are dear to us can get through the day safely and not be bruised by society's rampant and uncontrolled lawlessness. And by that I don't mean lawlessness in the legal sense, necessarily, but just the lawlessness of how we have come to treat each other, and how little the old rules of decency and kindness and consideration mean to so many people who go through life basically completely brutal and completely uncaring. It is terrifying. . . ."

He paused for a moment. They were all listening in rapt silence and, he knew, complete agreement. He felt a sudden surge of love for them all, these companions of youth come back for a few brief hours to this sentimental starting-place.

"So what does one offer in the way of hope when one looks around the ruins of this tattered century that began with so many high hopes and has ended with so many hopes in ruins and even the hope of a reasonably stable future for one's descendants entirely uncertain now?

"I have never been one, like Randy here and like some others of you who possess religious faith, to place my expectations in some sort of anthropomorphic God, compassionate, understanding, loving. I have seen too many tragedies in my life to believe in such a God. I believe in a fundamental order in the universe, so amazing in its infinite details that the mind cannot grasp how it ever came to be; it is what keeps the world going, and it offers what is probably the only valid hope that the human race will somehow, in some fashion, survive and, itself, keep going. But it will be, in my estimation, according to rigid rules of physics and genetics that we have only barely tapped so far, and probably never will understand in full. Certainly not in our lifetimes, probably not in our children's or grandchildren's, most probably never. We shall just survive; and maybe sometime, by some monumental fluke that will be the greatest fluke in all eternity, life will take on that truly generous, truly loving aspect in which the goodhearted have always believed and for which they have always striven. . . ."

He paused again, felt for a moment odd, in some way he could not define; dismissed it and began to conclude with a humorous air.

"When I was an undergrad, I went through a secret poetry-writing period, as I suppose many do. I was reminded of that the other day when, cleaning out some things, getting ready to move in with my Senator son, Latt, and his wife, Ti-Anna, who have kindly offered to look after me one of these days when I finally get old—"a rueful chuckle from everybody"—I came across the following, which I thought might fit this occasion."

He cleared his throat, again for a second felt suspended in space—out of balance—out of control—a sensation that again passed in a flash. His poem was brief and, as Willie always had been, wry:

> The course is run,
> The race is done.
> I hardly knew it had begun
> . . . Son of a gun!

Their rueful amusement turned to rueful laughter. In the middle of it his own laughter suddenly stopped. In some strange way he couldn't understand he seemed to be simultaneously looking down from the ranch over the great fertile San Joaquin Valley, coming down Palm Drive toward Memorial Church, and looking up at the Capitol dome gleaming pristine and pure in the deep blue of early evening. The Capitol was the last conscious imprint on his mind—so beautiful, so full of hope, representing such great dreams so earnestly espoused, so tenuously achieved.

"Willie?" Duke said sharply, and began to move toward him as he sank back in his chair and slumped over. Guy and North were quicker:

instinct had them on their feet at the first note of puzzled hesitation in Willie's voice. The others, paralyzed with shock and apprehension, sat immobile as the two doctors went about their practiced business.

Guy looked up, tears in his eyes. When he spoke it was with a strange combination of shortness of breath, anguish and a sort of weird, harking-back-to-flippant-youth humor that they all understood, as would Willie had he still been with them.

"Well, whaddya know," he said huskily. "Our golden boy is gone."

4   Thus it happens for millions every day. Survivors often remark to one another, "What a great way to go! I only hope I'm that lucky!" But confronted by the absolute, crushing finality of it, it is not that easy for those left behind, particularly when they are left by an old, dear friend like Willie, whose presence had dominated so much of their personal and political lives for so long.

There were of course major headlines and major stories across the country and around the world, television commentaries, newspaper editorials, analyses. He was recognized as an Institution, a Survivor, a Relic—"of long outmoded social and political philosophy" (Dr. René Suratt, fraternity brother)—"of staunchly balanced, moderate leadership in a wildly unwieldy time" (Anna Hastings, editorial, the *Washington Inquirer*).

A memorial service was held in the National Cathedral, attended by most of the Senate, almost half of the House and many members of the media who had so often criticized him so bitterly. Washington too was in the benign grip of beautiful Indian summer. Everyone agreed that the day of his final public honoring could not have been more lovely.

The President, who never missed an opportunity to demonstrate how firmly his feet were planted in all political camps ("He has more feet than a centipede," Tim remarked dryly to Latt), gave a brief eulogy. ("What the hell was I supposed to do?" Latt remarked in disgust to Tim. "The oily son of a bitch called me and said he would like to speak for ten minutes. How do you refuse a direct request from the President of the United States?") Tim delivered the principal eulogy, with considerable emotional difficulty, breaking down twice. The mourners emerged divided, as always, into the two usual camps about

Willie. Many in Washington and millions more around the country were genuinely grieved by his passing. An equal segment agreed with the private sentiments expressed ironically by the President to his wife in the limousine returning to the White House: "I only regret we couldn't drive a stake through his heart to make sure he's really dead."

It was a typical Willie day and a typical Willie audience divided by a typical Willie reaction, as Tim remarked to Latt.

"He would have loved every minute of it," Latt said. "Particularly the President pretending to be sorry and uttering all that hypocritical crap about how much he would 'miss my old sparring partner in all those great legislative battles we both loved so well.' "

Two days later he was interred in the family plot at the ranch, in accordance with his written instructions, which had rejected burial in Washington. Latt had hoped for that, as befitting his long career in public life. Willie in his last instructions had vetoed it in favor of going home. He also wrote that he had considered the option of having his ashes scattered equally over ranch, Quad and Capitol, but had decided that "this would be sentimentality carried to the point of being ridiculous. It's probably time to come home. I so charge my family and executors."

Latt, Ti-Anna and the only one of their three children still unmarried were there from Washington, Clayne and two of hers from Oregon. Nagatani and Katanian, both on canes and crippled with arthritis, but game, drove down from Fresno with their wives. Tim and Anna came out together from Washington in one of Anna's corporate jets. Everyone who had been at the Offenbergs' that night was also there. After considerable thought they had decided to go ahead with Sunday's picnic at the Andrades' in Napa Valley, a subdued and somber occasion but filled with much talk of Willie and the old days, a gradual easing of shock and pain, a growing acceptance—"a good catharsis," as Unruh remarked.

With the exception of Renny, who was not invited and whom no one even mentioned, they were all there; even Moose, for whom it was not easy but who told Diana he was "damned if I'm going to desert Willie on this occasion."

There, too, the grace of autumn lay on the land. The Valley, exhausted from the long heat of summer, rested. They, too, were somehow peaceful and rested as they said good-bye to the friend whose life had been so much a part of theirs.

Many were the editorials and analyses that sought to sum up his long public career. The three most typical were the ones the astute historians would seek out first when and if Willie's story was ever recounted in more formal pages. "My tale's soon told," he had written in one of his youthful semi-haikus. "Born old/Lived old/Died old." But someday someone might expand upon it at greater length, seeing in it the story of responsible statesmanship and stability he and those close to him saw.

"We suspect," said the Mother of All Newspapers on the morning of the memorial service in Washington, "that no element of the media has expressed more consistent criticism and opposition to the late Senator Richard Emmett Wilson of California than we have. Yet we also suspect that no element of the media has entertained a more genuine, if grudging (and with good reason, we've often thought) admiration for his courage and integrity.

"It was an often prickly courage, a sharply challenging, self-defensive integrity; yet, as he saw it, those qualities permitted him to serve the country well, in the ways that seemed to him best. We often did not agree with the political positions his personal convictions led him to espouse. But we, like the country, always knew that he said what he meant and meant what he said; and that the actions he took in pursuit of his convictions were equally forthright and unshakable.

"The power and influence of legislators such as 'Willie' Wilson go directly to personal qualities and the consistency with which they are maintained. These men and women belong to a special and necessary category: the independent thinkers who provide that extra leaven of common sense and sincere conviction that are so necessary to steady some of their more free-swinging colleagues. They provide strength and above all they provide balance. The country needs them and it is lucky that so many of them find their way to high office. The legislative process would be far less stable without their sound and moderating influence.

"We had many arguments with Senator Wilson during his long and distinguished career; yet we respected him and wished him well. History will someday assess him for what he was: a true American, earnest and honest and dedicated to his country's welfare. . . ."

The comments of the Daily Conscience of the Universe were less kindly and made less attempt to achieve deathbed balance. Like the President, they too were of the stake-through-the-heart school of political commentary. They came to bury Caesar, not to praise him; old enemies were not forgotten. They could not resist tossing a few last gobs of mud on his coffin as they consigned him, with pleasure and relief, to history:

"The late Senator Richard Emmett Wilson of California was one of those unique senatorial characters who come and go with fair regularity on Capitol Hill. Approve or disapprove of them—and we must confess that in his case we found much more reason to do the latter—they are always hard to overlook, often hard to understand and almost always impossible to support for any length of time, if one has any kind of broad and generous concept of what this country is all about.

"'Willie' Wilson was not an easy man to analyze or feel close to, at least not for those whose far-ranging and perceptive political views were different from his narrow and reactionary ones. He gave his critics short shrift and since we were often in the vanguard of his critics, we gave him short shrift. It was usually war between us. We do not regret these battles, whose results were usually pretty evenly divided. He invited controversy and seemed to thrive on it. We were always glad to oblige whenever this gave us a chance to oppose his views, which we believed were almost uniformly bad for America.

"We accord him his character, his integrity, his conviction that he was right. We only wish we could have seen his record through his eyes. It would have made it easier to forgive a career that we can only regard as having been, over all, detrimental to the best interests of this country. . . ."

"Graceless and tasteless as always," Anna Hastings (who gave as good as she got) wrote in a rare front-page editorial in the *Washington Inquirer,* "the usual vultures of politics and the media gloat over the grave of the late Senator Richard Emmett Wilson of California.

"Not content that he is gone and unable to defend himself—as he would certainly do, with his usual scathing vigor, were he here—his political and media enemies continue to heap calumny upon him. It is not enough that he will trouble them, physically, no more. They seem to be afraid that he can continue to exercise some sort of ominous influence from beyond the grave. They are apparently haunted, as well they should be, by the specter of a man whose integrity and courage never once buckled under their snide and irresponsible attacks.

"His character stands in glaring contrast to theirs. Therein lies his lasting triumph.

"All of us who knew 'Willie' Wilson admired his unyielding adherence to the beliefs and principles that strengthened him in his long public life.

"His enemies could only temporarily distract him. They could not permanently deflect or deter. In the long run their shrill, often hysterical, attacks were simply ill-mannered, boorish chaff.

"Senator Wilson was that rare thing, a truly selfless and dedicated public man, a servant of the Republic whose integrity enabled him to amass a long, constructive, worthy record, one of the best in recent senatorial history. He was a major example of staunchly balanced, moderate leadership in a wildly unwieldy time. He will be sorely missed, by the fellow Americans for whom he did so much, and by his featherweight enemies of politics and media who always hate to see what they consider a vulnerable target removed from their snide besmirchments. . . ."

On the hillside above the ranch house where he rested with his forebears and his wives, all of whom had asked to be there, Willie had the last word. He had asked for it in his instructions, even though his gravesite was so isolated that very few of his countrymen would ever see it. "But I think," he had written, "that it's a nice thought. At least it's some indication that I was what I've always liked to think I was, a decent and generous man."

It too went back to his youthful poetizing days. Latt had found it among his papers and had it chiseled, as requested, on the small granite obelisk that marked his resting place:

ALLEN DRURY

*   *   *

RICHARD EMMETT WILSON
1918–2000
United States Senator from California
*

You I have hurt, forgive me.
You I have comforted, remember me.
Stranger, think well of a stranger.

There he lies, facing down the long sweep of the Valley, while the heat of summer and the cold of winter and the endless vagrant winds of time pass over.